I Don't Mind Waiting

BEEGEE HILL

ISBN 978-1-63961-763-0 (paperback)
ISBN 978-1-63961-764-7 (digital)

Copyright © 2021 by BeeGee Hill

All rights reserved. No part of this publication may be reproduced, distributed, or transmitted in any form or by any means, including photocopying, recording, or other electronic or mechanical methods without the prior written permission of the publisher. For permission requests, solicit the publisher via the address below.

Christian Faith Publishing
832 Park Avenue
Meadville, PA 16335
www.christianfaithpublishing.com

Printed in the United States of America

This book is dedicated to the memory of my father Rev. Clarence L. Hilliard and my two sisters Ertie Nevels and Lynn Dodd, and to the living (the LOVE of my life) my mom Annie Hilliard. My brothers and my sister, Tia. You all shaped me into the woman I am today and I praise God for you all. My brother Phil who helped me through this process and made it ALL possible! To my mother-in-law, Clarine Thompson, my husband Dr. Ted and 3 children, Jason, Arik and Tedi, love you all immeasurably. My grandchildren, my neices and nephews and my two bestest friends in the world (besides my mom and Tia) Andrea Mitchell and Cynthia Holmes. And lastly, I want to thank my nephew/Godson DJ who constantly questioned me about getting this published. He said the world needs to read this! Thank you baby! Much love all! I couldn't have done it without you!!!

—BeeGee Hill

1

For typical Chicago weather, we had a seasonably mild winter this year. And thus far, spring was following right along in suit. If this was any indication as to how summer was going to be, then we're in trouble because I was imagining a real scorcher this year. I had just completed a nice casual visit with Mommy (as I did quite often) on this beautiful spring day. I live in the same town as Mom, just minutes away. And since Daddy passed away, my siblings and I were always hot on her trail, making sure she was all good.

There I was, heading home after my visit, when I saw flashing lights in my rear view. *Uh-oh! Somebody's in trouble. Let me get out of his way so he can go wherever it is he's trying to go. They're always in such a hurry, probably trying to go get a doughnut or something. Dunkin Donuts, here I come. They're not fooling anybody. Wait! He's pulling over behind me? Hold on a minute! I wasn't speeding. I signaled when I changed lanes. I haven't made a turn in a minute, so what is my crime? That's what I tell you about cops. You give them a little power, and they do as they please. OMG! He has really upset my day, always harassing somebody. But it's all good. I'm not going to curse and I'm not going to trip. I'm a Christian woman. But I can't imagine what it is that he thinks I've done. Let me think! Are my plates on point? Yeah, I did get that sticker, so go right ahead and run my plates, officer, I am legit, okay? All right, let me be cool and not make it any worse than it already is. Here he comes…*

Ooooooooh, DZAM! This brother is FINE! Ooops, I said I wasn't going to curse, didn't I? But *dam* is NOT a curse word. It's in the Bible, so it's cool. *Look at him. He has a silky-smooth complexion, like milk chocolate, bald head with a goatee, looking like he's a good six foot, four or five inches tall with a body. OH, to die for! This brother has muscles on top of muscles. He probably needs to invest in a bigger shirt because he's about to burst out of this one. Oh no, don't get me wrong. I'm NOT complaining. I am DEFINITELY loving the way this shirt is fitting. I do feel sorry for the buttons, though. They must be feeling a little nervous about getting lost. And his arms, mmm, he needs some elastic on those short sleeves. Them biceps are about to rip that cotton to smithereens.*

He's here! Roll down the window, girlfriend, and CALM DOWN!

"Can I have your license and proof of insurance please?"

Good gravy! Did you hear that? That voice...that voice is a nice solid baritone, I'm sure. Play it cool, baby girl, and breathe.

"Officer, what's the problem? I know I wasn't speeding. I can't even imagine what I could've done."

Give me a line, give me a line. I need to flirt right about now. He needs to know that I'm available without me seeming desperate. Something catchy. What can I say? You've got something in your eye? Nope, wrong movie. Let me give this man what he's asking for before I get on his nerves.

I reached in my purse, took out my wallet, grabbed my license and my insurance card. "Here you go, sir." Dang, I'm so mad at me. Any other time, I would've been giving advice, "Girl, you should've said..." And when it comes to me, I couldn't think of ONE clever thing to say to this specimen of a man.

"This looks like a fairly new car, and one of your tail lights are out."

Is that it? That's all? It wasn't a traffic violation? He's concerned for me. AWWWWW, that was so sweet.

"You may want to have your man take care of that for you."

Uh-oh, he's fishing. Okay, so HE's interested. Let's see. Let me help him out. "Well, I'll call my brother. He's the one that reminds me to get my oil changed and stuff like that. I'm surprised he didn't notice the taillight. Was that it, officer? I don't have a moving violation, do I? Everything else seem like it's in order?"

"Yeah, you're all good. So if your brother is going to look after that for you, does that mean you don't have a man? Or he's not taking care of you like he should?"

Mm-hmm! I told you, I got brother man fishing. He's interested!
"Well, officer—"

"Taj."

Val questioned, "Taj?"

"Yeah, like the Taj Mahal or Taj Gibson that used to play for the Bulls."

"Excuse me. Well, Taj, I don't have a man right now, and aren't you being awfully fresh? I bet my taillight is not even out, is it? You were only stopping me to get some information. Let me take a look-see." I got out and walked to the back of my metallic blue RAV4, and I accidently brushed up against officer "Good Body." Boy, that body felt just as I imagined: rock hard! *Breathe, Valeri, breathe.* "See, I knew you were trying to harass me. There is nothing wrong with my lights."

He looked down at my driver's license and said, "Ms. Wilson, your car is off. None of your lights are on."

"Oh, yeah, I did cut the car off, didn't I?" I gave a little embarrassed giggle. "Trying to preserve my gas. Gas is expensive these days." *Man, am I dumb, dumb, dumb?*

"It's cool. We all make mistakes, like I could've made a mistake about your taillights, but I don't quite remember right now. You ought to let me take you out and buy you a drink or dinner or something."

So Taj, can we leave right now? "Officer Taj, if MY memory serves me correctly, YOU'RE working. You can't take me anywhere in the squad car unless you're arresting me, and I don't think you're doing that, are you?"

"I wasn't exactly talking about now, Ms. Wilson—"

"You can call me Valeri."

"Well, Valeri, I was thinking about later on this week maybe. Let's say Friday?"

"That's awfully sweet of you, and I really would love to go—"

"Well, let's go. Don't follow that up with a but!"

"BUT as I was saying before I was RUDELY interrupted, I'm afraid I'm going to have to pass right now. I'm a Christian woman and I'm trying to live my life according to how God wants me to live it, and I think a relationship would complicate things right now."

"Dag girl, I didn't ask you to marry me. I was asking to see a movie and possibly dinner. Dinner would put a little complication in your life? How do you eat now?"

"Ha ha ha, I see you got jokes, Taj. I guess that did sound like you were proposing or something, huh? Nah, dinner wouldn't really complicate things, but how about this? If I should happen to run into you again, it's a date." *If it's meant to be, Officer Taj, we will meet again.*

"Fair enough, but you do know I have your address? So you know we will eventually run into each other once again. I'm a cop, remember? But without being too forward, let me say, that you are a very beautiful woman, and I look forward to running into you again so we can begin this 'COMPLICATED' process. Be safe out here till we meet again." At that statement, he gave me back my driver's license and insurance card.

He's so sweet! I think I love him. Look at how concerned he is. 'Be safe, till we meet again.' Hmmm! "Thank you Officer Taj, and you do the same." *Dam! Why didn't I just say yes? He can run into some of anybody between now and then and won't even remember my name. Lord, if this is what YOU want for me, make it happen because I don't want to do anything outside of Your will.*

2

After my meeting with Officer "Good Body," I went home. Had a little dinner and watched some TV. Well, if you know anything about me, I'm not much of a TV watcher. I like real stuff, like *First 48*, *Snapped*, and *Forensic Files*, the news—stuff like that. But you know, the news can be really depressing. I do like some movies, though. So I found myself snuggled up with my pillow in the bed, watching *Diary of a Mad Black Woman*. Kimberly Elise did such a good job in that movie, but why in the world did she go back to that piece of a husband she had? She almost lost out on Shemar Moore. I'm telling you, if she had messed that up, I would've been too mad at her.

Then at the end, when she said, "Ask me again, ask me again. I pray for you more than I pray for myself. When you smile, my whole world is all right. Ask me again." *Whew child, that's one of the best lines in ANY movie. I can watch that over and over again. And Shemar, if she doesn't want you, baby, I do. I can't breathe! WHEW!* I don't know why that movie gets me so worked up, but I love it!

A few days later, my best friend Toni and I were getting together for lunch. This girl loves to eat and stays so small. Don't you hate people like that? I mean, I'm a decent size, but I have to work so hard at staying that way. The pounds would start adding up if I thought about food like she does.

Anyhoo, we're having lunch today, and I have to tell her about "Taj." She's such a nosey little thing and has been trying to hook me up with somebody (anybody) for the longest.

*****

It's been almost two years since my last relationship, and the Lord convicted me, so I made the decision to live right. I started going back to church regularly, and I've been celibate since then. My last relationship ended after four years, and I'm not really sure why. I thought things were going well, and then out of the clear blue, he stopped calling and stopped answering my calls. I went out of town to visit my other bestest friend in the world (her name is Rhonda, but we call her Ronni), and he didn't call me one time. He wouldn't answer the phone when I called him.

I called his job when I knew he was the only one there, and he had one of his employees come in early and tell me he wasn't available. Do you know how miserable that trip was for me? I had no clue what was going on and why he was treating me like I was a stalker. I was miles away, and there was nothing I could do about it. Once I got home, he told me that he found someone else (I didn't even know WE were looking), but we could still be friends!

At that point, I didn't think I could go on. I lost faith in everything and everybody.

My Father passed away shortly after my ex left me, and that made this period in my life unbearable. My Dad was my hero. He and Mom were the best things since sliced bread, and he was taken away from me (I do still have Mom, though). I didn't blame God, but I was angry about his death. He meant the world to me. It took me a while to get back to church, but God saw fit to restore my faith in Him, which in return taught me to restore my faith in people again.

*****

Back to my girly, I told her that I had something to tell her when I talked to her the other day, and she has been sweating me about it ever since, so we set up this lunch date for today. She was the type that had to know EVVVERYTHING! "Okay girl, so when he called you, you said hi, and then what?" You know the type.

So I was sitting here at Chipotle, waiting for her. On any given day, one of us was going to be late. Sometimes I was there waiting for her, and other times, she was there waiting for me. Today, it was my turn to wait. I knew she got caught up at the office, running off at the mouth. Me being a physical therapist, I made my own hours, worked out of my own office, and could leave whenever I got ready—between clients of course. Well, in that respect, she made her own hours too (her manager was not in the same office as she), but she talked a lot as well!

Ahh, here she comes in her champagne Lexus, parking. And there she goes, looking at me sitting in my car, saying, "Come on, what are you waiting for?" like she'd been here all along. She's such a little witch, but that's my girl! I love her.

By the time I got out of my car and in the restaurant, she was at the register paying for her food. I can't stand her, but I guess she is on a tight schedule. She does have to get back to work (in what, two to three hours). When she gets back to work, her colleagues ask her, "Where did you go for lunch today, Honduras?"

She found us a table and was sitting down, eating already, and I was still ordering my food. *GREAT! Thanks for waiting, love!*

"Hey, girl. What took you so long? he he he he." She giggled.

"Yeah, whatever!" I told her. "What's up, girl? You were at the office talking when I called to see where you were, weren't you?"

"Girl, Anjoli was talking to me about something her and Chase had done the other day, and I forgot I was leaving the office. You know how she is when she starts talking about spending time with her kids. You called, and my tummy growled at the same time, and I ran out the office and answered the phone. I told you I was driving but hadn't even gotten to my car yet. SORRY!"

"So where did she take Chase? I may want to take my nieces and nephews when they're on spring break."

"She took him to the Holidome with the indoor water park. Girl, you think you slick. I have been waiting for days for you to give me some juicy gossip, and you got me talking about some dam Anjoli? Girl, who is it? What your Mom do now? Or was it your sisters? Tell me, what you waiting for?"

"Good gravy, Toni! RELAX! Take a deep breath. Geez, you're in such a hurry now."

"Ooooh, I hate you! You always do that to me. Fine, fine, fine, Val. What's up?"

"I got pulled over by the police the other day."

"Val, why you playing with me? I get pulled over at least once a week. What's the big deal? Oh, okay! I'll play along. Soooo what did you get pulled over for? Did you get a ticket? Were you speeding? What, what, what?"

Goodness, she seemed a little agitated right about now. "TONI?" I yelled and slammed down on the table with both hands and startled half of the patrons as well as Toni.

"WHAT?"

"Do I speed? Do I drive erratically? For one thing, I was heading home from Mommy's."

"Oh yeah. You are a Goodie Two-shoes when you're behind the wheel, aren't you? You have to make a complete stop at the stop sign," she said in a mocking voice. "Why did you get stopped?"

"There you go. That's the question you should've asked ten minutes ago… He thought I was cute."

"Giiiiirl, shut up!"

"No, YOU shut up!"

"You got a man? What's his name? What he look like? What he say? Are you two going out? OR YOU HAVE ALREADY BEEN OUT? Girl, you are so shady! You know, Val, I thought I was your best friend. You always want to tell me stuff months after it happened." She stopped eating and was now looking at me with DISGUST, like I had a big green broccoli stump stuck in my teeth.

"There you go again. Would you let me tell the story? Or you already got all the answers?"

"My bad, girl. You know I can't wait for you to get a man. You need to get you some. I'm so excited. I'm all ears. Tell me!"

"Okay, so I was visiting with Mommy the other day, and I did call you right after it happened, but I didn't want to talk about it over the phone. I wanted to see your face when I told you. So anyways, I was feeling pretty good and was almost home when I see the flashing lights in my rearview. Girl, I was ticked off because I knew I wasn't speeding or nothing."

"Yeah, we know GTS!"

"Whatever! But when old boy got out of the car and was heading toward me, MAN! Was he a specimen!"

"What he look like?"

"You know how I like a nice body, right?"

"Uh-huh, and don't tell me. Bald head, right?"

"Ooh, how you know? You know Taj?"

"Taj?"

"Yeah, like the Taj Mahal."

"That's his name? Ooh fancy!"

"Yep, or as I call him, Officer Good Body. Anyways he's built like a tank, like he LIVES in a gym. So I gave him my driver's license and stuff—"

"You know I need word for word. Okay, so how did you know he liked you?"

"Because he told me my taillight was out and told me to have my BOYFRIEND look at it for me. Now you know like I know if my taillight was out or the catalytic converter or whatever was acting up on MY car, or even if my washing machine needed fixing, Dwayne would've had that bad boy fixed by now."

"Or bugged you enough till you got it fixed. Girl, he was fishing like that? What did you have on? Were you cute?"

"What you mean, 'was I cute?' Like it's in the past! I'm always cute!"

"I know that, but…were you cute? What did you have on?"

"I'm not really sure what you're talking about because I am ALWAYS cute, BUT I had just got my hair done, and yes, if I must say so myself, I was cute! I had on a little yellow dress that I thought of you when I bought it, so I know you would love it. And more than that, HE loved it!"

"Whatever! So what did you tell him?"

"And you know what? I was so mad at me!"

"Why were you mad? What did you do?" At this time, Toni was looking at me like she was at Wimbledon and this particular volley had been going on for about five minutes.

"You know how I always got some kind of clever flirty line to say or a flirtatious look or something when I'm giving advice?"

"Yeah!"

"I couldn't think of nothing! Not ONE word."

"You're kidding?" And she started CRACKING up. "Not the female version of Will Smith, Ms. Hitch?"

I really didn't get it. What was so funny? Okay, so I'd given her advice here and there about what she should've said in a particular situation. And maybe I did give advice on flirting from time to time, but what did that have to do with MY situation? I told you she was a witch!

"I see my misfortune has caused you much pleasure, but regardless, Ms. Washington, I got the information from him without being the aggressor. So there, laugh all you want to, you little heifer!"

"Girl, keep your panties on! You know it's funny. I would never expect YOU to be the one to clam up when it comes to flirting. You're right. He was the aggressor. What did you say when he went fishing? You know what, forget it! Just tell me when you guys are going out. Tomorrow? Friday?"

"Well, when I knew that he was flirting with me, I called him on it. And then he kind of asked me out this Friday for dinner and a movie."

"Okay, so what are you going to see?"

"We're not!"

"But you just said he asked you out this Friday… What did you do? VALERI? WHAT DID YOU DO? You didn't blow him off, did you? Girl, you did! What's his number? Let me call the police department. I can find out who he is and connect you two."

"Dang, Toni, put the phone down! Can I respond to anything before you fly off the handle? And don't cry, what are you crying for?"

"Girl, I'm not crying, but okay…breathe, Toni"—and she took a deep breath—"Ahhhh. So what happened?" And you could tell she was somewhat woooooh-sahhhh-ing to herself.

"I did somewhat tell him…that going on a date may somewhat…complicate my life—"

She cut in, "SOMEWHAT?"

14

"Well, yeah!"

She started packing up her lunch, mumbling to herself about me growing up to be an old maid, never wanting to go anywhere because I didn't want to be a third wheel. I mean every situation she could think of! I couldn't even hear half the stuff she was saying. This girl really went off. She was cursing and carrying on. You know how when you see people talking, and you think they're talking to you because you don't see the Bluetooth that's in their ear and you may ask them what they said? Then when you realize they're on a Bluetooth, you feel kind of embarrassed because you know they're not crazy but you may be? That's how I was feeling, and people around us were looking at us, I guess wondering what on earth was going on. Like maybe WE broke up or something. "Toni, sit down. Sit down! TONI!"

She looked at me like she forgot I was there. I was waiting for her to say, *"Girl, when did you get here?"*

"Girl, what?"

"You can't leave. Let me explain."

"I'm listening!"

"Well, sit down first," I said. "Look here. This man was so fine. I mean tall, chocolate, muscle bound, AND A COP!"

"Your point, Val?"

"Do you realize how many cute women he may see on any given day? And you know how women love a man in uniform."

"And?" She was starting to soften up some. I knew she was kind of feeling my point and knew where I was going with this.

"I'm not trying to be 'THE OTHER WOMAN' or trying to get my feelings hurt or anything like that. I told him if our paths should happen to cross again, then I would go out with him. Now I'm praying about it. And if this is what the Lord wants for me, then He'll make a way for it to happen. I'm really scared of being hurt, and if I can avoid that, then I will. I haven't counted all men out. Kind of wish that Taj was ugly. I would feel a little better about going out with that body, BUT what God has for me, it is for me!"

"Baby, I'm so sorry that Kody did you like that. I'm with you whatever you decide. But believe me, if you don't happen to run into

Taj anytime soon, I'm calling the police department and asking for Officer Good Body, and you will run into him."

"Toni, the Lord doesn't need your help. Let Him handle it, PLEASE?"

"Girl, you know the Lord needs us at times to spread the Good News about His kingdom. And He uses us as vessels. He may want me to shoot a few Cupid arrows or something." She looked at my face and said, "Okay! Stop looking at me like that. That look is NOT going to work all the time. And you better hope it works on Taj!"

I'm not real sure of the look that I give her, but it does work every time. I think she was so used to me clowning around that when I got serious, she couldn't handle it. I'm sure glad it worked this time.

A couple of weeks or so had gone by. Toni and I planned to go bowling on Saturday. We were going early evening. The summer leagues hadn't started yet. I'm not much of a bowler. My goal when I bowl is to break a hundred and not roll any gutter balls. Toni absolutely loves bowling. I don't know why, but one good thing about it is after we bowl (which is Toni's thing), we can play pool, and that's what I love.

I'm not an expert pool player, but I can hold my own. Guys always challenge me, and for some reason, I seem to win. Not that I'm better, but they want to prove that they are so much better than me that they try a lot of trick shots while I simply try to get my balls in (by the way, I like the solid balls). I guess that way when I win, they have an excuse. I don't make excuses when I lose (I have lost before) and I even compliment them on good shots they make. But when I make a good shot, it's always luck. *Lord, what's wrong with men? Why on earth did you make them like that?* But it's not for us to question the Lord, and He makes NO mistakes. Oh well!

I met Toni at her place and rode with her. She ALWAYS drives when we go out together. I don't know if she doesn't trust my driving or if it's that I never know where we're going. She generally plans everything. I'm pretty easy going though, so naturally, I go along for the ride because it doesn't really matter to me what we do or where we go. Plus, she has that nice Lexus truck that she LOVES, and she loves her music!

Here we go, and she's playing her music. I can't tell you who it was or the song, but she said, "Girl, this my SONG!" She started dancing while she was driving. She had her left hand on the steering wheel and her right hand in the air with her pinky finger sticking up, as if she were drinking "a spot of tea." Next song that came on, and it was the same thing. "Girl, this my song!" I tell you the girl is nuts.

We got to the bowling alley, and she had her own little cute pink and white marble ball, pink bag, and these really cute pink and blue bowling shoes that look like sneakers. So you know she's got on some cute little blue jeans, trimmed in pink, and this really cute pink and blue button up shirt, cute little pink lacey camisole underneath. I hate her! I'm not that much of a pink person, but her outfit was adorable. She always made me want to go and get the same thing, but maybe a different color. Oh, but wait, I don't like bowling. Why would I get a bowling ball? *Disregard!*

I was chilling with my blue jean capris on (white K-Swiss with no socks). They had a cute little orange design on the right back pocket, so I had on an orange Tennessee Vols T-shirt that was tied in the back (Ronni's little brother played football for the Vols on a full scholarship). It had slits cut up the sides and a slit at the neckline. And no, Toni, I didn't cut the slit at the neck. I bought it this way. She was always talking about me cutting my T-shirts at the neck. She's probably whining about my orange and white Tennessee baseball cap too. She doesn't buy my clothes for me. Why would she worry about it? She is so outspoken. I hate her!

I had to rent my shoes from the alley, and I was okay with that. Look at her, she's flaunting her shoes and her outfit, parading around here in front of me. "Girl, go somewhere and sit down! Okay, yes, your outfit and shoes are awfully cute. Is that what you were waiting for?"

"Girl, no! Zani bought this stuff for me. You know how long I been talking about getting me some bowling gear and never did. I came home the other day, and he presented it to me. That's why I wanted to come bowling so bad. I want to try out my new stuff. And he was mad that I wanted to go with you to try it out and not him. So naturally, he doesn't know I'm here. Shhhhh, mum's the word!"

"He did a good job. It's real cute!" I'm not too jealous anymore, although Zani always did really nice and thoughtful things like that for her. He is her "BOYFRIEND." I guess he's supposed to do those type of things. Well, they did nice things for each other. It's cool. My time will come.

We started bowling, and I mean clowning. We really did have a good time. One time, I knocked down one pin, but because it wasn't a gutter ball, I was so geeked. We chest-bumped, "Blueberry style! Blueberries rock!" (That comes from the movie *A Bug's Life,* if you didn't know.) We had all the people around us joining in and encouraging me not to gutter ball and high-fiving me regardless what I did. I got a couple strikes too and quite a few spares. The problem was when I spared, I would knock down one or two pins immediately after that, which didn't help my score. She bowled way better than I did, but I must admit, it really was fun.

I tuckered out after two games. First game, I bowled a hundred and nineteen, which was great for me, but my second game was even better—NOT! I bowled an eighty-six that game. She bowled a hundred and twenty-five the first game and a hundred forty-nine the second. You are supposed to do better as you bowl. Not me! I always bowled my best in my first game. I should quit while I'm ahead, right?

After we bowled, I didn't feel like playing pool. I was really tuckered out, but I wasn't ready to go home and get in the bed, so we played pool anyway. We winded the evening down with a couple of cocktails, and of course, we had to order some chicken tenders and cheese fries with "Queen Snack-a-Lot" around. We sat in the billiards room, ate and drank, and shot a little pool in between. No serious games, just had fun. After we finished the game (I won, but it didn't matter; we were having a good time), we took a potty break. You know we had to freshen up the make-up and put a little lip gloss on before we could come back out.

This girl is so silly. As we were coming out the ladies' room, she started telling me this April Fool's joke somebody played on her. We were cracking up, not paying attention at all to where we were going, when who do you think we bumped into? It was Zani. He had seen her car in the parking lot as he passed by and was truly ticked off.

"So I thought you told me that you would try out your new gear with me, baby?" Zani was a decent-sized guy. He was about six-foot-one or so. He had a slender build but was muscular. I would guess his build was that of a basketball player as opposed to a football player. He was very nice-looking—caramel brown complexion with a short haircut. His pockets were nice-looking too, which translated to his finances being adorable. He was some kind of computer consultant or something like that. Who cares? He ain't MY man! Naw, I'm just playing. I liked him. He's good people, and Toni adored him. That was good enough for me.

"HI Zani," I cut in.

"Hey Val, how you doing?" He gave me a big hug and squeezed me kind of tight. It had been a minute since we'd seen each other.

"I'm good," I said, "How you durn?"

"I was great till I saw Toni's car in the lot." He turned his attention away from me and redirected it back to his girl. "So like I said, Toni, what's up with that?"

Toni was such a good liar. Well, not necessarily a liar, but she could come up with stories at the drop of a hat. I used to ask her for something to tell MY guy (when I had one) when I needed a tall tale. She was ALWAYS there to help, and she had Zani wrapped around her BABY finger. He believed EVERYTHING that came out that girl's mouth.

"Zani, we not bowling, we playing pool," she said.

"So you two are not bowling?" he asked, smirking.

"No! Here's our stuff in here." And we went back into the billiards room where our table was still set up. Our empty glasses and dishes were on the table as well. I started racking the balls, anticipating another game of pool.

Toni is a smart little cookie. I guess she had her little story figured out a long time ago. When we finished bowling, she had taken her ball and stuff back to the car. I was wondering why she had done that, but I guess she knew better than me.

Zani was looking around. I knew he was looking for her bowling bag or any remnants of us bowling, but there was NO evidence of it.

"Uh-huh! Did I hear an apology forming in your lips, Bay?"

"Wait, baby...so you didn't bowl at all tonight?"

"Didn't I tell you I would try out my stuff with you? Val doesn't like bowling anyways." You see how she never said no but eluded him to think that she hadn't bowled? That girl is good.

Zani, please don't ask me. I can't sell my girl out, but I'm not a liar either. "Nope, can't stand bowling," I said before he could ask me. I guess I'm pretty good too, huh?

Zani looked back and forth from me to Toni and gave her a hug. "I'm sorry, baby. You accept my apology?"

"Yeah, I forgive you. But you owe me."

"How can I make it up to you?"

"I'll think of something and let you know."

They kissed, and all I could think was, *SUCKER! Zani, you fell for the banana in the tailpipe. Why didn't you go check that girl's car? All her bowling stuff is pink and her outfit matches ALL of it, AND you bought it. DUH!* I told you he believed EVERYTHING that girl said.

"I knew I should've trusted you instead of jumping to conclusions. I forgot they had pool in here. Who's winning?"

4

After Zani showed up, I shot a little pool by myself. The two of them got caught up in a lip-lock. They were lip wrestling, and I couldn't tell who was winning. I knew that pretty much ended the "girls' night out" for us. I kind of ignored them as I ALWAYS did.

They're so lame. They're always hugging and kissing and acting like they like each other. We all know that relationships don't really happen like that except in the movies. One thing about it though, they do give me hope. After watching them for years and years, I guess my fairy-tale relationship could actually happen. There are a few examples that I have around me where I shouldn't be as negative as I am when it comes to relationships working out.

My Mom and Dad had a wonderful relationship. My Daddy used to come in the house and say, "Where's my girl?"

All four of his daughters would say, "I'm right here, Dad."

"No, here I am!"

"You looking for ME, Dad?"

"Here I come!"

And he would look at us and smile and say, "Where's my number one girl, my shugah bay-bee?"

And we would say, "Oh, you mean Mom. She's in the kitchen." He would never kiss any of the rest of us until he found his "shugah baby." I mean, that's what I call R-E-S-P-E-C-T. Nobody came before my Mom, EVER! That's probably why they were married for forty years and some change before that darn cancer took him out of here. Don't get me wrong, they argued and got mad at each other, but they kept God in the forefront of their relationship, and the anger that they felt toward each other never lasted very long. And they taught us to keep God first!

As a family, we had devotion twice a week where we read Scripture. Each of us gave our interpretation of what we read, then Daddy summed it up. Afterward, we gave prayer requests and prayed. It didn't matter what you had planned or who might've been visiting with us, but at seven o'clock on Saturday evening, we knew where we should be. Mom would start singing, and we would gather around the dining room table, and devotion would begin. And if any of us had friends over at that time, they were at the table with us. Sunday morning, we did an abbreviated devotion so we could eat and get ready for church.

Other examples that I have are my sisters. One of my sisters, Rena (pronounced Ree-nah), had been married for a good minute too (fifteen years or so). She and her husband Robert were just sickening. They LOVED each other more than life itself. I wanted to throw up when I looked at them ogling all over each other. The other two (Khaleesi Marie and Pearl Ann) were married too, but they didn't work my nerves like that one. They were not as public as Rena. They took their sickening behavior home.

I guess the real problem was that I was jealous. Well, not jealous because it's not like I'd ever been married before, seeing that I am the baby of the family and I really am happy that they have someone looking after them like they do. It's just that Rena was such a brat; she really needed someone to baby her like he did. I want someone to love me too and not put other people before me, kind of like what they had.

I had uncles that had been married for a good forty plus years too. So I did have positive examples around me. And I know that God is able, but Satan keeps slipping just enough doubt in my mind to make me negative toward relationships. I really wish he would take his ugly head and get behind me, but if he did that, he wouldn't be such a good devil.

Toni and I got our stuff together and left the alley. They didn't think I knew, but I was sure Zani was rushing over to Toni's to get the mood set for them to finish the lip-lock they started up in this piece.

Toni's mind was obviously not on me right now. She'd gotten quiet, and if you know anything about Toni, you know that quiet and Toni don't quite go together. And for some reason, she was taking the back roads to her place. If I'm not mistaken, this was the long way to her house. We were out in the quiet, country part of town, a secluded area. Zani must've needed a little extra time for something.

"Well, Toni, thanks for playing pool with me tonight. I had a good time."

"Girl, I was having a good time too, then Zani had to come and spoil our night out."

"Now Toni, you really don't expect me to think that Zani spoiled anything for you, do you?"

"What you mean?" she asked, all puzzled like. As soon as she said that, we noticed flashing lights up ahead. The police had someone pulled over on the opposite side of the street. Toni turned to me with her eyes all bucked. "Girl, you think that's Milk Chocolate? What's his name again? Let me slow down and see."

"Keep driving, Toni. It's too dark out here to be able to tell anyways."

But as we were approaching, the officer stepped out of his car, and the streetlight lit up his bald head. I could tell by the confidence in each stride that it was Taj.

"Is that him?" She looked at me, and I guess my expression gave it away. "Dam, girl, that boy IS gorgeous." She blew her horn at him as we passed, and he gave a slight nod as he was trying to hand the obvious lawbreaker the ticket that I'm sure they deserved. She began to slow to a stop and was about to blow her horn again when I stopped her.

"Toni, if you don't drive this car, girl, let me call Zani and tell him to check your car for your bowling bag." I grabbed my phone and dialed Zani.

"Val, don't do that."

"You said you wouldn't help God out."

She said, "Girl, I'm not. This ain't for God, this is for you. He is gorgeous!"

"Hey Zani, this is Val…"

She began picking up speed and whispering, "Val, hang up. You lost your signal out here. Hang up."

"Yeah, Toni wanted me to tell you…" I turned to Toni and said—"What did you want me to tell Zani, Toni?"

"Tell Zani I need him to pick up some wine coolers, Jack Daniels, Down Home Punch, some ice cream, and a little whipped cream before he gets to the house."

"Zani did you hear her?… Toni, he said he's on it and hurry up. Zani look, don't be rushing us now. We got another stop to make before she gets home… Boy, I'm just playing. Keep your shirt on… Bye Zani, and I got something to tell you later on when Toni's not listening…"

"No she doesn't! Hang up the phone, Val!"

When I hung up the phone, Toni narrowed her eyes, looking at me again with disgust. "Val, you told him if your paths should happen to cross again, you would go out with him. Your paths crossed. You supposed to be setting up a date with Mr. Man right now and shit, if you don't, I'mma set up a date for myself."

"He didn't see me anyways—and let me get this straight. You got a man, but you trying to go after what could be mine? I'mma get Zani back on the phone. You keep talking, keep giving me ammunition."

"What could be yours? You don't want him AND the deal wasn't if he saw you, the deal was if your paths crossed. You being the honest hoe that you are, it was your duty to wait for him to see you." At that moment, we noticed flashing lights behind us.

5

I shot Toni a look. Boy if looks could kill, Toni would be a goner. "Toni, I'm going to kill you, and I'm telling Zani. I'm definitely leaking this sh—"

"Val, just play it cool. It might not even be him. Maybe I was speeding as usual." Toni stopped the car and opened the door and bolted out the car.

"Ma'am, get back in your car. Close your door, and passenger, stay in the vehicle," the officer said over the loudspeaker. "Driver and passenger, place both hands on the dash."

"Toni, you see what you did? What if he starts shooting? He thinks we've done something wrong now! Why did you jump out like that? I thought you were about to jet!"

"Relax, Val. I was getting ready to intercept him, if it is him, so he wouldn't see you. 'I was just trying to help you, Ike.'"

"If HE doesn't kill us, I got you, girl."

Two other squad cars pulled up before we knew it and had us blocked in. I knew it was taking him a long time to get over to the car, but I was so upset with Toni that it didn't register that he wasn't here yet, but my subconscious self knew it was taking long.

"Look what you did! The man done called for back-up! Girl, you scared him silly, and now I'm nervous!"

Five officers piled out of the three cars and approached our vehicle with caution and with their hands on their weapons. Two officers came to the passenger door, two to the driver's door, and one was in front of the car. Toni rolled her window down. "Ma'am, can I see your driver's license and proof of insurance please?"

I would recognize that voice anywhere. I whispered to Toni, "That's him."

She looked up at him and said, "Officer, what's the problem?"

"You tell me, ma'am. Where were you going when you jumped out like that?"

She handed him her driver's license and said, "I was coming to meet you at your car to see what the problem was. I didn't know it was against the law to do that. I was trying to run interference for—"

I elbowed her as she was pointing at me.

He looked in and over at me, and a slight smile came across his face. "Is that Valeri Wilson?" He remembered my name! *Whaaaaat!*

"Yeah, you know my girl?"

The other officer asked kind of quietly, "This the girl you've been stalking... I mean talking about these last few weeks? The one whose house we rode past a few times? The one who owes you a date the next time you run into her?"

"Come on, Deuce, man! You ain't have to put my business out there like that," he tried whispering. I guess they didn't want the other officers to know what they were talking about. "Yeah, that's her."

"Ladies, I'm going to have to ask you all to exit the vehicle while we do a brief search." This was, I guess, the lead officer on the scene. He had on a white-collared shirt as opposed to navy blue and was in a car by himself. He originally was in front of the car but had walked over to the driver's side by this time.

"Sir, I know these women. I didn't recognize the car."

"So you're vouching for them? You're sure there's no contraband in this vehicle."

"Well, I know the passenger. We can do a search of the vehicle, sir." We got out the truck and stood off to the side of the road. Taj began talking to Toni, "I thought you two were having some sort of problem or were lost, being kidnapped or something. I saw you as you slowed down when I was giving out that ticket. You blew your horn at me and then stopped. I figured you needed something. But I see now that you were carrying precious cargo and was trying to get my attention." He turned to me and said, "Can I be of service to you, Valeri?"

27

The other two officers did a brief look through the car. Just a surface inspection but kind of detailed. I guess they were trying to make it look good since their sergeant was still there. When he got in his squad and pulled off, they finished their search and came over to Taj and his partner, Deuce, and told them that it was all clear. Taj could continue with whatever business he needed to handle with us, meaning if he was giving us a ticket, he could proceed with that. Backup was no longer needed, and we could get back in our car. They took off, and it was Taj and his partner left with Toni and myself.

Taj turned to Deuce and told him to "handle that." I guess he knew what that meant because he took Toni back to the driver's side, let her get back in the car, and started talking to her. I couldn't tell if he was flirting with her or dispersed to let Taj have some alone time with me.

I was so busy watching Toni being taken away by Deuce that I wasn't paying attention to Taj. I guess he had been holding his arm out for me to grab his hand so he could lead me back to the passenger side of the car for a minute. "You want my arm to fall off?"

No he didn't use one of my other favorite lines of a movie. Billie D said that to Diana Ross in *Lady Sings the Blues*, and this man sounded just as yummy as Billie D. Good gravy, I was in heaven. I placed my hand in his, and he helped me through the grassy terrain and to the passenger door.

"So, Valeri, can I be of service to you? Were YOU trying to get my attention?" he asked.

"Taj, my girl was trying to get your attention. I told her about our last encounter and had to pretty much make her promise she wouldn't call the police station so she could tell you where I would be, just to ensure us hooking up. I wanted it to be natural if we should happen to run into each other again, so no, I wasn't trying to get your attention."

I could tell that I kind of hurt his feelings by what I said.

"Look, if you don't want to go out with me, that's cool. I'm a grown ass man. I'm not going to cry. I would love to get to know you better and see where that takes us, but I'm not going to force myself on you or nobody else for that matter."

"That's not what I meant. I would love to go out with you. I wanted to make sure that's really what YOU wanted."

He said, "Look here, I can speak for myself. Wait a minute. Let's start over. Hi, Val. Can I call you Val?"

"Yes Taj, you can call me Val. How are you?"

"I'm good now," he said, and this big old Kool-Aid smile came across his face. "How are you?"

I was really caught up in his voice and that smile. He had a smile that lit up the darkness. It was so cute, and he looked like an innocent little boy that was about to get into some dirt for the umpteenth time. "I'm good too. You're not going to get into any trouble over here talking to me like this while you're on duty, are you?"

"Naw, I'm good. My boy is handling business if anybody rides past. You see how he put me on blast back there, don't you? I did ride past your house a few times, but I was only trying to make sure your street was safe. I WAS hoping to get a glimpse of you at some point, but after a while, I started thinking that I should let it go. But now that our paths have crossed again…will you marry me?"

We both cracked up. Here I was, thinking that we were about to set a date to go out, and he goes and pops the question. "Boy, you are too crazy," I said, still laughing.

"Okay, I'll take it slow…for you," he said, still smiling. "So when do you want to set this date for?"

"My schedule is pretty open, meaning I'm flexible. You tell me."

"How about tomorrow?"

"Tomorrow? Dang! You aren't wasting any time, are you? Well, I have to get home now so I can get in the bed because I have a big day tomorrow. I have to go to church in the a.m., and then Sundays are devoted to spending the day with Mommy and the rest of the family so…it will probably be a little hard for me to get away."

"Can I go to church with you?"

"WOW, you would do that?"

"I go to church regularly. What you trying to say?"

"I'm not trying to say anything. I wasn't expecting you to be willing to go to church with ME anytime soon."

"So is that a yes?"

29

"Taj, look here, I want to get to know you a little better before you meet any of MY people. My Momma would have us married with a baby on the way if she met you right now. So let's go out first, get to know each other a little better, and then see how things go. You may not even want to go to my church after you spend a little time with me."

"Nah, I'm a police officer. I've been trained to profile people and see what makes them tick, and I can tell that heaven is missing an angel right now because you're right here with me."

Awwwwww! That was really sweet. CORNY but sweet. This man is good and says the nicest things. Let's see if he feels the same way when he finds out I'm not giving it up ANYTIME soon. "As Michael Jackson would've said, you're a smooth operator. Daddy always told me to look out for fellas like you. Let's see if you feel that same way after a while."

"All right, I'll give you tomorrow all to yourself, but that's it. Monday, it's me and you lady. Is that cool?"

"Monday it is. What time and where bouts?"

"Can I come scoop you?"

"That's fine. What time should I be ready? Wait, you don't have to work Monday evening?"

"I usually work the day shift. This is overtime for me. I didn't have anything else to do. Why not work? Is six okay for you?"

"Six is fine." But I was thinking to myself, *Why you don't have anything better to do on a Saturday night? This gorgeous specimen, and he doesn't have a lady already? Hmmm, I'll find out Monday for sure what the problem is.*

He took my hand and kissed the back of it and said, "Till Monday, girlfriend."

"Till Monday," I said.

He opened the car door for me, shut it behind me after I got in, and walked away. He walked alongside of our car and, around to the driver's side of the squad.

Toni was sitting in the car, looking at me while I was watching him walk away. I had forgotten all about her. "You didn't eff it up this time, did you?"

I didn't answer. I simply looked at her; in fact, I glared at her. And there she goes, fussing again.

"You know the things I do for MY friends. My man is sitting at the house, waiting for me to put a little moonlight in MY night, and I'm trying to make sure that MY girl is going to be all good, find HER a man, and look at the thanks I get." She started driving away. "Boy, I tell you about some folks." Her voice changed, and she said, "Make sure that I'm the maid of honor and that your family knows that I made this all possible for you. Okay, honey?" she said as she patted me on the leg.

I shook my head and said, "Just drive, heffa!"

6

After Toni let me off at my car, I realized I didn't get Taj's number. Suppose something happens and I can't make it or something happens and he can't make it? I started to call Toni and let her know. I know she would've gotten in touch with him somehow and either got his number or given him mine, but nah. It's all good. I'm still at the place where if it's meant to be, and God is leading this thing and not me, then it'll work itself out.

I made it home safely; daydreamed the whole way. I couldn't seem to focus. All my thoughts were about this man. I don't know right now if this is God leading me or Satan. I had some real impure thoughts going through my mind, and for the longest, I couldn't think of anything but Taj. He said the sweetest things, was absolutely adorable, had a great body, beautiful smile, and a nice voice—the whole package, for an impressive first impression. I know I don't know the man, but he seemed too good to be true and more than likely if it seemed too good to be true, then it probably was.

As Daddy warned, he was probably one of those slow walkers. According to Daddy, a slow walker is a man that says and does all the right things until he gets what he came for (which in most cases is some nookie. Or in layman's terms, sex), then it's a done deal. They don't know you anymore. His main objective is to get into my pants, I'm sure. *"Lord, I'm asking You to be the head of EVERYTHING that I do, and right now, my mind is not focused on You, so I'm asking that You would redirect my thoughts and help me to relax, get some sleep, and be ready to get in Your Word and refuel my spirit with You in the morning. In the name of Jesus I pray. Amen."*

I was able to sleep after that. Praise God he relaxed my mind, body, and soul and gave me a good night's sleep.

Sunday, worship service was ALL good. The preacher spoke on giving God praise in everything you do, regardless of the situation. If it's trouble and turmoil that you're experiencing in your life, give Him praise. If you're having the best time in your life, give Him praise.

Wow! I never thought about praising God when I'm down and depressed, but I guess giving the Lord praise during that time would help you come out of it quicker than without Him. My sister, Pearl Ann, always has a positive word to say. For instance, before I got my RAV4, I had this car that was in the car clinic at least once a month. Yeah, Robbie (that's what I called my red Dodge Shadow) was ALWAYS sick. I would get so upset because I was spending a lot of money to keep her running. As soon as I got a little extra piece of money in my pocket, I had to spend it on her. Pearl would say, "Well, praise God you had the money to get her fixed. You could've been in a situation where you would either be without a car or borrowing the money or something."

At first, I would think to myself, *Shut up, girl! Ain't nobody trying to hear that!* But when I really sat back and looked at it, I would have to give the Lord some praise because she was right. She helped me get to a point where I praise God for everything that I have. I would get a few extra dollars in my pocket and make plans to do something for ME with it, but as soon as I got that little bit extra, one of my nieces or nephews would call or come by and ask, "TT (that's what they call me), you got a few dollars you could spare?"

God gave me the spirit of sharing which I got from my Momma. Well, Daddy used to share too, but you better believe if you borrowed money from my Daddy, he was expecting to get it back and NOT have to come looking for you to get it. And so of course, if I had it, they had it. And whenever they were in need, the Lord saw fit to hand me a little extra so that I could share. Praise God for my family. And now with the preacher preaching on it, it's just confirmation. So whatever you're going through, good or bad, give Him praise because your situation could be worse.

Dinner at Mommy's was like dinner most other Sundays. First of all, it was scrumptious. My Momma does not play when it comes to throwing down on some food. Those greens were some of the best-est old greens I have ever tasted before in my life. Yum yum! Rena and Robert were their usual pain in the butt selves, all lovey-dovey and carrying on! Khaleesi Marie and Jonah were there of course. They don't usually stay too long. They were usually gone before sundown. I guess because they had a little distance to travel, and Khaleesi does not play. The kids have to be in bed by eight o'clock EVERY night. They can get her up as early as they need to, but you better believe that her and Jonah are going to have their alone time after eight. That's probably why they've lasted so long too.

Pearl, Jesai, and their kids were there as usual. So all four of Mom's girls were there as well as three of my brothers and their families. The other two boys live a good ways away and only come over once a month when the whole family gets together.

After dinner, the guys get a game of bid whist going, and the ladies get the kitchen cleaned and chill out with Mom for a while. We take care of Mom's hands and feet. Today was my day to give her a pedicure and polish her fingernails. She works so hard and never does a lot to pamper herself, so her girls try to make sure that's taken care of for her. And believe me when I say she is NOT going to PAY (or let YOU pay) to have them done.

It was pretty nice outside, so the kids had a good time playing across the street at the park, and the girls sat on the porch, enjoying each other's company and enjoying the weather. You know, I praise God for my family. I'm not saying that we are any better than anyone else's family, but I praise God for mine. We're not perfect. We have our faults and make mistakes, but when push comes to shove, we are always there for each other. We can sit down, play cards, converse, and enjoy each other's company without arguing, drinking, or acting plum fools. That's because Mom and Dad always taught us how to love and be there for each other. *Thank you, Lord for the family You gave to me. You didn't have to do it, but I'm so glad You did.*

Khaleesi and Jonah stayed for a long time today. It had gotten dark and was almost ten before they left. The kids were on spring break, so she gave them a little more time to play with the rest of the crew, or should I say Jonah gave Khaleesi a little more time to play with us. She had us playing Yahtzee and Boggle. She won most of the games of Boggle, but we gave her a run for her money with Yahtzee. The only way Jonah got her out of here was because he convinced Robert to take Rena home. Two of my brothers left a while ago.

I had such a good time with the family that I hadn't thought about Taj till I got home at about ten-fifteen and turned on the news, and of course, there were stories concerning the police. I started thinking, *I wonder what he's up to? Is he thinking about me? And that smile…who is he showing those pearly whites to today? Lord, I need to get to sleep. Will You help me, please?*

7

Today's the big day. I had two massages to do before noon and two for the afternoon. I tried to keep my mind occupied on my work and was doing a good job till Toni called me while I was having lunch at twelve-thirty.

"So what you wearing?..."

Now I'm wondering if she was really trying to be helpful or if she was being her usual NOSEY self? "I'm not sure, Toni. Do you have any suggestions?..."

"Well, where are you all going? Is this a jeans night? Or should you be a little more classy?..."

"Aw man, I forgot to find out how I should dress. I didn't get his number, so I can't call him and I know what you're thinking, and NO! You cannot do my makeup for me. Maybe I'll throw on my blue jean jumper, which should be pretty neutral. It can go for casual or for something a little snappier, depending on the shoes. So what shoes should I wear with that?..."

"You sure you don't want me to do your make-up?..."

"Positive! What shoes did you say? Never mind, I'll wear my orange lacey camisole, orange sandals, and my orange purse..."

"Orange sandals?..."

"They're not really orange. They're a rust color, like cognac or something. I like calling them orange, though. Don't worry about it. I got this!..."

"That boy is going to think you a dam pumpkin and get to running. You had on orange Saturday. Can't you wear something else?..."

"Oh yeah, I did. I'll wear my red pumps with my red purse..."

"Now he's going to think you're a hooker and run..."

"Toni, I'll talk to you later…"

"Wait, wait, wait! Val?…"

"Yeah?…"

"I'll be by there in a few…"

"Nope, I'm not home…"

"You'll be there in a little bit. I'll meet you there…"

"Toni, look. I'm not trying to go above and beyond to impress anybody. If he likes me, he'll like me if I was wearing nothing…"

"Now that's what I'm talking about, baby girl! Go to the door wearing nothing, and he'll be hooked for life! You got a banging body!…"

"You are so silly! You know what I mean! I got this, Toni. I'll get it together without you…"

"Okay, I won't say anything. Just let me come by and sit while you get ready. I'll leave by five-thirty, I promise…"

"Goodbye, Toni…" and I hung up the phone. I knew she was going to be at the house when I got there. She probably worked half a day, and this was MY date, not hers. NOW how am I supposed to focus on work? *Okay, so Lord, it's me again.*

I finished with my last client about three o'clock. I went home, and praise Jesus, Toni was NOT there! I got in the tub and soaked for close to an hour with candles lit all around me and RELAXED. I started to have a glass of wine while I soaked but decided against it. I wanted to have ALL my faculties when I went out on my date. Didn't need anything to alter my thought process or decision-making. I got out the tub around four-thirty, dried off real good, and put on lotion and body spray. Mommy gave me some Mango body butter for Christmas that I absolutely loved. I'd run out of my Christmas present and had to go stock up on my own. I did not want to run out of that stuff. It smelled scrumptious.

I pulled a few outfits out the closet and was sitting on the bed, chilling in my undies, about to start trying on stuff when I could hear someone trying to get in the front door (Toni had a key to my place. I was somewhat forgetful, what can I say? I had the dead bolt on or whatever it's called, which is why she was having trouble. My big brother, Dwayne, hooked it up for me. He was so protective of me. Anything that needed fixing or that he thought I should have, he was "Johnny on the spot" with his drill and his tool belt, always ready to hammer or drill something. I called him Mr. Fixit! I am the baby, though, so I'm not mad at him.)

When I heard her struggling with the door, I went and opened it for her but didn't let her in right away. I kept my foot behind the door and told her to go home. "Toni, why are you here? Didn't I tell you not to come? You're NOT doing my makeup!"

"Would you open the door for me, please? And why didn't my key work?" I looked at her. She's so worrisome. "Val, you know you going to let me in, so stop playing and open the door. You wasting precious time. Plus, I gave you time. I could've been in the house waiting for you when YOU got off work, but I let you have some alone time."

I let her in. She looked me up and down as she passed by me and mumbled, "You smell good BUT you should've been dressed and ret to go, then I would have nothing to do." She headed straight for my room. "Let's see what our options are for today."

"Toni, I'm going basic. If we hit it off, I'll have plenty of time to show off my wardrobe. I'm going to wear this jean outfit right here."

She looked past the clothes I was pointing at and the other stuff I'd pulled out and started looking through my closet. "We got these pants here with this silk blouse, or if you'd like to add some color to it, we can do these slacks with this top right here."

I went into my bathroom and sat down at the vanity to start applying makeup, so I couldn't see what she was pulling out, and she didn't realize that I had started my makeup which was a good thing for me. I had been contemplating on what to wear, but seeing her helped make my final decision, so my mind was made up, and I wasn't about to stress over it any longer. I'm not one to try to do a whole lot of impressing. I'm a simple girl, and if I like it, then there it is!

I've come to realize that I have to be happy with me. Once you start trying to impress people, you have to continue with those airs, and when they find out you're not the person they thought you were, then what? Yeah, no thanks! I'll do without that. I am going to be me till I die, and either you're going to like that person or you're not. But all the pretense, I don't need it.

I could hear her still in the closet, rambling through my clothes and talking to herself. I wondered when she was going to realize I was on the next phase of getting ready to go. I was almost done with my eyes when she started calling me. "Val?" She came into the bathroom where I was and startled me, yelling out my name, "VALERI NICOLE WILSON! I have been in that closet, pulling out outfit after outfit, and you're halfway done with your makeup! Girl, you are wrong! So what are you going to wear? Did you see anything I pulled out for you? How are you putting on makeup without knowing for sure what you're wearing?"

She asked question after question, and I simply ignored her. She did almost make me smear eyeliner all over my eyes when she scared me, though. I'm glad I had JUST pulled it away from my eyes. I would've had to do them all over again. My eyes were complete; all I was doing now were the finishing touches of mascara when I noticed the look on her face. I could tell she was disappointed. For whatever reason, she really thought I was going to let her apply my makeup.

"I can't believe you didn't let me do your makeup."

"Look here little lady, I understand that you don't like how I put MY makeup on, but guess what? I like it, and right now, that's all that matters. If this was a special date or something, then maybe I would let you, but right now, I'm satisfied. Thanks but no thanks!"

"Then why did you let me come over here?"

"Girl, I told you no!" And I was about to let her have it when I realized who I was talking to.

"You told me I could come over and do your makeup and help you pick out an outfit." Then she started with her acting skills and started whining and acting like she was crying. "You used me. You got me over here and your makeup is done now and I'm sure you're not going to wear either of the outfits I picked out for you. You used me. You absolutely used me!" And at this point, she went over the top and started really sobbing, "I thought I was your best friend! Friends don't do friends like that!" She ran out the bathroom, and I could hear her jump on the bed, and she was kicking and sobbing out loud.

I continued with the makeup, put on my blush and lip liner. She came back in the bathroom. "You weren't even going to come check on me?"

"Toni, you need Jesus." And we both started laughing. That girl is so silly. She was the type that you either thought was hilarious and you really liked her or you hated her. Most of the time, I hated her. Just joshing, she cracks me up.

I took my time getting dressed, put my little Derréon jeans on. They had sky blue threading on them, so the halter top I was putting on was sky blue. I wasn't going to put the jacket on till he got here. And I wore a pair of black ankle boots. We went back and forth on me wearing one of the outfits she picked out for me, when I finally put her out.

"Toni, go home."

"Okay Val, I'll be quiet. Just let me stay till he gets here."

"Nope, I don't want him thinking I needed you here to dress me or whatever. Go home. I really don't want you here when he gets here. Besides, YOU said you would leave by five-thirty. It's quarter to six. AND you promised!"

"Girl, don't be expecting bruh man to be on time. You know how colored folks are?"

"Goodbye Toni, I'll call you later."

"Fine, I'm gone. But if I don't hear from you by ten-thirty, I may be in your living room, waiting for you when you get back."

"I will call you before then and let you know what's going on, but don't—I REPEAT, DO NOT—come back to my house tonight unless I call you and tell you I need you."

She started mumbling again, "Well, I can't make no promises, but—"

"Give me your key."

"Okay Val, I won't come over. GEEZ LOUISE! Relax!"

I opened the door to let her out. "Out Toni!" And guess who was coming up the stairs? I looked up and saw Mr. Man and looked back and glared at Toni again.

8

"Did somebody call the po-po? Intruder in the house?" Taj said, walking up to the front door.

"Hi Taj, you're early."

"Hi, baby doll, I'm impatient. I been around the corner for about ten minutes and decided fifteen minutes early is cool."

Toni peeked her head out the door. "Hi Tee." She turned around and looked at me and said, "He's on time, hmmm! What do you know?" She looked back at Taj. "Don't you look dapper? Did you all plan to dress alike?"

"Toni, don't stop with just your head. Let the rest of your body follow your head out the door." I turned to Taj and said, "Toni was just leaving."

"Hey, Toni!" Taj said. Then he turned to me and said, "You ready to go? We should be leaving too."

"Yeah, I'm ready. Let me get my purse and jacket. Bye Toni, I'll talk to you later."

"Bye Toni, she'll call you later on. I'll make sure of it."

"Bye girl. Glad I could be of help to you today. Tee, don't make me have to come looking for either one of you. Take care of my girl, and y'all be careful. No drinking and driving." She hit him in the chest as she walked past him and headed down the stairs.

"Yes, ma'am!" he replied.

I walked away and back into the house. I don't know why Toni needed to be known for whatever she does. She's GOT to be recognized, under all circumstances, even when she didn't do anything. Taj followed me into the house and stood by the door.

"Nice place you got here."

"Thanks," I said as I went to get my jacket and purse out the bedroom. "You can have a seat if you want. I'll be out in a minute. Just have to grab my stuff." When I came out, he was sitting in the living room on the arm of the couch. "Do I need to change my clothes since we do kind of look like we're trying to dress alike?"

"Naw, we're good. You live here by yourself?"

"Yeah, I'm renting right now. It's one of my brothers' properties. You ready?"

"Yeah, let's hit it."

We went outside and got in his black on black four-door Avalanche. He was such a gentleman. Naturally, he opened and closed the door to the truck for me. I got a chance to get a good look at him as he crossed in front of the car. He looked awesome. And the truck smelled really good. I couldn't tell if it was his cologne or air freshener. When he got in, I could tell that it was his cologne, and it smelled great. His music was nice and soft. I guess it would be considered smooth grooves.

"So...how was your day today?" he started off the conversation.

"Well, you know, I can't complain," I said, but I was engulfed in his voice. I could listen to him talk all day. "I had a good day. I didn't work too hard. How about yours?"

"My day was good too. I got off at three and relaxed for a while. I'm not going to lie, I've really been looking forward to getting together with you today, but before I take off driving all over the place, where would you like to go eat?"

"I'm good. I can eat anywhere. Where do you want to eat?"

He said he'd been thinking about some good old-fashioned soul food, so he took me to a restaurant on the west side called MacArthur's. I had been there before, but not in a while, and I had never eaten inside before. So we sat down and ate in the restaurant.

We had good conversation, and the food was awesome! We talked about his family. He has three sisters and a brother, and he was the oldest. Both his parents were alive and well, and he was a true "Mama's Boy" by every sense of the phrase. He talked a lot about his Mom and Dad, but his Mom was his number ONE girl! That's one reason he didn't have a steady girlfriend right now. He said the women he'd been dealing with lately had a problem with his and his Mom's relationship.

I thought it was cute the way he talked about his parents. I knew he loved them. How could anyone NOT be crazy about their parents, especially Mom? I loved my Mom just the same (actually, I think I love mine more). And Daddy always told us, you can tell how a fella is going to treat you by how he treats his momma! Well, praise Jesus! I hope this is a GOOD indication.

He had no children, but one of his previous girlfriends had an abortion (against his will) a few years back. He did explain that he had "FRIENDS," but nothing serious. His Mom was really looking forward to him settling down and bringing in some grandchildren, which he was not ruling out if the right one came along. He also explained that his friends were something that he could live without. I took that to mean that if he had a reason to give up his friendships, then he would. I could be wrong, though.

Anyway, our conversation was really good. I didn't talk much about myself. Every time he tried to get me to talk about me, I would tell him he wasn't finished and ask another question. We sat there, talking for a while, getting to know each other a little bit. Then we decided to leave. He asked me if I had a problem sitting outside, taking in some sights. My only concern was that I might get a little cold, and he told me not to worry, but he had something really nice he wanted to share with me.

He pulled my seat out for me to get up, and as we were leaving out the door, I got to the door first and opened it myself and held it open for him to grab it and thought no more about it. When I got to the car and went to open it, he shut the door back and held his forearm against it. I looked up at him. I noticed a look on his face, and he didn't seem very happy with me for some reason.

"Look here Val, I'm not sure what kind of guy you're used to kicking it with, but when you're with me, I open doors. My girls don't open doors for me. So if this relationship is a friendship or turns into anything else, just know that you WILL allow me to be the man that MY Daddy taught me to be, and we'll be all good. Otherwise, we're going to have a problem. Capiché?"

"My bad, Taj, I didn't mean any disrespect, but I'm used to opening doors myself and doing things for me, even when I did have a man, so it may take me a minute to get used to this. Be patient with me?"

"Just so that you know, the quickest way to get on my nerves is to do MY job for me."

"Are you done scolding me, Taj? I'm getting cold. Can I get in the car now…SIR?"

"Are you going to behave?"

I looked up at him again, and he put this big old smile on his face, put his arms around me, and gave me a nice firm hug. He squeezed me tight and lifted me off the ground and asked me again, "Are you going to behave?"

I was almost eye level with him and was barely able to squeeze out these words, "I…can't…breathe." He squinted his eyes at me, and I said, "Yes…I'm going to try."

He put me down, and I held on to him long enough for the oxygen to travel back to my head while he rubbed my back. When I was good, he opened the door for me, and over exaggeratedly, helped me in like I was really hurt or something.

Once he was settled in the car, I asked him, "Is it okay if I open the door when you're not around? I mean, I would hate to get on your nerves when you're at home, chilling, and I'm at work wanting to get in the bathroom or something."

"I thought you said you were going to behave? I see I'mma have to deal with you."

"I'm just asking. I want to be sure we're on the same page."

"By all means, you may open all the doors necessary when we are apart. Smarty-pants!"

"Thanks, officer," I said with a smirk on my face and laughing to myself. I was somewhat of a smarty-pants, if I might say so myself.

We talked a little bit more while we headed off to whatever it was he wanted to show me. Although I still didn't do much talking about myself, I found it to be fairly easy to talk to him. It seemed as though we had known each other all our lives. We were laughing and clowning around and enjoying each other's company so much that I wasn't paying attention at all to where we were going. Toni would be so disappointed in me. She always told me to pay attention to where I was in case I needed to know how to get myself home. And when I talked to her, she was going to ask me where we went, and I was not going to be able to tell her a thing. Dang! Oh well.

Before you knew it, we were at some spot further into the city that was secluded and quiet. He parked and came around to the passenger side and opened the door for me to get out. I don't know when he grabbed the blanket, but he was carrying it in one hand and held my hand with the other and led me to an area through some trees where you could see Lake Michigan and the Chicago skyline. We sat down on a grassy slope on the blanket, wrapped the rest of it around us, and sat there, looking at the scenery.

I have been in the Chicago area all my life and have NEVER seen the city like this before, except on postcards. We sat there for about ten to fifteen minutes without saying a word, taking in the sights. He put his arm around me, and I leaned my back onto his chest. It felt like I was lying on a rock. His chest was oh so firm, but it felt oh so good, and the scenery was breathtaking.

"Taj, this spot is beautiful and quiet. How did you ever find this place?"

"I am a police officer. There are a lot of little nooks and crannies that I know about that the average person doesn't."

"Yeah, and I'm sure this is where you bring ALL your women, huh? I know…you don't even have say anything because you figure once they see this spot, you got 'em. It's cool."

"Oh, so you judging me now, huh? Look here, baby girl, I haven't had to bring NO woman out here to GET them. Just being with me has been good enough. You know how women are these days?"

"Okay, Mr. Conceited."

"And that wasn't to be conceited. It's a mere fact. Look here, I stopped a woman one day for running a red light, and when I got back to her with her ticket, she was handing me her drawers and asked me if I wanted to settle this over dinner and spread her legs. Now tell me I'm wrong and women don't throw themselves at men. Or maybe they just throw themselves at me."

"Somebody actually did that to you?"

"Yup."

"And what did you do?"

"I handed her the ticket and told her to have a nice day. I also told her to be careful, mosquitoes are out, and they're carrying that West Nile virus. You might want to close those."

"Close what?"

"Her legs!"

I found that hilarious. "What did she do?"

"She closed her legs and drove off with an attitude."

"Aww, you hurt her feelings."

"That's not all I was going to hurt. I started to pull her ass out the car, cuff her, and take her to the station. Indecent exposure or something. Propositioning or trying to bribe an officer. I could've come up with something. She pissed me off!"

"Well, I'm glad you didn't."

"Yeah, but my point is that women throw themselves on men."

"So is that your way of saying that you never brought another woman up here? Or is that your way to avoid answering the question?"

"Do you want me to answer that truthfully?"

"If you want to answer it, then yes. But you don't have to. And truthful is the ONLY way I would want you to answer any question!"

"I have brought one other person out here, but she didn't appreciate the sights. She was whining about sitting in the grass and stuff, one thing after the other. She said she had seen the skyline before. She took the taste out of my mouth for this spot… I knew that you were one that would have a deep appreciation for stuff like this. Tell me this: do you like watching the sun rise and set? Actually, you don't have to tell me. I know you do. You like seeing a rainbow and the colors in the sky as the sun is rising or setting. I can see that in your eyes. And you DO have beautiful eyes, by the way."

"Thanks Taj, and I do deeply appreciate you bringing me here. And yeah, you're right. I LOVE looking at all the beautiful colors God puts in the sky. And this place? I could sit here and look at this all night. It's so serene."

At that point, we began to gaze out at the scenery again, not really talking but making a few comments here and there about what we were seeing. We had a nice time. I was beginning to fall asleep when he noticed the time.

"Say, baby doll...wake up you, it's eleven o'clock. Your girl is going to start looking for you any minute now. Let's get going. You can call her in the car."

"It's eleven already?"

"Yup, let's go."

He took his arm from around me and got up. He pulled me up and gave me another hug and said, "Thanks for appreciating my efforts."

I put my hand on the back of his head and his neck and pulled him down and whispered in his ear, "Thanks for making me feel special and sharing this with me. I had a really nice time today." Then I kissed him on the cheek.

We got back in the truck and headed for home. There wasn't a lot of conversation on the ride home. He did remind me to call Toni, though. "Baby doll, call Toni now before you forget."

"I'll call her when I get home."

"Well, call her now and tell her you'll call her again when you get home. She might be waiting at the house for you when you get there, remember?" I told him about that when we were in the restaurant.

"You're right." So I called her. "Hi Toni!... No, I'm not just getting home... I'm actually on my way home now, so I'll call you when I get there... I'll call you when I get home, love...in about fifteen minutes or so... Actually, give me about thirty minutes, and I'll call you... Well, if I don't call you, then you call me... Goodbye, Toni... I'll talk to you in a few... Bye!..."

"You know your girl is a mess, don't you?"

"Yeah, I know, but that's my girl."

"Before I forget again, give me your number."

"Oh yeah, good thinking, officer. I guess that's why you're the boss, huh?"

"I am? Good, that works for me."

He gave me his number, and I called his phone. Shortly afterward, we pulled up to the house. He grabbed my hand and kissed it and said, "Stay put, I'll get the door for you." He came around, opened the door, and walked me to my front door. "I enjoyed myself tonight. Can I expect another date this week or what?"

"You can call me, and we'll discuss that."

"Cool, I'll call you tomorrow. Is that okay, Val?"

"Sure, that'll work. Thanks again for a great night, Taj."

"My pleasure, beautiful, thank you. Get on inside."

So I went in the house, went to my room, got ready for bed, and headed straight to la-la land (beddy-bye for those of you who don't know—dreamland, sweet dreams).

My phone rang around twelve-thirty. Actually, when it rang, I had already missed two calls. I had been sound asleep, having a rather pleasant dream (I might add). You know the kind where you don't quite remember what it was about, but you wake up smiling, trying to remember?

"Hello!..."

"Heffa, I'm sitting at home, waiting for the thirty minutes to be up, and you drooling on your pillow? I know he ain't there with you, is he?..."

"Toni, I'll call you tomorrow. I'm sorry I forgot to call you when I got in but I had a really nice time, and that's ALL I was thinking about. Talk to you tomorrow..."

"Val, is he there?..."

"No, goodnight..."

"I'll call YOU in the morning..."

"Fine, goodnight..."

"Nite, heffa..."

9

My alarm and my cell phone both went off at six Tuesday morning. I answered my phone without looking to see who it was because I already knew it was Toni. "Good mornting, Toni!…" I sung it the best way possible being the first words I spoke today.

"Wake yo dusty ass up! How was your date? Where did you go? Never mind. Lunch today, eleven-thirty this morning, Chipotles?…"

"And how are you this lovely mornting?…" I said, still singing.

"Val, don't play, and there is no 'T' in morning…"

"Tell that to Muh-to the dam D-E-A!…"

"Whatever! Can you do lunch at eleven-thirty or no?…"

"Well, I'm glad to hear that you're doing so well this mornting. Let me check my 'SHEDULE' and see if I could possibly squeeze in a lunch date today so EARLY in the mornting?…"

"You know Val, you play entirely too much. If you can't go, just say you can't go. What time IS good for you?…"

"Toni, let me get back to you on that. I have to get ready for a wonderful day at the office. I feel like throwing in a few discounts today. You sound a little tense. You need to come in for a Swedish massage today? Half price for you, of course!…"

"Keep playing! Sounds like you had a good time last night, unless it ended for you sometime this mornting. Just remember, when YOU NEED your FRIENDS to be there to hold your hand and comfort you, let's just hope you can find one. Maybe Ronni will come in from ATL when you're down and out. I'll be at Chipotles at eleven-thirty…"

"I'll check into that when I get to the office and get back to you, okay, doll face?…"

"Bye, Val!…"

"Bye, hun…" *Hey, she hung up before I said bye! What kind of stuff is that? She's so sensitive!*

I did have a wonderful date yesterday, and I was going to spend a lot of time today thinking about it, I know. *Why can't things stay like this? Why do relationships have to change after you get to know one another?* It would be so nice if a relationship could remain the same way it started off when you were courting each other. *But You know, Lord, I'm going to put it ALL in Your hands. I'm going to praise You for the good as well as the bad. And You know how they say take your burdens to the Lord and leave them there? Well Lord, You got 'em. I'm dropping this relationship thing off in Your lap. I know that right now, it's not a relationship, and I'm guessing that he likes me, although he never even tried to kiss me or anything like that I did get a couple nice hugs, though. But as of right now, I'm going to go with it and have a good time until You tell me differently. I'm keeping my eyes and ears open so I can hear You LOUD and CLEAR speaking to me. You know what I want, Lord, but if my wants and Yours are not one and the same, then remove MY wants from me, and in your own time, give me what I need.*

I love You Lord, and I thank you for hearing my cry, and before I end this prayer to You Lord, I want to thank you for a wonderful night last night. I'm giving YOU the praise, the honor, and the glory right now, Father God in heaven. In the sweet name of Jesus, I pray. Amen! Now should I call him? Huh, Lord? You say don't push it? Okay, I'll relax and wait for his call. Dang! But I'm listening, Lord, and I heard You. Thank You, Lord!

*****

I got to the office around eight. My first appointment wasn't till eight-thirty. This client here was for physical therapy. He broke his ankle playing basketball on an outdoor court. He was in his early twenties, not a bad-looking guy, and on his way to recovery. This was his third visit since he'd gotten his cast removed, and he was progressing well. His name was Allen, but he was known as AJ. I guess he was pretty good at basketball. He was going to school on a full scholarship but had to wait till after next season to enter the NBA draft after this injury. Wouldn't you know that in the middle of this session with him, Toni showed up to my job?

My secretary came to the therapy room and told me I had an important call from a Dr. Somebody. I wasn't sure what the doctor's name was that she had mentioned. It didn't sound familiar to me, but I excused myself from AJ and went to get the phone.

My secretary was also my niece, Tia. She was my parents' first granddaughter. We had boy after boy till Tia came along. She worked for me part-time and was in school part-time. When I stepped out of the therapy room, she said, "TT, Toni is here, and she said it's very important that she speaks to you right away."

"Let me talk to the doctor first, Tia."

"Auntie, Toni is here. There's no doctor on the phone."

"Khitia Lee, are you kidding me? There's no doctor on the phone?"

"No, Toni made me do that."

"Val, don't be mad at Tia," Toni said, coming through the door. "You said you would call me when you got to the office and checked your 'SHEDULE' and I quote! And you didn't call."

"Toni, I am coming up to your job and getting YOU off one of YOUR conference calls or business meetings. You KNOW that ain't right!"

"Don't act like this is the first time I've come to your job. And who's going to fire you? Your business associate? Y'all just share this office. Stop tripping, and you KNOW YOU can escort me to my job right now if you wanted. You coming, 'DOLL FACE?'"

"Girl, you not right. Tia, the next time you let Toni get you in trouble like this, you're fired! Or better yet, I'm calling yo Momma!"

"Whatever Val, are you meeting me?"

"Toni, I'll be there. Bye heffa!"

"Val, you mad, huh?" Toni whispered to me as I opened the door to the therapy room.

I could hear Tia talking to Toni as they walked back to the lobby area about Toni getting her in trouble. They both knew I wouldn't fire her, but Tia better get it together. If I called my sister and told

51

her that I was going to have to let her go, she would have a fit all over Miss Khitia Lee Johnson. And that's what she was afraid of.

Anyhoo, I got back to AJ. I had him doing a few exercises while I was gone; nothing too strenuous, just a little something to keep him busy. I finished up with him. Tia better keep her eyes open. Allen seemed like a nice catch, and if he was as good as they said, he'd be in the pros soon.

I had another physical therapy job at ten and was heading to lunch when I finished with that client. I was a little irritated with Toni and started not to show up, but I knew that she would either come back to my job or blow my phone up if I didn't. That's all right. I'll have my chance to get under her skin again soon. She always gives me that opportunity.

When I got to Chipotles, who do you think was already sitting in the parking lot? And it wasn't even eleven-thirty yet. When I saw her car, I tried to sneak into the lot, but the little nosey heffa had already spotted me. She got out of her car and started signaling to me that there was a spot right next to where she was parked. I took my own sweet time getting there, and she stood in the empty space, waiting patiently for me. Yeah, right! Toni and *patiently* would never go in the same sentence together unless you were speaking of a different Toni with a different spelling even. Maybe Tony.

She didn't even race me inside. She stood there, waited for me to park, gather my purse and keys and a book (in case I got a chance to read) so we could walk in together. "Hi there, best friend," she said. I'm guessing that she was feeling me out to see if I was angry with her.

"Hey, Toni," I replied.

"What you bring a book for? You are not going to have time to read."

"You don't know what I got time for!"

"Lookie, lookie! I know you don't call yourself having an attitude with me when YOU didn't call ME back last night like YOU said you would. Nor did YOU call me back this mornTing when YOU got to YOUR office, like YOU said you would. Needless to say, I came to your house yesterday to offer MY services to YOU because that's the type of friend I am. Got totally pushed aside, but did I let that upset me? NO! Also, I stayed away from YOUR house last night at YOUR request because that's how I do ME! That's the kind of BEST friend YOU got, and YOU can come to lunch sporting an attitude with me. Okay! Yeah, I'd like a chicken bowl for here"—and she placed her order in the same breath—"with LOTS of rice and just a little bit of chicken and some vegetables. Yeah, put some of that salsa on there and a Sprite with a little bit of ice. Oh, and I need the top and some chips, please."

What am I going to do with this girl? I placed my order and went and sat down at a different table than where she was sitting. She jumped right up and came and sat at the table with me. "Girl, it's so funny, I thought we were sitting over there." And she pointed to the table she had been sitting at. "I don't know how I got so confused"—and she started mumbling—"thinking we were sitting over there. WHEW! I don't know what's wrong with me."

I shook my head. Something is truly wrong with her. BUT the girl cracks me up. She never broke a smile, and she really seemed disoriented or something. I hate her! "Girl, YOU are a mess!"

She said, "I know! So how you doing, Miss I-had-so-much-fun-I-don't-know-how-to-call-nobody?"

"I'm good Toni, how are you, Miss schizophrenic, paranoid, classified, grade A NUT!"

"Heeeyyyyyyy, that's not very nice! But I'm good. Details. Tell me everything starting with him coming in the house! What did he say about the way we decorated the house?"

"He said I had a nice place."

"That's it? Did you take him on a tour?"

"A TOUR? Girl, NO! My place ain't but a blink long! He sat on the couch while I went in the room and got my jacket and purse."

"Hmmmm'kay, what next?"

"We left."

"And went where?"

"We got in his car and went—"

"Oh yeah, that was his black Avalanche?"

"Yeah."

53

"Nice. What did it smell like?"

"Him!"

"Good. What kind of music did he play? Or was he listening to the radio?"

"Smooth grooves, a little of the Isleys, Luther, Brian McKnight, India—"

"Got it! Okay, where to?"

"MacArthur's."

"Really? Hmmmmm! Now that could mean one of two things. Either he's broke and that's all he could afford."

"Or?"

"He really likes MacArthur's and wanted to share that experience with you, which means he really likes you."

"Alrighty then."

"Which one do YOU think it is?"

"Toni, I don't really care."

"Yeah, but which one do you think it IS?"

"I don't think he's broke, but it doesn't matter to me."

"I don't think he's broke either, which means he REALLY likes you. Awwwwww, give me hug!" She got up from the table and came around to hug me.

"Toni, if you don't get away from me, I'm-onna punch you in the throat." She put her hands on the side of my face and thrust my head into her chest.

"I'm so happy for you."

"Sit down, please!"

She went and sat down. "Have you talked to him today?"

"Nope."

"Uh-oh!"

"Toni, please shut up!"

"Okay, okay! Don't panic. All is not lost. You got his number, right?" I looked at her with disgust, I might add. "Right?"

"Toni, I'm NOT calling him."

"No, but I will! Did he kiss you? Never mind."

I pulled out my book and started flipping the pages to where I had left off.

"Put the book down. Okay, so you haven't talked to him today. It's okay. How was the food?"

I kept skimming through the page as if I were reading.

"Val, put the book down."

"Are you going to behave? Because if you do that to me again, I'm done talking about it. You'll find out whatever as time progresses."

"Valeri, am I your best friend? Am I? Never mind, don't answer, I already know. Then have no fear. I got you. We'll figure this thing out together. How was the food?"

"Food was good, conversation was good, time—"

"Wait a minute! Did you give him any background on Kody?"

"I didn't talk about me at all."

"Oh, I was going to say maybe that scared him off."

"TONI!"

"Proceed."

"What?"

"What did you talk about?"

"He talked about him. He talked about his family. He's the oldest of two boys and three girls. He loves his Mom and Dad and is truly a Momma's boy, and that's why he doesn't have a steady girlfriend right now. They can't handle his MOM being his NUMBER ONE lady."

"Cute! What else?"

"He did some talking about his lady friends, why he doesn't have any children, previous relationships, and things of that sort."

"So he HOGGED the conversation?"

"NO! I kept reversing the conversation back to him!"

"Oh, okay, cool! Sounds like you had normal conversation. He didn't want to know anything about you?"

"Yeah, but I kept telling him he wasn't done."

"I see. How long were you at the restaurant?"

"We left about nine."

"Wow, you were there for a good minute talking about nothing much. Were you all struggling for conversation? Or was it easy to talk to each other?"

55

"It seemed like we had known each other forever. Not a struggle at all. He's got a good personality and kept me laughing."

"Good, good! Where did you go after dinner?"

"He took me to this spot where...wait a minute. I didn't tell you how he snapped on me."

"He snapped on you on the first date? Hey, what's that's about?"

"Girl, I guess I opened the door and didn't let him do it, and he snapped. Wouldn't let me get in the car. Then he gave me a BIG hug and held me and almost squeezed the life out of me till I said I would let him open doors for me, even if we just stayed friends."

"OKAY! He checked you like that?" You could tell she was kind of impressed with that.

"Yeah!"

"Well, I ain't mad at him!" she stated, kind of chuckling a little.

"Whatever!"

"Now you know Kody would've let you open all the doors you wanted to. He let you carry chairs, bags, and boxes, whatever without EVER offering to help."

"Yeah, I know. It was cool. I kind of appreciated his 'take chargeness,' although I do like breathing!"

"All right, well, at least we know you got yourself a REAL man who LOVES his Momma, which is ALWAYS a good sign. If they treat Momma right, then they're bound to treat YOU right too. So where did you go after that?"

"This is the best part. Well, not really the BEST part because the whole night was good, but he took me to this spot downtown where we sat at the lakefront with a blanket and gazed at the skyline and lake. We simply watched the scenery and chilled till I started dozing. I had never seen Chicago like that before. BEAUTIFUL! Absolutely beautiful!"

"Really? Where was this?"

"Oh yeah, I meant to tell you not to ask me where he took me. You know, I wasn't paying attention to where we were."

"Girl, you haven't learned a thing from me, have you?"

"Yeah actually I have. I learned how not to be a pain in the butt from you."

"Wow, well, that's good. I'm glad I taught you something."

"I knew that would go right over your head." Just then, my phone rang. "Uh-oh, I have to take this. Good Mornting! I'm good, how you?…"

"Girl, who is that, and don't you know it's afternoont, not MORNTING? We're in the middle of some in-depth conversation. You ain't got time to be entertaining anybody else."

"Naw, I wasn't doing anything. Having a little lunch, but I'm good…"

"GIRL! So now I'm 'doing nothing?' Okay!"

"Yeah, that's Toni!…"

"Who is that asking about me? That Khaleesi? Tell Khaleesi Marie I said hey girl, hey!"

"Naw, it's cool. I can talk to HER anytime…"

"YOU can talk to your SISTER anytime. This is MY time, Val."

"YOU know she thinks she's got to know everything? I'm giving her an outline. Not details…"

"OHHHHHH! Is that Mr. Wonderful? Mr. Chicago Skyline himself? I like your moves, Tee. You got skills, baby."

"Can I call you back in about twenty minutes?…"

"We're not going to be done in twenty minutes. You going to blow me off for a MAN?"

"Well, call me back when you get chance later on. SHE won't be around…"

"That's right Tee, call her back. We're busy talking about last night!"

"Okay, I'll talk to you later, bye!…" I gave her the evil eye!

"WHAT? What I do now? And that concern I had earlier, don't worry about it. It's gone, you in the house, girl."

"I hope you've enjoyed this conversation because this is the LAST time I will give you information like this. You talk entirely too much. I'm telling Zani that we bowled on Saturday. Let's see what's going to happen to that little gift he's supposed to get you to make up for accusing you."

"Relax Val, why don't you have some chill with your pill?"

She thought I was kidding with her. "Toni, why don't you have some be with your quiet and some shut with your up? You talk too much. You see how I had your back with Zani, but that's okay. I got something for you."

"Val, you know I was just clowning with you and Taj."

"Yeah, but Toni, he doesn't know me. And right now, he thinks I'm going to tell YOU everything that happens between me and him. I don't know what he expects from me. You could've waited till we'd been out for a minute before he knows how we are. But that's okay. I got you, girl."

"You're right, Val. I'm sorry. Call 'im back."

"I have to get back to the office. I'll talk to you later."

"Val, don't be mad. I didn't mean anything by it."

"It's all good. I'm out."

"You haven't even finished eating."

"I'm done. I'll take the rest home."

"I really am sorry, Val. I didn't mean to upset you."

"I'm good, girl." I packed up my stuff and headed out the door. I hadn't noticed, but Toni packed up too. When I got in my car, she was coming out the door and walked up to my window.

"Girl, I'mma call you later. You can tell me what he wanted then."

"Toni, you stupid!" I wasn't really mad at her. I just wanted her to think sometimes. She talked a lot without thinking and she needed to think before she spoke. So if she thought I was mad, she'd behave for a little while at least. She might even buy me a makeup gift like she'd done time and time again. Last time, she got me a necklace and pair of matching earrings to make up for messing up, so I was all good.

I called Taj back when I got in the car. I figured he was still on lunch since that's what he was doing when he called me a few minutes ago. "Taj, hi! It's me, Val…"

"Hey, baby doll. How are you?…"

"I'm good, thanks. How are you?…"

"I'm all right now. You done telling your girl about your date last night?…"

58

"Taj, I'm sorry, but you knew last night that's what she was trying to find out. You know like I know that she wasn't being OVERLY concerned for me…"

"Yeah, I knew what she wanted, it's cool. Calm down! When I got some stuff for OUR EARS ONLY, I'll let you know…"

"Okay!…"

"So when can I see you again?…"

"When would you like to see me again?…"

"Tonight…"

"Really? And what would you like to do tonight?…"

"Not much, just chill at the house. I was thinking about stopping to grab us a little something to eat and maybe watch a little TV, maybe a movie. I won't stay long. I'll let you get to bed early so you can get your beauty sleep…"

"Well, I was planning to work out when I get off work…"

"Cool, I'll meet you there. Where you go to work out?…"

"LA Fitness by my house…"

"What time you going to be there?…"

"Around four-thirty or five…"

"Is it okay if I meet you there?…"

"As long as you're not going to stifle my workout…"

"If you don't stifle mine, I won't stifle yours. I know you want to watch me workout. She just wants me for mah bah-dy!…"

"Okay, Tow-Mater. Yes, I saw the movie *Cars* too. Something's wrong with you…"

"Nope, I just believe in having a good time…"

"All right, well, I'm back at the job, so I'm going to…"

"Ho', Ho', Hold up, Shorty, you talking on the phone and driving?…"

"Well…yeah!…"

"I see me and you are going to have to talk. I'mma need you to understand my rules…"

"Wait, you hold up, Gymshoe! I moved out of my PARENTS' house, and now I make up MY rules as I go along…"

"Don't get a spanking, Miss Thing!…"

"I don't plan to…"

"We'll talk when I see you this evening…"
"Looking forward to it…"
"Bye, baby doll!…"
"Bye, sweet pea!"

10

My afternoon went by slowly but surely, and after work, I headed to the gym to get my cardio on with some tiresome elliptical exercise. I didn't see Taj when he came in. I guess he came in while I was in the locker room, changing clothes, or maybe I came in while he was in the locker room. It was probably me that came in later because I didn't check the parking lot for his car. I'm sure he would've spotted my car out there if I came in first. He IS a police officer, and they are trained to be aware of their surroundings. That's just a cool way to say they are extremely NOSEY. But it's all good. I did my usual workout of an hour on the elliptical stepper and was going into my weight machine exercises when I spotted Mr. Man in the free weight room. I knew how good he looked fully dressed, but dam…to see this body with a tank top and shorts on—SHAZAM!

Now I understood his conceited comment when he said, "Don't YOU stifle MY workout." He was all sweaty, and his muscles were ripping out of his skin, glistening. *Dam, dam, dam!* I wanted to pull up a chair and watch him bench press five hundred pounds or do some curls or just go sit on his lap and rub all OVER his body.

I realize we were not going to be able to workout at the same time EVER again. I was NO good right now, so I engaged myself in a conversation, with me. *Girl, you better relax and act like you don't see him. So why did I just wave? Girl, go ahead and do what you came here to do. And how do YOU propose I do that? First of all, you can stop staring. Shoot, I was staring, wasn't I? No, not was, you still are.*

Okay, okay, breathe, Val. He's just another man! Yeah, but he's a man that looks like THAT! That's NOT just another body. A body like that doesn't walk past you every day, AND THAT body wants to kick it with me! OKAY, I must be pretty decent myself. Let me look at me! All right! I see me, I see what I'm working with. I am kind of cute, though, but DAM. Don't look, girl, just keep going.

Lord help me! There are thoughts going through MY mind. Well, Lord, YOU know what they are, and YOU know they are NOT pretty. I'm going to need an intervention! Relieve my mind of these sinful thoughts, Lord. You know my goal, and if YOU don't step in RIGHT NOW, it's ALL over. LORD! I thought I asked you to step in? Here he comes!

"Hey, beautiful, when did you get here? I didn't think you were coming."

"Hi! I've been here for over an hour?"

"An HOUR? How come I didn't see you?"

"You tell me, Mr. Observant!"

"I guess I must've really been into my workout."

"How long YOU been here?"

"I got here about an hour ago too. I would give you a hug, but as you can see, I'm a little sweaty right now."

"A LITTLE sweaty?"

"Oh yeah, you the one with the little smart mouth. I'mma give you a hug anyways."

"Taj, don't—" And right then, his chest was on the side of my face, and those beautiful WET arms were wrapped around me.

"I'm not going to let you go till you hug me back. Aren't you glad to see me? I thought you said you were looking forward to it?" Then he leaned over and wiped his face off on mine. I HAD dried off after getting off the elliptical, BUT—

"That was soooo wrong of you, Taj."

"My bad. I'm really glad to see you, that's all. You're looking awfully cute in your little workout clothes. And I do mean LITTLE."

"Yeah, well, whatever! I need my towel."

"You didn't bring one? Well, let me help YOU out!" And again, he started wiping himself off on me. "Ewwwwww, you nasty!"

"Thanks Taj, I needed that." And I took my towel and began wiping OUR sweat off me.

"You done working out?"

"I am now! I have to go shower for real now. I was GOING to do it when I got home, but thanks to a certain someone, I'mma take care of that now."

"You sound like you complaining. I can help you out again." And he started toward me.

"No, no, no, no, no, I'm good. Thanks, though!"

"Aw, okay. Well, I guess I'll head to the showers too."

"Thank YOU!" I said under my breath.

"Did you say something, baby doll?"

"Nope, just thinking to myself. Shower, here I come."

"Cool, I'll meet you back out here in what, twenty minutes?"

"TWENTY MINUTES?"

"What, that's too long?"

"TOO LONG?"

"Val, don't make me have to come in there after you. You know I can, I'm a cop. I can pretty much go anywhere I want to."

"I'll be out in nineteen. Don't make ME have to go in there after you. I'm not a cop, and I may get taken advantage of by a nice body. I am at the gym."

"Yeah, okay! Play crazy if you want to. You hurry up because me and you really have to talk, Miss Thang!"

"Hurrying!" I went in the locker room, got my stuff together, took my shower, lotioned up, and got dressed. Naturally, I had to redo the makeup after I washed his old nasty sweat off me.

I forgot about the time, and after about twenty-five minutes, I heard someone right outside the ladies' locker room, yelling, "Valeri, you still showering?"

"Oops, I forgot about the time. Have no fear, here I come!" I yelled back.

"Harry up, girl!"

"I'm coming!" I was done at that time anyway. I did the quick simple job on the makeup, but I was all good.

Taj was standing right outside the locker room in uniform where you couldn't have missed him. I guess he wanted to make sure I saw him. But when I came out, he was talking to some stank woman in her skimpy workout clothes. Of course, I didn't know who she was, so I walked right passed him and headed for the exit. I put my headphones in my ears. I didn't turn any music on but acted like I was jamming to the beat.

"Val, hold on a minute. Where you going?" he yelled to me. I'm not sure if he wanted me to come back to him so he could introduce me or what, but I wasn't thrilled with seeing Mr. Man over there, talking to that hoochie, so I kept going like I didn't hear him.

When I got outside, I cut the music on and he came running out, calling me, "Baby doll, what's going on? Oh, now you in a hurry all of a sudden?" He caught up to me when I was about to get in my car. "Val, what's up?"

I took the earpiece out of one ear and said, "I'm sorry, were you talking to me?"

"So you didn't hear me calling you?"

"Nope, I didn't hear you calling me or talking to what's her name back there."

"Oh, I get it! You're jealous! Ain't that cute?"

"Taj, I'm not jealous. You don't owe me nothing. We're just friends, right?"

"Baby doll, I have on my uniform. What's her name was asking me a question pertaining to my job. Is that okay with you, lovebug?"

"As I stated previously"—I got real formal with him—"there's no allegiance here! You don't owe me a thing. We're great!"

"Awwwww, come here." And he reached his arms out for me to hug him.

"I'll take the hug, but I'm all good." So I hugged him.

"So you're not jealous?" he said as he was holding me.

"I didn't like it, but like I said, we're just friends. I don't have the right to be jealous...yet!"

"YET? Mmm, I like that. And you called ME conceited!"

"I didn't mean it like that."

"How did you mean it then?"

"I'm just saying."

"Saying what?"

"Forget it, Taj, we all good."

"Ummm-hmmmm, well if I saw YOU in there or anywhere talking to some stud, I would be jealous. In fact, I would be dam pissed, and I would check both of you! And for dam sure wouldn't have walked away!"

"That's what makes you, you, and me, me… Hold up, you would be PISSED?"

"YUP!"

"You're right, we do need to talk."

"That's why I'm headed straight to your house right now."

"So am I."

"What are we eating? I'm starving."

"I don't know."

"You cooking?"

"Negative!"

"I'll pick up something on the way."

"Okay, see ya in a minute." I got in the car and took off. I left him standing there. Oh well! But how do you like that? He would have the nerve to be jealous if he saw me talking to some "stud." Yeah, we better get this straight.

11

I got home and changed my clothes. I had brought my workout clothes to the gym and planned to leave in them since I thought I was going to shower at home. So upon completion of my workout, I had to change back into my work clothes. So I got nice and comfy with sweats and a T-shirt, chilling clothes. I'm sure Toni would probably be upset if she knew I was entertaining company with sweats on. It's a shame that I need THAT chick's approval on my attire, makeup, behavior—oh and the list goes on! *Oh well, she ain't my Momma! She'll be all right.* And my phone rang.

"Hellur!..."

"What you doing?..."

"Well, Toni, I'm playing hopscotch in Uganda..."

"Who's winning? I wanna play..."

"Girl, what do you want?..."

"Can't I call to talk to my BFF Jill?..."

"You most certainly can, so why did you call me?..."

"Touché! You're funny, so I guess you're still mad?..."

"I'm fabulous, thanks! What's up?..."

"Okay, so listen, I didn't get a chance to tell you earlier because you hogged the conversation at lunch. Anyways, Zani came over last night and brought me these beautiful pearl earrings and matching necklace. It's his makeup gift to me. I love 'em! I've always wanted some authentic pearls. And now that First Lady Michelle brought them back in style, I finally got me some. Ain't that nice, girl? I'm going to have to show them to you..."

"That's Zani's makeup gift to YOU for HIM being right about YOU trying out YOUR bowling gear with ME and NOT HIM? HUH? HMMMMMMM!..."

66

"Well, when you put it that way, it does sound a little dishonest, but yeah!…"

"Well, I'm glad that you're happy with them. That's good old Zani for you…"

"Isn't he a good guy? That's my boo! So did you smooth things over with Mr. Wonderful yet?…"

"There wasn't anything to smooth over…"

"Did you talk to him since you left me?…"

"Yup!…"

"Is he mad at you?…"

"Nope!…"

"Are you going to see him again this week?…"

"Yup!…"

"Are you going to give me any details?…"

"Nope!…"

"VAL?…"

"Yyyyyyyeeesssss…"

"You know you can't do me like that. I don't usually tell your business. I was so happy that you two sounded like you were hitting it off that I got carried away…"

"You may not tell ALL my business, but you talk TOO much. And you always tell things by accident. Example: 'Yeah because when Kody cheated on Val… You remember? Oh, yeah, you probably didn't know, but anyways…' That sound familiar Toni? AND you were talking to my sister when you divulged that info…"

"Okay, I did that ONE time, but in my defense, I kept that secret for a good year before I told anyone…"

Just then, my doorbell rang. I was so caught up in the talk with Toni I forgot Taj was on his way.

"Girl, was that your doorbell? Who you expecting? Ooooh, it's Tee, ain't it? So you two are really hitting it off, huh?…"

"Toni, I have to go. I'll talk to you later…"

"Girl, go get the door and tell me who it is. It could be a killer, and you may NEED me to be on the phone with you for details…"

"You are so nosey…"

"Just take me to the door with you, and when you find out who it is, I'll let you go…"

"Who IS it?"

"It's the police."

"You satisfied, Toni? It's Taj… Come IN! I'll talk to you later…"

"Goodbye Val, tell Tee I said hi and call me later…"

"Nope, bye!…"

Taj came in with Popeye's chicken, some red beans and rice, and corn on the cob. "Did I just hear you on the phone?"

"You did."

"What did Toni want now?"

"How you know that was Toni? She's not the only person that I talk to, you know."

"So was it Toni?"

"Affirmative!" We both started laughing.

Taj and I sat there, watching a little TV, eating our Popeye's chicken and having light conversation till we finished eating. It just occurred to me that he still had his uniform on, so I asked, "Are you on duty? Why you still wearing your uniform?"

"Nope, I'm not STILL on duty, but I AM still an officer."

"And?"

"I need to give you a little background first, is that cool?"

"Alrighty then, I'm ONE big ear listening."

"Like I told you before, Val, I have friends. I have always had a lady, so it's not like I'm hard up for women or anything like that. But I find something special in you. I'm like most men and not the type to put my feelings on the line, but for whatever reason, I'm going to with you. I don't know what it is about you, but something tells me that this relationship is different."

"Oh, this is a relationship now?"

"Can I finish? Even if we remain friends, that's a relationship, ain't it? Smarty-pants."

"Sorrrry, Mr. Sensitive! You're right!"

"I know this is early in the RELATIONSHIP, but I don't think there's any sense in waiting around to get to know each other better.

I want you to be my lady. You be exclusive to me, and I'm going to be exclusive to you."

"But Eric…this is all so…so suh-den!"

"I'm sitting here, bearing ALL my feelings to you, and you're reciting lines from *The Little Mermaid*."

"Taj, I'm feeling you. Relax, boo!"

"Yeah, but I don't want you playing with my emotions."

"Well then I may not be the one for you because I play a lot. I get serious at times, but life is too short to be taking everything so seriously. I like to have a good time in the meantime."

"Okay, so if YOU were bearing your feelings to ME, and I was clowning around with you, YOU would be cool with that?"

"HAYELL NAW!"

"So then why YOU playing with me?"

"Because I can. Like I said before, that's what makes you, you, and makes me, me. I can't do everything you can! I can't bench press two hundred and fifty pounds nor can I pee standing up and write my name in the snow, and believe me, I've tried. And you can't do everything I can, like have a baby or clown around when I'M being serious with you."

"You're right! Maybe I better rethink this."

"Rethink it baby, because this is what you get."

"Does that mean you'll be exclusive to me?"

"Let me give you a little background on me before YOU make that decision."

"Okay, shoot!"

And I began giving my background. "My last relationship hurt me really bad. I put my feelings out there. I was faithful to him and let it be known that I wanted NO ONE but him. I thought everything was going good, and out the clear blue, bruh man told me he had someone else and didn't want me anymore. We didn't have a fight, an argument, nothing! I thought we were ALL good, which leads me to believe that he had this dip on the side, possibly the whole time. I wasn't ready for that, and he almost destroyed me. While I was dealing with that, my dad—my hero, the love of my life—passed away from cancer. NOW it may be a little difficult for me to buy into everything you say. I'm probably wrong for this, but I don't trust you!"

"Wow!"

"Don't get me wrong. I like you and think that you are absolutely adorable! Your looks, your body, DAM!" I stopped talking briefly and began to fan myself. "Is it getting hot in here?" I asked. "Oops, sidetracked." I continued the conversation, "Your charm AND that voice, goodness! And I would love nothing more than to parade MY trophy off to the world and be the woman that YOU display. You seem like the perfect man, too good to be true. But when it seems too good to be true, it probably is. AND it's hard for me to believe that after ONE date, I'm the woman of your dreams. I'm not trying to hurt your feelings or nothing like that, but there's no sense in me NOT being honest with you. I'm an honest hoe, and all my hoes are honest. The Lord is dealing with me and helping me through my feelings and insecurities, but I am in NO WAY healed."

"Wow, even when you're bearing your heart to me, you quote movie lines. *Harlem Nights*? Della Reese, right?"

"Yeah, that's one of my favorites."

"Got it. BUT first of all, let me say I'm sorry for the loss of your dad, and I'm not going to act like I know how that feels because I don't! And believe me when I say that I'm sorry that old boy hurt you so bad, and now I have to work extra hard to get you to see that THIS is the real me. What you see IS what YOU get."

"I hear you, cousin."

"Okay, well let me ask you a question."

"Go for it!"

"You go to church regularly, right? I mean, you're talking about the Lord dealing with you, so you're a Christian woman, right?"

"Affirmative!"

"You don't think that God can be leading this thing rather than you or ME?"

"Yeah, right now, that's the ONLY thing I trust."

"Then how do you know that this is NOT of God."

"I don't. How do YOU know that it IS of God?"

"I don't, but I do know this. When I stopped you about your taillight, I stopped you because I thought you were cute and wanted a better look. But after that, I couldn't stop thinking about you. I asked God why He kept bringing your face back to my mind, especially if I was not going to see you. I actually asked Him to take that picture of YOUR face out of my system, and you know what He did? He took your face out but put the rest of your body in my head. That cute little yellow dress, the RAV4—everything. Then I asked Him WHY He won't take you off my mind, and if He's not going to remove you, then let me see you again. And the next day, I stopped a Lexus truck that had YOU in it. So when I say I don't know what it is about you, I don't, but I'm figuring that the Lord does."

"Well, sir, I can't argue with God. And if this is His doing, then there's nothing that either one of us can do, except go with it. You're going to have to be patient with me and understand that I'm not TRYING to be difficult. Well, sometimes I am. I can't help myself. And I'm really scared of being hurt again."

"So is that a yes, baby doll?"

"So you still want to try this?"

"I do!"

"Then, yes, I will be exclusive to you. Are you going to be exclusive to me?"

"Yes."

"Oh, wait a minute, I forgot one thing."

"What's that?"

"I don't plan to give it up. Meaning NO SEX before marriage."

"Dam!"

"Rethink it, Gymshoe!"

"I can live with that…I think!"

"Well, I'm going to need you to be strong and resist the devil."

"Well, I'm going to need YOU to be strong and resist the devil."

"Well, I can't make any promises."

"Good, then we straight. Can your man have a kiss?" So he leaned in, and we engaged in a nice passionate introductory kiss. "So now your man is about to step knee-deep in your behind."

"Wuh-ohh!"

"Yeah, yeah. You see this uniform I'm wearing?"

"Yeeessssss!"

"You don't talk on your cell phone while you're driving. That's a definite no-no. You don't drive and text, nor do you drink and drive. Do you understand? It's my job as a police officer to keep the streets safe. It's my job as YOUR man to keep you safe as well. I don't want to hear that you're talking and driving again. I just got you, and I want to keep you as long as possible, capiché?"

"Geeeez, you are NOT my daddy!"

"You know what? I'm glad that you're feisty. That way, when I have to break you down, I won't feel so bad."

"You threatening me? Isn't that a criminal offense? A legal issue?"

"Not when it's your man doing the threatening, and baby doll, I'm serious. I don't want you talking or texting and driving. I need you to be safe. You need to remember, I see accidents on a regular. People texting or talking on the phone and driving. Then they crash because their attention is diverted. It's not a pretty sight, and I need you to make a conscious effort. I'm going to take you at your word, though. Will you promise me that you'll stop that?"

"I get where you're coming from, and I never thought about it from you guys' perspective, but I'll work on it. I'll try not to text and drive, but talking on the phone…hmmmm, that's something I will really have to work on, BUT I'll try because YOU asked me to."

"I can go for that for right now, but after a while, I'm expecting you to have mastered that. Okay?"

"Yes, sir!"

"One more thing."

"Dang, what else I do?"

"You call me by another man's name, and I won't be responsible for my actions."

"When did I call you another man's name?"

"When you quoted *The Little Mermaid*. I know you were kidding with that, but for the future, I just want you to know that could get you hurt."

"You do a lot of talking about jacking me up. You hit women?"

"Nope, never have hit a woman, but I will do a lot of talking about it."

"Okay because you are a little too big to be hitting somebody."

"And you are too little to have such a flip mouth. I can back up all the noise I talk. Can you?"

"I have ways of backing up what I say too, boo."

"We'll see about that."

"Yeah, we'll see. You done fussing at me?"

"For now, but I can tell that won't last too long."

"Okay, so I got something for you to mull over now."

"Go for it!"

"How YOU going to get mad at me and snap on me if you see me talking to a guy? So I'm not supposed to talk to NO other guy ever in life? What's up with that?"

"You belong to me now. You can talk to whoever you want to talk to, but if I don't like how it looks, don't think I'm going to walk away like you did today."

"As long as you're not going to act a fool, I'm good."

"I'll have to see what you consider acting a fool."

"I think you know what I mean."

"Yeah, well, I can get ignorant with the best of them if I need to. But for the most part of it, if my questions get answered reasonably, then I'll be reasonable."

"Yeah, okay. So what now?"

"Can we watch a movie? I got one in the car I want to see."

"That's fine, boss."

He went out to his car and got *Star Trek* and some clothes to change into. We sat there on the couch all cuddled up and watched the movie. I truly enjoyed his company once again. I could've done without the movie but enjoyed chilling with my man. *Wow! That has a nice ring to it!*

12

O ld boy left my house at a reasonable hour. He stayed long enough to watch the news and bid his farewells. I got a nice solid strong hug (I love a nice firm hug) as well as a nice kiss. He had very soft kissable lips, which I rather enjoyed kissing. And once again, I thanked him for a pleasurable evening and for dinner. He agreed and said he would call me later.

We weren't going to get together on Wednesday because it was Sister Wednesday for me. Wednesdays were devoted to my sisters and I. The four of us (and sometimes our in-laws) got together every Wednesday. We took turns hosting, which meant we prepared a meal at our homes, and the host decides on our form of entertainment. If there was a movie that was at the show that we want to see, then our Sister Wednesday would have a field trip, go to the show, and out to eat. Otherwise, we'd decide on a DVD we'd like for the group to see and watch that. Sometimes, ONE of us (I won't mention any names, Khaleesi Marie) might have us play a game of Boggle, Yahtzee, or Jenga.

One of the other girls (mainly Pearl Ann, she was just like my daddy and loved to play cards) may call for a game of bid whist or something of that sort. There were other times that we ONLY talked. There might be a burning issue that we were dealing with, and we would confide in each other, give good solid counsel, and pray for each other. Those ladies are my best friends aside from Toni and Ronni.

Today was Rena's turn to host. Rena was the equivalent to Susie Homemaker. She watched ALL the cooking shows—Rachel Ray, Giada de Laurentiis and I'm sure anyone else who had a cooking show. She experimented with us on her fancy dishes all the time. She made some pretty weird stuff, but so far, I had no complaints. We generally do a cocktail of some sort too, and she was experimental in that aspect as well.

Today, we had au gratin potatoes, which was not a fancy dish, but the string bean salad was somewhat different. I was a little skeptical of the salad, but I got a second helping of both. So needless to say, the food was scrumptious. I can't remember what the name of the cocktail was (something minty and chocolatey), but it too was yummy. We ate and chilled and ended up watching *Twilight*. We were supposed to watch the second *Twilight* movie in the near future. I enjoyed the first one and was looking forward to the second and third ones.

Mommy generally came here when she got off work, and today was no different. She was another one of my bestest friends. I don't know what I'd do without these women.

Since today was Sister Wednesday, I knew I wouldn't be able to see Taj unless it was late. He called me earlier. It wasn't an in-depth conversation because my sisters had a fit when they thought that one of us was paying more attention to someone or something other than them. Therefore, I basically said hi, and we decided that I would call him when I got home so we could have a more in-depth conversation.

Once again, Sister Wednesday was a success. We enjoyed our meal, the movie, our conversation, and overall time together. Next week would be Pearl Ann's turn to host. Our day ended around 9:00 p.m. as usual. I enjoyed my time with them but was looking forward to getting home and calling Taj. I decided to call him on my way home.

I picked up my phone and dialed him and thought about our conversation yesterday. Dang, I told him I would try to respect his wishes and not use my phone while I was driving, so I hung up. My phone rang back, and it was him. I guess I didn't hang up before it rang on his end. I was still driving so, of course, I didn't answer. He called me three times within the next fifteen minutes it took me to get home. I called him back as I was walking from the car to the house.

"Hello, Val? Baby doll, why'd you call me and then not answer the phone when I called back? I hope you know I was on my way over there…"

"Hi back at you, Taj…"

"Why are you not answering your phone, girl?…"

"I called you once I left my sister's house, while I was driving, and thought about the effort that I promised you yesterday, so I hung up…"

"What you promised me?…"

"I WAS DRIVING, so I hung up. I thought you would be proud of me…"

"Oh, I get it. You hung up because you were driving?…"

"Uh, yeah…"

"Aww baby doll, attagirl! But why couldn't you pull over and answer my calls?…"

"Wow, I never even thought about pulling over. I was trying to get home so I could talk to you!…"

"All right, it's all good. We're going to take it one step at a time. And I am proud of you…"

"Thank you. I do what I can do when I can do what I can do…"

"You crazy, but next time, think about pulling over or calling me before you take off. That way, I'll know the situation before you get home…"

"One step at a time, sir!…"

"So how was your sister day?…"

I went on to tell him how Sister Wednesday was. I gave him some history on my family. It started with my sisters, and then he wanted to know about my brothers and then other stuff about the family. We had good conversation, and a lot of it was about me this time. He was looking forward to meeting my family. I believed he wanted information about my family so when he met them, he'd feel like he already knew them.

I asked him how his day went. We chitchatted for a good while. He was trying to come by as HE said just for a few minutes, but I turned him down. He was cute as all get out, and I really liked him so far. But he thought he was going to be the brains and decision-maker in this outfit. I was going to have to let him know that he was sadly mistaken. I'd let him think he was the boss for some things, but there were other things that I planned to rule over, just because I could. So he didn't come over because that's how I roll.

I have to admit, I'm not a woman that likes to be ruled or controlled. The only man that I will allow to tell me what to do is my dad, and since he's now gone, oh well, if God doesn't give me the "slow down" sign, then too bad, so sad. Kody used to try to control me, but those days were LONG gone! I could tell with Taj that I was going to have to ask God to help me with my attitude because it seemed like he was going to expect me to be somewhat submissive, and that's going to be a hard pill for me to swallow. I probably should have told him about this. This may have made him rethink our relationship too. God is able, though, if I really trust Him and fervently pray about it. He can do it IF that's how He wants me.

*****

For the next few weeks, we saw each other a little almost every day. We took in a movie here and there, watched a little TV, and chilled, getting to know each other a little better every day. We had good times with each other, still learning each other's personalities, and so far, everything had been lovely. I loved the way he made me laugh. We were both pretty goofy and liked to have a good time, regardless who was watching, and then it happened. I got to see a portion of his other side.

One day, after we left the gym, we stopped at a Long John Silver's in the neighborhood, and I still had on my exercise clothes, which means I was looking casually cute in my shorts and tank top. There was a young guy working there, and I could tell he liked what he saw when he saw me, and he was flirting. I tried to ignore his cute little young blood infatuation. Taj had walked away for something, I'm not sure what, but the little youngster felt this was his chance to put in his appeal, and he slipped me his phone number. I thought it was the receipt for the food. One of the other employees told him, "Twin, man, don't do that. You see she's here with dude."

Twin replied as Taj was heading back over to me, "F—, dude, I'm trying to get with her."

Now I ask, why would he make a statement like that with Taj coming back on the scene? Taj snapped. That's when I found out that I really didn't plan to purposely upset him. Taj said, "F—, dude? F—, dude?" He looked toward me and said, "Is that me he talking about?" He turned back to young blood and said, "My man, you DISRESPECTING me? You didn't see me come in here with my lady? With MY LADY? Hey, my man, why don't you step around this counter and show me how you plan to f— me?"

I was in the background, asking Taj to chill. "Bae, it's not that important. Let it go." I did finally get him to relax a little bit. I made him look at me. It was hard, seeing as though I'm only five feet, four inches tall, and he was a whole foot taller than me, but I grabbed his face, and he kept turning it back around, and EVENTUALLY, he looked at me and started coming around. He then tried to snap on me and asked what I did to instigate this situation.

And I told him, "Baby, I was born, what you mean? I'm adorable. Can you blame him?" That lightened the mood and got him to laugh a little bit. He agreed with me but was still somewhat agitated. At that point, I wanted to take the food and leave, but Taj insisted on eating in the restaurant. He had scared the daylights out of poor little Twin, so he disappeared in the back and stayed back there till we were out of sight. Then I made the tragic mistake of giving Taj the receipt along with the change, and he saw Twin's name and number on it.

"Oh, so you were going to call dude? Let's see. What's his name?" And he looked at the receipt and said, "Trent, huh? What kind of name is Trent anyways?" I guess Trent was his actual name.

"What are you talking about?"

"I'm talking about his name and number is on this here receipt! Don't act innocent."

"You're kidding, right?"

"So you didn't know he wrote his name and number on the receipt?"

"Let me see that!" He showed it to me but wouldn't let me hold it. "Let's be serious. Do you think I would've given it to you if I knew he wrote his name and number on it? Momma ain't raise no fool!"

He said, "Let me call old Trent." And he took out his phone.

"Taj, can you PLEASE let it go? He's a kid. Please stop messing with that boy. You probably already made him wet his pants."

"He messed with me when he disrespected me. If he wants to play big boy games, then he better be ready to suffer big boy consequences."

"You done already scared the poor boy half silly. Let him go."

"I'll let him go for now."

"Can I have the receipt, please?"

"Why, so you can call him?"

"Yeah!" I said sarcastically, but his facial expression told me to stop playing, so I continued real quick like and said, "No, so I can throw it away!"

"Nope, I don't trust you. You said you were going to call him. In fact, I'm going to pull out my badge and MAKE him come out here or go back there my dam self." He pulled out his badge and started for the counter. I tried standing in front of him, asking him not to do it. He picked me up and moved me out the way and went to the register. I left and went out to the car. I was afraid for little dude and didn't want to be around when Taj got to him.

When I got to the car, Taj was right behind me, which meant he must not have said anything to them inside. We sat at the car and talked for a few minutes prior to leaving, and as we were outside in the parking lot in the rear of the restaurant, Trent came out with a bag of garbage. He looked up and saw Taj and myself sitting on the car, talking, and took off back into the restaurant. I refused to tell Taj that he had come outside till after we got back to my house.

Later on that evening, Taj called him. He politely told old boy to be careful whose woman he tried to pick up because people were crazy these days. "Anything could happen. Be careful."

Twin apologized and said he let his hormones get the best of him. I was glad that Taj took a different approach to the phone call and used it as a teaching session as opposed to threatening the little guy. I tell you, men are something else when they think their manhood has been challenged.

13

I had a trip to Atlanta coming up. My girlfriend Ronni, had surgery, and I felt I needed to be there to help take care of her during her recuperation. I shifted my schedule around so I could make this trip. Taj wasn't thrilled about me going, but he understood. He gave me a "Behave yourself" speech the day I was leaving, like he was my daddy or something, and I let him go ahead with it.

"Baby doll, I know I don't have to tell you don't go down there and get yourself caught up with some smooth-talking 'country boy.' Don't be flirting with everybody you see. In fact, don't be flirting with NOBODY. I know you. You call yourself trying to be nice to everybody, and you add a little something to your niceness when there's a guy involved. So go down there, take care of your girl, and act like I'm sitting there watching the WHOLE thing. Meaning BEHAVE YOURSELF!"

So me being the person that I am, I had to tell him a few things as well. "Taj, first of all, do you trust me?"

"Look here—"

"No, no, no! Not 'look here!' The question was, DO YOU TRUST ME?"

"Yeah, baby doll, I trust you!"

"Then that's all there is to it. I told you I would be exclusive to you, and that's what I'm going to do. Now as far as behaving myself, I'm NOT going to do that, just because that's who I am. I don't behave myself when I'm here with you. I ALWAYS act up."

His facial expression changed drastically.

"Sweet pea, you know I'm playing, right? I'm going to take care of my girlfriend to the best of my ability, and that's all I'm going to do. She just had surgery, so I know we're not going to be going much of anyplace. I want you to pray for me and her both while I'm away. I need her to make a speedy recovery.

"And for number two, YOU the one that better behave YOURSELF, officer! You know I don't trust YOU. I do trust God, though, and that's who I'm depending on to keep us both straight!"

"Dam, girl! You a little too honest for me. You cut me deep with that."

"Bae, I'm sorry! And next time, I'll keep my honesty and my comments to myself. I'm not trying to hurt your feelings, but you know how they say, 'When the cat's away, the mice will play.' I HAVE to trust God."

"Naw, I want to know how you feeling, so be honest. I got broad shoulders, I can take it. I see I need to keep working to let YOU know." He grabbed my chin and tilted my face up to look into his eyes and said, "I found what I want."

There was a few seconds of silence, and then I said, "That was SO lame. What is this, a Kodak commercial? Where are the cameras?"

"Girl, you sure know how to ruin a beautiful moment. You are TOO sarcastic for me!"

"Yeah, yeah, yeah. Get me to the airport before I'm late for my flight… PLEASE, love."

"I should GET you over my knee for a good old-fashioned spanking before you go. You know, to give you something to remember me by, seeing as though I can't be nice to you."

"Oh, YOU can be nice to me. I'll take a hug for 200, Alex."

Taj took me to the airport. I absolutely abhorred flying. I guess he sensed my reservations about getting on that plane, and he held me, gave me a nice hug and a kiss, and told me he needed me to come back safe and in one piece. We prayed together, and wouldn't you know, the Lord came through once again for me. He showed up and showed out. He calmed my fears and relaxed my spirit, and even though there was turbulence, I had a pleasant flight. Praise God! You all right with me. I'm here to tell you, if you don't know the Lord, shame on you. He may not come when you want Him, but He's always on time.

My flight gave me time to think about how I treated Taj. I didn't mean to be difficult all the time. Sometimes, yeah, because that's who I am, but not ALL the time. So far, he seemed like a good guy. Not to say that he's perfect because none of us are. As Daddy used to say, "Ain't none of us sprouting no wings!" But what I've seen of him so far, I can deal with. I really do like him, and I don't want to drive him away with all MY faults, but it's so hard to trust. It's hard to trust ANY man. You know how men are. I know it's Satan sticking his little ugly head in again to try to keep me single, but I know the God I serve is able.

I hoped Taj would stick around long enough to see when the Lord dealt with me and fixed my heart. And just like He took that fear away from me on the plane, He could help me to trust again. *So Lord, I'm depending on You, to pull Your crazy child through.* I can admit that I am one of His CRAZY children. And you know that's half the battle!

I called him once I landed and told him about my flight. "Hello, Taj?…"

"Hey, baby doll, you made it, huh?…"

"Yeah, I made it. Bae, I want to thank you for taking me to the airport. I was so nervous before the flight that I'm sure I didn't tell you before I left…"

"I know, you all good, baby. It was my pleasure…"

"And…I want to apologize for being so difficult to you. I really don't try to ruin your mood or break your spirit down. This is hard for me, and I need you to be patient with me. God is able to remove all my doubts and fears. So don't let me run you off before you get to know me. Get to know me FIRST, THEN if you want to leave me, go for it. Okay?…"

"Baby, you are rough on a brother, I'm not going to lie. But I got you. I'm praying for you and for myself. We're going to be all good, and I'm not going anywhere. Like I said before, I've got broad shoulders…"

"Yes, you do! Thanks babe. I miss you already…"

"You still better behave…"

"Naw, you!…"

"Love you, baby doll…"

There was a pause, and I said, "You do?…"

"Yeah, I do…"

"Me too…"

"Talk to you later, have fun…"

"Thanks, baby, I will. Bye…" Wow, he said he loved me, but I'm not in love with him yet. I don't think. I did love him, but I was not IN love with him. Maybe that's what he meant. Okay. I must be doing something right.

Ronni's boyfriend, Andre, picked me up from the airport. I had met him before, so I knew who I was looking for. He didn't like me very much. I mean, we never had any kind of falling out or anything, but it seemed like he could do without being around me. I guess I kind of felt the same way. And probably because I felt that vibe from him FIRST. Not that I didn't like him because I didn't have to deal with him regularly.

Me and Dre had mild conversation on the way to the house. "Hey, Dre."

"Hey there, Val. You look like you done picked up some weight since the last time I saw you."

See what I mean? Now was that necessary? "Well, I didn't think you paid that much attention to me, but I guess you do, huh?"

"Naw, I'm just saying you look a little thicker since I saw you last, but it looks good on you."

"Well, thanks for noticing. Anyway, you been taking care of my girl, bighead?"

"Ain't nothing wrong with that girl. She just wants somebody to baby her."

"Well, have you been babying her then?"

"HAYELL NAW! I have to work and other things to take care of. Ain't nobody got time to be babysitting and worrying with some whining child!"

"Now you need to quit. She done already told me that she can hardly get you out of her face. She has to MAKE you go do something. ANYTHING."

"Well, if you already know, then why you asking?"

"You right, my bad. Let me give you a head's up, as soon as my girl gets on her feet, we both jacking you up. I mean, that's just to let you know."

"Why you have to wait for her? Go ahead and do what you have to do." So I whacked him, sure did. Backhanded him right in his chest while he was driving. "GIRL, what's wrong with you? Why you do that?"

"You told me to do what I had to do, so I did it. I'm being obedient."

"Let me hurry up and get you to the house before I have to tell Ronni that I couldn't find you at the airport and dump yo' little ass in the river somewhere."

When we got to the house, Dre went in, tattling to Ronni about me hitting him. I always beat up on him. Hey, maybe that's why he didn't like me? Naw, that's not it. I only started beating up on him because he acted like he didn't like me. Disregard. But if he ever hit me back, I would be a goner. He was a big guy, about six-foot-six or seven, and weighed a good three-hundred-and-twenty-five pounds or so.

I got my luggage out the car and went in. Ronni tried to snap on Dre for making me carry my own luggage. "Dre, why you got Val carrying her luggage? Go get it."

"Sorry, babe, can't hear you. You're going to have to speak up," he said, still heading up the stairs. Her voice was kind of frail right now, and he was taking advantage of that.

"Ronni, it's all good. I got it," I told her. I was glad to see her in good spirits. She was slow-moving but was able to greet me with a hug. We spent some time getting caught up with each other. She wanted to know how everybody back home was doing. She moved to Atlanta about two years ago. Her job packed up in Chicago and moved here to the ATL, and she came right along with it. After we talked about the family, she wanted to know ALL about Taj. We had spoken on the phone about him, but now she wanted details. I showed her a picture that Toni had taken of us.

"Val, he's cute, and he's a big guy."

"He'll do!" I said. "But he thinks he's all that and a bag of chips."

"So he's big-headed then, huh?"

"Naw, actually, he's really a sweet guy. The way these women throw themselves at these men, they don't have a choice but to think they all that."

"So then what's wrong with him?"

"You know, to be honest, he seems like the perfect guy. He's absolutely adorable, nice body, great voice, AND he's a gentleman. He doesn't want me opening doors or carrying stuff. So far, the only thing I HAVE seen is he's got anger issues."

"Like what?"

I told her the story how he scared that little boy at the restaurant.

"Yeah, but old boy had that coming. How you going to give somebody your number when you with your guy or girl?"

"Yeah, he had it coming, but Taj was out of control. I couldn't get the man to calm down. It's almost like he couldn't even hear me. I finally had to grab his head and make him look at me. Boy, men are something else when they feel like somebody's disrespecting them."

"So you haven't ever made him mad?"

"Negative."

"So why don't you do something to piss him off and see how he would react to you?"

"Nope, I'll pass. I'll piss him off eventually. He's always threatening me anyways."

"You scared of him?

"I'm not scared, but I'm not going to test him right now either."

"Girl, I know you don't let him run you. Do you?"

"Run me? NAW, he don't run me, but he ain't no punk either."

"Hold up, back in the day, me and you used to run things. We used to go where we wanted, when we wanted, with whomever we wanted, and wore what we wanted, and neither one of our guys had nothing to say about that."

"Yeah, that was back in the day. AND we're not with either one of those guys now. PLUS, I used to get dressed at your house, remember? And we withheld information about who we were going with. You don't remember all that?"

"Oh yeah, and you did used to put on some of my stuff once you got to my house, didn't you? I forgot about that, but still… Dre gets mad at me now for going to football parties with the guys, and most of the time, I'm the only female there."

"And you mean those size eighteen shoes let you?"

"What do you mean let me? I'm grown. These guys were there before Andre Deshawn Jamison came around, and they'll probably be there long after he's gone."

"Yeah, but Ronni, how would you feel if he was going to get-togethers with his female friends?"

"I would be cool with that."

"Come on man, you would be all right with that? And these are friends that HE had before YOU came along, and most of the time, he's the ONLY guy there? Because I wouldn't. Plus, I don't go anywhere anyway."

"You don't go out anymore?"

"Me and Toni do a little something something on occasion, but other than that, I'm either at Mommy's or with my sisters if I'm not home. Or as of recent, chilling with Taj."

"Well, yeah. I probably would have a problem with that since you put it that way. But HE knows better."

"Well, I have the same respect for Taj that I want him to have for me. So as of yet, I haven't done anything that he wasn't cool with."

"Dang, I'm not used to asking permission to do nothing. I can't imagine being controlled or having to submit."

"I don't think I'm going to be all that submissive myself. And I definitely don't plan on being controlled. We're going to have to come together and compromise."

"Shoot, I'm going to have to think about all this. And pray about it. I don't want to be displeasing in God's eyes, but yeah, He would have to convict me."

"Yeah, I'm having a little problem myself with that trust issue. I don't want to run the man off, but it's hard for me to trust him. So I'm praying about that."

BeeGee Hill

"Well, I think we gonna be some praying sisters. You pray for me, and I'm going to pray for you. But you can't run the man off before I get to meet him."

"Pray for me, girl!"

"I got you!"

"Cool, what we eating?"

"I don't know, but I'll send Dre."

Ronni and I did a lot of talking and praying while I was there. There wasn't a whole lot she needed me to do for her. The doctor wanted her to get up and move around and build her strength back up. So I was basically there to keep her company so she wouldn't have to spend all day looking at old big headed Dre. He pretty much stayed out of our way but ran our errands for us.

I called Taj each day so he could know we were all good. He seemed to be doing okay back at home but was acting like he really missed me. I could believe that because I was missing him too.

Ronni and I didn't do much of anything, except stay in the house, watch TV and movies, and talk. A few people from her church came by to check on her a couple times, and I let them know I would only be here for a few more days, so next week, she was going to need people to check up on her. They seemed like good people, and they didn't stay long, seeing as though I had everything under control for the time being, which was cool.

*****

It came time for me to pack up and leave. My time here with my girl had come to an end.

"Val, thank you so much for coming."

"Girl, I love you. You know I needed to know for myself if Dre was looking out for you or what. I came here, ready to take a beat-down for you if he wasn't doing what he needs to do."

"You so crazy, but I know what you mean. I'm all good, baby girl. I miss you."

"I know you are, and I miss you too. We're going to have to take a trip together or something."

"Hey, you never said anything about what Mom and them thinks about Taj."

"Well, they haven't met him yet."

"They haven't met him yet? Do they know about him?"

"Not really. I mean, they know I started dating again, but they don't think it's anyone in particular."

"So they don't know you got a man."

"Nope."

"Why?"

"I didn't think he and I would've been together this long. I know it's only been a couple months, but I been waiting for the real him to step out. I don't want to bring him around, and then he dumps me, and then I'm back to looking stupid again. My people thought Kody was the real deal."

"Val, you're doing a lot of 'I' talking. Are you letting the Lord lead you in this relationship or not?"

"I'm trying."

"You're not being fair to Taj. You're treating him like he's already hurt you. He does sound like a good guy because some brothers I know would've been out of there by now. Sweetheart, don't make Taj pay for what Kody or anyone else in your past has done. Relationships come and they go. You have some good times while they last, and then you go through some pain when it ends. That's called life, baby. Enjoy it while it's here, and if he's the man for you, and you all are letting God lead this relationship, then it WILL last. Don't lose him over some BS. And I see now this is more serious than I thought. Let me pray for you right now before you leave me, okay?"

"Girl, you know I don't have a problem with prayer. In fact, please do. And I probably shouldn't tell you this cause it's only going to make it worse, but we been together for what two and a half, three months, and he's never pressured me about sex. When things get a little steamy, he leaves."

"You mean you all haven't done the do?"

"Nope! I'm not doing that till I get married, and I told him that."

"And YOU haven't taken him to meet Mom yet?"

I shook my head no with a silly look on my face; she made me feel pretty bad.

"All right, let's do this then."

"Okay, but I'm going to pray too."

"Cool, I'll start. Dear heavenly Father, maker and creator of all things. I stand before you as humbly as I know how. I thank You for Your child that took the time out of her busy schedule to come and check up on me. But right now, Father, I need You to show Val that everyone is not out to get her. She's going to come in contact with some wonderful spirit-filled people that are going to love her because she's Your child. Taj seems like one of those people, and I don't think she's giving him a fair shot, Lord. But I know through You, ALL things are possible. Not some things, but ALL things, Father God. So in the Mighty Name of Jesus, I'm claiming that it is already done Lord. That You will mend her broken heart and let her start new with Taj. That whatever faults she finds with him will be faults that he himself has shown and not faults of someone else.

"I pray that she would lean more on You and not on her own strength and that if Taj is not for her, then You would break off that relationship NOW before it goes any further. And Lord, give her a relaxing and safe flight home, and bring her peace about it. I love You, Lord, and I thank You for hearing my cry. In Jesus's name I pray. Amen."

"Dear heavenly Father, I thank you first and foremost for Your goodness, Your mercy, and Your grace. Thank You for thinking enough of ME to send Your Son to die for my sins. Right now, Father, I thank You for putting people in my life who think enough of me to want to pray for me. I thank You for Ronni who let me come stay with her, not to take care of her because that's already done, but so that she could be a true friend to me. I pray for healing for her body. I know You're able to take away all her aches and pains, and if it's Your will, Lord, You do that.

"I'm looking for a miracle, and through You, I know I'll see one. And Lord, I ask that You direct her to be fair to old big headed Dre. If submission is what You want for her, then You lead her. Thank You for love. Be with my family back home, and continue to lead and guide me and Taj in whatever direction You see fit. Continue to bless Ronni, and let her know that she is truly loved. Be with me and my fears as I get ready to get on another plane, Lord. You be the pilot and calm my nerves. I'm asking for peace. In the Mighty Name of Jesus I pray. Amen!"

Ronni and I hugged and said our goodbyes. Dre had come downstairs while we were praying and had already taken my bags to the car. Wow! I guess maybe Ronni had given him a good scolding beforehand, and for once, he listened. Maybe not. Who knows? I'm glad for whatever reason he took them. Maybe he did like me after all.

As soon as we hugged and said goodbye, Dre started speaking, "Come on, ugly girl. I done already put your bags in the car. I want to make sure you get to the airport on time. You got your purse, your ID, your boarding pass? I don't want any excuse for you to miss your flight. Anything else you leave behind, we'll mail. You should have two good hours to make it through security. Y'all done already said goodbye, let's hit it." Well, that explains why he put my stuff in the car. My "like me" theory was gone out the window.

"Val, don't worry about him. I'll take care of him as soon as I'm better, and I'm going to keep praying for you. I love you, girlfriend."

"Thanks, Ronni. I love you too. I'll call you as soon as I land."

"That's sweet. Let's hit it, ugly. I got things to do, places to go, and people to see!" Dre came behind me and started pushing me toward the door.

"Dre, stop pushing her," Ronni was trying to yell at him. Her voice was still not back to normal yet, but it was getting there.

"Can't hear you, lovebug," and he continued till he had pushed me to the car door. He reached down and opened the door for me. I looked up at him, and he said, "Trying to help, that's it! No sudden moves!"

I turned around to say one last bye to Ronni, and Dre was pushing my head down, guiding me into the seat. You know how cops force their prisoner or whomever they may be arresting into their cars? That's how he did me. If my hair was fresh, we would've been fighting, but I had on a baseball cap. He shut the door behind me after he pushed my legs into the car. I didn't fight it because I thought I was smart and was going to open the door back, but he had put the child lock on the door. He ran around to the other side, got in, and started the car. I tried to put my window down, but he had that locked too. All I could do was wave back at my girl standing in the doorway. He had put a lot of thought into taking me to the airport.

Initially, I was a little ticked off, but all I could do was laugh. No one had ever outsmarted me like this before. I was going to have to remember this.

I called Ronni as we were pulling out of the driveway to tell her what her nut of a man had done to me, and he blasted the radio so she couldn't hear me, so we hung up. He said, "Uh-huh! I knew I would get you. Don't the good book talk about, 'He who laughs last, laughs best?' Well, hahahahahahahahahahahaha!" And he started cracking up.

"That doesn't come from the Bible, that's a proverb."

"So now they done took Proverbs out the Bible? When did that happen?" And he continued to laugh.

"You got me this time. It's cool, but you know I'll get you back."

"Regardless, I got the last laugh THIS time."

"Dre, why you don't like me?"

"What you mean?"

"You know, you don't like me. I want to know why? What did I ever do to you?"

"I do like you, girl, you the only one of Ronni's friends that I do like. The rest of them are too stuck up, too mature. I would've never been able to throw one of her other friends out the house like that! And they would've laughed about it? Never! They would've taken it personally. I started to pick you up over my shoulder and bring you out like that, and if you had of resisted a lot, that's exactly what I would've done. I only treat you like this because I do like you, crazy girl!"

"Oh, well, in that case—" And I whacked him right in his chest again. Then I started going upside the back of his head, popping him.

"Girl, let me hurry up and get you to the hospital. Oops, I mean the airport. But you hit me again, and we're going to detour to Grady Hospital."

So you know, of course, I hit him again. Once I got to the airport, Dre threw me out. He came around and opened my door for me, grabbed me by the hand, and pulled me out the car. He shut the door and locked it so I couldn't get back in; grabbed my luggage out the trunk and pushed it to me. He was running the whole time, like HE was in a HUGE hurry. Then he ran around to the driver's door, and I yelled at him because I was standing there with my arms out to give him a hug. "Dre, you really not going to give me a hug? You don't know when the next time you'll see me."

"No because you going to hit me. And I already got last lick AND my fingers are crossed!"

"Dre, come give me a hug. Please? I really appreciate the ride to and from the airport, even if you did abuse me to get me here."

"Okay, but I already got last lick," and showed me that his fingers were crossed. "Don't play." So he came around and gave me a hug. He gave me a bear hug, lifted me off the ground and everything. When he let me go, I was so lightheaded; I couldn't hit him if I wanted to. What's with everybody and these darn bear hugs? He stood there till I was almost back to normal, then went to the driver's side again. He opened the door to the car and said, "Lose some weight." He got in the car and pulled off. I'm sure he was cracking up because he really did get the last laugh this time. Next time, I'll be ready.

14

Once I got all checked in at the airport, I called Ronni and told on Dre. She said she should've figured something out. She thought he was being nice when he told her to make sure my bags were all packed and put by the door when they were ready. She told me she would take care of him.

I also called Taj and told him I was at the airport. I would be boarding soon and needed him to be at the airport when I landed. He assured me that he would be there waiting to greet me with open arms and a kiss. I told him he couldn't squeeze me too tight and told him what Dre had done. I was laughing the whole time, and he tried to get all protective and defensive of me. I had to tell him to reeeeelllaaaaaax! "Breathe baby, it's nothing like you're thinking." So he calmed down somewhat. He said he would calm down till he saw me.

He was acting so crazy about me hugging Dre and Dre squeezing the life out of me that I forgot all about being nervous on the flight. I was kind of nervous about seeing Taj. He was actually pissed off. I couldn't believe it because I asked the man for a hug and was messing with him, hitting on him and stuff? Wow! Men are some strange creatures. He should know I was not in the LEAST bit interested in Dre like that. I mean, he was a good-looking guy and all, but not for me! But then he asked me how I would feel if the man hit me back, and he, Taj, had to fly to Atlanta to defend my honor. As my brother would say, "Arjoo kidding?"

Just like I said before, the man gets totally out of whack when he gets upset. All I was thinking in my head was WOW! Maybe I shouldn't have told him all that, but I thought it was funny.

But then again, that could've been the Lord's way of keeping me calm about flying because not once was I concerned on this flight about anything but smoothing things over with Taj when I got home. Isn't it funny how the Lord works? He really is mysterious.

When I landed and got my luggage, Taj was outside waiting for me. Like I said before, I was a little nervous about seeing him, but I went to him like everything was all good, like I was so happy to see him and had really missed him, which I had. "Hi, baby! I missed you so mush!" I said in a little kid's voice as he was walking toward me to grab my luggage, but I intercepted him with my arms outstretched for a hug.

"Hey, baby doll," he said, wrapping his arms around me. He squeezed me real tight and lifted me off the ground. He wasn't cutting off ALL the oxygen to my brain, but he was coming close. He said, "Is this what old DRE did to you?"

"Baby, you're killing me," I squeezed out the best way I could.

"I just want to know if this is what you were talking about that YOUR man couldn't do to you when he saw you because some OTHER man had already done it." I kissed him, and his hold loosened tremendously.

I think the kiss must've thrown him off because he kissed me back very passionately. He must've forgotten he was reprimanding me because I certainly did. "I really missed you, baby doll. Did you have a good time?" he said as he was putting me down.

"I did, even though you weren't there, and me and Ronni didn't do much of anything. I still enjoyed spending time with my girl."

He gave me another hug and kiss and said, "I'm glad you had a good time with your girl and glad you made it home in one piece."

"Thanks love, because I'm glad I had a good time, and I really missed you too. Now I need you to do me a favor."

"What's that, Miss Lady?" he replied as he was putting my luggage in the car.

"I need you to run me by Mommy's before I get home. I missed her."

"You want ME to run YOU by your Mom's house?"

"Yeah! If that's okay. You didn't have plans, did you?"

"Naw, I'm good. And what? Stay in the car?"

"NO! Why would I ask you to stay in the car, Taj? I want you to come in and meet Moms. Now if you can't do it, then that's cool. Just drop me off at home, and I'll get in MY car and go see my Moms."

"Naw, naw, it's cool. I got you, and I would be GLAD to meet Moms."

"Cool, let's hit it, and Taj, don't show out over there." We didn't talk much on the ride home. I guess he was wondering what got into me.

We hadn't talked much about him meeting my peeps, but I knew that he was waiting for it. He had asked once or twice before, and I was dead against it. So he never did mention it again. I hadn't met his people either, but I was kind of leery about meeting them. I guess now that he was meeting my folks, meeting his was going to be right around the corner.

We got to Mommy's house, and I went in first, of course. Mommy heard me fiddling with the doorknob (I wasn't sure if it was locked or not) and yelled out, "Who is that coming in my house?"

I said, "Hey there, pretty lady. It's me, Valeri Nicole Wilson." My oldest brother and sister were there as well. "Hey, family!"

Taj followed me in, but she didn't see him initially. Mom was sitting in the living room in her chair, watching TV. I walked up and gave the little lady a kiss on her forehead.

"Hey, sweetheart. How was your trip? How's Ron doing?" Mom was always shortening or messing up people's names.

"It was good, and Ronni is coming along just fine."

"Why didn't you shut the door? Were you raised in a barn? The air is on," Mom said. Taj backed up and closed the door.

"Oh, well Mom, this is Taj," and I scooted over so she could see him. "Taj, this is my Mom, the love of my life. This is my oldest brother, Jason"—and I pointed to him—"and my sister, Pearl. Fammo, this is Taj, my boo." I walked over and hugged my sister and brother.

"Taj, your BOO?" Mom replied. "Since when you had a boo? Hi Taj, it's a pleasure to meet you."

"Hello, Ms. Wilson. I've been looking forward to meeting you."

My brother, Jason, stood up and shook Taj's hand and gave him a man hug. You know where they shake hands and bump shoulders and pat the back with the free hand. "What's up, man? Nice to meet you. So you taking my baby sis out, huh? You better take care of her, man."

"I plan to do just that as long as she lets me."

My sister Pearl said, "Taj, huh? You're a big guy. What you do, play football?"

"Not anymore. I'm a police officer. How you doing, Ms. Pearl?"

"Aww, a police officer, huh? Beautiful! I guess you're in good hands, huh, Val? I guess we're ALL in good hands now," Pearl said, like we had hit the jackpot or something.

Mom chimed in, "How long you two been a couple?"

Taj jumped in with an answer, "Ms. Wilson, we have been dating for almost three months, and I asked to meet you all a long time ago, but your daughter was against it."

"Val, you ashamed of your family?" Mom came at me, like she didn't know me.

"First of all, I told YOU to behave before we came up in here," I said, pointing to Taj.

He shrugged his shoulders and was shaking his head like, "What did I do?"

"Secondly, I am ashamed of some of your sons, Mom. Just kidding. I didn't want to rush it. I knew he would get his chance to meet the fam, but you DO know that some of your boys get out of pocket, and I don't want them tainting him."

"Three months, and I'm just now even HEARING about a boo? Well, I do believe its past time for you to meet the rest of the family, so how you feel about coming to dinner on Sunday? What church do you belong to?"

"I'm a member of Christ the Solid Rock here in the Woods. And personally, I would love to come to dinner on Sunday."

"Well, I'd like to first welcome you to come to service at ACBC. I'm sure Val has told you where the church is. And after service, you are more than welcome to come over for dinner."

"I accept and will be at both, if the Lord's willing—"

And Mom finished it with, "And the creek don't rise."

We sat around and chatted for about an hour or so. Jason left us about thirty minutes ago. He had some business to tend to before he went home. Taj was involved in ALL the conversations, just like on our first date. He seemed like he had known my family all along. I was a little nervous about my brothers Arik and Brian meeting Taj, though. They were both troublemakers. Arik was SUCH a male chauvinist. I could just see him tell Taj that he was going to need to go back to the caveman days with me. He was going to tell him that they (my brothers) would not be mad at him if he needed to slap me around a little bit to keep me in line. "A woman's place is in the kitchen, barefoot and pregnant," according to him, "and sometimes you have to slap them around to show them who's boss and to keep them in line."

And Brian, being the baby boy, was a certified nut. He was going to try to give Taj some pointers on keeping me in line, tell him where my weaknesses lie. I'm telling you, they were going to make me act out. So, oh well, if that's how they wanted it, that's how they'd get it. I'd be ready for them because they know I'm crazy too.

After we had been there for a minute, we were about to leave when Pearl asked Taj if he wanted to go pick up food for Mom. Mom loved fish and wanted some perch, so of course, Taj said he would do it. She called J & J and placed the order. Taj wouldn't take any money from them. He said he had it. He and I ordered fish as well. I was going to ride with him, but Pearl told me to let him go. He knows his way around and wouldn't get lost. I knew that was their way of getting rid of him so they could interrogate me.

"Baby doll, I'll be right back. You stay here, I can handle it."

"Yeah, okay Taj."

So Taj left to go get food, and as soon as he walked out, they bombarded me. Mommy started, "So you been dating him for about three months and you never said anything to us about him? What's wrong with him?"

Pearl jumped in, "He's a nice-looking guy and seems really sweet. I can't imagine why you haven't shared him with us before. Plus, I got a ticket that needs to be taken care of."

Mom said, "Where did you meet him? The two of you went to school together?"

"Um, hello? Would you all like me to answer any of your questions? Or are you going to keep asking more?"

"Go ahead, girl. I'm wondering what you waiting for," Mom said. She's so feisty.

"Well, Mother, I met him back in March leaving your house."

"Why didn't you tell us about him?"

"Ma, can I finish my story, please?"

"Go ahead, child."

"Well, he stopped me after I left your house because he thought I was cute and wanted a closer look, which, can you blame him? He told me my taillight was out. Anyhoo, he asked me out. And I declined. I told him I was trying to live right and thought he might complicate my life." They both kind of leaped forward and were getting ready to interrupt me again, and I kept talking. "BUUUUTTT, I also told him that if we should happen to meet again, it's a date. So a couple weeks later, me and Toni were at the bowling alley, and we saw him on our way home. To make a long story short, she got his attention, and he pulled us over, saw it was me, and asked me out. That was on a Saturday night. He asked if he could come to church with me the next day, which was Sunday, and I said no."

"You don't want him worshipping with you?" Mom asked.

"I didn't want him invading my space if he wasn't going to be in the picture long."

"So what now? He seems like he's going to be in the picture for a while longer?" Pearl asked.

"Actually, I probably have been unfair to him. You know how I am. I have a problem trusting men after Kody dumped me, and I've been treating him like he's the one that hurt me."

"Girl, I thought you were over all that. You going to miss out on a good thing if you don't get it together."

"Thanks Pearl," I responded sarcastically. "Actually, Ronni and I talked about it, and she prayed for me, and the Lord helped me to see the error of my ways. He really is a good guy. We've been together for almost three months, and one of the first things I told him before

I committed to being his girl was that I wasn't having sex before marriage, and not ONCE has he asked me to give in or pressured me or anything like that. If it starts getting a little hot and steamy, he leaves. He seems too good to be true, but as Ronni helped me to see, enjoy it while it lasts, and if it ends, get over it. Therefore, I left the airport and headed straight here. Am I growing up or what? Plus, until the Lord tells me differently, I'm going to go with it."

"Well, if you're letting the Lord lead you, baby, then you can't go wrong."

"Thanks Mom, we'll see how it goes."

"Well, he's back. Go open the door for your boo, girl."

So I went and let him in. He had stopped by the store and grabbed a couple of liters of pop. We sat there and ate, talked a little, and watched TV. We stayed for another hour or so before we left. When we left, Taj told Mom that he enjoyed finally meeting her and would be looking forward to seeing her on Sunday and kicking it with the rest of the family.

"Taj, don't be talking to my Momma about 'kicking' it with the family on Sunday. My Moms is not a hoodlum. You don't talk to her like that."

"I'm sorry Mrs. Wilson, I didn't mean any disrespect."

"Aww baby, don't worry about it. You go ahead and 'kick' it with my baby." We all laughed after she said that. I guess my Moms did have a little gangster in her. I wouldn't mess with the little lady.

He hugged my Mom and thanked her for the invitation and hugged my sister and told them both that we would see them on Sunday. I kissed Mom and told Pearl bye, and we left. When we got outside, I clocked Taj, punched him in the shoulder.

"Heyyyyy! What did you do that for?"

"Didn't I tell you before we got here not to come in here showing out?"

"I wasn't showing out. I was just being me."

"Yeah, well just being YOU is going to get you jacked. YOU didn't have to go in there, telling Mom that I didn't want you to meet them." I started talking in a deep voice, mocking him, "Mom, we been going out for about THREE months, and I asked her if I could come to church with her and meet the family. She said NO!"

"I wasn't telling on you."

"What you call it then, Taj?"

"I was getting myself off the hook. Your Moms was about to blame me."

I punched him again, and he laughed at me. "That's all right. I'll get you back, I'm not worried about it."

We went back to my house and chilled. I called Ronni while Taj was there and told her that I followed her advice and took Taj by Moms. She was glad for me, and we talked about how that went.

Taj felt like he was big stuff since he felt like he got in good with some of my peeps, especially Mom. "Oh, that was Ronni's idea? I like her. I need to meet my new little sister."

"Yeah well, she got me to see the light on certain situations. So I'm going to go with it."

"You know I'm going to marry you, right?"

"When? Tonight?"

"Mark my words."

"Mr. Taj Darnell Bryant, you need to stop playing."

"That's not my middle name."

"Well, what is it then?"

"Alexander."

"Well Mr. Taj Alexander Bryant, you need to stop playing with me."

"I'm not playing, but as soon as I hear from God, I'll let you know. Thank you for making me feel like you have faith in me. Like you trust me and know that I AM going to be around for a while."

The thoughts going through my head wanted to say, "There you go again, being lame." But seeing as though I was trying to turn over a new leaf, I had to say something nice. "Thank you Taj, for being good people. Oh, but don't forget, I haven't met your peeps yet."

"That's only because YOU made me promise not to take you over there till you were ready."

"Oh yeah, I did, didn't I?"

"Uh, YEAH!"

"Okay, REEELAX!"

"So you ready?"

"No time like the present."

"What? You want to go now?"

"BOY, NO! I'm just saying yeah, I'm ready, I guess."

"Cool!"

So we sat there, and I told him all about my trip.

15

The next day was Saturday, and we were supposed to double date with Zani and Toni. Actually, Taj set up the date up with Zani. Toni and I had nothing to do with it. And Toni called, "Hey, Val, where you at?…"

"Hi Toni, and how are you?…"

"Yeah, yeah, yeah, whatever. What you doing tonight?…"

"I'm fine love, thank you so much for asking. How are you?…"

"Fine Val. Hello Valeri, how are you today?…"

"I already answered that. What do you want?…"

"Girl, me and Zani are going out tonight. You should come…"

"Me and Taj are going out…"

"You can bring his old dusty Milk Dud head with you…"

"Heffa, Taj said we was double dating with you two…"

"Get out of here!…"

"No, YOU get out of here…"

"Are you serious?…"

"Uh, yeah!…"

"Why I don't know anything about this?…"

"You didn't know for real? I thought you were just kidding…"

"So Zani knows?…"

"Uh, yeah!…"

"Let me call him. I'll call you back…"

"Fine, talk to you in a little bit…"

"Bye…"

"Bye, heffa…"

She called me back in about ten minutes, still fussing. "Girl, how is Zani making plans like this without talking to me about it?…"

"Toni, what's the big deal? You were calling to invite me and Taj to come out with the two of you anyways. Why you tripping?..."

She began whining, "I'm supposed to be on the planning committee when we do something like this..."

"Oh, I get it, you mad because they planned this without your knowledge. You are such a brat..."

"Oh Val, don't be such a Goody Two-shoes. You act like nothing gets next to you. You're so easygoing all the time! Remember, I know the REAL you!..."

"My man told me we were double dating with you and Zani tonight. He's paying for whatever WE do. I don't have a problem with it..."

"Whatever! Well, since I didn't know anything about it, let's go see that new movie that just came out..."

"Um, I may be wrong, BUT I think they already have the night planned..."

"Don't worry about it. If I want to see the movie, then their plans will change to what I want..."

"Go for it, but I'm not tripping. I really don't care what we do..."

"Well, I'll see you in a bit, and if I need you to (which I won't), back me up on the movie thing, kay?..."

"You won't need me. See you in a few..."

"Kay, bye..."

We met up at a restaurant downtown for dinner. We had a pretty decent time. Of course, me and Toni had a good time with each other, and it was good to see Zani and Taj getting along too. This was the first time they had kicked it like this before, and it was all good. They seemed like old friends. They did some talking about high school days, playing football and basketball, being the stars of the team. Me and Toni boosted our men's egos by telling them that they were right. They were the bomb back then and are still the bomb today. "How do you think you both ended up with us? YOU must be ALL that?"

After dinner, we all rode together in Zani's Escalade, and Toni started her appeal to go see a movie.

"Zani baby, where are we going? Val and I wanted to see that new movie that's out now."

"Baby, I'm going to need you to sit back and enjoy the sights. We'll go see that another time, but Tab and myself got some other stuff planned for tonight."

"See Toni, I told you," I interjected in their conversation and then thought about it and said, "Who's Tab?"

Then Taj spoke up and said, "Baby Doll, I told Zani that my friends call me Tab."

I said, "Wow! I guess the saying is true. You learn something new every day, huh?"

Once again Toni began her appeal. "But baby, since you didn't let me know ANYTHING about what we were doing tonight, YOU don't think I should have a say in what we do? I really had my heart set on that movie."

"Bae, if you don't enjoy yourself this evening, I will totally make it up to you. Actually, me and Tab will let you ladies plan the next outing, and we'll go and do ANYTHING you two would like. Right Tab?... Taj?"

"My bad Zani man, were you talking to me? I got this fine honey back here whispering in my ear and kissing on me. I haven't heard a thing you said."

"Uh, Tab, you better stop clowning around with that fine honey because if my girl, Val, finds out, you're in BIG trouble," Toni said, being awfully funny. Taj found that to be hilarious.

"Taj, that was funny?" I asked as he was cracking up.

"Baby doll, I thought that was your girl. I ain't expect her to come at you like that. It caught me off guard." He cleared his throat. "Toni, watch yourself. My girl is not laughing, so no, that wasn't funny."

"So Taj, what's up? I told Toni if they're not satisfied with what we do tonight, we'll let them plan the next date. You cool with that?" Zani repeated himself to Taj, changing the subject to get his girl off the hook.

"Zee man, I think we may have to put some limits, some restrictions to what we let them come up with. Naw, but I'm cool with that because my girl is going to like what we do regardless. It's YOUR girl that's high maintenance."

"What you trying to say, Tab?" Toni snapped.

"I'm just saying. Ain't nothing wrong with high maintenance"— and then he mumbled to me—"if you like that type." We turned into Navy Pier.

"NAVY PIER?" Toni said.

I said to Toni, "Girl, give it a chance, please."

"Naw, I'm good. I like Navy Pier," she said, grinning. I hate her!

We parked in the parking garage and began enjoying the Navy Pier experience. I've been in Chicago my whole life, and this was another FIRST for me. After we walked around for a while, we took a boat ride around the lake. It was a beautiful night. There was a nice breeze blowing. We watched the sun go down and the moon come up with not a cloud in the sky. After the boat ride, we got on the Ferris wheel. There was a HUGE spider on the Ferris wheel, and Taj protected me. He put those big old tree trunks (arms) around me, and I felt safe from any danger, INCLUDING that doggone spider.

After that, we watched the fireworks, which were absolutely gorgeous. It was good to finally have somebody to hold on to while Toni and Zani were being their usual pain in the butt—ooops (did I think that out loud) I meant, lovey-dovey selves. We did a little shopping. Taj bought me a single rose as well as some jewelry—a necklace, bracelet, and earring set that Toni picked out for me. It was cute. I liked it and thought the rose was a very sweet gesture. I wasn't ready for my night to end. We had a really nice time, and I didn't mind Toni and Zani at all, but I had to get up early tomorrow for service, so Zani took us back to our ride.

Toni got out the car and gave me a hug. "Girl, I'm so glad you hung with us today. Didn't you have a good time?"

"I did."

"I know, girl. I'm so glad that Zani came up with this double date plan. He's so creative." Zani had gotten out the car and joined the party on the passenger side of the car at this time. He gave Taj one of those man hugs and told him they were going to have to get together again real soon.

Then Zani hugged me and told me to take good care of your man! "You got yourself a winner this time, Val. You take care of this one right here!"

"That's my plan, Zani!"

Toni and Taj hugged too.

"Toni, we out. I'll talk to you tomorrow."

"Kay, bye girl. Bye Tab. You be careful with my girl."

"I will, Toni. You behave."

The ride back to the house seemed to be quick. I rode home in the middle seat, leaning back on my man with that big old tree limb wrapped around me and had my eyes closed, chilling. I was replaying the night in my head. The boat ride was romantic, the Ferris wheel AS romantic—actually, that was a little scary if you let your mind wander. It moved so slow and went so high in the air, and that darn spider! But sitting all hugged up with those cobras wrapped around me, smelling his cologne, made me forget about the danger I could've been in. Then to top it off, he bought me a single rose. How sweet is that? But as they say, all good things must come to an end. WOW! Why did it have to end?

We made it back to my house, and I didn't want to open my eyes nor get out the car. I guess Taj thought I was sleep. He kissed me on the forehead and whispered in my ear, "Baby doll, we're home."

"Aww, do I have to get up now, Mommy?"

"Let's go, funny gal!"

I got up off him, and he came around to the passenger side and started pulling me up and out of the car. He shut the door behind me and held on to me as I gathered myself. He grabbed me by the hand and walked me to the porch. He stopped me as I got on the first stair and turned me around to face him. I was almost eye level to him, but not quite, and as we all know, almost ONLY counts in horseshoes. Anyhoo, he put his arms around my waist, and I put my arms around his neck. "Did you have a good time, baby?"

I looked into his eyes, and before I said anything, I gave him a very gentle kiss on the lips and said, "Taj, I had a wonderful time as usual. I want to thank you for making me feel special and for what it seems like to me, putting a lot of thought into making our time together exceptional." Then I kissed him for real.

He said, "Just to let you know, I enjoy doing things like this for someone who appreciates it. You make it easy to come up with things I think you'll enjoy."

"Well, I've been in Chicago all my life, and that was my first time EVER at Navy Pier."

"Really?"

"Yup."

"And you enjoyed it?"

"Very much so."

"What was your favorite part?"

"Uhhhhhh, being with you."

"Ohhh, baby, good answer!" And he hugged me tight and lifted me off the ground and started kissing my neck where I'm very ticklish, so I started laughing and trying to get away from him.

"All right, Shorty!" I said to him as I pulled away from him. Now that I think about it, he probably let me go. I guess I wasn't as BAD as I thought I was. "Now you know you not right for doing me like that?"

"What, like this?" And he tried to get my neck again, and I was fighting him off keeping my chin down.

"Baby, please stop. You going to make me pee on myself."

He said, "Saved by the wet pants."

"They not wet yet, but if you don't stop, they will be."

"I'll stop since you were such a good girl today, but I'm sure you'll act up, and I'll get my chance to torture you soon."

"Here you go! You should be happy that I behaved and had a really good time, but instead, you're looking forward to me misbehaving so you can torture me. See, you just can't do right! But seeing as though we had such a WONDERFUL time, I forgive you. And I really appreciated the time we had."

He told me to go in the house and get some sleep since we had a long day planned for tomorrow, which was Sunday—the Sunday that he was supposed to come to my church and come to Mommy's for dinner afterward. I didn't tell him what time service was or where the church was or what time I was leaving or NOTHING. He didn't ask, so I didn't tell him, but I'm sure we discussed it previously (at some point). I remember that because he was whining about 9:00 a.m. service. He had mentioned that he was glad that he had a choice of services to go to with his church. Whatever!

I enjoyed my service and my church, so nine o'clock worked out just fine for me. I didn't get down with big churches where the pastor would never know whether or not I was in service any particular Sunday. I liked to have a personal relationship with my pastor and the rest of the members. Hopefully, old boy remembered, or maybe he was planning to call me early in the morning to see if he should scoop me or not. *Oh well! Que sera, sera. Whatever will be, will be! I'm going to bed.*

16

Sunday morning! Ahhhhh, today's the big day! No call from Taj. It's all good, though! He's a cop. Meaning, he has a good memory (or should have a good memory) and will get to church at some point. I got dressed and ready for service, ate a piece of fruit, had some juice, and was leaving out of my house by eight thirty; service started at nine. *Well, I'll be dipped.* I came out of my house, and who do you think was parked outside? RIGHT! Taj was parked out front, sitting in the car. Now I wonder how long he'd been sitting out there…waiting.

I started walking to my car, and he rolled down his window. "Girl, where you think you going? Get over here in this car with me. What's wrong with you?"

I stopped dead in my tracks and cut old boy a look. He got out the car and opened the passenger door for me. I guess I gave the appearance that I was upset, well, I guess I was.

"What's the business, Val? You mad? You don't want me to go to church with you? You didn't tell me what time to scoop you or what time to be at church or NOTHING! What's the problem, baby doll?"

I didn't have a response. I'm really not sure why I was apprehensive about him coming to church with me. All I could say was, "Good morning to you too, Taj." After I got my Bible out of my car, I got in the car with Taj and started talking to God in my head. *Lord, I don't understand why I'm having such a big problem with this. Is this YOUR way of saying that this is NOT Your will or what? I need help and I need You to give me peace about this. Help everything to go off smoothly and relax me, or else I know that I'm making a mistake.* Before

I could end my prayer with *Amen*, I realized that Taj had been talking to me and calling my name.

"Baby, what's wrong? If you really don't want me to go to service with you and meet the rest of your family, I don't have to. I mean, I would understand, really, I would. Let me stop lying! I don't understand!"

Before he could finish his thought, I leaned over and kissed him on the cheek and said, "Good morning, baby. You look very—let me stress that—EXCEPTIONALLY good this morning. You must be trying to make a great impression on SOMEBODY today."

"Baby doll, don't be trying to butter me up. What's wrong?"

"I'm sorry, sweet pea! You're exactly right. I was expecting for YOU to ask me what time service is and all that other stuff, and all I had to do was tell you. Then I got an attitude because you didn't ask, didn't call, and then just showed up here this morning. It's just Satan trying to ruin a perfectly good Sunday morning. The weather is great, the sky is clear, my man came to pick ME up to share worship service with ME this morning, looking ever so scrumptious, my family is all fine and healthy—what should I have to complain about? I'm sorry, baby!"

"So we all good?"

"Splendid!"

"Well then, thanks baby doll. You look good too, but when is it that you don't?" He leaned over and gave me a gentle peck on the lips and said, "Good morning!"

Now let me explain something to you; when I say the man looked good, I MEAN THAT! He had on this medium gray suit with a long suit coat. Not dark and not light, but right smack dab in the middle gray. His shirt was a deep purple, and the tie brought the shirt together with the jacket perfectly. It had diagonal stripes of different shades of gray along with the same color purple of the shirt. His matching hanky was placed in the pocket where it was a thin horizontal layer of hanky showing over the top boarder of the pocket. It gave you the impression that the tip of the pocket was made out of the same material and pattern as the tie. He had on some nice gray shoes, and naturally, his socks were the same color gray with little bursts of purple. He was sharp! I'm cute too, but I think he got me beat today, but how can one tell? I'm cute ALL the time (not to sound vain, but when you got it, you got it). Oh well!

We headed to church, I gave him the general directions of how to get there, but he was already aware of where he was going. On the ride to church, he apologized to me for not asking about how we were going to handle things this morning. We were both expecting the other one to be inquisitive or informative as to how we were going to approach the day. When I sit back and think about it, THIS is probably one reason that relationships don't last. There's a breakdown in communication. But because I may have expected Taj to be the inquisitive one, and he expected me to be the informative one, why should that cause division? I'm so thankful that I have a God I can go to who can help sort things out and come through right when I need him.

"Thank You, Lord, for giving me the words to say. It was unnecessary for us to bicker about the lack of communication between us, and You showed that to me without me even knowing You did. You're such a good God, and I'm looking forward to giving You some praise in service this morning. Thanks, Lord. Amen!"

Naturally, Taj sat next to me in service. He stood up for visitors, introduced himself, and told the church that Mom had invited him. Pastor Phil's topic was "What Must I Do To Be Saved?" You can't just talk about being saved, and right now, you're in the process of being saved, BUT you're not actually saved till after you pass away. Also, you have to be active in your church; you can't only be a bench member. He gave all kinds of helpful information. It was a really good message. The choir was good. All around, service was truly fulfilling this morning. Taj seemed to enjoy it, but we hadn't talked about it much.

When service was over, we walked around and greeted one another. A bunch of my family members came over and introduced themselves to Taj and asked him if he was coming for dinner, and of course, he was glad to say yes, he would be there. Actually, he told them that he RARELY turned down a FREE home-cooked dinner.

Dwayne's response to that was, "From the size of you, I can believe that." He was always good for a laugh, and his audience cracked up.

Taj laughed too. "Yeah, this comes from collard greens and mashed potatoes." He flexed his bicep and was pointing at it with the other hand when he said that.

One of my nephews (we call him Guy) said, "Dang, I need to start eating me some collard greens and mashed potatoes." His comment brought in another round of laughter. We had a good time laughing and talking before we left church.

We stayed for Sunday School too, which in my church comes after worship service, which is not traditional in the Black church. It was fourth Sunday, so we had a Bible quiz. All of this was new to Taj. He wasn't used to having Sunday school after worship service, and he seemed to really enjoy the way our Sunday school was run. Our children play a big part in our church. Our assistant superintendent is a child as well as our Sunday school secretary. When our visitors were announced and asked if they had any words they wanted to say, he commented on ACBC getting their children ready to be leaders of tomorrow. He was impressed, which of course made me feel good. I do enjoy my church, but I'm glad to be wherever the Spirit is, and the Spirit of God is truly in this place! PRAISE GOD!

Taj brought a change of clothes with him, so we stopped by my house where we both changed and then went to Mommy's. By the time we got there, everybody was already there. It didn't take us a long time to get there, but nonetheless, we were the last ones to arrive. I guess everyone else came straight from church. I walked in the house and said, "Hi, fam, this is my boo, Taj and yes, like Taj Gibson. His nickname is Tab. Feel free to call him either. Taj, this is the fam. It's too many people to try to give you individual names, so y'all can introduce yourselves. When you see how crazy they are, some names will stick out quicker than others. You'll figure it out. I'm gone in the kitchen with the girls."

I reached up and kissed him on his cheek and was out. Yup! He's a big boy and can take care of himself, so I left him to fend for himself with those animals.

Just joshing! I love them knuckleheads.

When I got in the kitchen with the girls, Khaleesi Marie started in on me, "Uh-huh! That explains why you haven't returned any calls. People hardly ever see you anymore. So should we attribute that to the good officer?"

"Girl, what are you talking about? I have been here EVERY Sunday. I haven't missed a Sister Wednesday. And since when you been calling me and haven't been able to reach me?"

"Missy, I left you about three voice mails on your phone."

"I don't have any voice mails on my phone. You sure you been dialing the right number?"

"Girl, I know your number!"

"Wait, my home number?"

"UH, YEAH!"

"Leesi, why didn't you call my cell phone? I never answer my home number and always forget to check the messages. I only got it because it's free. Important people, like my family, call my cell."

"Oh, well...I forgot about the cell."

"Oh my gosh, girl."

"Okay, already, I said I forgot."

"Geeeeesh! Anyhoo, ain't he cute?"

Khaleesi was the first to respond to that question, "Girl, yesssss! He is adorable."

Pearl said, "I already told you the boy was good-looking. Did you give him that ticket I told you to give to him?"

"No ma'am, I haven't given that ticket a second thought, but YOU can give it to him now."

"Think I won't when I will?"

Rena's response was nothing short of what I thought it would be, "He's cute and all, I mean he ain't no ROBERT, but he's good for you. He's cute."

Khaleesi responded to Rena before I could say anything, "Girl, you think you got the monopoly on cute? Robert is okay, but God didn't stop making cute when he made old Rob. Good GRAVY! Jonah and Jesai are cute too, but she didn't ask us about OUR husbands. She just said ain't the man cute."

I chimed in with, "So there."

Rena had to defend herself, "I was merely making an observation, even if we do ALL know the obviousness of my observation, and I did answer her question."

"On to the next subject. So Val, tell us all about him and how y'all met and EVERYTHING!" Khaleesi changed the subject. Her and Rena could go on all day with that. I was glad she moved on to bigger and better things.

So I told them all about us, how we met, and how good he was to me and stuff. I told them how difficult it had been to trust that he really wanted me, but Ronni got me to see that I should enjoy the time we do have and if he's not the one, then be grateful still for the time we shared. I asked them to keep us in their prayers because I could be hard to deal with at times (although they already knew that) and I didn't want to run the man off because of that. I told them about my trip to Atlanta and how Ronni and I prayed and that she was the reason I brought him over on Friday.

Of course, they were very encouraging and had some good advice for me. "What God has for me, it is for me" is what they reiterated.

I also told them, "Well, I wasn't going to tell y'all this because I don't want to count my chickens before they hatch, but y'all always make me go further than my original plan."

"Girl, what is it? You know we got you." Rena was always the impatient one. "It's my money, and I want it NOW" is pretty much her philosophy.

"All right, keep your shirt on, girl… Well, I didn't put any stock in it when he said it to me because I can't let my feelings show like that, but—"

"Girl, get on with it. Give us the preliminaries later."

"Okay already, the man told me he was going to marry me as soon as God gives him the go-ahead."

"So that means he didn't ask you to marry him yet, right?"

"No, he didn't ask me, and actually, that was for Mom's benefit so that she could be praying for us, and if this is NOT what God wants, then we could go our separate ways. And Pearl, don't make me feel bad for telling y'all that."

"Naw, I didn't mean it in a negative way. I need to talk to him and get to know him a little better before he asks my BABY sister to marry him. That's all. You know you can tell us anything. And we going to be praying too."

Mom had been pretty quiet this whole time, but her silence had now been broken. "Sooo, if he asked you today, what would your answer be?"

"HHsssssssssssss," I sighed before I gave my response. "Well, I hadn't thought about it because I know that's way down the line somewhere, but I would NOT be able to say yes right now. He's just now meeting my family, and I have yet to meet his, but I guess my response would be that I have to pray about it and I'll get back to him. He would have to know that I need him to be patient with me."

"Well baby, as long as THAT would be your response and you would HONESTLY listen to His answer"—and she pointed toward the heavens—"then that's ALL I would ask for. You're on the right track, love."

"Thanks Mommy. Keep us up in your prayers."

"Always baby, and Terry does seem like a nice guy. I'm glad he makes you happy."

"Me too, Ma. But his name is Taj."

"What I call him?"

"Terry."

"Taj, Terry—same thing. You know who I'm talking about."

"Gotcha Ma!"

Mom called everyone in around the dining room table (as usual) for grace and asked my oldest brother, Jason, to bless the food. He welcomed Taj first and then said the blessing. Arik tried to make me fix Taj's plate, and I respectfully declined. He was trying to get Taj all geeked up to be like, "Yeah, babe. Go on ahead and do that for me," but Dwayne stepped in and said, "Yo Taj, let me show you how it's done. I'll be first, and you follow my lead." He backed everybody else up and said, "Y'all show some manners. Let our guest go first." He grabbed a plate and gave one to Taj, and they started loading up their plates.

I was surprised that everybody else backed up and let Dwayne lead the pack and feel like he was the man. My other brother, Louis (but we call him Red), went in the front room and got a tray for Taj and set his spot up for him and sat back, watching the Cubs game till the table cleared some. I was going to do it, but I was too busy making sure everything was straight on the table and getting the Kool-Aid made and put out.

I told Mom, "Mom, make sure you say your famous line."

"What famous line you talking about?"

And pretty much everybody said it at the same time, "WHATEVER YOU PUT ON YOUR PLATE, YOU'RE GOING TO EAT!" Everybody cracked up.

Mom said, "Well we have a guest, so I wasn't going to say it today, but since you all have said it then, Tim and everybody else, WHATEVA YOU PUT ON YOUR PLATE YOU BETTER EAT! Children in Africa are starving, and we don't waste no food around here!"

Taj was the only one who responded to that, and he said, "Yes ma'am!"

17

The rest of dinner went along pretty smoothly. Well, if you consider having to wait for all these people to get out of the way so you can fix your plate smooth, then it was smooth. My brothers and nephews were back for second helpings before I sat down to eat, but that's business as usual for me.

Taj seemed to be enjoying himself. As soon as he finished eating, he brought his plate in the kitchen and expressed to Mom how good the food was. "Mrs. Wilson, that food was soooo good. I haven't had a meal like that in I don't know how long."

"You mean my daughter doesn't cook for you?"

"Well, she's cooked me a little something something. But it was on a much smaller scale than this."

"Oh, I see. Well I'm glad you enjoyed it, baby."

"I did. Can I help clear the table and get the kitchen cleaned?"

Just then, Arik was coming in the kitchen. I'm not sure if he was getting seconds or looking for dessert, but he heard what Taj had just asked. "Look man, if you're going to eat here, you better get with the program. The MEN don't clean nor do we help in the kitchen after dinner. Now don't give us a bad name."

Moms stepped up and said, "Baby, don't mind him. I'm not sure where we got that character from."

"Aww, he doesn't bother me."

"Bother you? I'm trying to give you some pointers. You need to hang around me. I need to invite you over to MY castle, MY domain, and let you see how the MAN of the house is s'posed to run things."

"Arik, I wish Ms. Kiley Marie was here. Taj, he wouldn't be talking that same noise if his wife was here," I told him.

"Pssssssss, she know how I run MY house. I'm the king of MY castle."

"Yeah, whatever! More like she KNOW how you run yo mouth!" I said.

When we were done eating, me and a few of the women got up and cleared the table and cleaned the kitchen. When we finished, I went on the front porch with the rest of the women. Naturally, the guys were up front, playing cards along with Pearl Ann. I didn't know that my boo knew how to play bid, but he was hanging right along with the rest of them.

After a while, Jason left. He said his farewells to the guys, rounded up his crew, then he came outside and said his goodbyes to Mom and the rest of us. He whispered to me as he was leaving, "Looks like you got yourself a winner this time, baby sis."

All I could do was smile back at him and say, "Time will tell, but I'm enjoying it as long as it lasts!"

He said, "That's right. Take it one day at a time and stay prayerful."

"I got you, love. Thanks!"

He winked at me as he turned and walked away.

Taj came outside shortly after Jason left and said, "Y'all mind if I join you ladies out here?"

Khaleesi said, "Well, it's getting late. Me and my posse are about to head on out too."

Taj said, "I didn't run you off, did I, Ms. Khaleesi?"

"Now Taj, this is MY Momma's house. YOU can't run me off. Naw, we got a nice ride ahead of us. I would like to stay here and harass you a little, but I have to go. You got brothers and sisters, Taj?"

"Yes, I'm the oldest of five. I got three sisters and a brother."

"Oh wow, that's a nice round number," was Khaleesi's reply.

Mom chimed in with, "And where do they live?"

"Well, they're all in Illinois. My brother and one sister lives south suburbs, and then my other two sisters are not too far from Mom and Dad in the Bolingbrook area."

"Have you met them yet, Val?" Rena asked.

"Not yet, but I'm sure I'll meet them soon."

119

Taj jumped in with his two cents, "Yeah, she'll be meeting them real soon. My family knows ALL about her and most of y'all too. Well, they know as much about you all that I know."

"Oh wow! Is that right?" Mom replied.

"Yes ma'am, that's right, and—" But before Taj could say anything else, he noticed me looking at him. "WHAAAT?" he said to me, shrugging his shoulders like he really didn't know what the look was for.

"I didn't say nothing," I said.

"Yeah, but I can tell how you're looking at me that I'm in trouble, right?" He turned away from me and said to Mom, "Ma, now you see that, right? What did I say? I'm going to be in trouble when we leave here."

"Don't try to get Mom on your side, Bryant," I said to him.

Mom interjected with, "Tim, I'm sure you're fine. My daughter is not that petty. You'll be okay."

"Yeah TIM, you'll be fine," I said to him.

Pearl had left the card game too and joined in the fun with, "Yeah Tim, you'll be fine. You're not scared of li'l old Val are ya?"

Khaleesi, Jonah, and the kids were heading out just then, and Jonah jumped in the conversation to help him out and said, "Don't answer that Tee, and it's a trap. All right Mom, I'll see you later." And he kissed mom on the cheek. "Family, we'll see you all later."

"Bye, y'all," somebody on the porch said.

Taj got up from sitting on the stair in front of me and gave Jonah a man hug and thanked him for looking out for him. "Nice to meet you, Jonah, and good looking out," he whispered.

Khaleesi kissed Mommy and said her farewells as did the children, and they were gone.

After a little while, everyone was gone from Mommy's. It was almost nine-thirty when we left, and we were the last ones to leave. We had a good time with the family, and as far as I knew, my brothers had behaved themselves. I found out later on that Dwayne told Taj that he better not mess over his baby sis, otherwise there would be some consequences and repercussions. I knew if anybody had said anything like that, it would have been Dwayne. He was very protective of me. I didn't get the circumstances of how or why he said what he said. Was it just a friendly warning? Did he take him off privately and tell him? Or did he say it as a joke in front of the rest of the guys or what? Dwayne was known to be a jokester, and inquiring minds wanted to know. I'd find out.

Anyhoo, we said goodbye to Mom and my two nephews that lived there with her, and we were out. Mom thanked Taj (or as she calls him, Tim) for keeping her company all night and told him she looked forward to seeing him again, and he agreed with her. I was thinking to myself, "Yo, Moms, what about me?" But it's all good. I know she's happy when I spend time with her.

When we left, I scolded Taj for trying to make me look bad. Naturally, he didn't know what I was talking about, so I had to clue him in. "Do you remember that look I gave you?" And then I mocked him, "Yeah, my family knows all about Val and all y'all too, MOM!" He gave me a little sheepish grin. "And I know you was about to say something that was REALLY about to get you in trouble. I'm not sure what it was, but YOU better be glad you caught the look on my face and stopped talking!"

"Well thank heaven for SMALL favors!" he said as he looked up with his hands together like he was praying.

"Keep your hands on the wheel, funny guy," I replied as I whacked him in his chest. After he took me home, I thought he was going to drop me off and leave, but on the way home, he told me he needed to talk to me. I said, "Well talk."

He wanted to wait till we got to the house, so we waited. Once we got in the house, he began, "Baby doll, your family is everything I expected them to be. They're crazy! I really enjoyed dinner with you all."

"Well boo, I'm glad you did. So what did you think about church this morning? That's what I really want to know, and you haven't said a word about it."

"Baby, I thought you knew how much I enjoyed worship service. I REALLY enjoyed it. I can't believe you've kept that to yourself for so long. You know you need a whooping, and your brother told me it was okay to do it. I like him too. They all seem to know you so well. They know you like to show out and need to be checked every now and again, but in YOUR case, you're like Lucy Ricardo. 'LUCY, you got some s'plaining to do!'" he said in a Ricky Ricardo mocking voice. "You ALWAYS in trouble."

"I am NOT always in trouble. Who was the one showing out tonight, huh? Like Tony Montana says, 'YOU, das who!' You the one that had to try to tell Mom on me because YOU want to show out and run off at the mouth."

"Yeah, well—"

"Yeah, well whatever! Is this what you wanted to talk to me about?"

"Naw, but—"

"But my tail feathers!" I got up and smacked my rump roast with both hands when I said that.

"Baby doll, don't make me have to beat you down this evening."

"Boo, I'm just playing. Don't be so sensitive!" I was kind of tired and didn't feel like getting beat up right then, so I came down off my "want to be tough" soap box for the moment. "What's up, love?"

"Okay then." He was still looking at me with this, "I really want to jack you up and show you who's boss" type look. I know my family gave him that extra boost and a little more confidence in showing who was running this relationship.

Yeah, he was still pretty hyped about kicking it with my family, so I figured I better smooth things over. So I came and sat on his lap and kissed him on his neck and said, "What's up, baby? What you want to talk to me about?" I knew a nice mellow kiss would tame that savage beast.

He mellowed out and said, "Well first thing is I wanted to thank you for sharing your family with me. I had a good time, and everybody made me feel like I belonged. You got a really special family."

"Awwww, I'm glad you had a good time baby, and I praise God all the time for the family He gave me."

"Second thing is I think we should probably go to church with my mom and dad next Sunday and have dinner with them."

"That's fine with me, love."

"Well, just to let you know, Mom and Dad will probably want to go out to dinner somewhere as opposed to cooking. They're going to think this is a special occasion."

"Okay, that'll be fine too. Wait, what kind of special occasion they think this is?"

"I mean, baby doll, they've heard so much about you and your people, and NOW they're finally going to meet you, AND you're going to go to church with them. ALL that makes this a special occasion!"

"Okay, that'll work."

"Cool, then, I'll hook that up this week to make sure it's all good."

"Your brother and sisters going to be there too?"

"They'll probably come for dinner."

"Oba-kayba."

"Okay, third thing is—"

"Dang, how many things is there? I do have to work in the morning."

"There you go again, acting out."

"I'm just playing, baby. Take all night if you want, but if I start dosing, tap me."

"Okay, so I should just put you over my knee now, right? That'll keep you woke!"

"Boo, I'm good and woke now. Third thing is…what?"

"Third thing is one of my comrades, a fellow officer by the name of Thomas, needs a place to stay, and I offered my place temporarily. So I'm about to have a roommate."

"I see. What happened to where he was staying?"

"Well, I don't know for sure, but there's been some kind of nasty drama going on, and the residence thing has been a little shaky, so Thomas' home has been the Y for a little bit. Therefore, I offered my joint."

"That was really nice of you, boo. When is he moving in?"

"I knew I would be gone all day today, so I gave up my keys, and it should be a done deal already."

"So is your house two or three bedrooms?"

"Baby, you don't remember? It's three bedrooms."

"I was only in there once, and we skeeted in and skeeted out. Remember?"

"Oh yeah because you were about to make me late for my movie."

"Nooooo, YOU were about to make you late for that dumb movie. You the one that left your wallet at home."

"That's the only time you were there?"

"Yup!"

"Okay! Wait a minute, why my movie have to be dumb?"

"Well, let's see. What movie was it, baby?"

"Um, you know!"

"All I remember was that it was dumb. I went to sleep fairly early on it."

"You did, I remember. Why you do me like that?"

"Don't try to avoid the question. What was the name of the movie you took me to see that day? And who was in it?"

"Uhhh...baby, I can't think right now. Let me think about it, and I'll get back to you."

"You can't remember because it was a DUMB movie."

"Baby doll, you do not have to come at me like that, but yes, baby. I have three bedrooms—well, now I just have a guest room. My spare room has been rented out."

"Hey, why we haven't ever kicked it at your joint anyways?"

"Because my joint is a bachelor's pad. Your house is nice and homey. Decorated all nice and stuff. It's not all manly."

"Awwww, you like my joint, baby?"

"I LOVE your joint. And I love your joints, like right here" And he started kissing me wherever there was a joint, starting at my knuckles. "And right here" He kissed my wrist. "Right here." That was my elbow. He came up to my shoulder and kissed me gently there. "Oh and right here." He came up to my neck and said, "And this is one of my favorite joints right here."

I muffed him before he could kiss my neck and said, "Baby, the neck is not a joint, is it?"

He looked at me all puzzled like and said, "I don't know. We can Google it right after I'm done." And with that, he attacked my neck, kissing it. Trying to suck on it and give me a hickey.

I was squirming and screaming so hard. I'm sooo ticklish, and my neck is the worst. "Baby, please, bae, stop, PLEASE! I HAVE TO PEE! BABY, PLEASE, I'MMA PEE ON MYSELF. Please, stop! I love you!"

He stopped and looked into my eyes and said, "You love me?"

"Of course I love you, boo."

He said, "I mean, do you really love me? Or you just trying to get me to stop torturing you?"

"Baby, I love you. I'm in love with you and I'm in serious like with you, and you're always welcome to chill at my joint…ssss."

"That mean you want me to move in with you?"

"Negative, shorty. You straight at your joint!"

He sat back and kind of stared off into space for a minute, like he was really shocked at what I said. After he grasped a hold of my love statement and it really registered in his mind, he said, "Cool, cool. You're in serious like with me and in love with me, and I'm welcome at your joint anytime. Alrighty then! I know you better not be moving no OTHER stud up in your joint with you neither. Especially since I can't move in!"

"Relax big guy! We're ALL good. As long as YOU don't move no other stud up in YOUR joint with you. Uh, oops! You already did, didn't you?"

"Yeah well, I'm about to go home and check on my new roomy. And I have to get up early for work tomorrow."

"All right, Mr. Man. I'm sure you'll call me when you get home and let me know how Mister—what's his name?—Thomas is settled in and stuff."

"Okay baby… Wait, I can't do it!"

"Can't do what? What's wrong?"

"I realize I gave you the wrong impression, and I want—I mean, WE want our relationship to be built on trust, right?"

"Ri-i-i-ight!"

"Baby doll, do you trust me?"

125

"Baby, I'm giving it ALL up to the good Lord. He can fight my battles much better than I can, so yes, I do trust you (and God)!"

"Okay, well, my fellow comrade that's moving in with me—Thomas—is NOT a stud."

"HUH?"

I was still sitting on his lap, and he put his arms around me, kind of squeezing me, not real tight, but tight enough where I couldn't move my arms and said, "Baby doll, her name is Regina Thomas. You know how we call each other by our last names? She's a female."

"Sooooo, you got a BROAD as your roommate? And you tried to pass her off as a guy to me? Baby, that's deceptive, and you want me to trust you?"

"Look here, baby doll. I was going to go on letting you believe that Thomas was a dude, but I didn't feel right doing it. Thomas is a fellow police officer, and yes, she's a female, in which I have NO desire to be with. I want YOU and only YOU. I don't want some wannabe tough tomboy female (except for you). And baby, I work with her, so if I wanted to do something with her, opportunity is already there. I'm helping out my fellow man (in which this time my fellow man is a woman). I'm not going to lie, she's not a bad-looking girl, but she's NOT the one for me. Just trust that THIS is not going to tempt me in any way. I LOVE YOU and am looking forward to spending a lifetime with you. Trust me, baby!"

"Why you holding my arms? You scared I'm going to hit you?"

"Well, were you?"

"Yup, and I still am as soon as you let me go."

"I'm going to kiss your neck."

"I don't think so." I was pissed!

"You don't?"

"Negative!"

"Why?"

"Because I don't think I'm talking to you right now."

"You don't have to talk to me while I attack." Just then, Taj stood up with me still on his lap, threw me down (not hard, just kinda laid me) on the floor, pinned down my hands, and attacked my neck. I promise I tried NOT to react because I was REALLY ticked off with him, but I couldn't help it. I started kicking and screaming and begging and pleading. He stopped attacking long enough to say, "Unless you're going to tell me that you trust me and are going to give this a chance, you're going to pee on yourself. Sorry in advance!"

"OKAY, OKAY, OKAY, OKAY, BABY, we'll give it a shot. I trust you. Please let me go, baby!"

Taj stopped attacking but was still on top of me, holding my hands down, and said, "Baby, I'm sorry for being deceptive, and if you give it a chance, I'll prove to you that you have NOTHING to worry about. I promise!"

I said, "I'll give it a chance. My trust is in God who will NEVER leave me nor deceive me, regardless of the circumstances. So I guess we'll see how it goes. I never met Miss Thang before, but I hope I don't have to cut her or YOU."

18

As Taj left and went home, I had to pray. My spirit was uneasy, and I was angry! I kept imagining things that COULD happen, so I talked to MY Father in heaven. It was a simple prayer, but it was enough to settle my spirit for the time being! *Lord, all I can do is look to You and depend on You to keep my mind at ease so that I don't worry about this heffa living with the most beautiful guy in the world, MY man. But Lord, I know that You are able. And You know that I need You RIGHT now!*

He called me when he got home and had checked on his new roommate. "Hey baby doll, you miss me?…"

"Hey Bae, I guess you just got home, huh?…"

"I've been home for about twelve minutes and…" He paused as if he were looking at his watch. "Forty-six seconds. I wanted to make sure that my new roommate knew where everything was: the bathroom, towels, sheets, food—stuff like that…"

"You mean to tell me that that heffa can't find the toilet?…"

"Come on baby girl, I know you're not going to do that now, right?…"

"Do what? Oh, so now I'm wrong, huh?…"

"Baby doll, you don't even know this girl, and already she's a heffa. Are we going to get past this? Or are you going to make this a very difficult time for US?…"

"Okay, you're right. I'm not going to trip till I have a reason to. Did you let her know that you have a girl?…"

"Sweetheart, I cut mine and her conversation short because I told her I had to go call my BAY-beeeee. She knows, and if she didn't pick up on it, don't worry. She WILL know. I'm very proud of MY girl, and I want the WHOLE world to know…"

"Okay love, I'm going to bed. I guess I'll talk to you tomorrow…"

"Definitely, baby girl…"

"Oh yeah, how did I forget? I meant to tell you that one of my colleagues needed a place to stay, and previously, I said I would have to think about it and talk it over with my man, but in light of this new development, I'm going to offer my spare room to Chris. I'm sure you don't mind…"

"Baby, why you playing?…"

"I'm not playing. I'm serious. Do you mind?…"

"HELL YEAH, I MIND!…"

"OHHH, big boy! YOU mind?…"

"Val, I'm on my way back over there…"

"YO, YO, YO, little fella, stand down! Don't come over here. We can talk about this tomorrow. I'm going to bed…"

"Val, why are you playing with me?…"

"Baby, reeee-laaaax! We all good, remember? I trust you, and you trust me, right? We can talk tomorrow. Good ni-i-i-ight love!…"

"So what are we talking about EXACTLY tomorrow?…"

"My new roommate, Chris…"

"Yeah, OKAY Val!…"

"Of course, you're not MAD at me, are you Taj?…"

"You playing games, and these games are NOT going to go well for you, Val!…"

"I don't know what you're talking about, but I'm going to bed now. Night night, love bug!…"

"Goodnight, Val…"

Wow! No "baby doll," huh? Now I'm simply Val. Okay!

Naturally, I had no colleague that needed a place to stay as far as I was aware. I only wanted to put a thought in old boy's mind, whereas NEXT time, he'd be more careful how he treated me with regard to his NEW roommate. *I better dead bolt the door because no telling how (as Madea says it) mayett (mad in normal terms) that boy is. Well, I guess I don't need to bolt it. He doesn't have a key yet. I need to call Ronni because I do believe he is pretty mayett at me. We were wondering how he would react toward me when he's angry. Oh well, time will tell and I'll call her later. Right now, I'm calling Toni.*

"Girl, it's late. What you doing calling me this time of night?…"

"Toni, it's only ten-thirty, why are you tripping?…"

"I'm tripping because YOU don't call me at this time of night, especially when I'm sitting here with my man…"

"Fine, Toni, I DO call you this time of night, and you can't even say hi to me. First thing you want to do is start tripping because Zani is there? That's fine, though. Next time we talk, DON'T ask me to tell you what Taj did tonight. I'll talk to you later…" All while I was saying "I'll talk to you later," Toni was trying to cut me off, asking me what he did, but I kept talking.

"Heffa, stop playing with me. What Taj do to you?…"

"Oh, you want me to talk to you now, huh? What about Zani?…"

"VAL, tell me what Mr. Perfect did…"

"Hi, Toni!…"

"Uh, oh, ummmm, okay, hello, Val. How are you?…"

"I'm fine Toni, thanks so much for asking and for your concern. How are you, girl?…"

"Yeah, I'm fine too. Let's see, let me play along with this. Uh, so how's the family?…"

"Everyone is fine, thanks for asking…"

"Girl, if you don't stop playing with me! What did that bubble-head do?…"

"Okay, so you know he went to church with me today and came over to Mommy's for dinner, right?…"

"Girl, what he do? He made a fool of himself at Mommy's?…"

"Toni, relax. This is my story…"

"Oh yeah, but you take too long. Get with it…"

"Okay, so you knew that, right?…"

"Yeah, I knew that…"

"So church and dinner went fine. We had a good time, and actually, we're pretty much just getting home…"

"Okay, so what's the problem? He proposed?…"

"Girl, will you relax?…"

"FINE! I'll be quiet. Tell me what happened…"

"All right, so the man brought me home and said he wanted to talk to me. So he came to my house and told me how he enjoyed himself all day, yadda, yadda, yadda, bada-bing, bada-boom. So I asked the man if that's what he wanted to talk to me about, and he was like, 'Oh yeah, a fellow officer friend of mine named Thomas was having some drama and needed a place to stay for a minute, so I offered my place. In other words, I'm going to have a roommate for a little while.' So, you know, it was all good till after we discussed this for a minute, and he was about to leave. Then he decided to tell me that Thomas was actually a female!…"

"Oooooooooh girl, are you kidding? He done moved some hoochie, some skeezuh into his place?…"

"Yeah, but he tried to pass old girl off as a dude to me…"

"Dam, girl! He is so wrong for that. So what you gonna do?…"

"Well, I'm pretty sure he's mayett at me right now…"

"Hold up! He done moved some little SKEEZUH into his place without talking to you about it. He didn't talk it over with you first, did he?…"

"You know he didn't! Did I talk it over with YOU first?…"

"RIGHT! Then tried to pass old girl off as a dude, and now HE got the nerve to be mad at you?…"

"That's what I'm saying!…"

"So why is he mad at you?…"

"Well, I did kind of provoke him. I waited till he got home and called me, and I told him that one of MY colleagues needed a place to stay, and initially, I told them I would have to talk it over with him first, but in light of the new situation, I'm going to offer my joint to Chris. So now he's super salty…"

"So you got somebody that needs to move in with you? And who's Chris?…"

"Naw, nobody is trying to move in with me, and Chris is the first unisex name I could think of. I know he didn't really believe that, but now he's mayett. He said he was coming back over, and I told him NO. We could talk about it tomorrow!…"

"Girl, you may be skating on thin ice because old boy is not a little guy, but I could produce a Chris for you if you need me to. You know I got a cousin named Chris, but she's a girl. Or I could find you a guy if you wanted me to. I got boy cousins too…"

"Oooooh, that's a thought. But you're trying to get me killed. I don't want nobody hitting on me…"

"Well, wouldn't you need to know that now before things get too serious?…"

"Oooooh, you know what? I got it. What if you brought some boxes over here, which would make it look like somebody WAS moving in? You think you could do that?…"

"Girl, you know I got my winter stuff stored in boxes and other stuff that I got sitting in storage. You want me to do that tomorrow while you're at work?…"

"Hmmmm, let me think, let me think… Yeah, if you could, that would work, but I'm probably going to want YOU to be at the house by the time Taj gets here…"

"Hold up now, I'm not trying to get a beatdown either…"

"Girl, that man is not going to do a thing to you. You may have to dial 911 for me, though…"

"Yeah, well, I do want to see his face when he sees those boxes there. I got you, girl…"

"We so bad…"

"I like to think of us as being mischievous!…"

"Okay, so I don't have to remind you, do I?…"

"Girl, please! I'm looking forward to this!…"

"Cool, well have one of your cousins here with you when you come by. I want you to already be here when Taj comes. Just make sure you all are in the house…"

"Okay, let me see which one of my cousins is available tomorrow?…"

"Okay, surprise me. Hey, wait! Was Zani listening to what we were talking about? I don't want him to call Taj and give him a head's up…"

"Naw, he's in the other room, watching TV. If he hasn't called me, looking for me, asking why I'm not in there with him, then he's sleep…"

I Don't Mind Waiting

"Alrighty then, I'll see you tomorrow girl. Thanks Toni…"

"No problem, you know this is right up my alley. Tomorrow girl!…"

19

Monday morning, I went to work as usual. Well, I guess it was a little strange. I went ALL day without talking to Taj. He didn't call me, and I didn't call him, but I was pretty sure he was going to be at my house when he got off work. As it got closer and closer to time for ME to get off, I began to get a little nervous. I thought to myself, *Wow, I was really looking forward to playing this trick on Taj*, but now my mind was playing tricks on ME. I started thinking about him absolutely snapping if he saw some other guy at my place with his belongings. I could see him not asking ANY questions but just get to swinging and stuff. The thing that got me the most was when I started thinking about the fact that he already carried a gun. Boy, I got on that phone with the quickness and called Toni to back out, and the heffa wouldn't answer the phone! She knew I was going to chicken out, but I was not hardly trying to get ANYBODY killed, mainly ME!

"Toni, pick up, pick up, pick up," I said to myself, waiting for her to answer the phone. *Shoot, it's her voice mail.* "Hi Toni, it's me Val. Call me back as SOON as you get this!"

It was now three o'clock, and I was done with all my clients for today, so I was out of here. I'd have to come in early tomorrow to do my paperwork and make some phone calls. I rushed out the double doors and got to the outer door, and there was a squad car in the parking lot parked right next to me. I backed up with the quickness. *Oh shoot, the man done came to my job to kill me.* Instantly, I had to pee (I have a weak bladder). I turned around real smooth and went to the bathroom. I called Toni again. No answer.

"Toni, girl I done changed my mind. Answer the DAM phone. Taj is outside my job, and HE is going to KILL me. Call me back, I can't call 911 because he's a cop. You may have to come get me. I am absolutely terrified!"

Lord, what have I done? It was only supposed to be a joke to let him see how I feel, but now I'm about to die. They always told me I play too much. Lord, please help me. What am I supposed to do now? Think, think, think, Val. I don't hear any noise out in the lobby, so he must still be in the car.

I left the bathroom and peeked out the outside door. *Dam, he's still out there. Wait…wait, that's a white cop in that car. SHOOT! I done scared myself silly! That's a Forest Park police car.* I couldn't do anything but laugh at myself. See? That's why I don't do stuff I got no business doing because I ALWAYS give myself away. That man probably was not even thinking about me like that. WHEW! *Lord, let me get home and send Toni and her cousin on somewhere before I get us ALL killed.*

As I was getting into my car. I spoke to Officer Mitchell who was parked next to my car. "Hey, officer, working hard today or hardly working?"

He replied with, "Hi Val, I thought I saw you coming out a few minutes earlier."

"Yeah, that was me. Forgot something in the office and had to go back."

"I see. Well, hope your day was better than mine," he said.

"Oh, rough day, huh? I'm sorry. Mine wasn't too bad, but there's still time for that to change," I said, thinking about what I was about to be faced with if I didn't get home in a hurry.

"Well, you're off work now, so the rest of your day should be a piece of cake."

"I feel you, and I hope you're right. Well, I hope the rest of your day goes well for you, and you be careful out there."

"Thanks Val, I will. See you!"

He often parked in our lot and chilled or did whatever he did. WOW! I blew that WHOLE thing WAY out of proportion, completely forgot about him. But I still had to get home and intercept Toni.

It took me thirteen minutes to get home, and when I got there, Toni had already moved in seven or eight boxes and had some men's clothes in the closet in my spare room. Her cousin, Chico, was there with her. They called him Chico because when he was little he thought he knew how to speak Spanish and called everybody Chico, so that name stuck with him. He wasn't a bad-looking guy. In fact, he was darn cute. It had been a LONG time since I'd seen him. Shoot, this boy had to be much younger than us because I NEVER remember seeing a cousin of hers looking as good as he was looking as we were growing up. His complexion was that of maybe Morris Chestnut with a short cut. He had a full beard that was a little darker than a shadow and was lined under his cheeks at the bottom of the jaw line. He was about six-foot-one or two, and he wasn't as big as Taj, but you could tell that he worked out. His arms were nice and cut. I knew I had to get them OUT OF here before Taj got here.

I pulled up. "Toni, I changed my mind. Cancel ALL this, and why you not answering your phone?" I had to park on the street because Toni was in the driveway.

"Val, you remember my cousin, Chico, don't you?"

"Hey, Chico, how are you?"

"I'm good, thanks. You?" And he gave me a nice firm hug with that greeting. Dang, I PROMISE you I don't remember Chico looking and feeling this good.

"I'm good too, thanks. Boy, you done grew up, didn't you? Just a cutie pie! How many women you got?"

"Don't tell him that! He's already bigheaded enough!"

I redirected my attention back to Toni. "Toni, Taj is going to kill me if he gets here and sees Chris looking this good, moving in with me."

"Girl, my name ain't Chris!"

"Oh, Toni didn't tell you that for now, your name IS Chris? Toni, you already put boxes in the house?"

"Yeah, and Chris has clothes in the closet too. I knew you were going to back out, girl. We got this! Don't panic!"

"I am panicking, and YOU should be too. The man carries a gun! I saw a cop car parked next to my ride at the job and thought that he had come to the job to kill me. Oh, by the way, when you hear your voice mail, DON'T LAUGH! Chico, help me put these boxes back in Toni's car, PLEASE? And then y'all get out of here!"

I ran into the house, and they both followed behind me. Toni said real calm like, "Val, now don't freak," and I looked at her in a panic, waiting for her to finish so I could freak. "But Taj just turned the corner."

"Oh Lord, he is going to kill me!"

"Val, relax! Let me handle this! You stay here."

"I have to pee." I went into the bathroom and peed and asked the Lord to be in control and said, *"And please don't let this man kill us!"*

Toni went outside to intercept him.

Next thing I know, they both were coming in the house. Toni was trying to talk to Taj (I don't know what she was trying to tell him), but I kept hearing him say, "Toni, where's Val? I just want to talk to Val." He walked in the house and yelled, "VAL!"

I was coming out the bathroom, and his eyes met mine. He turned around and looked at Chico. "What the fuck is this, Val?"

"Baby, wait, wait. Let me explain!"

"Didn't you explain last night?"

When he said that, it made me remember the WHOLE reason I did this to begin with. "Hold up! You mad and having a fit at me when YOU the one in the first place that started this WHOLE thing? How's Officer Thomas doing?"

"Val, YOU'RE going to make me kick your little ASS all over this place! If you were going to move somebody in YOUR place with YOU, why didn't YOU tell me when I told YOU about Thomas?"

Chico went over to Toni and said, "I think I'mma step outside."

Taj said, "Wait a minute, PODNUH (partner in layman's terms)! Don't step NOWHERE! Val, who is this?"

"Taj, look here. I need you to relax and let me explain myself before you go any further, PLEASE!"

"Val, I'm cool. I'm all right. EXPLAIN!"

"Okay, Taj, this is Toni's cousin, Chico. After you told me what was up with old girl, Thomas (I can't remember her first name), I was pissed. I figured I would pay you back with the same type of scenario. Initially, I was just talking, but me and Toni got to brainstorming."

"Yeah, I should've known, you and TONI!" and he cut his eyes back and forth at both of us.

"Baby, we figured—I figured I could make it appear real to you. I know it was childish of me, and I tried to call the whole thing off because it didn't sit well with me at work, but I was too late. Toni and Chico, I'm sorry for getting you two involved in this, but I let my emotions get the best of me. And Taj, you know it's not Toni's fault. I wanted to let YOU know before you acted a fool. So there, Toni, you can take your boxes back and get the rest of the stuff out the room."

Toni told Chico, "Boy, help me carry this stuff outside. I'm sorry for getting you into all this mess."

Taj said, "Here, I'll help. Y'all can get the stuff out the room, and I'll start taking these boxes out."

Chico told Toni that he would get his stuff out the room and then come back and help with the boxes. I sat on the couch and was very nervous, so when Taj left out with the first few boxes, I told Toni not to leave right away. I was scared to be left in the house with him alone at this point. Toni said, "Cool." She would wait for a little bit before she left, but I could tell she was a little ticked off. I don't know why, though. That girl knew me. She knew before I did that I was going to chicken out. And what in tarnation did she want me to do? Was she expecting me to hold my ground and get an old-fashioned beatdown? PUUHHHH! I wasn't hardly trying to get smashed. Nope, not today, and DEFINITELY NOT like this! And the ice I was walking on now still seemed a little thin.

Taj got outside with the boxes, and Toni was still in the house with me, and he yelled, "Toni, unlock your door." So she pushed the beep-beep button on her keys, grabbed a box, and went outside. Chico came out of the room with his stuff in a garment bag and took them to the car. The guys made a second trip.

Then they came back in the house to make sure they got everything. Taj stood at the front door with his hand on it, like he was waiting for them to leave so he could shut the door behind them. Toni followed me into my room and in my bathroom. We left Taj and Chico out there. Toni said, "Okay, so Val, how long you want me to stay? And how long is Tab going to let us?"

"From the looks of things, I'm pretty sure he's waiting on y'all to leave now."

"Yeah, I think you're right. Well, I'm not worried about his big ass beating me down, so I'm going to go out there and talk to him before I leave."

"Toni, don't make it any worse for me, please."

"Girl, you going to be all right. That man is not going to touch you." As she walked past me, she kind of whispered, "I don't think."

"Thanks for the reassurance, Toni."

We left out my room and came into the general population. Taj and Chico exchanged a few words. I'm not sure what they were talking about, but I'm pretty sure it was small talk.

Once we came out, Taj immediately turned to Toni and said, "Thanks for having your girl's back, Toni, because I'm sure that's what you were here for, but I got it now. And I can take it from here."

"Taj, don't be coming at my girl. If you going to come at her, do it now while I'm still here."

"Soooo, you're what? Her bodyguard? You going to protect her?"

"I'm just saying, do what you going to do now."

"Toni, me and Val both are going to see you and Chico later. Chico, it was nice to meet you, man. Too bad it was under these strained circumstances, but it was still nice to meet you. You seem like cool people. But now take your cousin up out of here before I do."

Chico got up and fist-bumped Taj. He said to Toni, "Come on, cuz, Taj got this. Val will be all right."

Toni looked at me and said, "Heffa, you straight?"

I looked at Taj and said, "Am I straight, Tee?" He looked back at me and didn't open his mouth. "Wow! Uh, Toni, I'm coming with you all."

Toni and Chico started walking out the door, and I got up and tried to sneak out with them. Taj caught me by the waist, pulled me on the other side of the door behind him. He was shutting the door as they made it out, and I could hear Toni yell, "Call me, Val!"

I yelled back to her, "Okay, pray for me!" Toni and Chico sat in the driveway for about five minutes. Taj stood at the door, watching and waiting for them to leave. I knew exactly when they were pulling off because Taj turned around and glared at me, then I heard the car pulling out the driveway. *Oh darn!* was going through my head right about now. Again, he didn't open his mouth. He just looked at me.

"Taj," I started the conversation off. I couldn't deal with the silence and being glared at like that. "Baby, I am SOOO sorry for that stunt. Like I said before, it sounded good when we were first talking about doing it, but as time went on, I knew it could be disastrous. I was angry and wanted to pay you back." He still looked at me and didn't speak. "Okay Taj have YOU forgotten that YOU started all this?" Again NOTHING. "Look here, I've apologized, and I feel really bad for getting Toni and Chico involved in OUR mess, but that's it. If you going to keep giving me the silent treatment, then that's cool, but YOU could've left with Toni." I stopped talking and sat there, looking at him, and he stood by the door, looking at me with his arms folded on top of his chest. After a couple minutes, I sat back on the couch and cut the TV on. When I did that, Taj walked out the door.

Wow! I'll be dipped. That boy is really mad at me. He's got NOTHING to say, good or bad. No explanation himself, absolutely NOTHING! I picked up the phone to call Toni, and just when she answered, the door opened, and Taj came back in with a change of clothes. I hadn't even realized, but he still had his uniform on all this time. I simply hung up the phone. He glared at me for a few seconds when he came back in and went into the bathroom.

Toni called me right back. "Is everything all right? You called me and hung up…"

"Yeah, girl. I'll call you later…"

"You sure?…"

"Positive!…"

"Kay, make sure you call me back!…"

"I will. Thanks again, Toni, and I really am sorry!…"

140

"I got you, girl! Talk to you later…"

"Kay, bye…"

Taj came out the bathroom, looking all fresh and adorable in his cute little shorts and wifebeater on. He still had a stern look on his face. I looked at him for a minute, then I went back to watching the news. I was hoping the shirt was no inclination of what was about to happen! He came and sat on the couch next to me and leaned over me. I thought he was trying to make up with me and give me a hug or kiss or something and leaned toward him, and he took the remote out of my far hand and cut the TV off. "Wow! So I don't get a hug or a kiss or nothing, huh? I just get the remote taken from me? What if I was watching that?" I kept my face peeled to the TV, like it was still on.

He gently turned my face toward his, still looking pissed, and said, "Baby doll, if you ever pull another stunt like that—"

"Baby, I said I was sorry."

"But I want you to understand, if you EVER pull another stunt like that—" He put his bottom lip in his mouth and bit on it.

"I know, I know. Wasn't NOTHING nice going to come out of that. I realize that, and I apologize. I love you, boo!"

"I love you too!"

"You forgive me?"

He leaned over and gave me a gentle kiss but never verbally responded. Right now, I was taking that as a yes. I laid back on his chest, and he cut the TV back on.

Now my thing is this: Why did I have to be the one apologizing like that? I mean, yeah, I was wrong. I take FULL responsibility for my actions and ALL that was unnecessary, BUUUT I wasn't wrong by myself! I guess he didn't feel he had ANYTHING to do with MY behavior. It was ALL on me. Well, seeing as though I like my general looks and am not the BEST friend of pain, I was going to go ahead and be the bigger person and stick with MY apology and NOT wait for his, but that's bogus. It's all good, though. Like I said before, "Momma ain't raise NO fool!" We didn't say too much after that. Just chilled.

20

We sat there, watching nothing really, for a couple hours, both of us dozing off. That ordeal we had was really draining whereas we both were exceptionally tired. Neither one of us could keep our eyes open. After a while, we ordered a pizza and ended up falling asleep on the couch, intending on watching TV. He didn't get up and go home (and I didn't make him), and I didn't get up and go in the room. I woke up close to three and went right on back to sleep. He was sitting on the recliner end of the couch, and I was across the couch with my head on his lap.

He woke up at five and woke me up. "Bae… Baby doll." He was nudging me. "Wake up. I'm about to go home and shower and get ready for work."

"What time is it?"

"It's five. You have to move, baby. I have to go to the bathroom."

"My bad." So I got off the man, had me a good stretch, and went in my room, used the bathroom (and brushed my teeth). I laid across my bed after I was through.

After about five minutes, he came in my room, fussing, "So I suppose you didn't know I was out here waiting for you to come out so I could say bye to you, huh? I told you I had to go get ready for work."

"No sweetheart, I didn't realize you were waiting for me. I thought you were still in the bathroom. Again, my bad!"

"Get over here and give me kiss." So me being the person that I am and NOT wanting to be in ANY more drama at this point, I got up and fell on him. He caught me. "Girl, what's wrong with you?"

"Nothing," I said. "I'm just falling for you."

"You so silly. I'll talk to you later on, okay?"

"All right! Behave yourself today."

"Yeah right! You trying to beat me to the punch." And he popped me on the buttocks.

"NOOOO, I just want you to BEHAVE yourself today." And I popped him on the buttocks.

"Yeah, okay!"

I gave him a kiss and a hug and walked him to the front door, and he left. Boy, he's so demanding. In a couple days (after I'm SURE he'd calmed down), I'm going to have to check him on his behavior because THIS is unacceptable.

I went back into the room and laid across the bed again and decided it wasn't really a need for me to try to go back to sleep, so I decided to take a nice long bath. I guess I was more tired than I thought because next thing I know, the alarm was ringing, telling me it was six o'clock (time to make the donuts).

Well, there goes my nice LONG bath. I had paperwork and calls to make at the office, so I knew I had to get there early. I had to take a quick bath and get to work.

Shortly after I got to the office, Toni called me to make sure everything was all good with me. "Heffa… Whew, girl! You're still alive! That is some good news…"

"Good mornting, Toni…"

"Val, what's so good about it? Huh? I mean, really! Think about it. What's so good about it?…"

"Toni, you didn't have to wake up this morning, and more than that, I didn't have to wake up this morning. You better give the Lord some praise and tell Him thank you for another day!…"

"Oh yeah, I guess you would be saying that, wouldn't you? Just tell me this. Did you see your life flashing before your eyes yesterday? Because you know that's what people say happen when you're about to die!" She started cracking up. "Girl, I heard your voice mail yesterday. You were scared to death. If I wasn't so mad at you for chickening out, I would've felt sorry for you…"

"Once again, I'm glad that I give you so much pleasure…"

"Laughter is cleansing to the soul. You should try it sometime…" She was still tickled by the whole ordeal.

"Toni, I'm fine thanks, and I did tell you not to laugh when you heard the message, didn't I?..."

"I don't recall, but even if you had, that would've been close to impossible to do. Just wait till you hear it because you KNOW I saved it. You're going to laugh at yourself..."

"Yeah, well, whatever!..."

"Okay so Val, what happened? How did you guys end up?..."

"Girl, I apologized to him. You remember how he was giving me the silent treatment before you left?..."

"Yeah..."

"Well, he continued. He didn't say nothing for fifteen to twenty minutes after you left. I apologized, and when he didn't say nothing, I told him, 'Let's not forget why I pulled this stunt in the first place,' and I mentioned that girl living in his apartment with him—Thomas or whatever her name is—and the man STILL had nothing to say. I said ALL that I had to say, then I told him if he was NOT going to talk to me, he should've left when you did. So he left..."

"He left? Stop playing!..."

"Yeah, well I thought he left, so I called you, but then he came back in with a change of clothes, so I hung up..."

"Girl, he playing games with you..."

"Then he played me to the left because I started watching TV after he was ignoring me, and old boy came and sat next to me and leaned across me. I thought the man was apologizing and giving me a hug and a kiss, so I leaned into him and puckered up, and guess why the man had leaned across me?..."

"You mean he didn't kiss you?..."

"No, guess what he did?..."

"Wait a minute! You were sitting there, puckered up for a kiss, and he DIDN'T kiss you?..."

"NO!..."

Well, now she was done. I couldn't even tell the girl why he was all on me because she was laughing so hard. That girl is really hard to take sometimes. But after a minute or so, she had me cracking up too. Laughter is contagious, and she was laughing and screaming and carrying on so that I started laughing. When I think about it, I would love to have seen what the whole thing looked like, me sitting there all puckered up, and he didn't even kiss me. We laughed for a while, and then the girl said, "WHEW! I can picture your face all puckered up with THEM soup coolers, waiting for him to plant one on you and apologize! That was a good one. I needed that so bad, Val. Okay, let me see, so he didn't kiss you. What DID he do? He didn't hit you, did he?…" And you could hear in her voice how she got serious all of a sudden.

"Naw, girl. That boy ain't THAT crazy!…"

"Well, you sure can't tell it from YOUR behavior. So what did he do?…"

"Grabbed the remote from me and turned the TV off. Now he could've gotten the remote before he sat down, but he's so dramatic! I guess he needed that little special effect!…"

"Wow! And you thought that was your makeup kiss?…"

"Yeah, I did…"

"So what then?…"

"Then he told me if I ever pull a stunt like that again…"

"WHAT? What he gone do?…"

"Well, that's all he said. And he said it twice. If I ever pull a stunt like that again. So I told him that I wouldn't and apologized again, and THEN he kissed me…"

"So for all practical purposes (and knowing you), I can assume that you won't be playing like that again, right?…"

"Ya dam skippy!…"

"So you never did talk about how he did you the night before?…"

"Nope!…"

"Wow! Girl, I tell you, men are a trip! They can do the same things we do, but then when WE do it, all HELL breaks loose. We have to call the National Guard and everybody else. I mean seriously Val. That boy had you SCARED to call the police…"

"Yeah, you're exactly right. I'm going to tell him about himself in a couple days…"

"Well, I'm going to tell him about himself too. That's bullshit!…"

"I know, but you know me. The Lord can fight my battles better than I can, so when he gives me the go-ahead and gives me what to say, I'm going to deal with it. That boy is entirely too big to be hitting somebody, and I promise I am NOT going to be scared to upset my man. That's all a part of life, but then again, men go crazy when they think their MANHOOD is being challenged. Lord, thank You for thinking enough of me to make me female! Now how would I look going completely BONKERS because of that chick living in his house with him?…"

"I don't know how you would look, but me and Zani would still be fighting if he pulled some shit like that with me. I have to give it to you Val, you're a better woman than I am!…"

"Not really. I think the thing that really got me was when he told me that they work together already. Time and opportunity is already there if he wanted to do something with her, so BAM! Why make a stink about them living together? Plus, I don't trust him, but I do trust God, and I don't think He brought me this far to leave me. I gave it to Him, and I'm leaving it there…"

"Yeah, well you both are better than me…"

"Well, I know He is…"

"Okay girl, when I grow up I want to be like you, but for now, Zani knows he better not pull no stuff like that with me. But I have to go. I was actually just checking to make sure you were still alive! LOL!" And she started laughing again. "I'ma call you later, kay?…"

"All right, thanks again Toni, for everything. I'll talk to you later…"

"Bye girl…"

"Bye…"

21

The rest of that day went by pretty fast, and Taj called me at his lunchtime to make sure I was all good and, I believe, to let me know that he put yesterday behind us.

Later on that night, I called Ronni. "Hello?..."

"Hey Val, how you doing girl?..."

"I'm good Ronni, how are you?..."

"I'm feeling pretty decent, thanks. So how did church and dinner go with Taj and the fam?..."

"Everything went fine. He SAID he enjoyed church..."

"What, you don't believe him?..."

"Naw, I do. He seemed impressed during service and stuff, so yeah, I do believe him..."

"Then what's wrong?..."

"Nothing! I didn't mean it to sound like that..."

"Oh, okay. So he enjoyed service. Dinner?..."

"Yeah, he really seemed to enjoy dinner. He came in the kitchen with the ladies after dinner and offered to help with the cleanup, so naturally, Arik had to try and taint him for offering to help. Dwayne told him not to mess over his baby sis. Brian told him it was okay if he needed to slap me around a little bit to show me who's boss..."

"They were on a roll, huh?..."

"Yeah, they were their usual pain in the butt selves, so we had a good time..."

"See baby, I knew it would work out for you..."

"Yeah, it was all good...till later on..."

"Uh-oh! What happened later on?..."

"Well let's see. Taj told me that he had a fellow officer moving in with him..."

"Is that the bad part?…"

"You tell me. His fellow officer, 'Thomas,' is a female…"

"Oooooh, no he didn't!…"

"Oh, so that is the bad part, huh?…"

"He moved a female officer in with him and told YOU about it AFTER the fact?…"

"Uh, yeah…oh, but that's not even the bad part…"

"There's more?…"

"Well, the first thing is that he deceived me, making me think that old girl was a dude…"

"What you mean?…"

"All while he was telling me that one of his comrades was moving in with him, I was under the impression that it was a guy. He said the name was Thomas. Now how many girls YOU know named Thomas? Then all while we were talking about it, I was referring to that person as a him, and he never corrected me UNTIL he was leaving. THEN he couldn't take it anymore and came clean and told me that her first name was Regina…"

"He ain't right. So how did YOU handle that?…"

"Now this is the part where YOU came in…"

"Uh-oh, what did I do? And I'm not even there!…"

"When I was there with you in the ATL, YOU told me I need to do something to piss him off to see how he would handle it, right?…"

"Oooooh, what did you do? Just tell me, did he hit you?…"

"Anyways, when he left my place and got home, he called me, letting me know he was home, and I told him that somebody from MY office needed a place to stay too and that INITIALLY, I told them that I would have to talk it over with my boo thing first, but in light of what HE had done, I was going to tell Chris it was ALL good…"

"Who's Chris?…"

"That was the first unisex name that came to mind…"

"Oh, I see. So naturally, you didn't really have anyone that needed to move in with you. You were being vindictive?…"

"I wasn't being vindictive. I wanted him to see how it felt…"

"That's being vindictive, gal. So how did he take that?…"

"Well, let me finish the story because I did something REALLY dumb…"

"Something ELSE? Oh my goodness girl. What did you do?…"

"I called Toni, and she created a Chris for me (which was her cousin, Chico). By the time I got off work, Toni and Chico had moved some boxes in. Chico had stuff in my spare room closet, and the girl wouldn't answer the phone. She knew I was going to back out. Girl, by the time I got off work, I had scared myself to death almost. One of the cops is always parked in our lot at the job, and I just KNEW it was Taj that had come to MY job to kill me. I was in a straight up panic…"

Ronni was on the phone, making some kind of noise. I wasn't sure what was going on.

"Ronni? What's wrong? You okay?…"

She gathered herself together enough to say, "I'm still here, Val…"

"What's wrong?…"

"Nothing girl. Finish your story…"

Then I realized that she was laughing. "Okay, I see. You're laughing. Well, by the time I finish this story, you won't be able to contain your laughter. Anyhoo, I tried calling Toni to tell her to pack up her stuff and leave, but again, she wouldn't answer. So I left work in a hurry to try to intercept her and Chico and send them home before Taj got here, but he showed up before we could move one box…"

"And how did he take seeing…what's Toni's cousins name?…"

"Chico…"

"Girl, what he look like?…"

"Young and adorable. Nice body and all…"

"So tell me, how many times did Taj tag off on you?…"

"By that, I guess you mean hit me, right?…"

"But of course, and I'm kind of thinking you deserved to be tagged a few times!…"

"He was very upset with me, but I came clean really quick and explained everything to him. He was NOT pleased with me at all, AND he threatened me a few times because I tried to tell him that he started the whole thing to begin with, but that was about all…"

"So how you feel about the whole thing?…"

"I'm going to have to talk to him later in the week because he has GOT to understand that I refuse to be with someone that I am absolutely terrified to upset. That's all a part of life…"

"Yeah, I feel you girl. But I can tell that you were really scared…"

"Girl, I was. That man is TOO big. I'm scared for him to give ME a love tap, PLUS he carries a gun…"

"So y'all cool now?…"

"Yeah, pretty much, but what's YOUR feelings about the whole thing?…"

"Well, you know if you had of called me, I would've had different advice for you than Toni did. Not saying anything bad about your girl, but it would've been different…"

"Yeah, I know, and I started to call you. You were my first choice, but I needed instant gratification! I decided I'd give you the end results…"

"Gotcha! I kind of got mixed feelings about the whole thing because I do believe that Taj was wrong for moving a female into his place without talking to YOU about it first. And then he was being deceptive by passing her off as a guy, BUT I think he ONLY did that because he felt like YOU have the ultimate trust in him. Plus, y'all together way too much for him to have time to get with anybody else…"

"Regardless if I DO have the ultimate trust in him, THAT's no reason for him to do what he did! AND that's the ONLY reason that I wasn't AS mad at him as I could've been. Not that we're together all the time anyway, BUT he explained to me beforehand that she's a cop. Opportunity is already there if they wanted to do something! BUT if he LIVES with old girl, that's WAAAAY more opportunity, regardless if we're together all the time or not! We don't live together!…"

"That's true! I said he was wrong! BUT of course you know that I think YOU were WAY out of line for what you did too?…"

"That's probably why I called Toni and NOT you. You're too mature for me sometimes!…"

"And how did that work out for you? I'm just going to tell you. You came over my mind real tough this WHOLE weekend. I didn't know what the deal was, but I started praying for you right away. I thought it was because I missed you after spending a week with you. And I asked the Lord to give me peace about you, and He did that. I've also been praying for you and Taj, and I believe that y'all going to be all right…"

"I believe so too, but Brother Man is going to have to understand that he better relax about stuff and stop getting soooo dagum mayett!…"

"Work with him baby. You know men have to be trained. It takes years to get them like we want them…"

"That's funny because Rena always says, 'You think Robert came that way?'" We laughed about that. Then she asked me what else was going to have her laughing, and I told her how I thought he was making up with me, leaning over to kiss me, and took the remote from me. We both laughed so hard. Well, she laughed as hard as she could, having just had surgery. I had to tell her that she asked for it.

*****

The rest of the week went by pretty quick. Taj and I got together on Friday to play some pool at a spot that he was familiar with. While we were out, he told me how Sunday was going to go, getting together with his peeps. "Okay now baby doll, you know we're going to church with my parents on Sunday right?"

"Uh, okay. That WAS the plan, love."

"What you mean WAS the plan?"

"Nothing, it was an observation that that WAS the plan."

"That's it?"

"Uh, yeah! Geeeez, relax little fella!"

"Cool, well their service starts at ten-thirty so I was figuring I could pick you up at eight-thirty. We can go have breakfast, then head on to the church afterward. Does that work for you?"

"Whatever you say, boss," and I saluted him.

"All right then, that's what I say." Naturally, I was kicking his butt on the pool table, so he kept trying to distract me when it was my turn. This time, he did a good job at distracting me. "Bae, did I tell you what Thomas said to me the other day?"

"No, who's Thomas?"

And I was concentrating on my next shot, measuring it out, about to take it, and he said, "My roommate, Regina?"

I stood straight up, forgetting about the game, and said, "Now what was the original question?"

He said, "Did I tell you what Regina said to me the other day?"

"Naw baby, you didn't tell me."

"The day we fell asleep on your couch, I went home to shower and get ready for work, right?"

"Riiiiight!"

"This chick told me she was worried about me. She told me next time I was going to stay out all night to give her a call so she won't stay up all night, worrying." He was tickled by that and then said, "Ain't she crazy?" He looked at my face and saw that I hadn't found a thing funny with that. His laugh stopped immediately, "What, baby doll?"

"Ain't she crazy?" I asked, mocking him.

"Yeah, that's what I'm saying. She crazy!" And he started laughing again.

"So that just tickles you pink, huh? Because she's concerned?"

"Baby, I thought it was funny. Kind of cute, but more so funny."

"You know she has a thing for you, don't you?"

"THOMAS? A thing for me? Naw, I don't think so."

"Mark my words LOVE she has a thing for you."

"Okay, go ahead and take your shot baby, so I can finish whooping you THIS game."

"Yeah, I bet you do want me to take my shot now, don't you? What else did Ms. Thing say to you?"

"What are you talking about, bae?"

"Come on. I know she said some more stuff to you. She cooked dinner for you yet?"

"Baby, take your shot."

I looked at him for a minute and saw that he was done talking about her and took my shot. I guess I was a little more ticked off than I thought because I ran off four shots once I turned back to the table, almost cleared ALL my balls. "I guess you wanted to finish this game off quick, huh? Was it something I said, baby doll?"

"I'm waiting for you to finish whooping me. Isn't that what you just told me?"

He took his shot and missed. I had to really be in his head because that was a straight shot. He hadn't missed one of those ALL night. "Hey there, little fella, was it something I said? You haven't missed a shot like that all night. I must be onto something, huh? It's something YOU not telling me, isn't it?"

"Look here girl, you're making me sorry I mentioned her in the first place!"

"You don't have to be sorry for that, but I'm going to let you know right now, I DON'T LIKE HER! I don't like how you set this whole thing up. You're going to tell me about her moving in with you AFTER the fact! Make it seem like she was a dude, and then when your CONSCIENCE got the best of you, THEN you tell me she's a girl. You get absolutely BESIDE yourself when I turned the tables on YOU. You threaten me, had me SCARED TO DEATH. You had ME scared to call the police, did you know that?" I kept talking before he had time to answer. "And then had ME apologizing to you left and right, like I was the mastermind of this whole thing. I never did get an apology. An 'I'm sorry, baby doll' from you for what YOU did. And now YOU think it's funny because old girl got a thing for you?"

Taj came around the table, took my pool stick along with his, and laid them across the table. He took me by the hand and sat me down. "Baby doll—"

I interrupted him, "So now I'm baby doll again, right?"

"Baby, don't do that."

"Taj, I am definitely NOT happy with you right now. I don't know what to do with myself. And another thing I'm going to let you know is that YOU'RE gone have to do whatever it is that you're going to do because I will upset you again! It's called life. It's a 'fairy-tale' relationship if we think that I'm not going to upset you and you're not going to upset me! And I REFUSE to be scared to piss you off because of what I think you may do to me! You're going to have to do you love, because I'm definitely doing me. I'm done walking on eggshells."

"Baby you're right, and I DO apologize."

I wouldn't look at him; I was looking up at the ceiling with a pissed smirk on my face.

"Baby, I'm sorry. Look at me."

I didn't look at him right away, but I cut my eyes at the ceiling and faced him. This time it was me with a stern look on my face. Now see? That's why I didn't want to look at him in the first place. He is so cute. It's hard for me to stick with the angry face, and I'm soooo glad he doesn't know what's going through my mind right now, but I'm going to do it. I have to stay strong! I have a cause!

"Baby doll, I know I should've talked it over with you before I gave her the okay to move in, but we were at the job talking, and she was crying and everything. Talking about she wished she had someplace else to go, and before I knew it, I told her that I had an extra room at the crib that she could crash at till she could do better. By the time I realized what I had done, I had already committed my place to her. Initially, I was going to continue to let you think she was a dude. It's not often you're at my place. I don't have a home phone, so I know I could've kept that lie up for a while, but I didn't feel right about doing that, so I came clean with you. My bad. But then again, I felt like YOU could handle it. Me and you are together ALL the time."

"We're not together ALL the time."

"We're together a good portion of the time, and I told you I'm going to marry you. Doesn't that count for anything?"

"First of all, we're NOT married. We're NOT engaged! We don't LIVE together! You go home to old girl at night! We're simply boyfriend and girlfriend. There's NOTHING legally binding us to one another."

"So you want us to live together?"

I wouldn't even dignify that question with an answer!

"Baby doll, you ARE going to marry me, so you might as well get used to it!"

"Yeah, well, whatever! Time will tell."

"And about that other stuff?"

"What other stuff?"

"You making me mad."

"Yeah, well let me give you my undivided attention." I put my elbows on the table and sat my chin in my hands and looked dead at him, like Eddie Murphy did in Beverly Hills Cop when he was talking to Victor Maitland at the country club.

"Baby doll, I don't EVER plan on hitting you. Now understand what I'm saying."

"OH, I got what you're saying. You don't PLAN on hitting me. That's NOT to say that you WON'T ever hit me."

"Prior to this situation, I didn't think I WOULD hit you or anything like that. But when I came in and saw old boy, I was going to strangle you! I'm going to put it to you like this: I hope I NEVER feel like that again, and I PRAY that it NEVER comes to that. In fact, I can tell you ALL day long that I WOULD NEVER put my hands on you in a serious manner, but when OLD BOY called himself moving in with YOU, and YOU were bullshitting with me, all I saw was red. I don't know what I would have done if you hadn't come clean with the quickness."

"Well, let ME put it to YOU like this: if you EVER put your hands on me, not only are we done, but also you better not EVAH let me cook grits for you. You know I watch a lot of Madea movies, and I take my lead from her. And to take it a step further, you better not EVAH go to sleep around me because I will pay you back. Although I know that me hitting you isn't really going to hurt you, I WILL NEVER hit you when we're angry, and I expect the same from you."

"Baby doll, promise me this. Promise me that you won't TRY to make me jealous or anything like that. I can control myself with any situation as long as there is no other hard leg involved."

"I'm not going to play those kind of games with you ever again Taj, but I can visualize you acting a fool in everyday type situations where I'm not trying to get next to you. You're going to have to learn to control yourself. I love YOU boo. And I'm not trying to be with ANYBODY else. You're going to have to trust that and look to God more."

"I feel you and I understand that those are YOUR intentions, and believe me, I do trust you. But any other dude come up on you baby, and I know HIS intentions are different, and if anybody ever hurt you, I'm going to jail. I can't imagine somebody taking something from you that I haven't had yet. YOU'RE not giving it to me. I KNOW you're not about to give it to anybody else either!"

"Ain't nobody trying to get with me, MAN!"

"Yeah, well, don't make me have to choke you!"

"You know what? I am going to make you jealous, then we'll see how you're going to handle things!"

"Yeah right Ms. Badass! Get over here and give me a kiss!"

"Naw, you'll be all right. Let me finish whooping you on this game."

I got up to finish our game of pool, and he grabbed me as I walked past him. He put his arms around me and said, "Baby doll, do YOU forgive me?"

"Man, move and let me finish this game so we can go."

He repeated himself like this was the first time he was saying it. "Baby doll, do you forgive me?"

I looked at him and said, "Can we finish the game, please?"

He squinted his eyes at me. "Baby Doll, do you FORGIVE me?"

"I'm working on it," I said. My feelings were still a little hurt, and he needed to know that I was not forgetting about it just because he was cute as all get out; I wanted him to know what he put me through. But then again, he is just a guy. He'd probably never get it! And the Bible DOES SAY to forgive your brother seven times seventy. "You're forgiven, Taj." *Four hundred and eighty-nine to go.*

"I love you baby doll!"

"I love you too, boss!"

He leaned over to kiss me, and just as he got to my face, I moved and said, "Move and let me finish whooping your tail!"

He put his hands around my neck as if to choke me. "Awwww, look at this cute little neck. You know you make me want to wring it, don't you?"

"I'm sure I do," I said in a voice as if he were applying pressure to the choke. He put his thumbs on my chin and lifted my head to his and kissed me. Naturally, I allowed it.

22

Sunday morning came pretty fast. You know how when you're nervous about something, it comes real fast, but when you're really looking forward to something, it takes forever for it to get here? I guess that means that I'm a little nervous, huh? Taj called me at six-thirty to make sure I was up. "Hey baby doll! You ready for the big day?…"

"Baby, what time is it?…"

"It's six-thirty, get up…"

"I'm not getting up till seven, MAN!…"

"My bad! Well, it's too late now, so get up!…"

"Good night, Taj!…"

"Get up, baby doll. I'll be by to get you in a little bit!…"

"You're not coming by here for another two hours. Go back to bed!…"

"Don't make me have to wait for you, baby!…"

"Goodnight, sweetheart!…"

"See you in a little bit…"

"Bye, man!" Now all while I was talking to him, my eyes were closed. I figured that I wasn't really woke if I kept my eyes closed. I was off the phone now, and guess what? My eyes were wide open! Dang! Why didn't I keep them closed? I might've been able to get back to sleep. Well, heck! I was still going to try. I laid there, with my eyes closed, trying to go back to sleep. My mind kept playing forward to what type of day today was going to be. What were his parents going to think about me? Was I going to have to fight to stay woke in church today? What should I wear?

When I realized it, fifteen minutes had gone by. *Oh well, I guess I might as well get up and start getting dressed.* I got up and took me a nice long bath. I had my devotion while I bathed. Me and the Lord had wonderful conversation while I was in the tub. I love the way He speaks to me. He gave me such a peace about meeting (as Taj says it) my future in-laws. It's reassuring to know that if you take time out for the Lord, He'll take time out for you. I have so much to be thankful for, and right now, I'm thanking the Lord for MY personal relationship with Him. I wonder where people who don't know Christ turn to when they need help. Who do they talk to? Praise God that's not MY dilemma!

I decided to wear my grey skirt with a little split at my left thigh. Don't get me wrong. I know I'm going to church, so it was not provocative. I wore a basic white blouse with it and some charcoal grey sandals. I had a matching jacket to the skirt, but it was late July. Was I really going to need the jacket? I'd bring it just in case. It may be cool in the church (or restaurant).

I had a few minutes to spare after I got dressed and put the finishing touches on my makeup, so I made me a cup of coffee. Before I could take my first sip, I heard a car pull into the driveway, and I'm pretty sure it was Mr. Man! I looked outside, and sure enough, Taj was here. *Oh well, there goes a perfectly good cup of coffee.* I didn't spill it out right away.

I went to the door, and Taj was getting out of the truck. "Is it time to be pulling off?" I stepped onto the porch and asked him. I didn't think it was possible, but this combination that he had on today looked as good, if not better, than last week. He had on a navy-blue suit with a bright pink shirt. Well, it was more of a melon than a pink, kind of salmony. Child, I don't know what color it is, but naturally, his tie had the same color blue and the same color pink in it with some white or grey or something thrown into it. *Good GRAVY, that man is fine! Can I sit here and just admire MY man?*

He stopped at the passenger side since he realized I was ready, "You ready to go, love?"

"Yes, sir!" I replied.

"Well, let's hit it then, beautiful! Your chariot awaits!"

I grabbed my purse, Bible, and jacket and went outside. "Good mornting, handsome!"

"And good morning to you, beautiful! You look rather smashing, m'lady! As always." He used a British accent when he said that. Ooooh, this man is a dream!

"And you sir, look absolutely adorable. You sure are confident in yourself wearing that pink shirt, aren't you?"

"Well, sweetheart, besides your Momma and my Momma, I'm escorting the most beautiful girl in the world. That in itself is a confidence booster, don't you think?"

"I declare, Taj, you say the sweetest things. Thanks for including my Moms in that!"

"I call it like I see it. But besides that, my Momma gave me this shirt and tie for my birthday last year, and she's never seen me wear it. So now is as good a time as any."

"I see, well, those are exceptional reasons for being confident. And I'm glad I could be of help to you on that." He opened the door for me, gave me a little peck on the lips, and closed the passenger door behind me, and we were off. We went to Cracker Barrel for breakfast. I hadn't really supported Cracker Barrel much since we were victims of racism a while back, but we went today and had a splendid time. Good conversation, and the pancakes were on point! It's always good to have a good breakfast before going to the Lord's house. I would hate to be in service (especially with strangers) with a loud stomach!

By the time we finished breakfast, it was time to head over to the church. We got to church around ten twenty-five. I went to the ladies' room to make sure my makeup was good before heading into service. Taj's Mom and Dad were already seated when we got there. His Dad was in the front row because he was a deacon. His Mom was fairly close to the front. We sat toward the back of the church. I wanted to go closer, but Taj preferred the back, so that was that. Once we were seated, he pointed his parents out to me. Naturally, I couldn't get a good look of anything but the back of their heads.

It wasn't a big church, but it wasn't a small church either. The service was good. The choir did a real nice job, and the pastor preached a good message. Well, as much of it as I could hear. Taj kept talking to me during the sermon. He was telling me funny stories of different people in the church. For instance, he showed me one of the mothers of the church that loses her top teeth often when she testifies. Well, her top teeth are always loose, so she'd just take her teeth out to finish her testimony. Then one of the deacons wore a toupee, and when he knelt at the front bench to pray, it flapped over. Now why did he know that? He should have his eyes closed and head bowed when they were praying. He's so bad!

I kept telling him to hush so I could pay attention, but he had a lot to talk about. One of the ushers finally came up to him and whispered something to him. I assumed the usher told him to be quiet and said to him, "Now see there, somebody has to come over and tell your grown behind to be quiet in church? Now hush!"

His response was, "The usher, Brother Palmer, told me to look at Deacon Robinson up front. His shirt is buttoned up wrong."

These people were terrible! Here I thought the usher came by to tell him to hush, and he was instigating. What was I going to do with them?

Service was pretty much over at that time, and the pastor was opening the doors of the church. That's why Deacon Robinson was up front. After the benediction, Taj took me around, introducing me to different people, leading me to the front. This was the church that he grew up in, which I hadn't known before. I was wondering why he knew so many people here. I figured that he visited a lot but soon found out that wasn't the case.

We got around to his Mom and Dad, and his Mom popped him on the buttocks. "Boy, you were going to get it. I sure didn't think that you came today. What time did you get here?"

He kissed her on the cheek and said, "Hey, Momma! Now you know your baby boy is NOT going to let you down."

And his Dad said, "Yeah, we know HE won't, but we're talking about you!"

We all laughed. I see his Dad is a comedian, which must be where Taj gets it from. Taj said, "That's cold, Pops. I guess I stepped right in that one, huh?"

"Yeah, I guess you did," he replied, and they hugged.

Taj then turned to me and said, "Mom, Dad, this is my girl. This is Ms. Valeri NICOLE Wilson dash Bryant!"

I gave his Mom a hug and said hi, and Mom said, "Hi, sweetheart. It's so nice to finally meet you."

"Yeah," I said, "it's nice to finally meet you too."

His Dad said, "Okay, Shirley, let me get some of that too."

Again, we laughed, and Taj said, "Oh yeah, I forgot to tell you that my Dad is a pistol."

His dad said, "Shoot! I don't know what you talking about, I'mma double-barrel SHOTGUN! Come on and give me a hug, girl."

"Yes sir!" I said as I went to hug his Dad.

"If she is as sweet as she looks, then ya done good, my boy!"

Taj looked at me and said, "She's sweeter!"

"Well all right!" I said. "I come from good stock like Taj does!"

"Well, you sho' been taught right."

"Thanks," Taj said, "I've been doing my best to teach her, show her the ropes. And I almost have her just like I want her."

Taj's Mom hit him again and told him, "Hush up, boy! Ain't nobody talking about you! Did you two greet my Pastor today?"

"We were on our way, and we got hijacked by two old people," Taj said.

Now it was my turn to hit him. "If you don't behave yourself, you know you gonna get it."

His Mom said, "Thanks baby, Alexander knows he gonna get it. He always talking stuff. You better hope you get my age one day, boy."

He said, "I am hoping, but until then, I'm going to talk about YOU!"

His Dad said, "All right Junior, you better leave ya Momma alone. She can't stay young like US forever. But she's still sweet as fine wine!"

Taj turned to me and said, "See, I told you. And the sad part about that is he really believes that he's still young!"

"Get up there and speak to Pastor Riley before I beat you!" And he got into a boxing stance.

Taj grabbed me and shielded himself with me. We went and spoke to the Pastor. We told Pastor that we enjoyed his message, and Pastor stated that he was glad to have us. They talked for a little bit. Pastor was giving Taj an open invitation to come back as a member here anytime and feeling him out to see if he was a faithful member of his own church. As I was standing there, listening, Taj told Pastor that the Lord may be moving him in a different direction but that he was being still and quiet to hear what the Lord had to say.

"Isn't that what you always told us, Pastor? To never make a move till you're sure that it's the Lord leading you?"

"Yeah, that's what I told you. Glad that you were listening."

We left church and went to Taj's Mom and Dad's house to wait till it was time to eat. His parents had a nice home. Well, I guess so. His dad was a retired engineer from Ford, and his mom was a local high school math teacher. They lived in the same house that Taj grew up in.

She pulled out some photo albums. I saw pictures of the whole family and of Taj's childhood. I must say he was an awfully cute little boy too. Well, his parents were both nice-looking, so he was bound to be adorable. His Dad was at least six feet tall. He got a nice grade of hair, naturally curly, and he was gray at the temples. He was really nice-looking now, so I know back in the day, he was a ladies' man. Not that he was a womanizer, but that all the women were probably attracted to him.

His Mom was adorable too. She was a red bone, as they call it, meaning she was light-skinned. She had pretty brown eyes. They were so brown they almost looked black, like black pearls or something. She wasn't a small woman, about five-foot-seven or eight, and somewhat thick with some hefty curves. Yeah, she was a brick house in her younger years.

After chilling at the house for about an hour, Taj's brother, Jackson, and his best friend, Duss, showed up. "Hey, Bubba!" Jackson said to Taj.

After they hugged, Taj put his brother in a headlock and said, "You thought I forgot, didn't you? I told you I was going to body slam you!"

"Momma, call ya son before I hurt him," Jackson pleaded to his Mom.

"Taj, get over here and stop playing before y'all break something," Mom had spoken. Immediately, they stopped, but Taj grabbed him in his collar and said, "Momma's not going to be around you always, boy."

Duss came over and said, "Taj, don't make us jump you. You better be glad you got on a suit. Otherwise, we had you."

Taj put his arms around both of them and led them to me and said, "Baby doll, this is my little brother Beavis and his sidekick, Butthead."

His mother jumped in really quick, "Val, my baby boy's name is Jackson, not Beavis! I don't know what you have done to that boy, but he is really showing out, and I'm about to whoop him!"

"Now, Mrs. Bryant, why I got to be the blame for Taj cutting up? You should see how he acts with me. In fact, let me tell you how he threatened ME the other day."

"Baby doll, meet me in my office. I forgot to give you ground rules before we got here."

"Oh, you don't want me to tell that, and now we got ground rules, huh?"

"Nah, Tab! We ALL want to hear this," Jackson said.

Taj cut me a look, bit his bottom lip, and squinted his eyes at me. "I'll tell you later," I whispered to Jackson. "Hi Jackson, how you doing?"

"I'm good, Val. Let me be the one to tell you that if MY big brother gets out of line with you, you can always call me, and if ME and my boy, Duss, have to handle Tab, then that's EXACTLY what we'll do. He don't want none of us."

"Thanks Jackson, make sure I get that number before I head home."

"Gotcha, girlfriend. Oh, this is my guy, Duss, also known as Fred."

As Fred and I were speaking, all three of Taj's sisters showed up. They all came in saying hi to Mommy and Daddy, and the oldest girl came in. "Hey, Mommy and Daddy, where she at? Where's my big brother's flavor of the month?"

"Nay Nay, how you gone act?" Taj said.

"Aw, so it's like that, Taj?" I asked. I wasn't really bothered, but I could clown with the best of them if need be.

"Baby girl, these are my sisters, Shayna, aka Nay Nay, Delilah (named after my grandmother, aka Dee Dee), and the baby of the family, Tedi Lonnese. They're also referred to as Moe, Larry, and Curly."

"Okay Tab," Shayna was speaking again, "she's cute, but then again, you don't mess with no ugly girls, now do you? How long this one going to be around?"

"Momma, can you shut that daughter of yours up?" Shayna was REALLY working Taj's nerves.

"Baby girl," Daddy was now getting involved, "stop messing with your brother and his lady friend. You're going to have plenty of time to hassle him, but you have to leave Val alone. She's special!"

"Uh-oh, y'all! What she done to my Daddy?" She went over and gave her Dad a hug, and they had a brief private conversation over there.

The other two girls had already come and spoken to me and gave me a hug. Shayna was too busy giving Taj a hard time that she didn't formally greet me. Mom said a few things to Taj which seemed to relax his nerves a little, and then she made us get ready to leave for dinner. She said she was hungry. Mom and Dad rode in the truck with me and Taj. On the way to the restaurant, Mom told me not to worry about Shayna. According to Mom, she was probably a little bitter because she recently broke up with her boyfriend. "She must've drank a WHOLE bottle of HATORADE before she came over here today. That's what y'all call it, right? Hatorade? After a while, she'll mellow out and be all right."

We ended up going to Red Lobster, which is MY favorite restaurant. Me and crab legs are BEST friends. I had Taj on one side of me and Mrs. Bryant on the other. Mr. Bryant blessed the food. Dinner was wonderful. Initially, I was inhibited about the conversation, thinking I wouldn't be included, but it ended up not being as bad as I thought. They told a lot of stories about their childhood. Jackson told the story about when Taj was in about the fifth grade and was on the phone with a little girl that he liked. He didn't know that Jackson was listening on another phone in the house, and Taj asked the girl if he had big muscles. Back in the day, he talked with a lisp, so he actually asked her, "Do I have big muthelth?"

It was hilarious the way Jackson mocked him. We all laughed pretty hard at that. Naturally, Taj said he had the last laugh now. "Because look at this!" And he flexed one of his arms. "Do I have big muscles now?" Well, who could argue with that? He had HUGE muscles (love them)!

Jackson was not half-stepping himself. He was a little thick guy too, but not as tall or as big as Taj. HE started flexing too, but nobody was paying any attention to him. All in all, we had a good time. Our server asked if we saved room for dessert, but we had eaten enough. No one wanted any, so she brought us the check, and Dad grabbed it. Taj offered to pay for it, but I'm sure he already knew that his dad had it. Other than Taj, Delilah (Dee Dee) was the only other person that offered any money.

Like Mom said, Shayna had calmed down a lot. When we were leaving, she grabbed me by the hand and apologized for giving me and Taj a hard time. We exchanged numbers. She hugged me and told me to look after her little brother, which helped to lighten the mood. We laughed about that, and she said he needed somebody that was going to be good to him. I was glad to see that she was looking out for my baby.

The rest of us headed outside and were saying our goodbyes. Jackson asked me for my number and called me right away so I could save his number. He told me that I shouldn't have anything to worry about with Taj. He's a big teddy bear, all bark and no bite was what he thought. I hoped he was right. I don't know if Taj knew that we were exchanging numbers or not or if he was all right with that. He was handling the bill with his dad, and they hadn't come out yet. It wasn't too long before they came out, though, which was good because nobody had left yet, so Taj had a chance to say bye to his peeps, and then we headed back to take Mom and Dad home.

They asked us to come in for a while, so we did. We decided to take advantage of their theater room, so Taj convinced his parents to watch *Welcome Home, Roscoe Jenkins*. They had never seen that before. They both loved the movie, and Mom compared characters to people in her family. She had a person for each character, and of course, Taj was Michael Clark Duncan (may he rest in peace), and Shayna was Monique: "It just ain't sanitury!" She had really tickled us with her comparisons.

She mentioned some of her extended family too, who of course I didn't know, but I guess it was funny because Dad and Taj were in tears, laughing so hard. We had a little ice cream for dessert after the movie, watched the news, and were out. I thoroughly enjoyed my time with his family. They weren't as loud and wild as MY family, but that's only because it was not as many of them as there were of us. We laughed and talked about different things in the course of the day all the way home. I was glad it was over, and PRAISE GOD I made it through!

23

Monday morning, another day, another dollar—*"time to make the donuts."* I was going to have to tell Ronni about my Sunday with the Bryants. She was going to be so proud of me. Since my time in sunny Atlanta, I'd introduced Taj to my family, I met his family, and most importantly, I pissed him off tremendously. WOW! Was I ever growing up? Just joshing! Pissing him off was NOT the most important thing. But because of Ronni, I was taking it one day at a time and enjoying it while it lasted. And most importantly (for real this time), I was looking to the Lord to lead us EVERY step of the way. Praise Him for my friends. But calling Ronni would have to wait till this evening. First things first, I felt a lunch date coming on today. *Let me call Toni.*

So yeah! I set up a lunch date with Toni for one o'clock. For whatever reason, she had to do a late lunch today. And when it came to Toni, if she was not at lunch by eleven-thirty, then it had to be one or after. She didn't like to be caught in the lunch rush. Well, it was cool with me. I had a slow afternoon today. I'd had several cancellations. I think it might have been due to the weather. It was gorgeous outside.

Right at eleven-thirty though, there was a knock on my office door. My niece Tia peeked in the door. "Ms. Val, you have a visitor." Guess who showed up at the job? Taj! "Hey, boo! What are you doing here?" I asked him. He showed up, bearing lunch. He brought me a grilled chicken salad from Lucky Dog. How sweet!

"Hey there, baby doll! Your man missed you. I was thinking about you and wanted to see you. Is that all right with you?"

"Lovebug, that is absolutely fine with me. This is your first time ever coming by the job to see me, though. I am pleasantly surprised."

"Well sweetie, I wanted to let you know what Mom and Dad really thought about you. I figured I could kill two birds with one stone and see my baby in the meantime."

"Oh yeah! I didn't think you even had time to talk to them yet."

"Yeah, Shirley couldn't wait for me to get home and call her."

"Okay, so what did they say?"

"Of course, you already know that my Dad, Deacon Canton Lee Bryant, found you extremely adorable."

"I know that's how he acted, but he really thinks I'm adorable?"

"Of course! Who doesn't?"

"Good call!"

"My brother thinks you're adorable too. Actually, that's why I was going to beat him up when I saw him. He told me that he was going to take you from me. And he promised me that he would leave with your digits."

"Oooooh!" and I covered my mouth.

"What's that about?"

"Baby, was I NOT supposed to give him my number?"

"You gave him your number?"

"Well, yeah! You heard him say I needed to get his number before the night was over."

"That's got nothing to do with him having YOUR number, baby!"

"For real, is that a problem?"

"Are you attracted to him?"

"Baby, you know I want you and NOBODY else. I definitely wouldn't get with your brother, EVER!"

"Then we all good! But let me know if he starts flirting with you. I'll kill 'im!"

"Whew! Don't scare me!"

"We all good, baby doll, and Mom thinks you're lovely! She didn't tell me, but she told Pops that she had a good feeling about you."

"Why didn't she tell you?"

"She told me that you appeared to be a lovely girl. She said that you were really cute and seemed different than the last gal I was with."

"That's all she said?"

"She said a lot of stuff, but that was the gist of it. Pops was all excited when I talked to him, and he told me that Mom said she had a good feeling about you. She told him that she believes that this is it. 'That's going to be the mother of my grandkids!'"

"Wow! That's awfully sweet of her, but time will tell."

"Don't play with me, girl!"

"I'm just saying, love!"

"Yeah, okay! The rest of them thought you were down to earth and all that. I had to tell them that's MY girl. Would I be with someone that wasn't down to earth? And Nay Nay, of course, had to remind me of a blast from my past."

"Don't tell me THAT blast was the one that wasn't feeling the lakefront thing?"

"Yeah, among other things, but we're not going to spend any time reminiscing on old girl. I want to think about my main flavor!"

"What's that supposed to mean, Taj?"

"I'm just playing, girl." And he grabbed me and put his arms around me. He hugged and kissed me and said, "Can we eat now?"

"Of course! You're the one that had so much to talk about."

So he blessed our food, and we sat there and ate lunch in my office. He gave me a little scolding for threatening to tell his Momma about our little falling out that we had last week. "I told you I would get you back for always showing out when you get around MY peoples. You didn't like that, did you?"

"You seem to forget that your brother gave me permission to whoop you?"

"Nah, didn't forget. I wasn't going to tell!"

"Attagirl!"

"But I'm glad that your people thought I was good people!"

"Yup, they did."

So we finished our lunch, and he left. He had to get back to work. I had some office work to do before I headed out. I guess

I'd be done with everything anywhere from two to two-thirty. My cell phone rang at one-fifteen, and it was Toni. "Hey girl, how you durn?…" I said.

"Val, where are you?…"

"What you mean? I'm at work…"

"Were you not supposed to meet me for lunch at one?…"

"Oooooh! Toni, I am so sorry! Taj came by here and brought me lunch, and I forgot I was supposed to meet you! My bad, girl!…"

"So I get played for a pretty face, huh? Girl, you so shady!…"

"Toni, I'm sorry. You know what? I'm on my way…"

"Val, you already ate, remember?…"

"I can still come and meet you. Give me fifteen minutes…"

"No! I'm picking up my lunch and heading back to work. Thanks for letting ME know that I play second fiddle to Big Boy!…"

"Well, that's true! When you start helping me pay my bills and spend some of your money on me, I'll move your status up…"

"You bogus, but that's okay!…"

"Toni, I said I was sorry. Taj has NEVER come by my job before. It threw me off. He wanted me to know what his people thought of me. So I guess he was a little geeked. He didn't call or nothing, just popped up here…"

"Oh, so you met them?…"

"Yeah, yesterday. That's why I wanted to have lunch with you today so I could tell you about it…"

"And I forgot that YOU were the one that asked ME to lunch. That makes it worse…"

"Whatever, Toni, I'll call you later on…"

"I'm going to be busy with my man, don't bother…"

"Okay, which reminds me that I've been playing second fiddle to Zani for HOW long now?…"

"Girl, don't be so petty. I'll call you later on…"

"Uh-huh. Bye, Toni!…"

"Bye, girl…"

My bad. Taj got me so turned around coming by the job that I COMPLETELY forgot about my girl, Toni. *Oh well, she'll be all right.* So I finished my work and headed out. I stopped by the health club before I got home and did me a quick workout, which was a good cooldown to a great day.

I stopped by Mommy's after my workout. It was nice to see her, seeing as though I didn't see her at all yesterday.

"Hey, Pearl." That's what I call my Moms when I'm trying to be grown. That's her middle name.

"Hey there, sweetie, missed you at church yesterday. How was your day?"

"Well Mom, I had a really good time with Taj and his family. His parents' church wasn't mine, but I had a good time. How was church?"

Mommy and I sat there and had good conversation about the service that I missed at MY church, and I told her all about Taj's family and how our day was. Mom was glad that I enjoyed my time with the Bryants. So after I sat there and chilled with Mommy for a little bit, I left and went home. Guess who was sitting on my porch when I got there? No, silly, it wasn't Taj. This time, it was old crazy Toni.

When I pulled up, she stood up and acted like she was watering my plants. She's so lame! When I got out the car, I could hear her humming as if she was really doing something.

"Girl, what are you doing here at my house?"

"Oh, so you finally decided to come home, huh? And where's Mr. Man? I knew he was going to be hot on your tail."

"Hi, Toni. I thought we were going to do lunch tomorrow. I guess now we don't have to, huh?"

"Girl, bring your tired self in the house so you can tell me about your church date yesterday." I grabbed my keys, getting ready to unlock the door, and Toni said, "Uh, the door's unlocked, sweetheart." I looked at her, and she said, "What? I've been here for almost an hour."

"Look here ma'am, I gave you keys in case I lock myself out. NOT for you to use at your disposal."

"Yeah, right! Well, I thought you were locked out. How's that?"

"Heffa, why are you here?"

"UH, I'm so offended. My BEST friend is NOT happy to see me. Give me hug, baby!" She said that like Eddie Murphy did in the bar in Beverly Hills Cop.

I laughed at the little nut. "Girl, you know you crazy."

"Yeah, I know. So how was your dinner yesterday?"

We went in the house, and the first thing Toni did was go into the kitchen, grab a bottle of Moscato, and two wine glasses. She had already had cheese and crackers on the table, poured us both a glass, came and lit a candle, sat on the couch next to me, and said, "Let's hear it."

Why we had to be sitting there like we were about to get intimate, I don't know, but if that's how she wanted it, then cool. "All right, so Old Boy came by my house and picked me up at eight-thirty. Actually, he was a few minutes early because I had just made myself a cup of coffee that I didn't get to drink."

"Girl, give me the quick version. I already know that you got up and brushed your teeth and things of that sort. Details, but not so detail-y."

"We went to breakfast, church, where he talked during the WHOLE service. I met his parents who are absolutely adorable. We went to their home, which is very nice, and then went to dinner." I pretty much said that without taking a breath, and when I looked at Toni, she had that "You getting on my nerves" look.

"You know, Val, if you didn't want to talk to me, why didn't you just say so? I can take a hint, REALLY."

I yelled, "NOT!" and scared her. After that, I told her to let me do this MY way and gave her the details about dinner. I told her about how Jackson told me to call him if Taj got out of line with me again. I also told her about Miss Nay Nay and her attitude in the beginning. I gave her all the details that I could think of.

Toni, being the person she is, had something to say about Shayna. "Uh, ma'am, what did YOU say to Miss Nay Nay?"

"What do you mean?"

"I mean, you let her come in there talking noise about YOU and his past relationships?"

"Toni, that child didn't bother me. I'm confident in who I am, and I'm not going to let nobody come in and make me second-guess myself. I'm cool."

"Yeah, well, I would've had to tell Miss Thang a thing or two."

"I'm sure you would've. But you know me, it's not necessary to get into no stuff with her or nobody else. Now if it so happens that Taj and I DO get married at some point, THEN if I need to check somebody, I will. But only if it's necessary. I'm not mad at her for looking out for her brother. That's what I would do."

"Yeah, but YOU wouldn't go in there talking crazy either."

"Naw, I wouldn't, but she's not me."

"Well, you know how I feel."

"Yeah, you'll be all right."

"I know I will. Enough about you. Did I tell you what Zani bought me the other day?"

Toni started talking about ONE of her favorite subjects, which was Zani. Her other favorite subject was Toni, and I didn't feel like getting into either one of them subjects. I had my own NEW favorite subject to dwell on, so I sat there and acted like I was engaged in the conversation, but my mind kept drifting off to my baby and all the wonderful things that were happening between us. I wanted to call Ronni and give her the update on us and thank her again for being such a good friend to me, BUT I had to wait till Toni left to do that, so I sat there, sipping on my Moscato, reminiscing and occasionally chiming in with, "Girl, for real? You playing? I know that's right." Sorry, I don't have more information on Toni and Zani right now, but I had been listening to their saga for three years now.

24

Toni stuck around and talked about her and Zani for at least another hour. I did finally get back into the conversation, and we were comparing notes. I turned the TV on, and we watched the news and *Wheel of Fortune* till close to seven when Taj called me. I was wondering what was up with him. Generally, I would've heard from him sooner, but he got held up at the job with some kind of big incident there. He went straight home, but I guess Toni thought he was calling to tell me that he was on his way, so she ended up leaving.

"Girl, I know your man is on his way, so I'm going to head on out. Maybe MY man is waiting on me at my place."

"Taj, let me call you right back... Yeah, that's Toni you hear in the background... I'll tell her... Toni, Taj said, 'What's up, girl?'"

"Yeah, yeah, yeah, tell Tab I'm getting out of his way so he can head on over."

"Yeah babe... I know she's rude... Yeah she could've said hi to you, but I'm going to call you in a minute... Love you too, boo... Bye!"

"Oh, my bad, when you call BOO back, tell him I said, ''Sup.'" (And she threw her head back like bruh man—from the fifth flo'—off Martin.)

"I'll make sure I tell him. So you gone?"

"Well, not yet, but I am leaving. I'll call you later on."

"All right, well, thanks for coming by, girl."

"As always, it was a pleasure. We haven't been out in a while. We going to have to go kick it one day. Maybe play some pool or something."

"That sounds good. I'm always up for some pool."

"All right, I'll see you." We gave each other a hug, and I went out on the porch and watched her as she pulled off. And then I actually DID water my plants. I'm glad Toni reminded me. I'd been neglecting them since Taj had been hanging around. *Let me call my girl.* But first things first, I grabbed my phone and sat on the porch, and I called Taj to see what he was talking about. With all the excitement at the job, he was tired, so he headed home to rest up. I was cool with that. We'd been together almost every day since we started dating, and I did see him earlier today when he brought my lurnch. Anyhoo, hey, can somebody tell me why Madea has to put an R or a T in all her words? Ain't no R in lunch or hello, and ain't no T in morning, but that's my girl. I love her.

When I got off the phone with Taj, I called my girl, Ronni, and gave her the 411. After I gave her all the information on dinner with the Bryants, I said, "Ronni, you should be proud of me. I have taken your advice on just about everything since I left you there in ATL. I introduced my man to my family, I've met his family, and I pissed him off tremendously..."

"Val, I am proud of you. I been praying for you guys, and you forgot something..."

"What's that?..."

"Have you been looking to the Lord?..."

"Oh yeah! I have AND I been taking it one day at a time. Enjoying it while it lasts..."

"And you're going to be enjoying it for a lot longer too. You going to end up marrying that man, and you better make sure that I'm in the wedding too..."

"Taj keeps telling me that same thing, and first of all, Ronni, wouldn't be no wedding without you. You know that..."

"Now you're talking..."

"Yeah, and ONLY time will tell..."

"Okay, keep fooling yourself..."

"I'm not fooling myself. He hasn't asked me yet, AND it's only been a few months. AND most importantly, I haven't gotten confirmation from the Lord. I would love nothing more than to become Mrs. Tim Bryant, as my Momma would call me..."

"Yeah, well, I got confirmation…"

"Does that mean that you and Dre are getting married girl? Congratulations!…"

"HA! Funny. I got confirmation on YOU, girl…"

"Yeah, well, I'm still waiting…" Me and Ronni talked for a little while longer. She had some stuff going on with Dre and some other folks in Atlanta that she was venting about, so we ended up talking for a little more than an hour.

I thanked her for being a great person and friend to me, and she took a line off the movie *Soul Food* and said, "You my sister, girl…"

Yeah, she is my sister. All sisters are not necessarily bound by blood but can be bound by love! Praise God!

*****

Taj and I got together throughout the rest of the week as usual. But Thursday, when he came by, he stayed in the car longer than usual. When he came in the house, he was pretty tickled. "Baby, what's got you so tickled?" I asked him.

He gave me a kiss and said, "Hey, love."

"My bad baby, hi sweetie. How are you today?" I asked him.

"I'm just fine, baby doll. I can see that you're fine too, but how do you feel?"

"I'm good sweet pea, thanks for asking."

"Well, you know I have to ask. I can see that you're fine. Just have to know how you feel physically, though. I was laughing because my girl, Thomas, called me as I was getting out the car and wanted to know what time I was coming home. She was cooking like she did the other night." Men are slow! This man is sitting here talking about his roommate that he KNOWS I have a problem with. He was just talking away, like everything is cool. HIS GIRL!

Lord, I don't know what You were thinking about when You created man, but I can see that You weren't too particular about what You placed in their heads because they are really lacking in the brain department. I'm here to tell You, they don't think worth a dime. But I was playing it off because I wanted to get ALL the information I could get about him and his roomie.

"You remember Monday night when I didn't come over here, right?"

"Yeah, I remember."

"Baby, I went home, took a shower, and crashed."

"Okaaaay."

"So Thomas was there in the kitchen, cooking. I was laying down by seven fifteen, otta der [that means he fell asleep—he was out of there]. About eight, I hear old girl yelling something. When I finally gathered myself, the girl was in my room, talking about some, 'Honey, it's dinner time, time to get up.' I told her, 'Five more minutes?' And we both laughed. It was so funny the way the whole thing happened. I knew she was cooking, but I didn't know she was cooking for me too, which was cool because I was starving. Anyways, I got up, washed my face, and went in to eat."

"Cool, so what did she cook?"

"We had some shrimp alfredo stuff along with some Mexican corn and some garlic bread. Then we topped it off with Kool-Aid and some Heineken. Everything was really good."

"So what you have for dessert?"

"Oh, we had some hot apple pie a la mode. Store bought, not homemade."

"That's it?"

"Yeah, don't you think that's enough? So she was calling just now because she was going to cook again tonight. I had to tell her that I was going to eat with my BAY-BEE." And he put his arms around me and squeezed me real tight. "So what we eating?"

"Hold up, PODnuh!" And I pushed him back off me.

"What?"

"So that's ALL you had for dessert the other night?"

"What do you mean?"

"I mean, you didn't have some Regina a la mode along with your apple pie?"

"Baby, don't tell me you going to start tripping like that again?"

178

"Taj, you know that girl likes you, AND I'm not giving it up, so there's always that possibility you getting it from somewhere."

"We're just roommates and colleagues, and I'm going to tell you this ONE time and ONE time ONLY. I have NO desires to be with that girl, and I'm not sure, but I don't THINK that girl has a desire to be with me. Don't come at me like that about that girl again, and I'm NOT playing!"

"Whatever! And that might be what you two are to you, but that girl is trying to get into your pants. Mark my words."

"Yeah, right! Well, whatever. You heard what I said. Now I'm hungry. You cooking?"

"Why? Because if I'm not, you can go home and eat with THOMAS?"

"You know what? I'm going to stop telling you stuff since I see that you can't handle it."

"Baby, I'm fine. Believe me, I can handle it, and I definitely don't want you to stop telling me stuff because when she UNDENIABLY comes on to you, I want you to tell me."

"Right, so you can say, 'I told you so?' Whatever man. I said what are we eating? Why don't you call and order us a pizza?"

"I can do that." And as I crossed over him to get my phone, I punched him HARD in his shoulder.

"Awwww, my baby doll is jealous. Well, you better step it up in the kitchen…if you want to keep that status." He mumbled the last part of the sentence like I wasn't supposed to hear him.

"What did you say?"

"Huh?"

"YOU HEARD me."

"Baby, I don't know what you talking about. Make sure you get some onions and black olives on the pizza. You know how I like it."

"Yeah, well if you going to make a statement like that, you better be prepared to back it up. I am who I am, and either you like it or you don't. And either you going to deal with it or you not."

"Girl, ain't nobody trying to hear all that. I know what I'm doing and I know what I want. And right now, I want some pizza (unless you gone cook). So ORDER my DAGGUM pizza or be prepared to throw down!" And he put up his dukes, like he was ret to fight.

I don't know what he thinks this is, but this ain't that! Trying to tell things to me! You watch! That girl's going to do something, and then he'll see what her true motives are, but in the meantime, I'm not going to worry about him or her. If they getting it on or whatever, the Lord's going to reveal it to me. But that man is so slow; I really don't think he has a clue what she's up to. He thinks it's all innocent. Me being a woman, I know what's in that little feeble head of hers because I would be doing the same thing if I was interested. For the time being, I'm all good. Time will tell all!

25

After we finished the pizza, I kicked Taj out the house. Let me stop playing. You know I didn't throw that BIG thing out my house. We would probably still be throwing down to this day. The next day, Toni and I took our men to play pool. We went to an actual billiards place where we ate and drank and were merry. Initially, we had two tables, and the ladies played against their men. I don't think Zani and Toni were engaged in serious competition. They were hugging up and kissing too much to really be competitive.

They are so nerve-racking. They kind of set the bar as to how our night was going to be. Now Taj was over here, acting like he was teaching me how to hold the stick and take shots. Even though I already knew how to do all that, that big old body around me felt awfully good. And he smelled scrumptious as usual. After we clowned around for a while, we decided to play couples. Us two against those two lames, HATCHOOOOO! I'm allergic to lames.

Zani made the suggestion that when we missed a shot, we would have to kiss one of the opposing players. Taj was trying to get a clear understanding of what the man was talking about, "So if I miss my shot, I have to kiss YOU Zani?"

"Naw, man. If you miss your shot, you have to kiss Toni and vice versa."

Now me, personally, I wasn't going along with this idea at ALL. I was NOT into swapping mates and I was NOT about to be putting my lips on NO other man, ESPECIALLY with this nut present! Heck NO, but I wasn't going to say anything because I wanted to see Taj's response to this. Toni seemed like she was all good with it. "Oh yeah, bae, that would make it really interesting," she replied.

Taj looked at me and said, "What YOU think, bae?"

"Naw! What do YOU think, BOSS?" And I bowed at him when I said that.

So Taj said, "Well, what kind of kiss we talking about? Are we talking about just a peck on the jaw like this"—and he kissed my jaw—"or a peck like this?" And he gave me a gentle peck on my lips. "Or we talking about a KISS, like this?" And he put his arms around me and looked into my eyes and gave me a very long and passionate kiss.

Zani said, "DAM, man! We was just playing to see how you two would react to that, but I didn't expect to be grilled nor did I expect to get that type of demonstration. How about you kiss YO girl when YOU miss, and I'll kiss MY girl when I miss? Ain't going to be NO girl swapping round here." Me and Taj were still engaged in "the kiss" while he was talking.

He came over and broke us up. "Shoot! Maybe we should skip this game and just go home. That kiss done got ME a little worked up."

Taj said, "How do you think I feel?" He was still looking into my eyes, and I'm here to tell you, THAT WAS A KISS. If we were at my house right now, I would've been in a world of trouble because it just got REAL hot in here. "At least YOU can go home and fix YOUR situation. I'm heading to the bathroom RIGHT now." He pecked me on the lips and whispered in my ear, "Baby doll, I'll be right back." Him and Zani headed toward the bathroom while he was adjusting his situation in his pants. Zani actually went to the bar.

Toni came over to me and said, "Girl, you still ain't giving that man none? How in the WORLD do you do that?"

"Toni, shazam! Let me just say that I'm glad we were not at home. After THAT kiss, my goals would be shattered. Is it HOT in here or is it just me?" She thought that was really funny. I didn't because I was serious.

"Well, I know what I'm going home to do," was Toni's reply.

After I gained my composure, I noticed one of my physical therapy clients walked in to the pool hall. It was Allen, the basketball player that broke his ankle playing on an outdoor court. He was with a few other young guys. He spotted me and came over and gave me a hug, and we started chatting. "Hey, AJ, what you doing in here?"

"What do you mean, Ms. Val? This my spot!"

"Oh, okay, how's that ankle doing?"

"My ankle is almost 100 percent, thanks to all your help."

"Well, praise God! Allen, this is my bestest bud, Toni. Toni, this is a former client of mine, Allen. I had to nurse this ankle back to health so he could get in to the NBA, what? Next year?"

"Hi, Ms. Toni. Yeah, after I have a good season this year, I'm expecting to enter the draft next year. Thanks to Ms. Val here."

"NBA, huh? Do you have to a girlfriend, Allen?"

"Uhhhhhh…"

I jumped in before he could respond, "Toni, leave that boy alone. He is WAY too young for you."

"I'm not talking to you. I'm talking to Allen."

Taj had emerged from the bathroom and IMMEDIATELY jumped to conclusions and came over with a TALL attitude. "My man, you didn't hear my lady when she said she was here with her man?"

"Taj, this is one of my physical therapy clients, Allen. He plays ball for U of I, Champaign, and more than likely will be heading to the NBA draft next year. Allen, this is my EVER so jealous, EVER so jumping to conclusions man, Taj!"

AJ attempted to shake Taj's hand, and Taj gave him a firm fist bump instead. AJ said, "I mean NO disrespect, sir. I saw Ms. Val over here and was only speaking." He turned to me and said, "I'll be heading back to school in about a week or so, Ms. Val, and I wanted to thank you for nursing me back to good health with all those strengthening exercises you gave me."

"Yeah, I bet you do!" Taj said mockingly.

"It was nice meeting you all. I'mma head back with my boys and beat them in some pool," he said as he was walking back to his crew he came in with.

"Yeah, you do that!" Taj said.

I nudged Taj to be quiet and said, "No problem, AJ, and you make sure you take good care of yourself in school. I'm wishing the best for you and praying for the Lord to have His way with you. Say hi to your Mom for me. Your Mom and Dad."

"I will, and thanks again for everything."

"Yeah Allen, make sure we get some locker-room passes when you make the pros," Taj said as he was walking away. AJ gave a slight head nod.

I was so mad at Taj that initially, I simply looked at him, couldn't speak, just looked. I was mortified by his behavior and couldn't believe this attitude that he was displaying. And then he had the nerve to ask for locker-room passes? "You know you ought to be ashamed of yourself, Taj. You don't give me the benefit of the doubt for NOTHING! I have an innocent conversation with a client of mine, INNOCENT conversation, work-related, but then you want to act like I'm so wrong for asking YOU a question about the woman that YOU live with or reacting to something you tell me about you and old girl? I'm ready to go! I'm done playing, y'all!"

"Val, lets finish playing this game. Me and Zani were going to whoop up on you and Taj."

"Y'all can play. I'll be in the car." I went to grab my stuff. Taj came over and stopped me.

"Baby doll, you're right, and I'm sorry."

"Yes, you are!"

"For real, baby. You know how I get. I JUST had a really nice kiss from you and then can't satisfy my urge, so I have to go cool myself down, and I come out, and you sitting up here laughing and talking with some YOUNG stud. I didn't even go off, but I had to ask the question because I know YOU told old boy that you was here with me!" He grabbed a hold of my hand and kissed me on the cheek. "Let's finish enjoying the night with our friends, baby, and I'll try to refrain from jumping to any further conclusions, PLEASE?"

"Toni, I'll talk to you later. I'm gone. Can I have the keys to the car please, Taj?"

"Ahhh, well you forgot I was driving, huh? I'll give you the keys in a few. Stay and have some fun. I'll make it up to you!"

I got my purse and went and whispered to Toni, "Toni, let me sit in Zani's car because you didn't drive, did you?"

"Naw, I didn't, but Val, don't leave. Please?"

"I have to go. He gets on my nerves. You was standing here talking to Allen too, and you were flirting. Zani didn't come out here tripping, did he?"

"I got you girl, come on. We going to the ladies' room," she said to Zani, "I'mma try to get her to stick around. Y'all go ahead and play a game till we get back." So Toni and I walked toward the bathroom, and I exited out the door. When Toni realized I wasn't with her, she came outside too. It was about eight o'clock in mid-August, so the weather was pretty nice, and it wasn't dark yet, but the sun had set by now. I started walking down Grand toward River Road because I was about to be out of there. "Val, what are you doing? I know you not walking?"

"Toni, go back inside. Tell them I'm still in the bathroom and enjoy the rest of your night."

"Val, Tab is going to kill you for walking and leaving him when he finds out, but before he gets to you, he's going to kill me for letting you go by yourself! Are you kidding? Get back in here!"

"Bye, Toni."

"Well, let me get my stuff. Here I come."

"Toni, go back inside. You're going to draw attention to me if you go inside and get your stuff. Go back, I'll be fine." I kept walking, took my earphones out my purse, and started jamming to the beat. I tried to keep my mind off of things, mainly Taj. But I was really bothered by the fact that he has such double standards. He actually could TRIP about me having a conversation IN public, in front of him and our friends, but the stuff that him and OLD GIRL do BEHIND my back, I'm supposed to be cool with. If he could react like this in THIS type of situation, I can envision him really reacting (since as HE says, THIS was mild) and going off and truly CLOWNING on the most INNOCENT of conversations. I can't deal with this. He is going to have to do some serious changing because I don't know. I mean, I love him, I really do, but I am NOT going to deal with his insecurities like this.

I didn't get too far up River Road before I was accompanied by someone who came walking on the street side of me. It was Taj. I was so bothered and deep in thought and listening to the music that I didn't hear him walk up on me or anything. "What are you doing?" I asked him.

"What do you mean what am I doing? What are YOU doing?"

"I'm going home. Now what are you doing?"

"So you that mad at me that YOU don't want to ride with me, huh?"

I stopped walking and turned to him, "First of all Taj, I asked you for the keys to YOUR car which you wouldn't give me. I told you I was leaving! But just so you know, I AM really that mad at you! I'm really bothered by the fact that you have these double standards. Not to mention the fact that you don't trust me, you jump to conclusions, and you're insecure. It's okay for YOU to play house with what's her name, and y'all do whatever it is that y'all do and… You know what? Forget it, I'm done talking about it. It IS what it is! I need some air."

"Well, you can have all the air you want, but get the air you need once you get home. You came here with me, you going to leave here with me. Get in the car!"

I looked at him, and he had a stern look on his face whereas I knew he wasn't playing. Now the question was, was I THAT mad whereas I want to tempt him and make him enforce his manliness-ism? Or should I go along with him and not cause a ruckus? He probably sensed some rebellion inching up inside of me and said, "You already mad at me. I got nothing to lose. Test me, and this is going to be REAL ugly, Ms. Wilson. I parked right over here in this lot…after you." There was a Motel 6 or something right on the corner that I hadn't even noticed before, so being the person that I am and NOT wanting to make a scene out here, I headed into the lot, spotted his car, and walked over to it. I tried to get in, but it was locked, so I turned around and leaned my back on the door with my arms folded across my chest.

"Val, I have apologized to you already and I realize that you do have a point, and I want you to know that I didn't mean to mess up a perfectly good evening. Like YOU have some things to work on and…what's her name in Atlanta? Ronni? Yeah, Ronni helped you through some issues YOU were having, I got some things I need to work on."

My music was still playing in my ears, but I could hear him talking to me. Well, should I say, I got the gist of what he was saying. I guess he realized I was reading his lips, and he pulled the earphones out my ear and listened to see if music was playing and said, "So you not even listening to me?"

"Taj, I heard you."

So now I guess he was a little ticked off because he stopped talking, unlocked the door, waited for me to move off the door, opened it, waited for me to get in, and closed it behind me. He came around to his side and got in. He put the keys in the ignition but didn't start it right away. After a minute or two, I turned to look at him because I was thinking maybe I missed it and the car wouldn't start. "What's the problem?" I asked.

"Val, we need to talk. I understand that you are pissed off at me, and that's cool, but let me explain something to you. I hope you understand that it took a lot for me to come and walk beside you instead of picking yo' ass up when I spotted you and carrying you to the car and dumping yo' little ass in this truck. I had some real vicious thoughts going through my head. I thought about cuffing you, choking you—I mean…those were my initial thoughts. I had NO intention of walking beside you and ASKING you to get in the truck."

"You didn't ASK me to get in the truck."

"Well, compared to what I had in mind, that was asking. Don't do this again. You can get mad at me all you want to. You can even call yo'self done with me, if that's what you choose to do. But if you ride with me somewhere, then be prepared to ride back with me. Handle your anger in a different manner."

I didn't respond. I knew the man was serious, and I could only imagine him tossing me over his shoulder like a sack of potatoes or something and being choked or handcuffed—wow! My imagination wouldn't even take me there. I guess I really was going to have to adjust my thinking. I have jumped out the car with Kody a million and sixteen times. That man just let me go and went on home. Didn't make sure I was good or nothing. I mean, he scolded me the next day or something, and I knew what I had coming after the first time, but NEVER did I feel like, "Oops, I should not have done that" like Taj was making me feel. I'd have to keep this in mind. Was it worth being manhandled or treated like a criminal?

After my mind took me all those places (I imagined the outcome of a whole bunch of different scenarios, and none of them ended very nicely), I looked up, and we were sitting in front of my house. I didn't know how long we had been sitting here. Neither one of us said a word, I don't think. Well, I know I didn't say anything. I was too deep in thought, and if Taj said anything, I was in a whole other world. Again, I looked at him, and he looked so pitiful. I wanted to hug him and kiss him and tell him I forgive him; he is so absolutely adorable. I guess he had time to think on the way home, and his anger had turned back to sorrow.

He finally spoke, "Baby, should I let you get the air you needed now or can I come in?"

"That's up to you, Taj."

So he got out the car. I was still sitting there. He came around and opened the door for me. I took my time getting out the car, and by this time, it was just shy of being completely dark out here. He said, "You see how dark it is out here now? And that was in the car after driving. Imagine if you had still been walking? You wouldn't be close to home at this time. Ain't nothing nice about this world, Val. And I would NEVER forgive myself if I allowed you to walk and something happened to you." It had turned to a mellow moment for us.

And I wrecked the moment and lightened the mood and blurted out sarcastically, "So if it was broad daylight, then I could walk?"

Initially, he just glared at me with a smirk on his face, then he said, "Hayell naw!"

"I was just asking."

"Well, I just answered. Now get in the house, girl!"

"That sounds like a direct order, officer?"

"DIRECT order!"

"Yezzur!" There was no need in continuing on in that angry state because for one, it was hard for me to stay mad; and for two,

I was hoping and praying that SOMETHING spoke to him about his insecurities. Like I said, I was not one to wallow around in pity or to stay angry. I liked to make my point and be done with it. I was sure I'd see a change if for NO other reason than MY God being a GOOD God (ALL the time)! He'd help him to see the error of his ways and make some changes. Besides, he already acknowledged that he needed to work on this!

26

We went in the house, and naturally, the mood had shifted from both of us being angry and testy. Once we got in the house, he asked me for a hug. "Baby doll, can I have a hug?" I walked into his arms and looked up into his eyes, and he said, "I do apologize for this evening. Do you forgive me?"

Ooooooh, he makes me sick. He put that extra deep Barry White tone to his apology, which was so unfair. He knew that melted my heart. And if he took off this shirt and made his bosoms dance, I was a goner. And wouldn't you know it? He didn't take his shirt off, but with my face against his chest, he did make his pecs jump one at a time. So me playing hard to get took my arms from around him and put my hands on his chest, camouflaging it as if I were trying to push away from him. He held me tighter and asked again, deeper this time, "Baby doll, do you forgive me?"

I'm pretty sure I started perspiring. This man absolutely turned me on. And he was a cheater. He knew I couldn't handle it when he did this to me. Now who needed to cool off? "Yes, baby, I forgive you! And just so you know, you're forgiven, but it's definitely NOT forgotten! And only because I know you're going to work on that jealousy, right?"

"I'mma pray about it and ask the Lord to deliver me from that evil because I know me. And I know I can't work on a dam thing. Just thinking about some other dude talking to you, making you laugh, trying to get with you"—and he put his hands in my armpits and lifted me eye to eye to him and shook me—"I can't handle that! Now if I was knocking your back out from time to time, then I'm sure I could take it better, but since that's NOT the case and imagining somebody else rocking your world...whew! Let me pray about that right now."

He put me down and held my hands and started praying, "Dear heavenly Father, master and creator of every good and perfect gift, I want to thank You for sending Your Son, Jesus Christ, who sacrificed His life for a poor sinner like me. Lord, this beautiful specimen that is standing here before me drives me crazy. You know that. And I don't want to lose her due to MY insecurities Father. So I'm asking for divine intervention because without YOU I'm lost. I need you to soothe my loins and help me and the fellas to be patient and know that in good time, this woman right here WILL one day be my wife and the union of the two of us becoming ONE and me KNOWING my wife will truly be worth the wait.

"But until that time, I need for You to relax my spirit and help me NOT to react if and when I see her talking to another guy. I can't do it by myself, and You said ask for what you want, and I'm asking Lord. Thank You for the spirit of communication that You have given to both of us, and continue to strengthen that bond that we share. Stay in the forefront of our relationship, and we can't go wrong. I love You, Lord! In the Mighty name of Jesus, I pray, and we both say amen!"

"Ament! That's why I can forgive you because I know you want to do better. I love YOU, boo. And I'm not trying to get with nobody else."

"Baby, you're not who I'm worrying about. Here's the thing. Now suppose, just suppose—I don't want you tripping! But suppose Ms. Thing that lives in my house wanted to get with me? And suppose that she made up in her mind that she was going to have me regardless, even if she had to take it. Would that be feasible? Ain't NO way that little woman is going to overpower me and take my virginity [as your girl, Madea, would say it]. Now on the other hand, if some dude, let's just say the guy from today, what's his name?"

"Allen."

"Okay! Let's say that Allen had that same thought process, would he be able to overpower you and take what he wanted? Of course, you don't weigh a buck fifty. What you weigh, a hundred and forty pounds?"

"That's not your business, Taj."

"Oh, but it is. If the AVERAGE guy wanted to take what you got, it ain't a whole lot YOU could do about it. So my problem is not that I don't trust YOU, but I do know what guys think. Not ONLY because I'm a guy, but you have to remember, I deal with stuff like this on a regular. I am a POLICE Officer."

"Okay, with that being said, so now what? I shouldn't speak to anybody, huh? I should close down my business and what? Stay in the house now? Taj, we can't live life according to what could've, should've, would've, and might happen. If somebody wanted me bad enough and you were right there by my side, they could take YOU out or disable you and have their way with me. Where there's a will, there's a way. That's why it's so important to take God with us EVERYWHERE we go! Don't you understand that? If and when it's MY time to go, the Lord could take me right here, right now, IN your presence, and there is not ONE thing YOU or I could do about it.

"Think about it, Taj, all you need to do is be a presence. Come out the bathroom, come over to me, and let me introduce you. I'm going to introduce you AS my man and look at you. Unless somebody wants a HUGE fight on their hands, they're going to look the other way. Don't nobody want to tangle with a real live silverback."

"You're right! And I am going to work on it. 'I can do ALL things through Christ who strengthens me!'"

"That's what I'm talking about, bae!"

"I love you, girl."

"I love you more, boo. Now make Tom and Jerry dance for me again, please?"

Naturally, he was glad to jiggle his chest for me because he was glad we were at a good place. I could tell he knew that he messed up and was worried there for a minute, but now that we were good again, he raised his shirt up and gave me a good show. He flexed for me and everything. I'm glad my temperature rising didn't show like his because things were really happening to me. *Ooooh, let me go pee.*

27

After we sat around chilling for a little bit, we decided that the night was still young. It was close to 10:00 p.m., so we went and got some ice cream (I had to have my mint chocolate chip hot fudge sundae), and then we drove around downtown sightseeing for a little bit. We first went to Buckingham Fountain. We sat and watched for just a little while because old boy was parked illegally. We continued to drive around. Then he took me on an actual sightseeing tour.

We rode over by the spot where he brought me on our first date. There were a few people over there. I don't know if that's why we didn't get out or if it was because it was only a tour. He showed me where different famous people lived, like Oprah's building, where Derrick Rose used to live, and a few other people. He named a few athletes, but I didn't know these people, PLUS I didn't know if he was telling the truth or not. He had me cracking up talking about folks, so he could've been making this stuff up. They were pretty ritzy-looking buildings though.

He topped off the tour with a ride by President Obama's neighborhood. Naturally, we couldn't get too close to his house because of all the security, but I was inclined to believe that he may have been telling the truth about other folks too. Well, whether it was the truth or not, we had a good time.

As we were closing out the tour, Taj's brother texted him and asked him what he was doing. We were already pulled over, so we called him.

"What up, Jack?…"

"Naw, I'm not. I'm out with my girl Val… We just finished sightseeing, about to head back now… Val, Beavis said hi!"

"Hi, Jackson, how are you?" I chimed in.

"He said he's good. He said they're over Mom and Dad's about to watch a movie and wants to know if we want to come."

"Taj, it's late. I'm not going over your parents' house this time of night."

"Yeah, JC, We'll be there. Let me run her by her place so she can grab her toothbrush, and we'll be on our way…"

"You know what? YOU are absolutely terrible! I don't have a say in this at all, huh?"

"Sure you do, baby doll, but I'll tell you what your say is, kay booger?"

"Wow! I'm telling."

"Who you going to tell?"

"Yo Momma!"

"Watcha self, girl!" And he cut me a look. "Okay, so for real, is there a problem? What you have to do in the morning?"

"Wake up and brush my teeth, shower, eat—"

"So far, you haven't said anything that you can't do at Shirley and Canton's house."

"So you don't think it's rude to go over there this time of night?"

"Girl, if I know my parents like I do, Momma and Daddy probably already had a nap and are in the theater room waiting on us. Somebody is fixing popcorn, they got the cooler all set up with the drinks in it, they've already decided on a movie, and the spare rooms are made up and ready to go. And knowing my Momma, she probably already put those little chocolate mints on the pillows. So now if that's your ONLY dilemma, you're going to be spending the night in Bolingbrook tonight!"

"Yeah, okay. I got something for you."

"Oh, so then I guess we're going to be at your house a little longer than expected, huh? It won't take me that long. Cool!"

"What won't take you that long?"

"You said you got something for me. I thought we were going to wait till we get married, but I guess we can expedite this process. Seeing as though you ARE going to be my wife."

"Boy, you are full of jokes tonight. That was soooo funny I forgot to laugh."

"Oh, that's not what you were talking about?"

"Only in your dreams."

"Yeah, well, I've had a few of those. You the one missing out."

"I guess I'm just going to be that one then."

"Oh well, suit yourself."

"I shall."

"Cool, do it then."

"I will!"

We continued arguing like that pretty much all the way to my house. We so silly. When we pulled up to the house, he said, "I'm going to come in with you to make sure we speed this process along."

"Not necessary, boo. I got this. Don't we need to stop by your house to get your toothbrush because I know that dragon be HUMMING in the a.m.?"

"No ma'am, I am going to MY Mommy's house. Everything I need is already there. I keep a spare. Never know when I may need it."

"Alrighty then." As soon as we got in the door, Taj threw me over his shoulder like a sack of potatoes and first started walking around the house like he was looking for something. "Taj, what are you doing? Put me down, please."

He said, "First of all, this is how I'm going to do you if you ever try to walk out on me again. That's the first thing. Secondly, I want to know what you got for me. I have a feeling you're going to show out when we get to Shirley's house." He started spinning around with me still on his shoulder. "You ready to talk or shall the torture begin?"

"Taj, please?"

"I'll take that as a no." So he spun me around till he got to my room and dropped me down on my bed. As you could imagine, I was somewhat turned around, the room still spinning and all. While I was trying to gather my faculties together, he pinned my right arm beneath himself, pulled my left arm over my head, and was holding it at the elbow, and his leg was across mine. He had his right hand in the air, ready to attack my armpit, I guess. I was very vulnerable at that point, so wherever the attack was coming was not going to be good, I'm sure. He first started very gently tickling my neck. "You ready or as YOU say, you RET to talk? And please, don't give in too fast. I would like for this to last for a while."

"Boo, I wasn't talking about nothing in particular."

"Good! That's the answer I was expecting." At this point, he started tickling me all over—my underarms, my side, my neck. It was a complete disaster for me. Pandemonium, I tell you!

I begged and pleaded with him as much as I was able to talk. "Baby, please. Okay, okay, okaaaaayyyy!"

"Think about this very carefully, baby, and if you need to, you better make something up that sounds really believable to me or else I'm not stopping till you pee because I know you got to."

"Okay, baby, please let me catch my breath."

"You mustered enough air to say that. You got ten seconds. Ten, nine, eight, seven, six—"

"Okay, and this is the truth! I was going to tell your Mom on you for how you acted tonight with my client, Allen, so there. Scouts honor."

"I believe you."

"Thank the Lord! So will you get up then?"

"Well, hol, hol, hold up just a minute there, little lady. Now the penalty for tattling on me is slightly harsher than what you just received."

"Baby, but I didn't tattle on you."

"Yeah, but you were going to."

"Sweetheart, I hadn't made up my mind what I was going to do yet. It was merely a precautionary warning to you."

"Yeah, well, I don't take too kindly to precautionary warnings."

"Baby, I learned my lesson. I promise, my lips are sealed. Please forgive me for the mere thought of telling on you. I'm healed."

"Yeah, but there's nothing like the actuality of being tortured to teach one a lesson for futuristic measures."

"Baby, now I forgave you for your thoughts and your behavior with a CLIENT of mines earlier today. You can't find it in your heart to forgive me for MY thoughts? I really don't want to change my clothes, and I do need to pee, BAD! And we need to go before it gets too late, please, baby!"

"Oh yeah, I forgot about that. Maybe just a brief torture?"

"You going to make me pee, and I'mma have to shower before we go, then it's going to be REAL late."

"Okay! Get your stuff, I'm out front." He gave me a kiss, then got up and sat on the bed. As soon as he cleared me, I jumped up to run to the bathroom, and he grabbed me as I tried to skeet past him. "Baby doll, if I need to, you know I'll torture you AT my Momma's house, right?"

"Baby, please! I said I was good. Trust me!"

He had his arms around me as he was talking, so I gave him a nice kiss for reassurance, and he said, "Okay!" and let me go and then popped me on the buttocks as I passed by him. He is such a bully, just because he's bigger than me. I'll find a way to pay him back, though.

28

I got my stuff together, and we headed to the "in-laws'" place. I should stop playing like that, shouldn't I? We headed to Mr. and Mrs. Bryant's house for movie night. I didn't know how good I was going to be watching a movie. I was already ret to hit the hay. This big bully had drained all the energy from me. So if I did go to sleep, I was going to blame him.

When we got there, everybody was there; everybody but Shayna. We ran into the two girls, Dee Dee and Tedi, in the kitchen first. They said Shayna was out of town with some friends for the weekend. They also told us that Jack and Duss were around there somewhere, and Mom and Dad were in the theater room. We walked into the theater room, and before Taj could say hi, he started clowning his parents. "Uh-uh, Canton, you know that's my seat, and Shirley Lynn, where's my girl going to sit if you in her seat?"

His Dad got up immediately and yelled, "JC and Fred, y'all get in here and help me take down this intruder. I would handle it myself, but I don't want to upset your Mother. You know how she gets."

Mom stood up and came over to me as if nothing else was going on. We hugged, and she said, "Valeri. How are you, honey? Glad you two could make it."

"Hey, Mrs. Bryant, I'm good, thanks. How are you?"

"Baby, I'm fine. Had my nap earlier, and I'm ready to enjoy a good movie."

"Well, I hope our timing is okay with you. I thought it might be a little too late to be coming by to watch a movie."

"Ooooh, I was right. I told Canton that you weren't going to feel comfortable coming over here this time of night. Sweetie, it's fine. If EVER you need to or just want to come by, YOU ARE ALWAYS welcome. We got plenty of room here, and if you don't feel like driving home, then let me know, and the guest room will be ready for you."

"Thank you, Mrs. Bryant, I'll keep that in mind." In the meantime, the guys flew past me and Mrs. Bryant and had Taj surrounded and were about to throw down. "You really going to let them fight?"

"Child, they do this all the time, and as long as they don't hurt their Dad, then I'm okay. Usually, my husband fights by himself, and Jackson will join in after Taj is down. I guess with YOU being here, Canton wants to make sure they GET him down! Taj MAY want to put up some resistance. Show off a little bit."

"Dude, you don't come in here, disrespecting my father. Not sure what you did, but I'm sure it wasn't good," was how Jackson brought himself into the equation.

I called Taj's name to tell him to behave, and when he looked at me, Duss went for his legs, and Jackson leaped at him up top, and Taj was down. Oops! My bad! That wasn't my intention, but oh well. He wasn't putting up too big of a fight. I don't know if that was because they hurt him or his pride was broken or he didn't want to hurt anybody, but once he was down, Daddy pounced on him and began with the body shots. Not too hard, though.

Mr. Bryant called out to me, "Val, sweetie, come here, please."

I ran over to them, thinking somebody was hurt, and he said, "Here, honey, we got him down for you. I know you want a couple good licks off old boy, don't you? Well, let him have it."

Ooooh, the thoughts that were going through my head! He did deserve a few good licks. How did Pops know? I bent down to him, not realizing he was looking dead at me, giving me that squinty eye look. Just as I was drawing back, Taj said, "This I gotta see. Come on, baby, give me a good lick."

I caught a glimpse of his face at that point and thought about the torture that he promised me if I showed out over here, and I said, "Y'all ain't bout to get ME killed. Y'all better let that man go, he crazy!"

199

Jackson said, "So you got the little lady scared, huh?" And gave him two nice shots to his chest. I must say, he didn't hold back too much. It seemed like they hurt.

"JC, you know I'm going to kill you, right?"

"What are you talking about? Those were from Val."

"Yeah, okay. She knows better. I got you, though."

Just then, Duss gave him two thigh shots. "Compliments of the little lady, Tab."

"Butthead, you just signed YOUR life over to me too."

"Well, let's see what's in store for me," Pops said, and he slapped him around a little bit. You could tell he didn't hit him hard, but it sounded like he did.

"Canton, you know you wrong for that, but I'll find somebody to take those out on. You got a couple more stored up in you some-where so that I could add on to Beavis and Butthead's whooping they got coming?"

"Naw, I'm good. That'll learn ya!"

"Well, y'all ready to end these shenanigans?"

"Ready when you are, big bruh," Jackson said, and everybody got a good grip on him.

I guess that was his sign that he was getting up.

"Pops, I don't want to hurt you, so you may want to get up because I'm getting up RIGHT now!"

"I wanna see this. Go for it, my boy!"

Taj arched his back and sat straight up, knocking his dad over who was sitting on his abs. Jackson had let go of his upper body and was heading to the door. Duss was still holding on to his legs, which gave him the leverage he needed to sit up. When Duss saw Jackson take off, he headed toward the door right behind him. "Hey, where y'all going? The party is just getting started!"

He stood up and helped his Dad to his feet, and they hugged. "Hey there, fella, glad you could make it."

"My pleasure, Pops. Glad to see that you still got it."

"And you know it."

I was still standing fairly close to them from when Pops called me over, and Taj turned to me and said, "You ret, little lady?"

"Ready for what?" I said reservedly.

Pops stepped in front of Taj and said to me, "Did you have a hug for the old man, little lady?"

So I gave him a hug and said, "Of course I do. Taj didn't hurt you, did he?"

"Naw, I'm good. He knows better." He kept his arm around me.

"I know he does!" And I kept my arm around him.

"Uh-uh, don't hold on to the old man! You got a little something coming from me, baby doll!" He started pulling me away from Pops.

"Baby, what are you talking about? I didn't do nothing."

"Taj, you better have some love for that girl, and THAT'S IT!" Pops said to Taj.

"Oh, I got NOTHING but love for her." I was in a tug-of-war at this time.

"Baby, you know I know better. I was trying to help you, Ike."

Mom came over to us at this time and popped Taj on the butt, "So you been in MY house for fifteen minutes now and haven't spoken to me yet? I know YOU know better."

"Hey, Momma! The number one lady in my life, how are you?" He let me go and gave his Mom a big hug.

"Don't hand me that. We ALL know who the 'NUMBER ONE' lady in your life is right about now. Momma don't hear from YOU half the time I used to before Ms. Val came around. And I'm not mad at you. Just stating the facts!"

"Nobody could ever replace that number one status that YOU got, Momma!" and he started kissing her on her neck, making her squirm and squeal. "This girl trying to keep me on lockdown, that's all. She knows you're numero uno!"

"Taj STOP!" she said.

"Mrs. Bryant, believe me, I know. Because he knows he'll never replace MY MOMMA'S status. The difference is, I either call or see my Momma pretty much every day."

"Oh, is that so?" And she gave Taj a dirty look.

"Momma, let me inform you that I'mma beat Ms. Val up here in YO house before the night ends."

"YOU will do NO such thing." Mom and Dad were standing in front of me, letting Taj know they weren't having that. Taj's dad was in his boxing stance, and Mom was spanking Taj's hands. Mom continued with, "Why Taj? Why you going to beat her up? Because she calls or sees her Mom every day? All YOU got to do is follow her lead. You can call and check in with me on a regular. You don't have to come see me. I know we don't live right next door to you."

"That's not why she going to get it. She knows why."

"Believe me, Ma, I don't have a clue what he's talking about, but I'll make sure he calls you regularly."

"Thank you sweetie, I know you will. See baby? That's all I want. Just let me hear your voice regularly. You're a police officer. Anything could happen to you on that job, and at least if I hear your voice, I can relax a little bit. You keep me on my knees praying for you, but if I heard from you, it wouldn't be a prayer of worry."

"You're right, Mrs. Bryant. We both going to do better, right baby?" I said to him.

Taj was standing over there, looking at me, biting his lip, which I knew wasn't a good sign, but when Mom looked up at him, he jumped in really quick with, "Yup baby doll, we BOTH going to do better, huh?" but I could tell that BOTH had double meanings. I think I messed up.

Taj hugged his Mom again (squinting his eyes at me the whole time and threw me a quick fist), then whispered in her ear, "I got you, Mom. You ARE still my number one girl! Love you, Lade!"

She patted his back and said, "I know you do, and don't you mess with that girl!"

"Please, Ma?"

"NO! I like her. But if you want to beat somebody up, you can go find that last girl you had and give her a whack for me. What was her name? Sabrina?"

"All right, let's change the subject. Ain't it time for the movie?"

"Uh-huh! Now you want to change the subject."

Taj let go of Mom and skeeted around her toward the door and yelled out, "MOVIE TIME. Bring it on!"

Daddy cosigned with Taj and whistled for everybody to get in here and everybody came running.

It was now after twelve-thirty. Taj took me by the hand and brought me to the back of the room. The room had about fifteen reclining leather seats in it with one reclining loveseat right in the back, which was the seat Taj and I claimed. There were three wide stairs like at the show and plenty of room to bring in other chairs or have people sit on pillows if they wanted to have a real live movie night. I already had plans in my mind of getting both families together to do a MAJOR movie night. *When I grow up, I'mma want a room like this in MY house.* Taj asked, "What are we watching?"

Jackson said, "We got a movie in honor of the old people here, so we're watching *Red*."

"Y'all going to stop talking about ya Momma. I done told y'all. Jackson, don't have me sic the fellas on YOU!"

I see now that Mr. Bryant was really serious about not being old, and I was in total agreement with him. You're only as old as YOU think and feel, and he thought he was a spring chicken. *I'mma be like him when I grow up.*

After a good laugh, we grabbed our snack trays (everybody fixed their own tray—we had popcorn, nachos with all the fixings [meaning sour cream, olives, ground beef, jalapeños, and cheese], and different kinds of candy, juice, pop, or bottled water; I felt like I was at the show with the exception of paying an astronomical fee for all this). When everybody was all set, we dimmed the lights and started the movie. I was glad we were watching this movie. I had never seen it before, and I was thinking I may be able to stay woke. I heard it was really good.

29

So there; we watched the movie, and I thought it was all right. It wasn't what I had expected, but I enjoyed it and was able to stay awake. Mr. and Mrs. Bryant seemed to like it too. But when I looked over at old boy (Taj), he had the nerve to be sleeping. I didn't expect that at all. I guess that wrestling stunt actually worked him over.

"Uh, Shorty, you may want to finish that in the bed. It's night-night time!" I said nudging him.

He woke up and said, "Dang, the movie went off? What happened at the end?"

"Man, I'm going to bed. You'll have to talk to somebody else about that."

Mrs. Bryant came over and said, "Well, that was a pretty decent movie. Did you enjoy it, baby?"

I opened my mouth to answer, but before I could say anything, Taj said, "Yeah Mom, I enjoyed it. Thanks for asking, though. I did miss the very end. What happened?"

"Boy, ain't nobody talking to you. I was talking to Valeri. Baby, how did YOU enjoy the movie?"

Taj put his hand over my mouth and replied once again, "Mom, I told you I liked it. You going to tell me what happened at the end?"

"Boy, get your hands off her mouth. We don't know where your hands have been." Mom pulled at his hands. "Don't have me call your brother over here. They already beat you up once tonight."

"Now Mom, that's bogus! You know them boys ain't do nothing to me. Go ahead, call 'em." In the meantime, he got up off the couch and started toward Jack.

Mom grabbed him by the wrist and told him, "Show our guest to YOUR old room, PLEASE!"

"And now you giving away MY room? Where am I supposed to sleep? Oh, I get it. You're giving me the okay to stay in the room with my girl. Atta girl, Lade" And he kissed her on the forehead and overexaggerated a wink.

"Your room has the bathroom in it. Don't want to put her through running into anybody first thing in the morning. Plus, you're a grown man, you do what you want to do. Momma knows YOU ain't no angel!"

I interjected, "Mom—oops, I mean, Mrs. Bryant, he knows the deal. He can stay in there if he wants to, but ain't NOTHING happening."

"I do, huh?"

"Don't play. You heard me. You can stay in there if you want to as long as—"

"As long as what, Tab?" Jackson came over, instigating. "Mmm-hmmm, you want to explain that? Naw, it's cool. I got it. I think we ALL got it. Look at MY big bruh. You setting a good example for me, bruh." He patted Taj on the shoulder, adding fuel to the fire, getting Taj all riled up.

"I owe YOU a butt-whooping anyway, don't I?" And Taj lunged at Jack and had him in a head lock before anybody could intercept him.

"Taj, leave Jack alone, and show me to your room like yo' Momma said. PLEASE!"

By this time, Dad was over here. "Taj, kill your brother in the morning, son. It's late for all this noise, and I'm going to bed. Plus, this sweet little lady right here has spoken. Don't make her have to get ugly out here because when she gets ugly, that's going to get ME riled."

"Listen to your pops, Tab," Jackson said, hoping to be free from Taj's grip.

"Tomorrow dude. Don't think you got off easy," Taj said, giving Jacks neck one last squeeze before he let him go. "C'mon, baby girl.

Let me get you settled in." He popped Jack on the back of the neck as we passed by.

"So you're not just a bully to me, huh? You know, one day, me, Jack, and Duss are going to jack you up." I mumbled the last part of that sentence.

I guess he didn't hear me too good. "What was that, bae?"

"Nothing, I was talking to Jackson. GOODNIGHT ALL!" I said.

He grabbed me by the hand and walked me to his room. Jackson yelled to him, "You better watch how you grabbing on my girl, boy!"

I knew Taj was about to turn around and head back after Jack, so I got a good grip on his hand and stuffed it under my arm and kept going. "Taj, I don't know which room is YOUR old room, so please keep walking. I'm tired, lovebug."

"Don't you need your bag?"

"Can't you take me to the room first and then get it for me, PLEASE?"

"Gotcha, baby doll!"

We went to his room. It was nice and roomy. There was a couch in there along with a queen-sized bed and still had plenty of space. There was a fifty-inch flat screen TV on the wall. The color scheme was blue and lime green, so the bathroom was lime green and blue, which I thought was really cute. "I know you didn't decorate this room. It is WAY too cute."

"How you going to act? You know your man has taste."

"Of course you do. You picked me, didn't you? But YOUR place has no similarity to the décor in this room. You can try to claim the credit for it, but you will NEVER get me to believe YOU did this. Sorry, babe!"

"Well, it didn't look like this when it was MY room. But I have these same type of visions for my place."

"Riiiiiiiiight! Go get my bag, please, so I can put my jammies on."

He came over and wrapped his pythons around me and squeezed me and said, "You really don't have to wear any if you don't want to."

He whispered in my ear, "There's a lock on the door." And he gave me a devilish laugh like Bernie Mac's nephew.

"Behave yourself, Taj. Even if I was giving it up, it would NEVER happen HERE unless we were married sweet pea, so don't get ANY ideas!"

"Rats! I'll be right back."

"And don't mess with anybody on the way, especially if you run into Jack or Duss. Behave yourself!"

"Yes, Mother."

When he came back to bring me my bag, he had on gym shorts and a wifebeater. *Dang, this man is adorable, and he's all mine. Thank You, Lord!* He laid across the bed and cut the TV on and turned to that MMA stuff (*Ultimate Fighter* or something). "Now see, that's why you always want to fight somebody. You definitely shouldn't be watching this stuff."

"You know I could do this, right? I was a state finalist in high school wrestling, and I got belts in Tae Kwon Do."

"I got belts that were made in Japan too. The closest YOU going to get to that MMA stuff is what YOU and Jack and 'em do. Give it up, bruh."

"Bring yo rump over here so I can put you in the rear naked choke. Never mind the choke. I just want to put you in the rear, naked, ha ha ha." We both began to laugh.

I stopped laughing abruptly and said, "Get out! You can't behave yourself for nothing, huh? Go, head on before I call your Dad in here."

"You like acting up. I should put you in the kimura. Come here."

"Babe, please, I'm going to sleep. First, promise me you won't make me yell or nothing here at your parents' house. I'm serious, promise me you WON'T beat me up here. Promise!"

"I'm not promising you that. You like to act up."

"Baby, I'm not going to act up till we get home."

"Home, huh?"

"That's not what I meant."

"I think it is, but if you behave here, I'll behave here. Deal?"

"Works for me. Now get out."

"See, you can't behave for nothing, can you?"

"I was just playing love, but if you staying in here for a while, could you move over, please?" And I got in the bed. That man is such a smart a—, but since I'm not a swearer, I'll say he's such a smart butt. He moved over all right, but toward me, not away from me, and he laid his python across my neck, trying to kill me. "Can I breathe please sugar plum?"

"Oh, sorry! I didn't think you wanted to."

"Yup, happens to be a necessity. Night night, sweetie," and I got comfy, snuggling my behind all up to him, facing away from him, of course.

He politely turned me around to face him and planted soft sweet kisses on me, starting at my shoulders, and worked his way up to my lips. "Goodnight, ladybug." Then he passionately whispered in my ear, "Baby, I love—" He paused, and I looked into his eyes, knowing he was about to get mushy on me. He finished that thought with, "Watching *Ultimate Fighting*. I'll leave when it goes off." He had stopped whispering and turned me back around (away from him) as he finished his thought.

"And you call me bad. You the one they ought to call 'Cain't get right,' but in YOUR case, it should be 'Ain't gone do right.' Love you too, Tab. Goodnight."

"Shhhhhhhh! I cain't hear," he said, smacking my tush at the same time as he moved himself away from me, I guess so he could concentrate on that fighting stuff. I closed my eyes, and next thing I know, I was sleep.

30

When I woke up the next morning, that big brute was laying in the bed next to me. He was still on top of the covers in the same position he had been in when I went to sleep. The TV was still on, and I know he was going to have some kind of crook in his neck when he woke up. It was almost nine o'clock, which was late for me. I got up, went in the bathroom so I could do my essentials, which includes reading my scripture for the day and doing my devotion. I could hear stirring throughout the house, so I'm sure everyone else was up too. I started my bathwater running and came out to get my clothes and toiletries, and old boy was sitting up on the bed.

"You planning to hog the bathroom? Or can I go handle some business?"

"Well, good mornTing to you too, sleepyhead."

"Oh yeah, good mornTing baby doll."

"How much time did YOU need in there? My water is running, and I don't want it to get cold."

"Dang, is this what I have to look forward to when we get married?"

"It would be nice to have a master bath so that you could do YOUR thing and I could do mine. Just keep that in mind when you buy me a house, big boy."

"Can I brush my teeth, love?"

"By ALL MEANS, PLEASE do, and kind of cover your mouth as you walk past me. Don't want to unleash THAT dragon."

"Ha ha! You so funny I forgot to laugh. Let me inform you that I learned some moves that appear to be excruciating to the person being moved upon. YOU keep THAT in mind."

"Gotcha sweetness, take ya time."

"I thought you'd see it my way."

"Can you cut my water off for me while you're in there, please?"

"My pleasure, baby girl."

This man didn't need any MMA moves to put a hurting on anyone, and I promise I was NOT in the mood to be begging and pleading for him to stop abusing me here at his parents' home, even though I knew it was all in fun. I don't mind being checked and reminded who the boss was (or should I say, who THOUGHT they were the boss) from time to time. It kind of turned me on, and I would hate to have a wuss as a man! But right now, I would rather it be a verbal reminder as opposed to a physical one, and it appeared as though he and his brothers' relationship had him in a fighting mood. Obviously, this was how they grew up because it didn't faze his Momma at all, but GOOD GRAVY! Was I going to have to deal with this with my kids when I had some? I don't know how his Momma does it because their Dad is as big a kid as those other two. I believe I'm going to be on my best behavior from here on out, but it's so hard.

Anyhoo, he spent a good five to seven minutes in the bathroom. I read a little further in my Bible while I waited. It was always good to be able to get into the Word, and it helped relax that spirit that was in me that wanted to remind my boo that I was a grown woman. *I say what I want to say.* So by the time he came out the bathroom, I was very docile, meek, and humble. I walked up to him and hugged him. He bent down to me, and I did him like he did me last night, starting at his shoulders, then I kissed his neck (as he bent down for me), then sucked his earlobe a little bit (which drives him crazy, and I wasn't trying to get him riled, so that was VERY brief), kissed his chin, then his cheek, and said, "Good mornting, lover boy."

He gave me a very sweet and gentle kiss on the lips and said, "Good mornting, sweetie pie," and hugged me real tight and said, "Girl, I love you… Will you marry me?"

I started squirming. The man done gone and made me nervous. I'm sure he was just playing, but I needed for him to let me go right now. "Taj, stop playing."

He looked square into my eyes and said with a straight face, "Val, will you marry me?"

"Baby, you really need to quit playing and think about what you're saying. Let me go so I can finish up what I started in that bathroom." I couldn't tell, but I think I may have hurt his feelings. His grip started gradually loosening, and he never took his eyes off mine, and as he was letting me go, he kissed me again. He didn't say a word, just let me go and walked over to the bed. Oh my gosh! What am I supposed to do? I need to call Toni or Ronni. I need to talk to somebody QUICK!

I went into the bathroom and sat on the toilet seat and looked up to the ceiling. *I have to talk to somebody quick! One of my girls... Jesus... SOMEBODY! Dang!* I couldn't call anybody right now. I left my phone by the bed. Don't get me wrong, the Lord was the best one to talk to, but I needed an answer from somebody with the quickness, and the Lord takes His time responding for the most part. *Lord, Lord, Lord, whew! Where do I start? Okay, so, God, You know that Taj just proposed to me, right? I mean, first of all, I don't think he was serious, was he? I think he got caught up in the moment and went with his emotions. But Lord, why? Men don't get caught up in their emotions like that, do they? That's our job. Okay, so what now? Naturally, ME, I want to say yes and tell him he can't take it back. You said it, now deal with it (Black, black, no change back! You shouldn't play so much!). Then again, I want to say no. Am I ready for that? It's only been four months. Do I really know him? On the other hand, how long are we going to be able to refrain from doing the do? I just want to be pleasing to You, Lord. And secondly, You never gave ME any confirmation on my response to that question if I was ever asked.*

And after he thinks about what he said and stops playing, is he going to retract his question? And did HE get the okay from You to even ask me that? But he couldn't have been serious, right Lord? Lord, I've got so much stuff going through my head right now, am I making any sense? All right, all right, breathe, Val (WOOOOOOOOOSAAAAAHHHHHH). Okay... I'm going to take it slow because You haven't given me the okay to say yes to that question, right, Lord? Lord, calm my spirit, and You take the lead. Whichever direction You direct me in, that's the way I'm going. Can You give me a hint of what I'm going to say when I go back out there though? Be patient, okay. Gotcha! Breeeeeeeeeeeeathe! Okay, okay (whoooooooooooooooo), I'm breathing and I'm relaxed, and I'm getting in this tub. Thank You, Lord! Love you! In Jesus's name. Amen!

I got in the tub, and the bubbles relaxed my spirit and soothed my soul. *Aaaaaaah! Feels soooo good!* So I soaked in the tub for a good fifteen to twenty minutes before I washed up. I cleared my mind of ALL outside forces and began to meditate on the goodness of the Lord. I got my health and strength, my Momma's doing well. Everybody else in my family was good. Praise God! I forgot about everything and everybody else and relaxed. I used some orange ginger bath and Body Works body wash and lotion, which is supposed to energize you, and I felt absolutely cleaned and energized when I got out the tub. I left my clothes in the room in the sheer panic of a proposal, so I peeked out into the room, and the room was empty. So I locked the door, grabbed my clothes, and dressed really quick.

I put on a smidgeon of makeup and went out to see what was going on with everybody else. The girls pretty much had breakfast finished. Mom, Dee Dee, and Tedi were all on it. They had pancakes, eggs, grits, hash browns, bacon, and sausages all prepared. "Good morning, Val," Mom said, "how did you sleep?"

"Good morning, Mom, Dee Dee, Tedi. I'm sorry, Mrs. Bryant, do you mind it if I call you Mom. To me, it's a sign of respect. Believe me, I'm not trying to be disrespectful or something that I'm not."

"Baby, its fine. If YOU don't have a problem with it, I don't have a problem with it. I think I know your intentions."

"Well thanks, and I slept great. I don't remember a thing once I closed my eyes till this morning. Is there anything, I can help with?"

Tedi greeted me with, "Heeeey girl, hey! You can get the glasses out the cabinet and get some plates. Mom, we letting everybody come in here or do we have to set the table?"

"Naw, everybody is home folks. They can come in here and fix their plates and go to the family room or wherever to eat. Dee Dee, go see what the guys are doing, and tell them to come in for the blessing. See where your Daddy is too."

"Yes ma'am, I'm on it. Morning Val."

Taj was in the room with Jack and Duss. They were talking, I guess. I didn't even know they talked at all. All I'd ever seen them do was wrestle. But when they came in to eat, Taj had his arm around Jack's neck, and they seemed like they were engaged in actual conversation. "Good morning, ladies." All three of the guys gave their greeting when they came in, and Jack said, "Mom, where's the big guy?"

"Dee Dee just went to check on him."

"Moaning, moaning, moaning, everybody!" Dad said as he stepped into the kitchen.

"Mom, Daddy was out in the garage. That's where I found him."

"Honey, what were you doing in the garage?"

"Well, I already watered the garden and the grass and was about to check your car to see what that noise is that it's been making lately. But I was saved by one of the most beautifullest girls in the world. Thanks, baby!"

"Thanks, Daddy!"

"Well, you were the beautiful messenger, but you got your direct orders from the little lady of the house who is the MOST beautifullest girl in the world. All the rest of y'all are a short second place to ya Momma."

The guys started chiming in, acting like they were toasting each other, "Here, here!"

Daddy blessed the food, and we ate.

After we finished eating, the guys gathered up the dishes and actually cleaned the kitchen, which had me in sheer and utter disbelief. Now THERE was a major difference between my people and his. I don't think a guy has washed a dish in my family since I was a teenager. Shazam! Mom already told everybody not to go anywhere. We had to watch one more movie before we were released from the Bryant household. I was still in the kitchen with the guys, trying to offer my assistance before they finally kicked me out and told me to go find Tedi if I didn't have anything else to do. So I found my way to the theater room where Tedi and Dee were vacuuming and getting everything straight for the next movie. They refused to let me help and told me to enjoy my time as a guest because the next time I come, I wouldn't be considered a guest, and they would expect me to pitch in, which I don't have a problem with that. That was the same rule that applied at Mommy's house. Besides, my parents always told me to be prepared to carry my own weight. *Don't sit back and have people do for you all the time.*

Therefore, I don't believe someone should have to do all the cooking and cleaning too. So if you assist with the cooking, it should be a whole different crew for cleanup. And, generally, it's enough people around where the cleanup can be wiped out in no time if everybody pitched in a little bit. So I sat back and relaxed and got ready for the next movie.

The guys finished up and met us in the theater room around eleven fifteen-ish. Naturally, Taj came in there, talking much smack. "Tedi, you had my girl in here doing the cleaning? You know Momma don't play that."

"Taj, hush. Val didn't do one thing as far as the cleanup is concerned. Look here, we know that's your girl and all, but don't get me and Tedi on your bad side. You know we ALWAYS got yo' back. You want to change that now?" was Dee Dee's response to Taj.

Tedi didn't even get a chance to say anything, but I guess she didn't have to.

Tedi nodded and said, "So there, hmmmm!"

So Taj turned to me. "Bae, you in here being lazy? I know I taught you better than that."

Again Dee Dee spoke up, "Tab, what's wrong with you? Val came in and offered her assistance, and we told her next time. She's a guest right now. You want to try and come at us with something else, big boy?"

This time, it was my turn, so I nodded and said, "So there, hmmmm!" We all were quite amused by that.

Then Tedi said, "Val, I hope he doesn't beat up on you like he's done the rest of us. He is such a bully. Taj, you know I love you and I know I didn't get it as bad as the others, mainly because I tried to stay out your way and be on YOUR side, but I see you haven't grown out of that, huh? I know you, JC, and Duss ain't never going to stop acting crazy, but I need to know, do you still think you run everything and can always beat up on everybody?"

Taj got up from where he was sitting (with his leg propped all up on the arm of the chair) and said, "Well come on Sissy (which is what he called Tedi), let me show you some moves I learned on UFC last night. Then you should be able to answer that question yourself."

"Naw, naw, naw Tab, I was just asking. And I think I already got my answer. Val, I feel sorry for you, girl. And you really LIKE him?"

"Now you did it!" Taj jumped over the chair and was upon his sister before anybody could do anything. That boy is quick!

He was about to put her in the fireman's carry (if you don't know what the fireman's carry is, he would grab her right hand in his left, stick his right arm between her legs, and hoist her in the air across his shoulders) when I called out to him, "Taj Alexander Bryant, leave your sister alone and come sit with me, please!"

"But, bae—"

"Taj!"

"But I just want to—"

"NO!" And I went over to where he was and grabbed him by the hand and said, "Come sit over here with me, boo."

Tedi was very grateful for my intervention. "Whew, saved by the NEW and IMPROVED girlfriend! Thanks, Val."

Taj gave Tedi a hug and asked her if she forgave him. "Sorry, y'all, but I feel like a kid in the candy store. I'm really happy, and God is good! I'm here with my family, my parents are doing well, and my girl is right here by my side. What more can I ask for?"

"I feel you, baby. God is good all the time!" I said.

"HALLELUYER! We getting ready to have some chutch up in here? Should I go get Mom and Dad?" Jackson asked. We all laughed at him. That boy is silly.

"I'll put it to you like this: the Lord revealed a little something something to me that got me a little excited, that's all."

"Dang Tab, the Lord talks to you like that? I didn't even think he knew your name." We all were tickled and really giddy at this point, and EVERYTHING was making us laugh, so when Duss said THIS, we were over the top; his facial expressions and body language were hilarious. I'm learning that all the crew over here are comedians.

"Well, I guess He does know my name. The real question is, does He know yours, Butthead?"

Mom and Dad came into the room which settled everybody down a little. "What's going on in here? I could hear y'all all the way from my room," Mom said.

"Momma you know yo kids don't have no sense. Jack, get out of my Momma's seat. What we watching, Lade?" Taj asked.

"Ya Momma got us watching a chick flick. But I heard it was pretty good. It's called *Jumping the Broom*," Daddy said. "Let's get this party started."

Everybody got into their movie positions, killed the lights, and got the movie started.

31

I absolutely loved the movie. It had such a good message to it with an unusual twist. We sat around, discussing it a little once it went off, and everybody pretty much had similar sentiments. I know one thing: Loretta Devine was a HOT mess. That's all I'm going to say about it, except that it was confirmation on MY behalf that I made a good decision.

Taj and I left shortly after we watched the movie. I guess we kind of set the mood because once we decided to leave, then everybody else decided to leave as well. Mrs. Bryant wasn't ready for our time together to end. She was trying to get a board game started. It was either Monopoly or Life, but I didn't want to wear out my welcome and was ready to get home, so Taj and I were definitely out of there. I mean, it was fun while it lasted, but I wanted to leave on a good note.

We said our goodbyes, and I thought that Taj and Jackson had grown up a little and were going to be able to part without incident, but when I went to Taj's old room to make sure I had grabbed all my stuff, they were back at it—Taj had Jack in the MMA submission hold called the kimura. As of yet, he wasn't killing him because Jack wasn't yelling, but Taj was saying something to him. I think it was more or less to show Jackson who was the boss. And Jackson was actually very receptive to the lesson he was receiving. I didn't know where Duss was at this time, but I politely went in the room and told Taj to stop torturing his brother so we could leave.

Taj was pretty good about it because he jumped right up. Jack got up too and shook his shoulder out a little bit, and as I was making sure I had everything, the two of them had a few private things to say to each other because they were whispering.

"What are you two whispering about? First you want to kill each other, and next you're all private, whispering to each other like little girls. What's the business?" I asked them.

"Baby doll, can't two brothers share a private moment with each other without being little girls?"

"Yes sir, you most certainly can. But the way you two fight ALL the time, I didn't think y'all EVER talked."

Jackson shot Taj a look and said, "Every now and again, my big bruh feels like he needs to teach me a little something about life, and as the little bruh, it's my duty to make his job as difficult as I can. And I've been doing JUST that ALL my life. Ya heard me?"

At this time, Taj had his arm around Jack's neck and was pretending to be educating him. I walked out the room and said, "Bye, Jack. It was good seeing you again."

Again, we said our goodbyes to all and were en route back to the western suburbs.

"I had a good time with your family, baby. Thanks for sharing that with me."

"Aww, baby doll, I'm glad you enjoyed yourself. All the family is in LOVE with Miss Valeri Nicole Wilson, dash Bryant."

"Is that right? Well, they seem to be good people." I didn't comment at all about my hyphenated name because I was scared where this conversation might lead.

"So baby doll, you didn't say anything about the name."

"What you want me to say, sweet pea?"

"Well, are you going to hyphenate your name or just be Mrs. Bryant?"

"Okay, well since we're on the subject, why you play so much?"

"What you talking about, baby doll?"

"When you asked me to marry you?"

"Who said I was playing?"

"So...you were seriously asking me to marry you?"

"Baby doll, the Lord revealed to me ONCE AGAIN that YOU are going to be my wife! He's revealed it before, but I wasn't sure, so I asked for specifics, and specifics are what I got. You WILL be my wife, lovebug. And I didn't mean to scare you and I'm not going to rush you. You can run from it if YOU want to, but at SOME point, there will not be a place you can go. And I'll be waiting."

"Well, you know I can't answer that right now."

"Yeah, I know. That's why I said you can run from it if you want."

"But baby, I'm not running. I would love to be able to say yes, Taj. I will marry you, but I can't make a move till the Lord tells me my next step."

"Baby doll, I understand. We all good."

"Bae, I don't want you to think that I don't want you."

"Naw baby girl, I don't think that. I'm going to wait for YOUR word to come through. I'm a patient man. But now, in the meantime, if you want to go head and take our relationship to the next level and let me KNOW you, as in the biblical sense, seeing as though you WILL be my wife, then I'm cool with that too!"

"You know what Taj? I have NEVER experienced love-making without shame. I'm looking forward to the day when I can experience it in the manner that God intended: to be shared between a man and his wife."

"WOW, baby doll! That's deep! And I never thought of it that way before and I will make a promise to you right now with God as my witness, I will not add to your shame. The next time I ask for it, you'll be wearing a white dress. And I don't mean Women's Day at the church!"

"Really baby?"

"Really!"

"What if it takes years?"

"If it takes years, then I'm going to wait years, BUT I'm going to pray that the Lord moves a little quicker than years. He's ABLE!"

"Yes, He is!"

"Let's table the question till YOU get the confirmation that YOU need. Next time I ask, I'll know that YOU are ready to answer me in a favorable way. And I'll have the ring in hand."

"All right, Reverend!"

"Not yet! But we'll see!"

We made it back to my house, and Taj stayed for a minute before he headed home. I guess he needed to check in with old girl. Let me quit playing. If I thought that's what he was doing, I wouldn't have let him leave. I went to check on Mommy when he left.

32

A couple weeks passed by without much incident. Labor Day weekend, I generally go out of town to Michigan for my church family retreat. I was hoping that old boy would be able to go with me this year, but he had to work over the holiday. Oh well! We leave out on Friday before the holiday and come back on Labor Day. As expected I went with the church and much of the family. He didn't have a problem with me going on this trip, I guess because he knew that I would be there with Mom and the rest of the family. He probably talked to Arik and had some stuff worked out with him as far as me getting out of line. *Yeah right! I'm going to be me.*

Ronni was able to come to the retreat this year. Her dad's birthday was coming up, so she coincided her vacation with our trip to Michigan. YAY! She'd FINALLY get to meet Taj face-to-face once we got back. Nice!

Our trip was really nice. It was very relaxing, but more than that, it was truly refreshing to my soul being out there in God's beautiful creation. And simply being able to reflect on how GOOD God has been to me and my family throughout the years was absolutely amazing! Breathing that fresh clean air and being away from city life, if only for a weekend—nice! I enjoyed myself immensely. Ronni and I had a great time catching up too.

Only one thing was missing. I missed my boo thang!

I didn't get a chance to see him when I got home Monday night. He was really busy and ended up working a double, so I didn't see him till Tuesday (after work)—RATS! But Ronni being here helped to fill that void (a smidgeon). She was visiting with some of her family while I was at work and met me back at my place around three. We were sitting on the porch, chatting, when old boy pulled up. "I would imagine that this is the officer pulling into your driveway like there's a fire somewhere, huh?"

"Well, you know what they say, Ronald, 'absence makes the heart grow fonder!' Hey, boo!" I said, standing up and moving toward the stairs. "Come give me some love. I missed you!" I said as he was exiting his vehicle.

But him being the JERM that he is, instead of walking toward me, he stood on the running board of his truck and said, "Can one of you lovely ladies tell me where the love of my life is? I seem to have misplaced her somewhere in Michigan for the weekend."

Awwwwwww! My man done redeemed himself; he's not a jerm! But before I could respond, Ronni jumped up and said, "Here I am, boo!" And they ran toward each other (almost in slow motion) like you see people do in really touching scenes on TV. They embraced, and he lifted her off the ground and began to spin around.

"You two are so lame," I said, shaking my head at them as I went into the house to get some more ice-cold water—*aaaaah, refreshing!*

They both walked in a minute later. Taj had his arm around Ronni, and the two were talking like old friends. He turned to me and said, "Hey baby doll! Give me kiss!"

"Oh, so now you want a kiss from me? You and Ronni were looking all chummy, get one from her."

"Ronni, what do you say?"

"Boy, you play too much," and I pushed Ronni out the way and punched him in the gut, but I guess he knew what I was about to do and tightened his abs. Therefore, I hurt my hand, but I acted as if I didn't.

"Uh-huh, hurt your hand, didn't you? You know what happens when you punch a brick wall. Don't you, baby girl?" He turned toward Ronni and said, "Well, if you didn't before, now you do!" They both started laughing.

"No dear, I didn't and still don't. I never have hit a brick wall before. AGAIN, Momma ain't raise no fool!"

Taj pulled me close to him and said, "Well, now you have. Let me kiss the baby's broke hand." After he hugged and kissed me, he grabbed my hand and kissed it for me. "Is that better, baby doll?"

I said, "Plant one more right here"—pointing to my lips—"and I'll let you know."

Ronni had taken a seat at this time and said, "Awwwwwwww! Now who's the lame one, Val? It's going to take me a minute adjusting to this side of you. But I guess finally meeting Taj, I can see why you may be somewhat more of a punk than you used to be. Cops are crazy too girl, so that's an added word of caution to you, but I guess I don't have to warn you, do I? You've had your share of scares from him."

"Ronni, don't start nothing. You're supposed to be on MY side anyways."

"Val, I got you girl! Besides, I think we can take him. You know me, I break bottles if necessary."

Throughout this whole conversation, Taj was still holding onto me, kissing me. Kissing my lips, kissing me on the jaw, kissing my ear when I turned my head, kissing my neck, simply ignoring me and Ronni like we hadn't said a word—till she mentioned breaking bottles and me and her laughed about it. "Wait, hold up! What's this breaking bottles thing supposed to mean?" And he pushed me away from him so that I was arm's length from him. "That's like an inside hypothetical joke, right?"

"No, really, it's not. Me and Ronni were out one day many, many moons ago, mind you. And Ronni was going to fight some girls."

"Tell it right, Val! Them girls were ignorant and thought I was a punk. And I was about to whoop some you know whats!"

"Okay, Taj, here's the thing. I realize that you don't know EVERYTHING about me, but it's NOT intentional, so don't get mad. Okay?"

Ronni had this DUMB look on her face because she knew she just opened up a can on me, and now she was sitting there talking about some, "Oooooooooooh, you gone get it!" She pointed at me, looking like Pam did Gina on *Martin*. I really wanted to punch her. She talks so much. But she was not as bad as Toni.

"I'm ONE big ear, baby doll!"

"Okay, well, can we sit down please and get comfy? Maybe we should go sit on the porch."

"Val, why do I have the impression that you're stalling? Sit down right here, right now, and get to telling me what you failed to tell me about earlier."

So we sat down, and I started talking, "Well, Ronni and myself went out one particular day. Actually, we used to go out EVERY Thursday night because it was stripper night at several clubs. Chocolate Shake, you remember him Ronni?"

"Girl, do I!"

"Uh-huh, stripper's night, huh? Well that's ONE thing I didn't know. Shall we go for two?" Taj stated.

"Again, Taj, this was some time ago."

"Yeah, okay! Proceed."

"Well, we went out. We got there fairly early, so we had prime seats right up to the stage. As time passed, all the good spots were gone, and the latecomers didn't have anywhere to sit, so some of them started piling ON the stage, and a couple of them got in front of us. As if that wasn't bad enough, these little witches actually came RIGHT in front of us and pushed us back off the ledge!

"I was ticked off and asked them to slide over, but they ignored me. Ronni, on the other hand, started straight snapping. She pushed them girls off the ledge and was talking much noise. Now it was just me and Ronni that was on our side, and the two girls had about five or six other girls with them. Ronni didn't care. She started reaching in her purse, talking about, 'Let me get my...'—like she had a gun or something in there—and finally, she took the empty beer bottle she had and cracked it on the ledge and was getting ret to cut one of them broads when security came and got her and the other girl that was scuffling with her. Needless to say, we missed the show."

"Dang, Ronni! You a little rough around the edges! So then what?"

"That was about it. They kicked us all out!"

"Okaaaaayyyy! For some reason, I think you missed something. What's the part of the story that I don't know you all that well? The part that you forgot to tell me some time ago? Because I must've missed that part."

"All right, Joe, relax! Well, I didn't get into the scuffle with them. I sat back and let Ronni do all the scuffling, and maybe it sounded like Ronni was on her own and I didn't have her back, but—"

"Yeah, I was kind of wondering. Y'all supposed to be thicker than thieves, Bonnie and Clyde, kind of…sorta."

"I was pregnant."

"WHAT? You was what?"

"Yeah, Taj. I got pregnant by Kody shortly after him and I got together."

"So what happened? You had an abortion?"

"No Taj, she lost the baby," Ronni defended. "Look here, I didn't mean to start nothing or to get my girl in trouble."

"It's all good, Ronni. I wouldn't have withheld that information from Taj willingly, but that whole time frame was something I erased from my memory, I guess. Bae, I was really mad at Ronni for putting me in that situation at the club because if something really went down, I would've HAD to get in it. All that really happened was some pushing and a lot of threats being thrown around, and it all happened so fast. I wasn't trying to lose the baby, but I did that anyway."

"So, baby doll, you were pregnant by old dude?"

"Yup! Not too many people know that I was. I lost it before I started showing and got around to telling anybody. Of course, my Mom and sisters knew. I ain't even tell my brothers. They may know now, but if they do, it's only because Momma or one of the girls told them. My Daddy knew too, of course. It wasn't something that I was proud of. I guess that's why I lost it. God's got His own way of doing things."

"But you're okay, right, baby doll? Because I do want kids one day!"

"There are no problems that I have physically that hinder me from carrying or having a baby. I guess the time wasn't right, and the Lord didn't want me bringing a baby into this world under the circumstances I was in. I don't even know if I ever told Toni that story."

"Well, I can understand you blocking that story out of your mind, and I'm all good. I would like to meet old boy though and thank him for being such a jerk so that I could have the chance to show you how a REAL man is supposed to treat his woman."

"Yeah, well I'm good with not seeing him," Ronni said.

"Me too, Ronni. You remember that time when he was going to fight you?"

"Yeah, how could I forget? Taj, he was really a jerk and thought he could control EVERY move Val made, and if he didn't like what she did, he would hurt her, and it didn't matter WHO was around. Well, I take that back. He didn't clown in front of her family, especially not her brothers. But he was about to beat her up in front of me one day, and I wasn't having it. So needless to say, he and I didn't get along."

"Well, let him walk up on MY girl NOW! I got something for him. That pisses me off. Ain't NO man got NO business putting his hands on a woman. I don't care what she's done."

"I am SOOOOO glad to hear you say that, bae. You keep that in mind the next time I piss you off."

"Baby doll, I love you. And I would like to think that I would NEVER put my hands on you, but don't test me. I'mma tell it to you like my Daddy told a guy he used to work with at the plant. Back in the day, my Dad was a real handful. He used to curse like a sailor. His mouth was so bad that out of all the guys that worked at the plant with him (and EVERYBODY cursed), this older guy singled my Dad out and told him, 'Boy, you got a NASTY mouth!'

"So anyways, once he found the Lord—and I mean REALLY found Him—and totally turned his life over to the Lord, people on his job began to challenge him. This one white guy cornered my Dad when he didn't think anybody was looking and told him, 'The Good Book says if someone slaps you, turn to him the other cheek. So if I slap you, you gonna turn the other cheek?'

"My Dad looked at him and said, 'Yeah, that's what the Good Book says, but I don't know if I'm that strong.'"

"So did the guy slap Mr. Canton?" I asked.

"Nope, he turned both his cheeks around and walked away."

After much laughter from the three of us, Ronni said, "So, Val, I guess the moral of that story is that you can test old Taj here if you want (and he would like to think that he would let you slide with a verbal lashing), but put him to the test, and he might have a different reaction."

"Wow, Ronni! You gathered all that from his story? I thought he was saying if a white guy challenged him, old boy would be in trouble." I started laughing really hard. I thought it was hilarious (I crack me up), but when I looked at Tab and Ronni, neither one of them had so much as a smirk on their faces. "Man, you two are killjoys!"

33

We sat around for a while longer, watching TV and clowning around. Actually, Ronni and I challenged Taj to a duel where we jumped on him. Sure did! We duked him up pretty good. I felt good about it, and he was so busy laughing at us that he couldn't do anything else. I know he could've put a hurting on both of us at the same time if he so desired, and if this had been me and Toni jumping on him, he would have hurt us both. He doesn't say it, but I know if he got the chance to put a slight hurting on Toni, he wouldn't hesitate. I know he still holds her responsible for that stunt I pulled when he thought I was moving someone into my place. But since this was Ronni. He was trying to be on his best behavior. He thought she was MY voice of reason and wanted to stay on her good side. I'm sure I'd pay for it later after Ronni was gone.

"Ronni, make Taj promise he's not going to take this beating out on me after you're gone," I said for a little reassurance.

Ronni said, "I know Taj is not that petty. He just got whooped by two beautiful women, and he's man enough to take his whooping like a man."

As he was chuckling, he managed to say, "Y'all done? Shoot, any man would love to have been in my shoes for the last what? Minute and a half? While you two did the best you could to hurt a REAL man. That was great! You two sure you're done? Oh, I forgot for a second you're women. You're tired, right? It's all good." He continued laughing and said, "Boy, I better watch MY behavior! I would HATE for you two to have to put another hurting on me!" Every time he thought about it, he laughed again. We really tickled his funny bone!

I hated that he was right, but I was absolutely pooped. I didn't realize that it took that much strength out of you when you had someone in a headlock. Yeah, I had him in a headlock while Ronni was punching him all over. Occasionally, she tickled him, which is why I thought he was laughing, but looking back on it now, I know the whole idea of us whooping him up tickled him.

The night came to an end, and Ronni decided to go to bed. She was staying with me while she was in town and said, "Well family, I'm going to retire for the night, but Taj, I want to thank you for being a good sport. Thank you for laughing at the attack of RVT minus the T."

"What's RVT minus the T?" he asked.

"Ronni, Val, and Toni, minus Toni," she replied. "Yeah, if Toni was here, we would've REALLY put a hurting on you."

"Ronni, I hate to be the bearer of bad news, but if Toni had been here, ALL three of y'all would've got hurt. I'm just saying I'm looking forward to getting my chance to put"—and he put his pointer finger and thumb together with just a little space between them—"just a little bit of pain on her. And I couldn't inflict a little pain on her and not you two. She would've known that it was one-sided."

"You don't like Toni?"

"Ronni, for whatever reason, Taj holds Toni responsible for that BIG squabble he and I had."

"Val, YOU know like I know that if you had NOT talked to that girl, you NEVER would've done that! Talking about moving another man in here with you. She egged you on, and YOU know it."

"Taj, I told her that I wish I knew somebody that could pretend like they were moving in here so YOU could see how it feels. I brought it up to her. The ONLY thing she did was provide me with that somebody, so YOU need to quit. I don't know why you don't think I could be devious if need be, but thank you. AND it was for pretend! I just wanted it to LOOK authentic when YOU saw it."

"Okay, so YOU can be devious when need be, right? You remember what I said."

"Which part, Mr. Bryant?"

"I don't know if I'm that strong. That part."

Ronni jumped in the conversation, "Well I know Taj, that if you let GOD control your life, you CAN be THAT strong. And by the way, didn't that whole situation occur because YOU ACTUALLY moved somebody in YOUR house and tried to make my GIRL believe it was a dude?"

"I don't remember, did I say I liked Ronni?"

"As YOU said, and I quote, 'I'm just saying!' AND, just to let you know, I speak it like the Lord gives it to me."

"My girl! Thanks Ronni, that IS what got the WHOLE thing started, isn't it, Tab?"

"Anyway, we put that behind us, Ronni. Why you got to be bringing up the past? As One Way says, "Don't keep bringing up the past!'" and he started singing "Something in the Past."

"Ronni, the voice of reason. Impulse? Toni," I said.

Taj grabbed me around the waist and said, "You, my lady, better stick with REASONING if you know what's good for you! That will guarantee LONGER life for you."

"Speaking of Toni, how is she? We all need to get together. She's always good for a good laugh," Ronni said.

"I'll call her. Maybe we can do lurnch tomorrow."

"Okay, well, I'm going to bed, but let me pray for you two before I go."

"Never was one for turning down a good prayer," Taj said.

We held hands, and Ronni looked at Taj and said, "Taj, let me let you know that you have a good girl on your hands. I know how she and I used to be together, and from what I've seen of her lately, there have been some very positive changes that she's made. Don't expect instant change, but appreciate the effort that she's putting forward." I was in the background, nodding my head in agreement with my girl, Ronni, when she turned to me and said, "Val!"

She startled me, and I jumped and said, "Yes!" I kind of felt like I was about to get a whooping or something.

"Val, from what I can see and the affirmation that I was given from MY Lord and Savior, Jesus Christ, Taj is a good man. Don't provoke him. Neither should you take him for granted. Don't take his kindness for weakness. And know that God is able to help you to do exceedingly and abundantly above ALL you could ask. Draw your strength from the Maker and Creator of all. Make sure that the two of you pray together and draw your strength from each other AFTER you've gotten it from God, and as a couple, you two can do MARVELOUS things. Let's pray.

"Father God, MY Father, MY God and MY King, thank you for being the just and gracious God that You are. And Father, it's not that we are so good or so deserving, but it all boils down to Your grace and mercy. And I thank You. We come to You this evening as humbly as we know how to first thank You for every breath that You've given us. We've wakened day in and day out, and our families are doing well. Thank You, Lord God, because You didn't have to do it, but I thank You that You did.

"Right now, I want to lift up these two beautiful people that YOU have brought together. Lord, I pray for wisdom and patience for both of them. I pray Lord that You would be in the forefront of EVERYTHING they do. That the two of them would draw their strength from YOU, and You would help them to be able to deal with each other. Love, Lord, is patient. It is kind. Love does NOT envy, it doesn't boast, and is not proud. It doesn't dishonor others. It's not self-seeking, it's NOT EASILY ANGERED, and it keeps NO record of wrongs. It doesn't delight in evil but rejoices with the truth. It always protects, always trusts, always hopes, always perseveres. Love NEVER fails.

"When things get rough for them, Lord, help them to turn to Your Word, 1 Corinthians 13, starting with verse 4. If they base their relationship on that, they can't go wrong. Thank You, Lord, for the opportunity to serve You. Watch over, bless, and keep us as we leave to do our own thing Lord. In the Mighty Name of Jesus we pray, and we all say"—and we all said—"amen!"

Taj said, "Reverend Ronni, when will you be preaching your trial sermon? Or did I already miss it?"

"You so silly," she said.

Ronni went to bed, and Taj and myself sat up, watching TV, and I was able to give him the rundown of how the retreat went as well as showed him pictures. He also told me how his weekend was. We had a good time together, but of course, we always did, and I was glad that he liked Ronni. I truly love that guy.

34

Wednesday (Sister Wednesday) was canceled for this week after just coming in town from camp. The three of us (RVT) got together for an early dinner, and Taj tried to crash. Me, being who I am, didn't have a problem with that, but the girls wanted "girl time ONLY." I agreed and told him I would see him a little later.

After dinner, we dispersed. Ronni went out with her family, Toni went to kick it with good old Zani, and of course, I went home to meet my boo, Taj. Before we split, though, we decided we would try to get the three couples together to take a cruise or a trip to Las Vegas (which was Toni's idea; she was dying to get there) in the near future. The good time we had together was kind of surprising, seeing as though the two of them don't really get along. Nothing ever happened between them, so maybe me thinking that they didn't care for each other was just in my head. Not that I think that the two of them would get together without me, but it was really refreshing to kick it with my girls, both of them. Maybe time had grown all of us up a little. Praise God!

When I went home—or should I say prior to me heading home—I called Taj and told him I was on my way to the house, and he met me. He brought me jumbo shrimp from Blue Island along with a bouquet of beautiful flowers that he insisted I put on the dining room table. I complied, but I guess he forgot that I just left dinner with my girls. "Boo, you are aware that I ate already, aren't you?"

"Well baby doll, actually, I did forget. You can save it for later, can't you?"

"Sure thing, I'll put it up. Maybe I'll take it for lunch tomorrow. But what's with the flowers? You've never brought me flowers before."

"Is that a problem, bae? I wanted to show my sweetheart that I love and appreciate her."

"No sir, I can always accept flowers from the man of my dreams. It just kind of reminded me of something else. Good looking out, baby!" He gave me a nice juicy kiss and a beautifully strong hug. Oh my gosh, did it feel good. But I couldn't let go of the feeling I had. "Wait a minute, bae! Did you do something? Are you trying to butter me up because you know you're in trouble?" I took a step back to look into his eyes.

"Okay baby doll, I do have something to tell you, but I want you to promise me that you won't get mad."

"Baby, I don't get mad, and that's a promise."

"Okay, so since when YOU don't get mad? Because I can recall a time that you were really upset with me."

"Well now, I didn't say I wouldn't get upset. I said I wouldn't get mad. Dogs get mad, lovebug!"

"So you going to do a play on words, right? In other words, you were going to wait till I said what I had to say, then you were going to snap, crackle, and pop, huh?"

"I can't tell you what I'm going to do. You'll have to wait and see my reaction, love. But why are you holding my arms? You afraid I'm going to hit you?"

"Actually, the thought did cross my mind."

"Shoot, this sounds like it's going to be a doozie. I better sit down." I started heading to the couch to sit down but stopped abruptly and turned around in a huff. "Hold up! You slept with old girl, didn't you?"

"Baby doll, I ain't slept with NOBODY since the day I met you, except for YOU!"

"You ain't never slept with me, Gymshoe!"

"We did sleep together at my Mom's house. Movie night?"

"Oh, you talking about sleeping in the room together."

"Were we not in the same bed ALL night long?"

"Okay, so now who's doing a play on words? I'm listening, and DON'T hold onto my hands. If I need to hit you, be a man and take it because you obviously have done something worthy of being hit!"

"Well baby doll, actually I did NOTHING, BUT here it is. I got off late from work on Saturday, right?"

"Sorry, I wasn't there. So I don't really know WHEN you got off work, LOVE!" At this point, I was being sarcastic because I couldn't IMAGINE what he had to tell me. When I was with Kody, he would buy me flowers after he hurt me or after I found out he was messing with somebody. To be honest I HATED getting flowers for that reason, but when Taj gave them to me initially, it felt different. Somehow now, that old feeling was rising to the top. "Taj, the suspense is killing me. Please get on with it. I need a drink." And I got up to get me some wine, but he pulled me back down.

"Okay baby doll, sit down. It's not that bad, but here goes. Okay, so when I got off, I was really tired, right? I came in the house, threw my stuff down, and headed to the bathroom to shower, and Thomas was getting out the shower. She had the bathroom door open and was standing there with the shower curtain open—"

"So she was getting out the shower? She had a towel around her, right?"

"That's what I'm saying. I don't know if she didn't expect me home so soon or if she forgot the towel or what."

"So you mean she was standing there, bucket naked?"

"Yeah! And she didn't hide, close the curtain—nothing. She stood there. The first time, I thought it was an error—"

"Hold up, PODNUH! What you mean the first time?"

"Oh wow! I said that out loud, huh?"

"See Taj? You playing around with my emotions."

"Look here baby, I'm really not. Here's the thing. Actually, THAT happened a couple weeks ago. I thought it was a fluke, but then THIS weekend, I was coming out the bathroom, and she was lying on her bed, the door WIDE opened, butt naked. When I saw her in the bathroom, I jumped back and apologized. I was thinking it was something I did. But now I kind of think this stuff is planned. So when I saw her in her room, I walked over and shut the door."

"So you didn't say anything to her?"

"No! I hate to say it, but I think you're right. I think she's trying to get with me, SOOOOO I was thinking that YOU probably need to say something to her! I think you need to stake your claim."

I started laughing at him. I looked into his face, and that little pitiful look made me laugh even harder. I wish you could've seen the look on his face when he had to admit that I was right and the look where he wanted me to talk to old girl. He was so absolutely adorable, but he got me ALL KINDS of twisted.

"Baby doll, what is so funny? I'm serious! You have to talk to her."

"Sweet pea, I don't do the 'staking my claim' thing. If that's what you want and who YOU want to be with, then by all means, YOU have my blessing. I will NOT stand in your way. My only thing is, don't think you're going to have both of us. So if it's ME that YOU want, YOU need to let old girl know what's up. Should I call Thomas and tell her that she wins? She's the better man?"

"Baby, don't play with me. Really? You're not going to say anything to her?"

"Sweet pea," I said, still kind of giggling a little bit, "it is YOUR job to let old girl know that that is UNACCEPTABLE behavior. YOU my friend, better 'stake YOUR claim' of me. Make your choice honeybunches."

"You play too much, but okay. I got you! Don't think that I would do the same thing if somebody was coming at you!"

"As a matter of fact, I was going to tell you that my roommate, Chris, that moved in here with me—"

"As Dr. Malcolm said to old girl in *The Lost World*, 'It is so important to your future that you DON'T finish that statement!'"

"Geeeeeeeez! Touchy, touchy, touchy!"

"So I'm waiting!"

"What you waiting for, lovebug?"

"I'm waiting for you to say, 'I told you so!'"

"Taj, I'm surprised at you! I am NOT that petty! I'm kind of surprised that you told me anything in the first place. So how you going to handle this, honeybunches?"

"I got it! Just don't YOU worry about it."

"I'm not sweet pea, as LONG as YOU know for sure what YOU want. I've had to share my man before. I don't plan to EVER do that again, so HONESTLY, if I'm not what YOU want, let me know now."

"Baby doll, I got this. I've told you EVERYTHING I had to tell you. Don't add any more to this story than necessary."

"Love you, boo!"

"Yeah, I love you too, girl!"

So I was right, huh? I knew old girl wanted him. Look at him! He's absolutely gorgeous. Beautiful complexion, all milk chocolatey, body like a Greek god (Zeus or Hercules), and a gentleman among gentlemen. Of course she would want him. And I would truly hate to lose him, but I believe what God has for me is for me! I feel in my heart that God has blessed me with Mr. Taj Alexander Bryant. God has confirmed it to me, even though He hasn't given me the okay for marriage yet.

And Taj has been so patient with me, knowing that I was NOT giving up the cookie (as Steve Harvey says). There are tons of females that would give him JUST what he wanted, but still he was sitting back, waiting for me. This man was EVERYTHING I had EVER dreamed of in a man. But if I'm not HIS first choice, then it's a done deal. I won't be his second. Time will tell.

I can't wait to tell Toni and Ronni!

35

Taj was gone by the time Ronni got back to the house but not without me making sure that he was still willing to wait for me and that I was what he really wanted. He assured me, and I could tell he was impressed that I wasn't a "told you so" type girl. I could also tell that he was a little disappointed that I wasn't going to fight for him. NOPE! Not at this stage of the game. I loved him, true enough, but the relationship was still early enough where there was time for him to change his mind if that's what he chooses to do. I definitely would be disappointed but I don't think he's going anywhere. I'm still pretty confident; or should I say that God has given me a peace about this whole situation. Besides that, the innocent look on his face when he was telling me this story was still stuck in my head. Oh, he's so adorable. Anyhoo, Ronni got to the house and called as she was pulling up. She needed to make sure I was home.

She came in the house and immediately noticed the flowers, "Awwwwww, somebody bought me flowers! How nice! Are they from you or do I have a secret admirer?"

"Girlfriend, you are always full of jokes, huh? What's the business? You don't think I'm worthy of flowers?"

"I know you are. Can't a girl wish?"

"Yeah, but you know what I thought when those flowers came in here, don't you?"

"What? You thought they were for me too?"

"Girl, forget you! Naw! Taj had some news to tell me. That's why he brought me flowers."

"Y'all still good, right?"

"Yeah, we good, but he wanted me to talk to his roommate cause she's trying to get in his drawers."

"You're kidding! What she do to him?"

"She keeps letting him see her naked, once coming out the shower and once lying across the bed, both with the door open."

"Wow! She needs to go! You going to talk to her?"

"Heck no! He better let old girl know that she's gonna have to go if she can't keep either the door closed or her clothes on. You know me. You know I don't do the run after the woman thing and put the blame on her. I'M his woman. He made the commitment to be faithful to me and ONLY me. She didn't. So if that changes and he wants somebody else, that's on him. He just better make sure he lets me know one way or the other."

"Wow, girl! You have really grown up! I remember the time when we would've been over there, RIGHT now, checking her!"

"That's you, girl! ALL day! I was NEVER the one to go after a female like that."

"You remember that time with Kody, when you and that other girl got into it?"

"Ronni, you don't remember how SHE came at me? He tried to hush her up, but she wanted me to know that she was sleeping with him. Me and you were together when she approached me. And if I remember correctly, YOU were going to fight her! I had to calm YOU down."

"Oh yeah! You never have been a fighter! Why?"

"Because I don't plan for NOBODY to EVER get the opportunity to hit me in MY face. I'm too pretty for that. You ain't know?"

"Well, yeah, you are pretty!"

"All right then!"

"When I grow up, I want to be like you, Val!"

"Pray about it, girl! God is ABLE!"

"I know that's right! So he's going to handle it?"

"He better!"

"I hear you, baby girl. Well, Daddy told me to tell you hi!"

I ended up telling Toni the whole story over the weekend. She had a slightly different reaction then Ronni. Toni wanted Taj's address. She said, "If YOU ain't gonna stake your claim for your man, I will!"

Naturally, I had to calm her down. She's the littlest thing, but is so feisty. And she thinks that I'm tooooo mellow. Well, maybe I am, but this is me. There's enough other folks out here acting a fool over their mates. If you don't believe me, watch *Snapped*. Life is too short to be wanting to fight all the time or whatever. Besides, old girl is a cop too. She carries a gun. Who wants to get into it with somebody like that? God can fight my battles better than I ever could.

*****

Later on that week, Taj and I went out to dinner with Ronni and her dad for his birthday. We had a good time. He gave me his stamp of approval for Taj. Her dad was a HOT mess, I tell you. He was flirting with our server as we were out and trying to get Taj to jump on the bandwagon with him, but old Taj was on his best behavior. He either felt like he was skating on thin ice or he was trying to make a good impression on Mr. Miller. Mr. Miller ended up telling me that if Taj could refrain from hitting on that young "tenderoni," then I picked a good one. I knew he wasn't serious. Ronni got her humorous side from him.

Naturally, Ronni couldn't head back to Atlanta without spending a Sunday with the Wilson family, having Sunday dinner and such. Even though we all spent the weekend together at the church family retreat, everybody acted as if they were seeing her for the first time in years. My family IS pretty goofy, though. Everybody had to catch up on new business and reminisced on old times. Taj was there as well, so you know he got his earful. He spent most of the time not saying much but laughing the WHOLE afternoon.

Mom was being Mom and wanted to know when she was going to be invited to Ronni's nuptials. And Ronni was being Ronni by telling Mom that no one wanted to ruin a good thing. "If it ain't broke, don't fix it." According to Ronni, marriage could destroy a good relationship. Hey, she was so busy pushing me in that direction I needed to see where her head was with this marriage thing for real. Mom took her off to the side and counseled her on the biblical principles of a relationship and ended up telling me not to let Ronni influence me.

All in all, we had a good time, and of course, the food was great. After dinner and the cleanup, we ladies went out on the porch and chewed the fat a little more, enjoying the weather, each other, and discussing God's many blessings. Now who could argue with that? God has been so good to us!

Mom was tired and called it an early night and went on to bed BEFORE it got dark. Wow! She must've been REALLY tired because her little nosy self was not going to miss much conversation. We stayed a little while longer, chitchatting on the porch, but kids had school the next day, so we shut it down on the early side too. Ronni had an early flight out on Monday, so we left and went by her dad's so she could bid her farewells.

*****

Monday morning, I got up with Ronni, but since she had rented a car, she didn't need a ride to the airport. However, I did get a chance to ask her about that marriage comment. Her response to me was that she knew that my family REALLY believed in marriage, so she knew I wouldn't dare be in a relationship without marriage being somewhere in the forefront. Also, she reminded me that I wasn't giving it up till marriage. RIIIIGHT! I had forgotten about that part. Oh well, time had come for Ronni to go home. We said our goodbyes AFTER we said a word of prayer. Man, I'm going to miss that girl!

36

The next few months went by without much going on here and there. Taj and I spent as much time as possible together, sometimes chilling at the house, other times kicking it at Mommy's (and not just on Sundays), and then going out occasionally. We were both pretty simple people. Although we did go to Navy Pier again with Toni and Zani, and this time, it was Toni's idea. We took a Segway tour once, rode the bikes another time, and then we took Zani and Toni to our spot on the waterfront, looking at the Chicago scenery.

You know, I think I would like to have my wedding here (at night) with the skyline in the background. To take a line from Darla off *Little Rascals*, "How romantical!"

We had our church's Halloween party whereas Taj couldn't come to that. He had to work late and wasn't real happy about it. He wanted to be there in case we needed some protection. He was not a big fan of Halloween. He initially thought that us as a church were promoting demonic behavior by endorsing Halloween with a party. I explained to him that you could make ANYTHING demonic if that was the spirit in which you chose to take. Halloween parties were good enough for me when I was little, and because there are people in the world that choose to do bad things on Halloween and any other day of the year for that matter, we should ban Halloween parties? Negative! Not on my watch.

We have a good time. We play games with the kids in the community, feed them (nothing big, just hotdogs and stuff), have prizes for the best costumes, for the winners of musical chairs (even the adults play musical chairs), and we play other games and we give them goody bags with a caramel apple. So it was good fun and a controlled safe environment for the young ones.

He soon understood my point and wanted to be there in case we needed some muscle. I had to tell him that we got all the muscle we needed. Again, I had to explain myself to the little insecure booger, meaning Jesus was all the muscle we needed at this time. No Taj, I was NOT referring to another man! But you tell me, why would I need to refer to another man when I got all this man right here? Good gravy! Dude needs to relax!

Thanksgiving came and went. We went to my Mom's house first and then went to his parents' home. We did it that way because we were spending the night with his folks, watching a movie with the family again. It was good times at both places. Everybody was pretty much used to seeing us together now, so there was nothing major to discuss. On the ride home from the Bryants' place, the thought hit me that I never had gotten any clarification as to whatever happened with his roommate, so I decided to ask what was going on with the Regina Thomas saga. You would think that I would've heard something by now. It had been a good two months since he wanted me to "stake MY claim," but of course, I had to inquire about it before I could hear anything. MEN! "Hey, Bae, I been meaning to ask you if you ever handled that situation with Ms. Thomas?"

"Oh yeah baby doll, I had been meaning to talk to you about that. "

"That's funny because I sure been meaning to hear about it."

"You're such a funny lady! I was talking to one of the fellas about—"

"Dude, you're stalling?"

"Okay baby doll, well actually, I hadn't said anything because initially, I thought this thing would blow over. I figured you...I mean WE"—and he gave a little sheepish grin—"were reading more into this thing than we ought to be."

"Oh really? So then something else must've happened. I mean, since this thing didn't 'blow over,' as YOU say? So what was it, big Tab? Did something confirm it to you that I—I mean WE weren't reading more into it than YOU thought we ought to be? What's the business? Speak up, sir!"

"Baby doll, I will if you let me—dang, man!"

"Oh he—... Oooh, I almost cursed. Hold up, so now YOU frustrated? Huh! I don't have anything else to say!"

"Baby, don't get mad!"

"Like I told you before, Taj, dogs get mad! Angry? Hmmmm, now that's a horse of a different color. First, I'm the one reading more into it than I ought to be, and secondly, I have to come to YOU about it? You didn't think enough of me to OFFER the information? Yeah, well, tell me or don't. It doesn't matter!"

"Okay, baby girl, I'm sorry, just listen."

I started playing Candy Crush on my phone. I was a beast on that game. I was almost to level three hundred. *Work it, me!*

"All right, I'm going to talk. If you don't want to listen, fine. But I'm going to say it. Really, it wasn't much."

"Oh, so that's why you failed to tell me about it, right?"

"Anyways, I came in one day and dropped my keys on the table because I was running to the can. When I came out and went to grab my keys, Thomas had them and asked me if I was looking for these. I said yeah and went to grab them, and she grabbed my hand and held onto it, THEN wouldn't let it go. In my head, I was thinking, *Girl, what is the problem?* But when I looked at her face, she had this funny look on her face. I believe it was a little seductive thing she had going on. I simply pulled my hand away and told her she needed to stop tripping. So the next time it happened, she grabbed my keys and put them in her bra and told me if I want my keys, I had to go fish."

In the meantime, I was sitting there, FUMING! The bra thing REALLY got next to me. I continued playing the game on my phone, but I couldn't concentrate. I was very anxious to hear how this story played out.

"At that point, I sat her down and told her that this wasn't cool. I told her that I was completely committed to the girl of my dreams." He looked at me as if I should be impressed, like maybe he deserved a treat or something, but I never even looked up. I could see him out

243

the corner of my eye, so he turned back around and said, "Since you don't care, I shouldn't tell you the rest."

I looked up at him and said, "Oh, I'm sorry. Were you saying something to me?"

"Never mind!"

"Awwwwww, the widdle baby got him feelings hurt? Awwwwww, you can finish your story. I heard EVERYTHING you said." He gave me a little look, and I said, "Go ahead... Proceed!"

"So you heard me?"

"You mean about the part where on TWO SEPARATE occasions—not ONE, but TWO occasions—old girl grabbed your keys, gave you a seductive look once, and—"

"I got it, you were listening."

I continued, "And on the SECOND occasion, Ms. Thang sent you fishing down HER bra to get YOUR keys! Believe me when I say I'm dying to find out how THAT fishing excursion concluded. Did you catch anything, honeybunches?"

"WOW! You really know how to finish off a good story!" Again, he gave a look which this time said that HE was impressed with my quick wit, but I guess he saw that I was NOT in the least pleased with his shenanigans, so he continued talking, "Baby Doll, I told old girl that I was very disappointed in her. I told her that from the beginning, my girl did not like the fact that I allowed her to move in. I told her that YOU thought she was interested in me, but I defended her till the end. We talked about her leaving doors open so I could see her naked. Then we talked about the key thing. I told her that she was going to have to leave if she couldn't control her longings for Big Daddy as Steve Harvey would say."

"So I want to know, did you go fishing for the keys?"

"Now baby doll, why would I need to go fishing with some little guppies when I got a pond of nice-sized catfish that I'm patiently waiting to devour?"

"That's the thing, Taj, you haven't attempted to go in that pond at all. And now a different pond is openly available to you, and your loins are allowing you to still be patient, sit back, and wait for whenever that date comes for you to fish in MY pond? So really, I'm supposed to believe that you didn't test the waters?"

"Baby doll, you're exactly right. I do expect you to believe that I didn't test those waters. And if you don't, then there's no reason to continue this relationship. Those waters are openly available to me if and whenever I choose to dibble and dabble in that pond and always have been, but where would that leave me and you? And to put it out there, I'm offended! My commitment is not only to you, Ms. Thing, but I'm also committed to my Lord and Savior, Jesus Christ! I'm on the same mission YOU on now."

"Good gravy, big fella, calm down! Don't get your panties in a wad!"

He gave me a look that said I was in some trouble, and for what? "You know I want to pull over right now and show you what kind of wad MY 'PANTIES' are in? I want to make sure I got this right. You did say panties, right?"

"Taj, you are entirely too sensitive."

"Too sensitive? Me? Naw baby doll, not me. But obviously you're confused as to whether I'm a man or a woman!"

"Okay, I get it! I apologize, lovebug. It's only a phrase. Geeeeez! You snapped on me because I questioned your faithfulness and considered ending THIS relationship, and so I was lightening the mood a little bit. Golly!"

"Well, I do realize that it's been a good minute since I kicked your butt."

Tartar sauce! I didn't realize that phrase would've caused a reaction like this. First, he questioned our relationship. Now he wanted to put a hurting on me because I said he had panties on… Hmmmmm, I guess I didn't think this out too well. "All right, baby, I replayed it in my head and realize that the panties thing didn't sound good. Please accept my apology! I was trying to save face because you questioned the relationship. I'm not trying to lose you over some bull like old girl, ESPECIALLY if you haven't done anything. And to set the record straight, I do trust you and won't question your actions again without something else substantiating my doubts. Give me kiss."

He looked at me, and I couldn't tell by the look on his face if he still wanted to kill me or not. But then he said, "All right, baby, I'm going to let the comment slide this time, but come at me like that again, and be prepared to throw down. I can show you what kind of drawers I wear better than I can tell you."

"And I wouldn't mind seeing them since I'm the one that's going to be shopping for your draws at some point…so do I get a kiss or no?"

He leaned in and gave me a nice smooch, which immediately I said, "Keep your eyes on the road."

He said, "Yeah, it's time for a nice butt-whooping. I'm glad we're almost to your house."

I tried to convince Taj to run me by Mommy's before we went to my house, but he felt like there was some business he needed to tend to before we ran any other errands. Let me just say, he wears cute boxers and not panties, and I don't plan on making that error again. Anyhoo, all in fun, though.

37

So now as we came into the Christmas season, Taj was trying to figure out how I was going to buy a gift for everyone in my family. I forgot that he wasn't around last Christmas (it seemed like I'd known him for years), so I had to explain it to him. There were too many of us to be trying to buy individual gifts; therefore, each Christmas, we did a grab bag. Yeah, we drew names. We got our grab bag a gift for their birthday as well as a Christmas present. We have a twenty-five dollar minimum for birthdays and fifty-dollar minimum for Christmas. The kids had a separate grab bag for themselves. This way, nobody got overwhelmed (we all had a year to pick up a gift for our grab bag person, and most of us spent more than the minimum). Of course, everyone got Mommy a gift.

This year was no exception as far as gift-exchanging went. Taj and I had decided to do a little something in exchanging gifts for each other, but nothing extravagant. I had seen a really nice gold necklace and bracelet that I felt would be absolutely adorable on his chocolate skin. It was white gold, and of course, I had to get him a nice pair of white gold diamond studs for his ears. Everything he wore was gold, as far as the color, so I had to spice things up a little with white gold. He gave me a nice Coach purse as well as a nice jogging suit with all the accessories to go with it—sneakers, socks, shirt, and hat. My guy! It was really cute too.

I had a series of dreams during this Christmas season that at first I thought nothing of. But after about the fourth dream, I woke up thinking about this particular dream, and all the other dreams came to mind (which startled me). I had to talk to somebody, so THIS time, I called Ronni. "Ronni, hi hun. How are you?…"

"Girl, what's wrong?…"

"Why something always have to be wrong? Can't I call my girl to see what's up with her?..."

"So nothing's wrong? You just decided to call me at seven o'clock in the morning—which, by the way, is six your time—on my off day?..."

"Girl, you're on Christmas break. You're off for at least the next week! Am I right?..."

"Okay, so nothing's wrong, right Val?..."

"Nothing is wrong, Ronni. I simply needed to speak with my girl for a hot second. Is that a crime?..."

"No crime as long as that's the truth!..."

"I need to run something by you..."

"Well, let's have it..."

"Okay, so I've been having some dreams, and I want to know what you think about them..."

"Scripture says run get Daniel, NOT Ronnie. I am NOT a dream interpreter!... My name is not Daniel!"

"Ha-ha-ha, so if you can't help me, then you can't help me..."

"Come with it then..."

"The other night, I dreamed that I was introducing Taj to my extended family, aunts, uncles, cousins. I can't place where we were, but one of my cousins asked me what my new last name was, and before I could answer, I woke up and immediately forgot the dream. Then I dreamt that I was at Mom's house, and somehow, I tripped and fell in slow motion. I don't know how. Maybe over the rug or something, but when I tripped, I knocked the Bible off the coffee table, and when I sat it back on the table, I opened it, and it opened to Ephesians 5. It was like everything else was blackened, but starting with verse 22, the words were clear: 'Wives submit to your own husbands.' you know the verses. 'Husbands, love your wife as Christ loves the church.' But all that was, like, highlighted. It was really weird..."

"You don't need to go ANY further..."

"You don't want to hear the rest?..."

"I don't need to, but if you want to tell me, then go head… Just tell me this, were the rest of the dreams similar? Did they have something to do with marriage and or Taj?…"

"Uhhhh…"

"Uhhhh, right! Just like I thought!…"

"Oh okay, so am I to believe that you have an answer for me, Ms. My Name Ain't Daniel?…"

"Val, you didn't need me for this. What do YOU think it means? You already know. That's why you called me because it scared you!…"

"Well, I did have a thought…"

"And?…"

"Ronni, I don't want to think that this is of God when the devil could be behind this. You know how Daddy used to say that the devil uses just enough truth to make you think it's of God? Satan knows Scripture too!…"

"Well, I know. I told you a long time ago that it was revealed to me, but if you want to be sure, pray a specific prayer… Girl, bump that! Call the man up and propose to him! That man is your future…"

"What specific sign should I ask for?…"

"Oh, you going to ignore me, huh?…"

"Wait, hold on a sec… Oh my goodness, it's him…"

"There's your sign, answer it…"

"I'll have to call him back…"

"Girl, answer the phone and call ME back…"

"He hung up. He probably thinks I'm sleep… Ronni, I'm scared…"

"Scared of what?…"

"What if he doesn't ask me again?…"

"Val, is this YOUR thing? Or are you allowing the Lord to lead you?…"

"You know that I'm not doing this on my own from beginning to end!…"

"Then stop worrying! God's got this! In the name of Jesus, Father God, I thank You for what You've revealed to my little sister. Father, for whatever reason, she's scared. I pray right now, in the name of Jesus, that You would give her peace, LORD, peace that passeth ALL understanding. I know that this is of You, Father, but I pray that You would confirm it to her, Lord, where there's NO denying it. I know that You can, and I trust that You will answer THIS prayer that I'm praying right now. In the MIGHTY name of Jesus I pray, amen!..."

"Amen!..."

"How you feel, darling?..."

"Now you sound like my sister, but I'm good, thanks baby girl..."

"Good! Val and Taj sitting in a tree, k-i-s-s-i-n-g..."

"Bye, Ronni!..."

"You aren't going to let me finish?..."

"Thanks for your help, and I love you sooo much, but I have to call my boo thing back..."

"Okay, well let me know how things go, okay?..."

"I got you girl, thanks again love! Wait, one more thing..."

"Yes, Valeri?..."

"So do I tell him yes? Do I tell him I got my confirmation? How do I handle it from here?..."

"Baby, be patient. He'll ask you again. Don't you say anything about it. Kay?..."

"You so wise..."

"Girl, shut up. You so silly. Now can I finish my song? Val and Taj..."

"Bye, Ronni!..."

"Congrats baby, love you!..."

"Not as much..."

Okay, so I got my confirmation. Wow! Mrs. Taj Alexander Bryant. Mrs. Valeri Nicole Bryant! That has a nice ring to it. *Okay, so Lord, if this is of You, I ask in the NAME of Jesus that You would give me peace about it! I pray that this whole thing would go into the deep recesses of my brain and that it doesn't keep me up, thinking about it, worrying about it, wondering when he's going to ask me. I would like complete peace, and when he asks me, then the memory of the dreams can come forth. I ask these things in the MIGHTY name of Jesus. Amen! Whew! Glad that's over. I'm going back to sleep. Nite nite, me!*

38

Again, time crept along. The winter was pretty brutal, but having a nice man to hold on to in those cold (almost lonely) evenings made that brutality of Chicago winters a breeze. We spent a lot of time inside, but then again, he told me to stop being a wuss on a few occasions and made me go out. He and I took a few of my nephews and nieces sledding on those not so bad days, which I must say was another first for me. I had never been sledding before. I didn't even know there was such a thing as sledding hills.

We made Toni and Zani come sledding with us on one of those occasions in which Toni whined the WHOLE time! I don't know what her problem was. Sledding and hot chocolate was a beautiful combination! Later, she confessed to me that that was one of the best times she had in a long time.

We also went to our spot at night to see the view of the skyline in the winter with snow on the trees and the lake frozen over. WOW! Now I want my wedding in the bleak of winter at night out here! NOT! It was beautiful and all, but I think I'll stick to a warm weather wedding.

On another occasion, we took a trip to Navy Pier (winter-style). I must say, I was pleasantly surprised that the spiders had retreated for the winter (hibernation, I guess)—SWEET! The scenery from the top of the Ferris wheel was breathtaking! *What a lovely city I live in!* And sitting there cuddled up with THIS hunk of a man was icing on the cake!

Valentine's Day ended up on a Sunday this year. This would be mine and old boy's first Valentine's Day together. The weekend leading up to Valentine's Day, he and I were having a conversation. He was trying to convince me to miss Valentine's Day service and go to brunch with him and his family. What he didn't realize was me, being the smart person I am, had invited his mom and dad and the rest of his family to church because even though it was Valentine's Day, it was also family and friends' month. My sister was the reigning champ for having the most visitors during February and I really wanted to dethrone her this year. I figured having his whole family come as MY guests, I'd be well on my way. "Um, baby, when did you make these brunch plans with your family?"

"It's a tradition, baby doll. I don't have to make special plans with them. They know what we do annually. Generally, it's been the immediate family, but this year, I'll have my BABY with me."

"You're probably going to have to adjust your plans."

"If you can't get out of service or don't want to go, that's cool. Believe me when I say my folks are definitely not going to change the tradition. Did you hear me when I said it's something we do EVERY year?"

"Maybe you should plan on an early dinner or something. Or better yet, you should call your moms."

"Why? Hol' up! You know something I don't?" He said this as he was reaching for his phone, giving me a look at the same time. I looked up into the air as if I were innocent, but what can I say? I'm a clever chick. That's one of the reasons he likes me so.

"Hey Momma, how's my favorite girl?…"

"Awww, Momma, you know that girl don't hold a candle to you!…" He put his finger up to his mouth as if to hush me, and pointing at the phone, trying to make me think he was trying to appease her.

"Really, Ma? So I haven't been doing a better job keeping in touch with the love of my life?… Oh my goodness! So you're going to give HER credit for me keeping in touch with you? It's cool, though. That's my girl, and I got broad shoulders. I can take it!… You'll see me at church tomorrow? What you mean?…" He turned around and looked at me like I had done something. "Oh, so she did huh? But Momma, it's Valentine's Day. We usually do brunch as a family on Valentine's Day!…" He directed his conversation to me, "Baby Doll, why didn't you tell me you invited my people to church on Sunday?"

"Taj, didn't I tell you to check with your family because I thought they may have other plans?"

"You could've told me they were coming to your church tomorrow?" But before I could respond, his mom was giving him the business on the phone. "Ma, I'm not fussing at that girl!… Yes ma'am, you did tell me to stop calling that girl 'that girl…' No ma'am, I don't want you to call Daddy to the phone. Ma, I was just playing. That girl knows—oooops, I mean, my baby knows what I think about her… So Daddy is going to take us out after church?… Well, yeah! I did think you guys could miss a day from church to spend with family! We're talking about ONE day, Momma!… No ma'am, I guess I didn't think that through all the way… Not a problem, Lade. I guess I'll see you guys at service tomorrow… I love you too, pretty lady… That's okay, I'll see Sir Canton tomorrow, so no, I don't need you to call him to the phone. Just tell my daddy I said hi and I'll see him bright and early in the a.m… Smooches back atcha, Lady Bird, bye…" Taj directed ALL his attention to me as he ended the call.

"So now why you looking at me like I did something wrong, Taj?"

"Baby doll, this is my FIRST time hearing this. You think I would be inviting you to Valentine's Day brunch if I knew?"

"Okay Bae, I can see how you're looking at me and I don't feel I deserve that. I talked to your mom and dad the last time we were out at their house and I told them about Family and Friends Month at church. They told me that first Sunday would be hard for them due to communion at their own church, but they should be able to make second Sunday. Mom told me to remind her about it the week before. I guess they didn't realize that second Sunday was Valentine's Day. I know I didn't! So now why you coming at me like I did something wrong?"

"You told them about this back then? I NEVER heard this before!"

"Yes, I did, AND you knew about it because you were telling Dad where the church was. It's right across the street from the restaurant. Remember? Because you were trying to remember the name of the restaurant as you were giving directions?"

253

"Oh yeah, okay. I do remember that. My bad, baby. I didn't realize it was for this Sunday, though. You off the hook, but you could've told me they were coming. I didn't have to call my mom's up like that."

"No, you didn't, but don't you think she enjoys talking to her baby boy whenever she can? Even if you ARE being a jerk?" I mumbled the jerk part.

"What was that, baby?"

"Huh? Oh, nothing, stomach growling a little bit. I was trying to cover up the sound."

"Uh-huh, okay! Well, I forgive you. Gimme kiss!" And he closed his eyes and puckered up the soup coolers.

Being the person that I am, I muffed him and said, "You forgive ME?"

"Baby doll, don't mess up a perfectly good day! Now if you really want to do this, we can. I'm all for it!"

I reached in and gave him a kiss. I wasn't in the mood for a wrestling match or a lecture. "Okay, well, I forgive YOU back!"

"Cool, what you wearing to church tomorrow? Maybe we can dress alike!"

"Really babe? You want to dress like me? I knew SOMETHING was wrong with you. I knew you were too good to be true."

"Baby, not like that. I'm talking about coordinating our attire… Oh, I get it. You're being funny! So I guess you didn't learn from the last time that I am ALL man here? There's another lesson to be learned, I see."

"All you think about is fighting me and teaching me a lesson. You must be the sweetest cop out there because you save all that built-up aggression for me, huh?"

"You the one with the smart mouth. Those folks on the job don't want to tangle with Ben and Jerry." He flexed his arms and kissed his biceps as he called out their names. "Besides that, YOU don't like for me to be nice to you."

"Oh, I do, okay, my apologies love. We can fight another time. I would like to sit up here with MY man as well as Ben and Jerry and watch some good old-fashioned TV or a nice movie while he lays his head on my lap and I rub that bald head of his."

"Well, that's cool and all, but you obviously don't know that I don't play those little girly games."

"Baby, I said I was sorry. Initially, that was the first thought that came to mind, and I went with it. Sorry! If I had any 'SERIOUS' doubts about you being 'ALL' man, I wouldn't be with you. Will you accept my apology?" I gave him a nice kiss, then started kissing him on his neck, then his cheek. I nibbled on his earlobe a little bit.

He jumped up real quick and said, "I have to go!"

"Really baby?"

"Don't act like you don't know what you're doing to me!"

Well, he shouldn't act like HE held all the cards. I got a few cards up my sleeve as well. "Can't you walk it off or go to the bathroom, man? I'm not ready for you to leave me yet."

"I'll see!" And he went in the bathroom to see if him and the boys could settle down.

Anyhoo, he was able to get a grip on his loins, so we watched a little TV before he got a call. It sounded official like it was from the police department or something. I'm not sure what it was. I was thinking maybe he needed to fill out some paperwork. I didn't know. All I knew was he ended the night early AND abruptly! Oh well, if you got to go, then you got to go.

I started playing on the computer after he left (needed to catch up on my e-mails; I didn't really do Facebook or Twitter). I stayed up WAY too late playing on that thing, but I was able to get up on time and be ready before my Prince Charming showed up.

39

*A*h, Sunday morning. His family and my family will FINALLY meet NICE! Looking forward to it. Hopefully my brothers won't embarrass me too much.

Taj got to my house like usual, looking EXTRA scrumptious, and guess what? We were coordinated. Yep! Looked like we planned this. With it being Valentine's Day, I had on a red dress with a black belt and black shoes and cute black overcoat so he didn't see what I had on. But he didn't have on a coat. He had on a charcoal grey three-piece suit with a long jacket (you know, the Steve Harvey look) and a red shirt. Who would've thought dude OWNED a red shirt? Grey tie with a splash of red in it. Anyhoo, he opened the door for me as usual.

"Good morning, beautiful! May I have the pleasure of asking the most BEAUTIFUL woman in the world, with due respect to the two women that birthed us, for a Valentine's kiss?"

Wow! Now was that a greeting or WHAT? "Yes, my love, you most certainly may." So we embraced in a lovely "FIRST Valentine's Day together" hug and kiss. I must say, it was absolutely passionate and very nice. Geeeeez! Took my breath away. I had to focus really quick on where we were headed because my EN-TIRE body was trying to go elsewhere.

Lord Jesus Christ, I need You to help me to focus on You. I'm not sure if I have loins right now. My head is absolutely scatterbrained, but whatever I have I need for You, Lord Jesus, to intercede as You have done so many times before and relax my spirit and help me to concentrate on the goodness of You so that I can go and worship for ALL that You've done for me and my family. Wooooooosaaaaaaaaahhhhhhhh! Lord, You are absolutely AMAZING! Thank You!

So I got in the car, and there were a dozen champagne roses. I take that back. There were eleven champagne roses, I think, and one red rose right in the middle sitting on the seat next to me with a card. I turned to Taj as he got in the car. "Taj? Are these for me?"

"Who else do you think they're for? The only thing is, I can't present them to you till after service. Then you get the flowers and the card."

"Awwwwww! How sweet is that? Well sweetheart, I can definitely wait. How romantical!"

"I do what I can do when I can do what I can do!"

"Show ya right!" I said, giving my man a little encouragement. Neither one of us said much of anything else on the ride to church. It was a pretty quiet ride, but the music got me good and ready for service.

We got to church about eight-forty. Devotion was going to be starting in a few minutes. Taj's family got there around the same time, everybody except Jackson and Fred. We did the little meet and greet thing. I introduced his parents as well as his sisters to my mom and then the rest of my family that was there. We got a few late ones in the bunch that would have to meet them later on. His mom explained to us at that time that Jackson and Fred were on their way, but they had to pick up Jackson's girl, Najah.

Service was about to start, and I guess Taj had to go to the bathroom or something. He disappeared shortly after he greeted his parents. I'm not exactly sure where he went.

Okay, so service started, and worship service was going along especially well. Jackson got there as we were finishing up devotion, so he made good time. Testimony time was good. The Lord was really doing some good things for people in the church. Not to say that only good things were happening. For instance (not to be putting people's business in the street like that, BUT...), one of the members had a son who was killed by a hit and run driver two weeks before the baby's eighth birthday. Now to some people, that would be a devastating blow, but to this young brother, he counted it a blessing that the Lord had given him eight good years with his son. He was blessed as well as the Lord considered his son worthy to call on him, and he answered the call. The last thing that father told little MJ was that he was his daddy's guy. He had other children as well, but that baby knew that he was something special in his daddy's eyes before he went home to be with the Lord.

To me, that was something powerful. It had me thinking that if anything were to happen to one of my family members, I would be able to handle it. I mean, the truth of the matter is why should we only accept the good from God, and as soon as something bad happens, we want to question, "Why me?"

Another member had been a smoker for quite some time and now had COPD and was on oxygen, but she was still here. She gave ALL the honor and glory to God for still being here. So you see, being a Christian doesn't keep you from trials and tribulations, but those same trials and tribulations make you a stronger person and help you to appreciate when all is well.

Young Reverend Dee and brother Pool on keyboards did an amazing job on the songs for praise and worship. My spirit was truly full right now! My guests (as well as the preaching) would be icing on the cake to a WONDERFUL service. When it came time for visitors to stand and mention who invited them, I was tickled pink. I had Mr. and Mrs. Bryant, Taj's three sisters, Jackson and Duss, as well as Najah (she was really cute by the way; I was proud of old Jackson; I hope she's a sweet girl). I got credit for Taj, and then Toni and Zani showed up. I got credit for eleven people on that day. Sweet! So after recognition of visitors and other announcements, Pastor said that we had a special testimony and asked for everyone to give this person their undivided attention.

I was waiting for the special testimony, and Taj got up. I tried to sit him back down and tell him not to leave out at this time (thinking it was a mistake), and Taj went up front to the pulpit. I was wondering, *What the Jesus! What on earth is he doing?*

Taj got the mic and started talking, "First, I'd like to give honor to my Lord and Savior for being as good to me as He's been. I'm not big on public speaking, so please bear with me. The Lord has put some new people in my life who have helped me to be a better man, a better son, a better brother, as well as a better Christian."

I started looking around at Mom and other family members, giving them the thumbs up because I was convinced they were who he was talking about.

He continued, "But right now, I'm in a little bit of a bind."

Now I was trying to figure out what kind of a bind he was in because I don't know anything about this bind.

"I'm up for a new job, and I'm not sure how that's going to turn out. I know it's going to be long hours as well as hard work, whereas I may have to do some cleaning and or some handyman work. Also, I'm going to be on call twenty-four hours a day. This job may take me out of town from time to time, and I have to be willing to go wherever this job takes me."

What the heck was he talking about? I was truly bothered at this point because I didn't know anything about this new position that he was trying to get. He didn't say a WORD to me about leaving the police force, and I thought it was bogus that he brought it to the church before he talked it over with me, his "so-called" woman. AND this wasn't even his church!

"The pay is not the best, but the benefits are out of this world. I brought this before the church because I need all the saints to pray for me. This is a job I would die for."

At this point, I was EXTREMELY ticked off. So this was a job that old boy would die for, possibly taking him out of town, AND he was going to be on call twenty-four hours a day, and I knew NOTHING about it? I guess we're not as close as I thought we were.

Someone in the audience asked, "What kind of job is it? And who is it with?"

Taj started walking with the cordless mic up the aisle, but to be perfectly honest, I was truly ticked off right now. Well, maybe not ticked off, but my feelings were really hurt. Let me stop playing. My feelings may have been hurt, but I was absolutely ticked off as well. *I was thinking my girl is here, listening to him, and she was going to ask me why I didn't tell her about this new position he was trying to get when, HECK FIRE, I didn't know nothing about it! I could hear her mouth already, and it wasn't cute.*

So right now, I was paying him no never mind. He stopped at my row and motioned for me, but of course, I had NO clue that he was trying to get my attention or anything. People around me started nudging me, and I didn't know why they were poking me (which added to me being upset). I was wondering what was wrong with these people. I had so much stuff going through my mind. Then Taj said, "Ms. Valeri, would you come here for a minute please?"

So I got up, realizing he was at our row. I started not to, but I didn't want to make a scene in the middle of church. I stepped over a few people and made it to the aisle with Taj, and he took my hand and walked back to the front of the sanctuary and said, "Ms. Val, I know you're probably upset because I didn't talk this over with you first."

"Uh, ya think, Taj?"

There was some laughter that came from the audience, and Taj said, "Baby, everything I do from this point forward I do with us in mind, so I need to know that you support me and stand by my decision, whatever that might be!"

"Baby, I'm all good with that, but we're in church. Why couldn't we have talked about this at the house or something?"

"Because I needed witnesses."

"Witnesses?"

"Ms. Valeri Nicole Wilson, it would give me great pleasure if you would allow me to take on my new position as being the head of your household, the man of the house, a husband and lover to you, father to our children, brother, uncle, son, and whatever other title that comes along with this new job."

I was in complete and utter shock and covered my mouth with my hands. Now here came the icing on the cake. Old boy broke out singing John Legend's song. He sang, "What would I do without your smart mouth? Drawing me in and then kicking me out. Got my head spinning, no kidding, I can't pin you down. What's going on in that beautiful mind? I'm your magical mystery ride. And I'm so dizzy, don't know what hit me, but I'll be all right."

He changed the words a little bit, "The Lord told me that you'd be my wife, I need you with me for the rest of my life. 'Cause all of me loves all of you. Loves your curves and all your edges. All your perfect imperfections. Give your all to me, I'll give my all to you. You're my end and my beginning, as long as you're with me I'm always winning. 'Cause I give you all of me. And you give me all of you, oh."

He stopped singing and said, "In the words of Martin Lawrence, I don't know what's in my future, baby doll, but I know that I have no future without you." He got down on one knee, took a box out of his inner jacket pocket, and said, "Valeri, will you do me the honor of being my wife and letting me be your husband? Will you marry me?"

By this time, pretty much EVERYBODY was on their feet cheering and clapping—HIS family, MY family. I looked at my momma, and she was crying. All I could do was nod my head yes because now I was crying too. Realizing that my daddy was not even here to see this, but I knew he was [as he would say] "sho' nuff" looking down on me with pride, telling me, "Dahlin', you done good. You better tell that man yes!"

He grabbed my left hand and put a beautiful marquise diamond halfway on my finger and said, "Was that a yes?"

I said, "Yes!"

He pushed the ring all the way on my finger, stood up, and we hugged, and he pecked me on my lips. He didn't pick me up like Shemar Moore did in *Diary of a Mad Black Woman*, but he held my hand in the air and said, "This woman wants to marry me, y'all!"

Pastor stood up and took the mic, quieted everybody down, and said, "Young people, let this couple be an example to you. Brother Taj and myself have been talking for the last few weeks, and he told me he didn't mind if I put their business out in the street because they have not consummated their relationship. And for you younger ones that don't know what consummate means, look it up. You're too young to be doing it anyways. They are waiting for their wedding day to do that. Ain't that how God planned for it to be? Awww, he's a good God. And according to Taj, it hasn't been easy, but God is able. 'Wait on the Lord, be of good courage, and He shall strengthen thine heart: wait, I say, on the Lord'" (Psalms 27 AND 14).

People were patting us on the back as we headed back to our seats. His mom and my mom met us in the aisle and hugged us both.

Pastor continued, "Y'all going to make it if you two can refrain from listening to the trash talk of Satan's disciples who are going to try to sway you, get you to question each other's actions AND motives. Awwww, then they got you! Believe none of what you hear and half of what you see. Happy Valentine's Day, everybody! If you can all turn with me in your Bibles to—"

Someone said, "Pastor, the choir didn't sing."

"Oh, my bad. This here couple got me all discombobulated. Come on, choir."

40

Well, I'll be. I am a betrothed woman. Can you believe it? And the ring is gorgeous. How did he set this up so quickly? Yesterday, he was whining about his family not going to the Valentine's Day brunch. Were they in on this? Oh my goodness, I had so many questions. I had NO clue what pastor was preaching about. I hope he doesn't call on me for anything, but why would he? This is not class. I am in AWE right now. And the ring—wow! It's on MY finger. I can't stop looking at it. I needed for service to be over. I need my Mommy!

Once service ended, everybody was coming by, congratulating us AGAIN and looking at the ring. I was finally able to get to my Moms, and she hugged me and said, "Congratulations, baby, I'm so happy for you! Let me see your ring." After she looked at it, she said, "I must say the ring looks much better on you than it did in the box."

"Ma, you saw it in the box? When?"

"When he asked permission to marry you."

"Momma, you knew he was going to ask? When did he do that?"

"One Sunday while you all were cleaning the kitchen."

"Ma, you told him yes? You like him?"

"Of course I did, and yes, I like him. I love the man too. He promised me that he would take good care of you. What mother wouldn't want that for her baby girl? I see how happy he makes you!"

"Well Mommy, why didn't you tell me?"

"Uh-huh, you think I can't hold water, huh? I can hold it when I want to, baby!"

Oooooh, she is not right!

Other people started gathering around. Pastor made an announcement, "I know everybody is happy and excited for the happy couple, but make your way up here to greet your pastor too." It ended up that we made our way round to see mostly everybody we needed to see—Pastor and the pastoral staff, all of my family, as well as his family. And instead of us going out to eat, Mom invited Taj's family (or should I say my new in-laws) home for dinner. So we were all headed over to her house for a home-cooked down South meal—to Mommy's it is!

It was going to take a minute for this to sink in. In ALL the excitement, I forgot that Toni and Zani were here. After we greeted everybody, I was thinking I needed to go home and call Toni and Ronni. We didn't stay for Sunday School, I was so excited. I HAD to get home. So we headed to the car, and as I was getting in, someone was yelling to me, "Val, Val! You that excited that you just going to forget about your girl, huh?"

I turned to look to see who was calling me, and it was Toni. Oops! Like I said, I had completely forgotten about her. I got out the car, and she started in on me, "Dang, girl! You got the rest of your life to be all up under this man. Can't you talk to your girl for just a second? I am still your girl, ain't I?"

"Toni!" We hugged, and before I could say anything else, Toni started tearing up, which started a chain reaction.

She got serious on me (for just a minute, might I add). "Val, I'm so happy for you, girl! You deserve it, and that was absolutely beautiful. When Taj called me up last night and told me to come to church today, I should've known something was up."

I wiped my eyes and said, "Wait, he called you last night?"

"Yep!"

"And said what?"

"Girl, he told me to come to church and help you win family and friends month."

"And you came? I've been trying to get you to family and friends month for years."

"Val, don't act like I don't come to your church on occasion."

"You have come before, but something always comes up when I REALLY want you there."

"Well, I do have my own church, Val."

"I know baby girl but…you know what? It's not even worth it. You came today, and that's all that matters right now. Have you seen this before like everybody else? Or should I show you?" I held my hand out so she could see my ring.

"No Val, this will be my first time seeing it. I guess Taj doesn't trust me…aw, man. This is beautiful. I must say, Taj, you do have good taste or did your sister or mom help you pick it out?"

Mr. Man had been standing here, chilling, watching the two of us. Him and Zani did their little man hug thingy, and Zani said, "Man, that's a hard act to follow. You pretty smooth, though. I have to hand it to you."

"Yeah, well, the good Lord gave me all the inspiration I need."

"Well, HE done good because you almost made ME cry in there like everybody else!" Toni said, giving Taj a hug. "I'm really proud of you, bighead! And you BETTER treat her right. Otherwise, it's on and popping, PODNUH!"

"Gotcha, little lady, because I'm REALLY scared of YOU! And yes, I did pick it out all by myself, thank you very much! But we all know I have good taste. Look at my baby doll!" he said, giving me a kiss on the cheek.

Zani said, "Can I get in on some of that action?"

"Oh, sorry Zani. Thanks for coming and bringing my girl out to worship with us," I said, giving Zani a hug.

"Congratulations Val, you seem very happy. I hope it stays that way for you."

"It better!" Toni said again, shaking her fist at Taj.

"Did Mommy invite y'all over for dinner today too?"

"Ooooooh Val, I didn't even speak to your Mom. I was so busy trying to catch you. Let me run in and say hi to her really quick before she tells me off in such a nice way. Come on, Zani."

"Okay, we'll see y'all at the house."

"It's Valentine's Day Val, we got other plans. But we got a wedding to plan, so I'll be in touch."

"Okay, well you kids have fun, and Happy Valentine's Day to you both," I said, and Taj dittoed me.

Once we got alone, I had so many questions. But before I could get to my questions, Taj said, "Now you can have your flowers and card. I wasn't sure if you were going to say yes or no, so you had to wait."

"Honestly, you thought I could say no to THAT proposal?"

"The Lord had given me 'peace like a river,' but then doubt stepped in, and Satan got a little bit of the victory. But it didn't last long."

I read my card, which mentioned being the woman of his dreams and us spending a lifetime together, so now I understood why it had to wait. The card would've possibly given the whole thing away. It was beautiful, and all I wanted to do at this point was give myself to him completely. As the Bible refers to it, "I wanted to KNOW" him fully. We pulled up to the house, and I leaned in and gave him a very passionate kiss and told him, "Thank you baby! You have made me the happiest woman in the world!"

He said, "Not yet, but I'm working on it. Don't move. I'll get that door." He came around and opened the door for me and helped me out the truck. We went inside, and I was absolutely floating on cloud nine, but I still had so many questions. He told me that he would give me the particulars after we changed clothes. I had to know how long he had this planned and who all was in on it.

He told me that he had it planned for quite some time (of course, after he got the okay from my Mom's), but the plan was to propose toward the end of the month. Okay, so the call he got last night that I thought was the job was actually his dad telling him that dinner after church would be a perfect opportunity for his proposal, but then the Lord gave him the idea to do it during service, which is why he left abruptly to get everything in order. The Lord also gave him the idea of how to do it. He then called Pastor and expressed his ideas to him.

Pastor felt like we were an exemplary couple, and this proposal would serve as a model for other young people in the congregation, so Pastor was glad to give him the time needed to do his thing during service. Nothing like this had ever been done in this church before. They set up the particulars, and after we got to church and Taj disappeared, he had gone to meet with Pastor. Pastor gave his blessings, they had prayer, and the rest is history, EXCEPT Pastor told him his next step was to become a member. Taj assured him that that was the next thing on his agenda.

Of course, I had to tell him all the emotions I was feeling as he was going through his spiel but how wonderfully surprised I was by the whole thing. I had NO clue that he was going to propose to me, especially not today. I must say, I was pleased, and God is good!

We realized that we left Mr. and Mrs. Bryant there at church. Wow! That was pretty tacky of us. We didn't give directions, make arrangements for them to follow anyone, or anything. Now I felt bad. Taj called his dad, and he told him not to worry. They had everything under control. I had to call my girl, Ronni, and tell her the WHOLE story. *But maybe I should call her after I get back home this evening. I can't wait, I'm calling her now. I'm sure she's home from church.*

41

"Ronni, Harry up and pick up this phone," I was saying as I called my girl. Taj made me wait till after I got home from dinner at Mom's to call her.

"Hello?..."

"Sooo, Ronni..."

"Hey, boo! What's wrong?..."

"Why something always have to be wrong, girl?..."

"Val, is everything okay?..."

"Ronald, everything is fabulous. Why do you ask?..."

"Okay, so what's up? It's ten my time and you know typically I'm not answering my phone after ten..."

"Yeah, well, it's not AFTER ten..."

"Oh my gosh, girl! You are so difficult..."

"I been waiting for you to tell me. So I would imagine you are none the wiser..."

"Val, what's up? I have NO clue why you are calling me. Uh, Happy Valentine's Day?..."

"Okay, well...Taj proposed to me today during service!..."

"AAAAAAAAAAAAAAAAAAHH!..." Ronni began screaming.

"Wait, don't you want to know what I said?..."

"I already know what you said. Remember those dreams you had a while back? I know you didn't turn that man down after the good Lord gave you confirmation!..."

"You're right! Oh my goodness, I forgot about that. Girl, my God is such a good God! I asked Him to take it off my mind till after he proposed, and He did JUST that!..."

"Give me EVERY detail, let's go." So I began. I gave her EVERY detail starting with Saturday evening. We both screamed at the very end, and there I go again, crying when I heard her sobbing, "I am so happy for you, baby. We have to set up a trip for the three of us. You think Toni would agree to that?…"

"Ooooh, I'm all for that, and I'm sure she would be too. We talking about a trip with us and our men, right?…"

"Yeah, can we do a conference call?…"

"Oooh, let me three-way her now…"

"Val, I wasn't talking about now. It's late…"

"Girl, hold on. You ain't doing nothing. Hold on, I know Toni is up…" So I called Toni, and when she heard that Ronni was on the phone too, the three of us started screaming. Then the tears started flowing. It was quite an emotional time for the three of us. Of course, Ronni being the voice of reason brought the conversation into being. She prayed a prayer for the three of us and reminded us of the goodness of my Lord and Savior. We couldn't decide if we should take a three-day cruise or go to Vegas for the weekend.

Toni was in charge of researching the Vegas trip while Ronni researched the cruise. We all had to check our schedules and see what would be a good time for our vacation, and then they wanted to know when we were thinking about for the wedding. I wasn't sure about the wedding time yet. Taj and I had not even discussed those details.

Before we ended the call, Toni had a question for me. "So, Val, how did dinner go with both sides of your NEW family?…"

"Val, you didn't tell me that you all had dinner together. Did Mom cook? Or y'all went some place?…"

"Okay, so ladies—well, Toni, you already know, but Mom invited Taj's family over for a down South Sunday family dinner, and it was great. You know Mom's house is not that big, but God made a way. There was plenty of room. Some of us were eating in the kitchen, some at the dining room table, and of course the guys were in the front room watching TV. The kids were all over the place in bedrooms and everywhere else…"

"So pretty much like ANY of the holidays?" Ronni asked…

"Right! Mom had also invited Pastor and his family over, so we had a HOUSE full. Food was great, of course. Mom and Dad Bryant sat at the dining room table along with Mommy, Pastor, and his wife. Jason gave Pastor the okay to bless the food, and we dug in. Dwayne and Arik were on their best behavior, but they also let the Bryants know that next time they came over, "the real them" would show up and not these imposters. But all in all, we had a really good time. The ladies sat in the kitchen, and we harassed Jackson's girlfriend, Najah. But I must say, she handled it in stride. She passed the test and seems like she'll do just fine for him. I really like her, but time will tell.

"The Bryants seemed to REALLY enjoy the food and the family and said next time, the family would have to meet out there in Bolingbrook. They said, 'Don't expect a meal like we just had,' but they would work something out. So yeah, it was a good time. Taj dropped me off here because he said he knew my fingers were itching to make a couple phone calls, and he needed to, as he said, rest his brain after the last couple nights he'd had…"

"Oh my goodness! He's such a baby!…"

"Yeah, but Toni, that's MY baby!…"

"You better say that, Val! Stake your claim, baby girl!…" Ronni said.

We got off the phone and decided to talk this weekend but divvied up the homework assignments before we concluded our conversation.

When I got off the phone with my bestest friends in the world, I HAD to call Taj. I needed to know if today really happened. "Hey baby doll, what's wrong?…"

"Nothing baby, I wanted to hear your voice before I go to bed…"

"Oh well, in that case"—he started singing—"goodnight sweetheart, well, it's time to go, ba ba ba ba boom, I hate to leave you, but I really must go. Goodnight, sweetheart, goodnight!…"

"Okay, one thing before you do go…"

"What's that?…"

"Did today really happen?…"

"Baby doll, you NOW belong to me, and I to you! What God has put together, let NO man put asunder. Our wedding day is simply a formality. The hard part is already over…"

"So it did happen?…"

"Yes ma'am, it did!…"

"Do you have a particular time you would like to make this official?…"

"No baby girl! Whenever you'd like!…"

"I'll keep that in mind… I love you, boo. I'll talk to you tomorrow…"

"I love you most, baby girl… Good night and Happy Valentine's Day!…"

"Nite nite, baby, and Happy Valentine's Day back atcha!" I hung up the phone and fell back on my bed and looked up at the ceiling. *Oh God, let me start by saying thank You! Thank You for watching over, blessing, and keeping through dangers seen and unseen. My family is well. You've blessed us UNCONDITIONALLY! And I know we don't deserve it, but because of Your grace and mercy, You've given us more time. Again, thank You! Lord, I asked You to take away the fears and thoughts I had about Taj proposing to me, and You did that! Why, Lord? I'm not complaining, but I wonder, what is man that You are mindful of him? There are wars, fighting, killing, stealing, liars, evil people left and right, but still You are mindful of us, and You answer even the littlest of prayers! Thank You! I just want to please You! Help me to be the woman and wife you've called me to be. I love You! In Jesus's name I pray. Amen!*

Huh. I don't have much time sleeping in my OWN bed ALONE! I better make the most of it. I started rolling all over the bed, kicking, bouncing, jumping like a kid, and having a good time with myself in MY bed. After I made a mess of the bed, I fixed the covers and laid down and went to sleep. Nite nite, me!

42

fter we researched, me and the girls INITIALLY decided to go on a Jamaican cruise over the Memorial Day weekend. But after Taj and I deliberated about the wedding and time off work, finances, and other things, we decided that we didn't want to spend a lot of money, so the trip was going to have to wait. We also didn't want to go into debt with a lot of expenses on a wedding venue and reception, tuxes, and whatever else went into planning a wedding, so I convinced him to have a small ceremony on our upcoming Labor Day retreat in Allegan, Michigan. We would invite the other two couples to kick it with us on our honeymoon to Hawaii and then have a reception where we could invite other people.

He was all for that because he was planning on wearing his uniform to the wedding anyway, which I told him no. He explained to me that he took his role as protector very seriously and wanted it known by all that he had a job to do, and he planned to do it. I explained to him that as long as he and I understood that, then that's all that mattered, but I agreed that if he just HAD to, he could wear it to the reception.

We also figured that getting married at our church retreat would assure heavier attendance at the retreat, and his parents and siblings would DEFINITELY plan to attend. I had Taj talk to Pastor Phil about it, and Pastor was good with the idea but said give him some time to pray about it and get direction from the Lord as well as talk to the camp director and make sure it was all good. We were both good with that.

After Pastor came back with a definitive yes, we set up time for counseling, and then he and I had to break it to his family, my family, and my girls. *Okay, big boy, who first?* was my thought. Since we would see my family first on Sunday (if not before), we decided to see what Mom thought about it. But then I decided I wanted to talk to her alone before her thoughts could be tainted by my siblings. I don't know why I thought I would get resistance from them. I figured they would think that it was corny getting married at the retreat, so Taj and myself went by mom's house on Friday after Pastor had gotten back to Tab about our plans.

We talked it over with her. She was home alone. She was a little surprised because she thought that I wanted a BIG hoopla of a wedding with twelve bridesmaids and twelve groomsmen in the bridal party, not to mention four flower girls and four ring bearers. "Geez, Mom! What makes you think I'm that high maintenance type? You know—or should I say, you SHOULD know that I'm a simple gal. I don't need the bright lights and spotlight on me. As long as I know that Taj's eyes are on me, I'm good."

"Well, you being my baby girl, I guess I had bigger plans for your wedding than you did."

"So Mom, does that mean you're against the idea?" Taj asked.

"Oh, no! I actually like it. As many times as we've been to Camp Lake Side, we always say how this would be a beautiful place for a wedding. I never expected it would be a wedding for one of mines, though."

"Really Ma? You think we could pull this off?"

"Baby girl, everything you're going to need for your wedding will be right there. And it's close enough where if people wanted to drive in just for the wedding and come home the same day, they could. Have you talked to your sisters? You know that Khaleesi Marie is good at planning stuff with her old creative self."

"Not yet. We wanted to see what you thought about it before we talked to them. They'll probably think it's corny."

"Well, you have my blessings. Besides, they don't have to come out of pocket for this wedding, so they shouldn't have ANYTHING to say."

"True that, Mommy. Thank you so much for being my Moms! I love you, girl!"

"Well, you're welcome! It has truly been my pleasure."

"I'm going to call my sisters and see if they're okay for a luncheon tomorrow. Mommy, you want to come?"

"I got too much work to do. You girls go out and enjoy."

"Okay, well I'll let you know what time to be ret and will be by to scoop you."

"Scoop me for what?"

"So you can go to lunch with us. I feel I'm going to need your wisdom. Your work will still be here when you get back, doll. You're GOING to lunch with us."

"Trae, I don't know why these kids think they are MY Momma. They ALWAYS think they can tell me what to do."

"Mrs. Wilson, do me a favor and be my baby's support at the luncheon. I know they're not going to let me come, plus I have to work OT baby!"

"Oh, and about you, why has neither one of you told me that you can sing?"

"Get him, Mommy! I found out the same time YOU did."

"Yeah, we're going to have to get you in that choir!"

"I love singing actually, but my schedule had been so hectic in the past that the choir thing simply slipped my mind. I have a little more freedom now. I may be able to work that out."

"Well, get to working on that! I could listen to you sing all day."

"I will, Mom, just for you!"

"Okay so Mom, I'll let you know as soon as I talk to my sisters."

"Fine, girl!"

"Love you, Mommy!"

"I love you too, and congratulations again to both of you. I'm one proud mother."

We left Mom's house, and I set up the lunch for one o'clock the next day at a neutral location for all of us. When I gave my sisters our wedding idea, they were all for it. Ideas were being thrown out left and right. Well, everyone except for Pearl. She was sitting there, taking it all in. When I asked her if she was opposed and if not, why wasn't she interjecting? She said that we had everything under control. She did say that this should give us some good numbers for our church family retreat. Seeing as though she was the retreat committee chairperson, her response didn't surprise me. She was always laying back in the cut in observation mode most of the time. Well, at least she was paying attention and not playing a game on her cellular device.

We got a LOT accomplished in this short time frame. My sisters expressed to me that since it was going to be a smaller affair that I should have my two best friends in the bridal party. They said if I added the sisters and in-laws, the wedding party would be forty deep with ease. They said they would make it easy on me by giving my bff's their blessings as my maids of honor (assuring that these two would be at the retreat) and allowing Taj's three sisters to be bridesmaids. They said that way, Taj should be able to get five guys there with ease. My niece, Tia's daughter, Mya, would serve as flower girl (being the youngest girl in the family at the time), and one of my younger nephews, Dwight, could be the ring bearer (as long as Taj was okay with these selections).

If weather permitted, we would have the wedding on the beach, and Khaleesi said she would make my dress for me and the flowers (she was blessed with the creative gene). She knew me pretty well and said she had a pattern that she knows I would love (nothing formal but very elegant). She brought the pattern to church the next day, and she was right. I absolutely loved it!

My sisters took a lot of pressure off by deciding on my wedding party for me, but for my reception later on down the road, they would be photographed and listed on the program as in the actual bridal party.

When I brought it to my brother's, they all were good with the idea. I asked my oldest brother if he would walk me down and give me away, and he didn't hesitate to accept.

Everything fell into place pretty good. Ronni and Toni were surprised that my sisters were taking a back seat and allowed them to be my maids of honor. (They know how close I am with my sisters.) Taj's sisters were ecstatic to be considered for the wedding party, and Taj had JC and Duss as his best men and three of his fellow officers were trying to get the time off to come and be groomsmen. The three officers that he had in mind wouldn't be able to stay the whole weekend, but they were able to maneuver things around whereas they would come out on Friday night with the rest of us and leave after breakfast on Sunday so they could be back for work on Labor Day. All I could say is that God is good ALL the time, and all the time, what is it? You're right—God is GOOD!

43

From February till September, there was lots of stuff going on. Since the wedding was going to be formal but informal, I allowed Taj to wear his uniform. He was advised that for the reception, he would be in a suit. My dress was not white but was champagne. It was a halter top that was knee-length and had a removable train that snapped around my waist. The girl's dresses were different styles, but all were short. They each picked out the style they wanted, but the color was the same, which was coral. And little Miss Mya's dress was similar to mine and was the same color too. She was a mini me.

All the men, including JC and Duss, wore police uniforms in which I found that out at wedding time. I thought Taj was going to be the only one dressed like that, and the killer part was my five-year-old nephew Dee 3 (that's Dwight's nickname) had on a police uniform too (badge and all). Taj was still going with the theme and wanted everyone to know that his job was to serve and protect. *Believe me, Taj, we get it!* Boy, was he serious about that!

The wedding was on the beach and was beautiful, if I must say so myself. The scenery was lovely, and of course, that was our gift from God along with the weather which turned out to be gorgeous. It was about seventy-seven degrees with a nice breeze. We had a photographer who was family. He was an in-law to one of my brothers who took fabulous pictures. He was set up on the dock and also had cameras set on the balcony, so he and his assistants had various vantage points. He also had a videographer.

My brother, Red, had the keyboard set up and played while a few of my nephews called Space's Thang sang for us. They did a really nice job. Space wrote a wedding song that seemed like he wrote it just for us. It was great.

Jason walked me down to Space's original song, "I Asked God for an Angel." So beautiful! He needed to be on the radio! He is so talented. And when it came time for Jace to give me away, each of my brother's stood up as well as my three brothers-in-law. They looked up to the heavens, and Jason said, "It's good, Reb? Cool!" As if Reb had answered him. Then they looked at the pastor, and all of them said, "We do!"

I saw Mom wiping away the tears. We were ALL missing Reb on THIS occasion. I know I was.

We exchanged vows that we had written, and Taj pulled a scroll out of his pocket that was super long and reached the ground, like he was about to read all that! It was really funny. We had our first communion together as one. When Pastor asked Taj for the ring, he turned to JC. JC felt his pockets and turned to Duss. Duss turned to Deuce. Deuce turned to DJ. DJ turned to Ace. And they all shrugged and started murmuring.

Pastor said, "You're kidding!"

My ring bearer, Dwight, tugged at Pastor's shirt and said, "Don't worry, Coach. I didn't drop the ball this time!" And he handed him the ring. Pastor also coached Pop Warner football.

Pastor said, "Y'all play too much!"

Again, we ALL laughed. We were having such a good time at this wedding. Pastor blessed the rings and asked if anyone objected to this union and introduced us as husband and wife. He told Taj to salute his wife, and Taj saluted me. Pastor said, "Naw man...now who doesn't know what I mean by that? Taj, kiss your bride!"

Taj licked his lips and planted a nice passionate kiss on me.

Pastor tapped him and said, "Bruthuh, this is a family show. Finish that later on!" Then Pastor added, "I present to you Mr. and Mrs. Taj Alexander Bryant!"

Everybody stood up and clapped for us as we walked out as husband and wife. As we were exiting, Space and his group sang another original song, "Beauty and the Beast."

We hung around for a little bit, took some pictures at the waterfront, and afterward, we changed clothes and went to orientation for our weekend at camp. Even though we were now husband and wife, I slept in the girls' cabin. I was counselor for the teen girls. Taj stayed in the cabin with the adult men. I wanted to leave the campgrounds and consummate my marriage, but Taj said, we waited this long, we could wait a couple more days. Besides that, he said he didn't want to have to rush or tone it down. When the time was right, EVERYTHING would be right. I must say, dude has a lot of self-control.

We completed the weekend at camp. His boys left on Sunday as planned. They said that they really enjoyed the time they had and would consider coming back next year. I think the ultimate tubing sold it for them. They were trying to stay till after tubing on Sunday, but Deuce had to work the night shift Sunday night, so they HAD to go.

Taj and his family expressed that they had a really good time too. We didn't ride the bus home. We rode home with Toni and Zani. Ronni rode with us as well. Dre was unable to make the wedding. He was meeting us in Hawaii. The whole ride home, we instant replayed the weekend. We laughed about the paddle boat race where Taj and myself were in one boat, and Zani and Toni were in the other. The two guys were being so competitive, so me and Toni let them do all the work since we could relax and enjoy the scenery. It WAS funny the way they were begging and trying to bribe us to help. Neither one of us helped though, because we wanted to ride around the lake and chill and enjoy the beautiful scenery. Oh my gosh! We almost forgot but then laughed so hard at Taj when he fell out the canoe, clowning around. His big self was out there in the middle of the lake, trying to recover his glasses and baseball hat, but since he had the life vest on, he couldn't go down in the water but kept trying and couldn't figure out why he was staying afloat. It was hilarious!

Then the two guys were trying to remember the words to our campfire songs, "Green Grass" and "Hi-Fi Lord." The lyrics they came up with were great. We laughed all the way home and was home before we knew it.

Had we thought about it, we would've had things planned to go straight to the airport since we were already together. But we decided to carry on the conversation when we met back up. We had a limo meeting us to take us to the airport. There were a few hours to spare before the limo would be here, which I thought was enough time for me to experience married life FULLY! BUT once again, my plans were foiled. I forgot that Ronni was staying with me! *DANG! "Really, Lord? Am I EVER going to KNOW my husband?"*

Just as I was thinking those thoughts, Taj snuck up on me from behind, put his arms around me, kissed me on the cheek and, as if he were reading my mind, said, "Baby doll, good things come to those that wait! Patience, my love, patience!" And as I looked up at him, he winked at me. *Oh, he is so sexy and ALL mine!*

The thought came to me that usually, when I come home from camp, I come home with poison ivy or maybe a cold, possibly even some fresh fruit from the farmer that came through camp. But this time, I came home from camp with a husband. And after my man spoke those words, a calmness came over me. I had to apologize to my Lord and Savior! *He's got this! And I'm sure it's going to be well worth the wait!*

We all showered, got changed, and sat around, chewing the fat for a little bit before Toni and Zani got back with their luggage.

The limo showed up shortly after Toni and Zani. We both called our moms to let them know we were off to our honeymoon, and BAM! Honeymoon, here we come!

We had a great flight! It was long but peaceful. Taj offered a prayer in the limo on the ride to O'Hare, and as usual, the Lord blessed. I was so appreciative of my husband. *Wow! Of MY husband! I like the sound of that!* And before I could even ask him to look out for Ronni since Dre wasn't with us, he was already on the job AND without slighting me. People on the outside looking in wouldn't have known which woman he actually was with. I was truly pleased with my boo!

And let me just say, the wedding, Hawaii, my TRUE introduction to the man of my dreams (va-va-va-voom!)—it ALL was well worth the wait. And one more thing: I can't wait to see what the future holds for us, but to put it in its simplest form, I don't mind waiting!

ABOUT
THE AUTHOR

Deborah A. Thompson (aka BeeGee Hill) was born in Buffalo, New York. She is the daughter of the late Reverend Clarence L. Hilliard (a world-renowned Evangelical leader who was noted for debating Malcolm X on the Buffalo State College campus in 1963) and Annie Hilliard. She is the eighth of nine children.

During her early childhood, the family migrated to the Chicago metropolitan area. Under the leadership and teachings of her parents, she developed an early-in-life relationship with Jesus Christ and learned ministerially that she had a penchant for grooming and nurturing young people during their formative years.

Mrs. Thompson has been married to Dr. Theodore Thompson for thirty-seven years. God saw fit to bless them with three beautiful children and eight grandchildren who keep her busy, young, and who truly captivate her heart!

Mrs. Thompson loves spending time with family, has a zest for life, and believes that laughter is a cure for what may be ailing you. She also believes if you see someone without a smile, give them yours. Life is too short to be serious all the time!

She is very active in her church community, Austin Corinthian Baptist Church (ACBC), which is located on Chicago's westside, and has served as its choir director for over twenty years among her other church responsibilities.

Although Mrs. Thompson has been writing for several years, this is her first published work, and her prayer is that God continues to supply her with inspiring stories that will bless His children for many years to come!

CPSIA information can be obtained
at www.ICGtesting.com
Printed in the USA
BVHW051802171122
652193BV00005B/130